L. NEIL SMITH

PALLAS

BOOKS BY L. NEIL SMITH

The Probability Broach
The Venus Belt
Their Majesties' Bucketeers
The Nagasaki Vector
Tom Paine Maru
The Gallatin Divergence
Lando Calrissian and the Mindharp of Sharu
Lando Calrissian and the Flamewind of Oseon
Lando Calrissian and the Starcave of Thonboka
The Wardove
BrightSuit MacBear
Taflak Lysandra
Contact and Commune
Converse and Conflict
*The Crystal Empire
*Henry Martyn
*Pallas

*denotes a Tor book

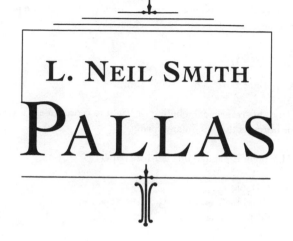

L. Neil Smith

PALLAS

A Tom Doherty Associates Book
New York

PALLAS

Copyright © 1993 by L. Neil Smith

This book is printed on acid-free paper.

A Tor Book
Published by Tom Doherty Associates, Inc.
175 Fifth Avenue
New York, N.Y. 10010

Tor® is a registered trademark of Tom Doherty Associates, Inc.

Edited by James R. Frenkel

Design by Lynn Newmark

Library of Congress Cataloging-in-Publication Data

Smith, L. Neil.
    Pallas / L. Neil Smith.
        p.   cm.
    "A Tom Doherty Associates book."
    ISBN 0-312-09705-0
    I. Title.
    PS3569.M37555P3   1993
    813'.54—dc20   93-26548
                                                              CIP

First edition: November 1993

Printed in the United States of America

0 9 8 7 6 5 4 3 2 1

This one could never have been for anybody except
Jim Frenkel.

Contents

Acknowledgment

The author wishes to express his heartfelt gratitude to Jeff Cooper and the American Pistol Institute, to Jerry Ahern, to J. B. Wood, to Jan Libourel at *Handguns For Sport & Defense*, and especially to Eldon and Marilyn Robison at L.A.R. Mfg. Inc., West Jordan, Utah 84084 U.S.A., for their kindness and assistance in the preparation of this novel. What he made of what they gave him, however, is entirely his own fault.

L. Neil Smith

PALLAS

WHILE WE ARE MEMBERS OF THE INTELLIGENT
PRIMATE FAMILY, WE ARE UNIQUELY HUMAN EVEN IN
THE NOBLEST SENSE, BECAUSE FOR UNTOLD MILLIONS
OF YEARS WE ALONE KILLED FOR A LIVING.
—**Robert Ardrey,** *The Hunting Hypothesis*

I

THE VOICE OF PALLAS

THE POLICE ARE LIKE PARENTS. THEY'RE NOT REALLY INTERESTED
IN JUSTICE, THEY SIMPLY WANT *QUIET*.
— Mirelle Stein, *The Productive Class*

Emerson Ngu wound the tuning coil carefully, following the instructions in the book he'd found in a Residence trash bin, and scraped the varnish off the wires
along the top.

Even in this secret, private place, he worked as quietly
as he could for fear someone might hear and report him to
the goons. He'd never suffered a shock baton "treatment,"
but had seen others writhe beneath the instrument of discipline, too agonized to scream. That there would be a first
time for him he had no doubt, but it didn't have to be here
and now, and wouldn't be if he could avoid it.

The variable capacitor had proven more difficult, and
from half a dozen alternatives suggested by the brittle-
paged paperback he'd settled on a strip of thin aluminum
covered with plastic wrap, over which he slid another
piece of foil, varying the area of their mutual effect. The
mechanical arrangement was inelegant, hard to keep ad-

justed, and the best he could do with materials at hand.

Reflexively, he glanced outward through the ragged-edged entrance to his private, secret place, watchful for the pale blue livery which stood out against the color of the local terrain as if dyed fluorescent orange. Seeing nothing but a handful of peasant colonists like himself, clad in off-white denim, and the endless brown furrows they tended—and feeling little relieved—he returned to his work.

The easiest part had been the detector, a lump of galena from an unworked area of the Project, wedged into a short section of plumbing copper. A wisp of the wire he'd used for the coil stood over that little chunk of lead ore, insulated with a bit of tape, to serve as a "cat's whisker," used to find a rectifying facet of the crystal.

The earphone had been hardest. The discarded "how-to" book had assumed that the hobbyist would buy one at some nearby establishment—which Emerson decidedly could not—but had included a diagram to show how they worked. He'd wound five different coils around the magnetic core of a carpenter's broken stud-finder, much smaller than the tuning coil he'd wound around a discarded toilet paper roll but with many more turns, before he found the correct "impedance"—whatever that meant. A small washer of foam wrapping plastic separated this field coil from its diaphragm, a tiny disk of steel he'd cut from a jar lid. The homemade earphone crackled whenever he attached it to the rest of his homemade radio.

Unable to stop himself, he looked up again—in the failing light at the end of the day, the goons might already be relying on the sickly green torches at the handle ends of their batons—and back down at what he'd accomplished in these stolen hours when nobody expected somebody like him to be able to go on working in the fields. Others of his kind would be off playing somewhere, one of the few

offenses overlooked by the goons because the only alternative was working children to death—or even worse, being
caught at it by visiting officials.

Just like the radio receiver he was building, Emerson's
kit of scrapers, cutters, measurers, and screwdrivers, his
mallet and flame-heated soldering iron, were homemade
out of little bits and pieces furtively salvaged from this
scrap heap or that garbage can. Nobody had ever told him
that having them, or having done with them what he had,
was forbidden. Somehow he knew it without being told.

Everything that interested him was forbidden.

It was the same with the stack of magazines and paper-
backs he'd salvaged, safe and dry in the niche he'd scraped
out for them at the back of the cave after others had tired
of them and thrown them away.

With a sigh compounded equally of excitement and
fear—of failure or discovery—he blew out the little paraf-
fin lamp he'd made last year from the bottom of a can. It
was the first such "forbidden" project he'd undertaken and
he was unreasonably fond of it. Familiar with his where-
abouts by feel alone, he took up another coil of wire—this
one long, loose, and with a weighted end—and emerged
from his tiny cave at the base of the crater wall just below
the Rimfence.

It was not quite dark, even here in the shadow of the
rim, and his pale lamplight would probably not have betrayed him, either against the setting sun—or what he
knew was about to follow. Still, he was careful to readjust
the clump of brush which concealed the entrance to his
cave, no more than a boy-sized bubble in what had once
been molten lava. He liked that brush almost as much as he
liked his cave or his little lamp. This was the same un-
tended section of the Project where he'd found the galena
crystal, and the wild plant had obviously blown here as a

seed from the Outside, where things like weeds were allowed to happen.

Holding the unweighted end of the coiled wire firmly,
he freed a couple of meters from the weighted end, swung
it experimentally around his head a few times, and heaved
it as high and far as he could up the crater wall, over the
Rimfence that stood above it. It would have been an impossible toss on Earth. Here, the coils flipped from his fingers as the weight sailed dozens of meters into the evening
sky until he heard and felt it thud to the soft ground on the
other side.

Immediately, he glanced around to make sure he
hadn't been seen. He'd already taken the precaution of
mottling the antenna wire's plastic insulation so that it
matched, as closely as possible, the carbonaceous chondrite soil it lay against, which was about the color and consistency of a slightly overdone chocolate chip cookie.
Emerson had never seen a chocolate chip cookie, but he
understood, again without ever having been told, that this
illegal antenna of his mustn't be conspicuous. Spending
hours at the mind-dulling task, he'd patiently camouflaged
it using a double handful of not-quite-exhausted marking
pens thrown out by the Chief Administrator's office. Now
he painstakingly added to its disguise with strategically
placed clumps of brush and dirt clods.

At last, pulling the free end of the wire inside with him,
he attached it to one side of his tuning coil, having
grounded the opposite side in the cave floor. He placed the
phone against his ear, wriggled the cat's whisker, and adjusted the flat capacitor and coil, hoping to hear more this
time than the mindless humming of the Rimfence or the
vagrant crackle of his own primitive circuitry.

*"—got a dozen fresh pan-sized trout she'd like t'swap for veni-
son. Better hurry, 'cause they don't keep and they never taste the
same after they been frozen."*

Even prepared as he was, Emerson started violently at the voice blasting amiably into his ear—and almost as violently at the grisly subject being discussed: the eating of once-living flesh. There was no way to adjust the volume, so he slid the commutator on the coil aside, detuning his receiver slightly to reduce the noise.

"Speakin' of swappin', C.W. Brown of Brown's Household Engineerin' here in beautiful downtown Curringer tells me he's got a handful of CPU chips he'd like t'get rid of for pistol ammunition. He's stuck with some old-fashioned caliber—nine millimeter Parabellum, it says here on the card—and can't get fodder for it. You reloaders better give him a call, 'fore he winds up socially nekkid."

So the goons hadn't been lying about that, either: the Outsiders *did* have weapons of their own. Emerson shook his head, not understanding half of what he heard—not even understanding a third—but knowing that it was wonderful.

"I'm gonna go get m'self another cuppa coffee an' inspect the plumbing, so you settle back an' listen as Jim Kweskin an' the Jug Band ask the musical question, 'Somebody Stole My Gal.' An' don't touch that dial, friends an' neighbors. There ain't no other station on the asteroid anyway. This here is KCUF—that's what we're callin' it this week—the one an' only radio voice of Pallas!"

A hideous, wonderful, terrible, beautiful thumping, twanging, slamming, and scraping noise commenced. All his fears forgotten, Emerson was completely overwhelmed. He'd never heard music—if that's what it was—like this before. All he'd known was the folksinging demanded of his family and the others as they worked in the fields—and of course the lifeless, insipid murmuring personally approved by the Chief Administrator and played over the compound's loudspeakers during meals and all day on Sundays. This was different. It made him feel happy deep inside for no reason at all. It made him want to

jump up and jerk his body around for nothing other than
the sheer irresistible pleasure of it.

Yes, it was wonderful. And so was this little crystal
radio he'd made. And so was KCUF, the one and only
radio voice of Pallas. Unlike most of his expectations so
• far, it had turned out to be everything he'd hoped it would
and more. Not only had he never heard music like this—if
that's what it was—he couldn't remember ever hearing the
words of a single human being who didn't live and work
inside the Greeley Utopian Memorial Project. But he
would remember this moment for as long as he lived. He
would learn all he could from it for as long as it lasted. And
he would come back for more until they finally caught him
at it and punished him.

And they would, sooner or later.

Emerson had learned that much personally, and
through the bitter experience of others, even at the age of
eight.

Remembering at last to glance outside the cave, he
could already see the eerie green torchlights, bobbing and
swinging in their carriers' hands, of the goons on their
rounds, searching field and furrow for slackers and strag-
glers. Their punishments for lying down or slowing work
at the end of the day were bad enough.

What would they do to him if they found him listening
to voices from the Outside?

II
A PLACE FOR EVERYONE

I'M NOT THE FIRST TO SAY SO, AND I CAME TO THE IDEA
PRETTY RELUCTANTLY MYSELF, BUT CONSIDERING ALL THE
CONSEQUENCES, THE INVENTION OF AGRICULTURE MAY JUST
BE THE WORST MISTAKE HUMANITY EVER MADE.
— Raymond Louis Drake-Tealy, *Hunting and Humanity*

Sunset had begun in earnest, differently on Pallas than anywhere else, prismatic brilliance racing across the heavens chasing complementary-colored shadows over the landscape.

As if the tolling of a huge bell had been suddenly made visible, vast feather-edged rings of violet, born within the dazzling diamond bead at the horizon, soared to the zenith, subtly fading. That alone might have made the Pallatian sunset the stuff of travelogues and tourist brochures, but it was only the beginning. Streamers of a fierce, deep blue arched out from the same hot pinpoint, lashing the sky. The pulsing emerald sinuosities that followed were only slightly less furious in their intensity and motion. Titanic loops of crackling amber, vast braids of actinic orange, each glowed in turn and dimmed.

At last, a broad band of purest scarlet arose from the dying of the day, its free ends racing around the silhouetted borders of the world until they met, annihilating one another, and vanishing into the velvety blackness of the night.

Gibson Altman—still "Senator" by courtesy despite everything that had happened in the past six years—shook his head. He always expected to hear explosions of some kind, but the spectacle was silent, produced by the plastic envelope they'd wrapped around this little world, an un-

foreseen effect of the specific polymer employed, the
stresses it was subject to, and its distance from the sun. No
one was entirely certain why it happened. There were
other things to do, so many other objects of scientific research that were more important.

That were everyday matters of life and death.

Altman stood alone on the verandah of his official residence, hands in his pants pockets, eyes adjusting to the
light of Pallas B, the tiny moon. With a feeling that was
almost satisfaction, he gazed out over the freshly plowed
and planted ground (not "earth") surrounding the building, realizing again that he was literally master of all he
surveyed. In the dark, and at this distance, he couldn't see
the Rimfence that marked the border of his fiefdom, nor,
many kilometers further off across Lake Selous, the lights
of Curringer, which in all respects represented the opposite of everything he hoped to accomplish here.

What he could see was what he'd accomplished so far:
order. A fair beginning at it, anyway. Stretching almost
eighty kilometers away in every direction, filling the vast
meteoric bowl that constituted the Greeley Utopian Memorial Project, lay hectare after hectare of lovingly prepared soil, its precisely harrowed contour lines accentuated by the rising moon and slanting shadows.

Closer in, set apart by neat concrete walkways too narrow to be called streets (nor would any motor vehicle ever
be permitted to defile them), tidy ranks of prefabricated
living facilities shone in the moonlight. Here, the Project's
ordinary colonists were learning to pursue a life that was
simple, healthy, and well planned. It was the Senator's job
to do that planning here on Pallas, second largest of the
solar system's "Big Five" asteroids—always within strict
guidelines, of course, set down by master planners back on
Earth.

The moon was bright tonight, presenting its broadest

face to the faraway sun. It was irregular in shape, too small to pull itself into a spheroid by its own gravity. Unlike the world it circled—and three-quarters of the asteroids in the Belt which were composed of carbonaceous chondrite—Pallas B was gray-white granite. Behind him, if he'd cared to turn, he might have seen his own reflection in the Residence's window glass. They were the only glass windows in the Project. The rest of its populace made do simply, with the translucent plastic their quarters had been constructed from. That was fitting and proper, he thought. Nobody else needed to look out from indoors to see what others were doing.

They only had to go outside and do it.

Had he cared to turn, he'd have seen the handsome face, somewhat younger in appearance than its forty-one years, of a former senator from Connecticut once regarded as the unopposed contender for the Democratic Union Party's Presidential nomination. Following the violent scandal which had dashed that aspiration—in a United States increasingly governed by neo-Puritanism and wracked by what the media were calling "The Great Depression II"—he'd been hastily removed from the spotlight. Some wag had observed that he might have gotten away with any one of the three acts he'd unknowingly performed for the benefit of a hidden video recorder, maybe even two, but that all three in the space of one night had simply been asking for catastrophe, if only in the form of a serious back injury.

Afterward, in the rooms (smoke-filled, of course) behind the proverbially closed doors, his angry, disappointed party leadership had offered him what amounted to a lifelong sinecure or—depending on who did the describing—exile in deep space. Like it or not, they told him, he was about to become the first interplanetary remittance man, officially Chief Administrator of an agricultural cooperative being established by the United Nations on the asteroid Pallas.

Hard as it was to believe, he had to concentrate to remember her name. Everything else about her was still fresh and clear in his mind—her eyes, her smile, the precise color, size, and shape of her—he cut the thought off savagely. It wasn't enough that she'd been impossibly beautiful, flatteringly willing. Almost instinctively, it had seemed, she'd given him everything he'd ever wanted, things he'd never known he'd wanted, things that were technically illegal in more than a dozen states. Things he'd have hesitated to ask of a prostitute.

Things that sometimes left permanent marks.

It wasn't enough that she'd been black. Voters on the wine-and-cheese side of the spectrum, the Volvo side of the spectrum—his own side of the spectrum—were always very careful to conceal their prejudices, but they were real nonetheless (otherwise, what political profit would there have been in appealing to them with three-quarters of a century's worth of condescending social programs?) and ran much deeper than the mere crude, open bigotry of the right. It was only later that he'd learned—because the press had informed him and the rest of the world in ten-centimeter headlines—that she'd been sixteen years old.

And she'd often brought her younger sister along.

Before six years of guilt and anger overwhelmed him as they'd done so often before, a feeling that was almost satisfaction came to his rescue. Out in the silvery moonlight, the first of his cultivation teams appeared in the distance, shuffling back from the fields they'd tended all day. And they were right on time, according to his grandfather's antique gold pocket watch which he consulted, as he always did at this time, from this very spot on the verandah. Return too soon and they'd lose valuable daylight and person-hours, an inefficiency that, repeated too often, might someday add up to disaster for the still-struggling colony. Return too late and the fleeting moon would set, leaving the night too dark for weary feet to find the narrow pathways laid between the furrows.

Even in this failing light he could see that the colonists' simple pullovers and loose trousers weren't quite as splendidly creased and spotless as they'd been this morning, lined up for assembly. That would soon be remedied. Accompanied as they always were by their Education and Morale counselors whose pale blue paramilitary outfits were nearly as wrinkled and dirty as their own, they would discard their work-soiled clothing in the Project laundry, step through the communal showers, be issued fresh white denims for tomorrow, and be led to their assigned seats in the Project kitchen for a simple, balanced, and nutritious meal. All three facilities were already in full swing—being put to use by clerical, maintenance, and other service personnel—in anticipation of the mass return from the fields. Some might have thought the mingled odors of laundry, showers, and kitchen disagreeable. For the Senator they had the smell of good things being done rationally, without a murmur of disturbance from anything or anyone.

The E&M staff were an International Peace Corps detachment on indefinite loan by the United Nations to serve as the Senator's hands and arms on Pallas. The shock batons swinging at their belts—once known as "cattle prods" before animal rights activists demanded otherwise—might be used on an occasional boisterous colonist (they could be such children, after all), but the presence of such weapons, he'd long since persuaded himself, was more for their protection from any Outsiders who might break in through the Rimfence. His colonists might be children. They weren't barbarians. They worked hard and obeyed, building a future for themselves and, he hoped, for all mankind, in which there would be no more Outsiders to disturb the peace.

In the midst of the compound, where the colonists could appreciate it as they ate, stood an heroic-scale bronze of Horace Greeley, after whom the colony was named, the nineteenth-century founder of the New York *Tribune*, a decent, inexpensive paper meant to uplift the laboring class. Greeley had hired some powerful journalistic talent in his day but his editorials had *made* the paper, supporting a protective tariff—an issue so hot it had sparked the Civil War—advocating governmental and cultural reform, and dabbling in experimental socialism.

The *Tribune* had been popular on the American frontier, many of its readers having acted on its famous editor's even more famous advice, "Go West, young man, go West!" Nor was this the first time Greeley's name had been tied to a project like this. The "Cooperative Union Colony" had named a town for him in 1870, a few dozen kilometers north of Denver. Mr. Greeley, however, had ignored his own advice, stayed East, and unsuccessfully run for President in 1872.

Altman suspected the name "Greeley Utopian Memorial Project" had been chosen by a Colombo bureaucrat who wasn't a native English speaker. With the new century, due to increasing hostility from rich Western countries, the UN had been forced to relocate to Sri Lanka. In any case, no American would have chosen the acronym GUMP.

In its way, the statue of Greeley was fully as incongruous. It had been commissioned on Earth and freighted here at an obscene cost, money that might have been better spent. The sculptor had either been a romantic fool or historically illiterate. Greeley, who'd also died in 1872, wore a spacesuit, holding the bulky mirror-visored helmet under one arm. None of the colonists had worn a spacesuit during their two-year voyage to Pallas, nor even seen a crewman doing so.

For some reason, the thought of his own seemingly endless voyage (two full weeks aboard one of the new fusion-powered constant-boost spacecraft) brought the Senator full-circle. He'd seen the aurora borealis once, on a Strategic Defense junket to Greenland. He realized now that it was a pale thing compared to a Pallatian sunset which was visible all over the asteroid. What was more, the same outrageous spectacle occurred each morning when the sun came up.

Unpredicted as it had been, the colorful display apparently harmed no one. Nor did it indicate any structural failure of the atmospheric envelope. It was *pretty*, he guessed. But with the notorious exception of various young women, he'd never cared much for pretty things as such. His publicly devoted, conspicuously long-suffering wife privately maintained that he had no poetry in his soul. For his part, he'd never claimed to have a soul, let alone one containing poetry.

The sunset was impressive. Some might call it garish. He felt that was appropriate somehow. It almost constituted the signature of the individual responsible for it. He, too, had been described as colorful, unpredictable, impressive, even garish. No one, however, had ever thought to describe the man as pretty.

What the Senator did appreciate, what the sunset mainly meant to him, was that an overbearing robber-capitalist and his pack of arrogant world-making engineers had proven imperfect, failing utterly to anticipate a phenomenon this . . . blatant. What else, in the name of suffering, bleeding humanity, had they failed to anticipate?

Pallas was half a billion kilometers from the sun, a quarter billion from Earth at closest passage. It was dark out here, he understood, and bitterly cold. Deep space was a living thing: hungry, vicious, determinedly clawing at a molecule-thin fabric which was their one and only protection against its ravages. And the frail lives of thousands upon thousands of helpless human beings lay in precisely the same hands whose owner had failed to predict this gaudy sunset.

Greedy hands.

Worst of all, the hands of an individual who would never have to live with the results of his failures, whatever they might be. Someone who would never take the same risks as those he'd schemed for all of his long, wasted life to exploit.

Dirty hands.

A dead man's hands.

The hands of William Wilde Curringer.

III
WHITHER THOU GOEST

KEEP YOUR OVERALL GOAL IN MIND ABOVE ALL. THOSE WHO
SWERVE TO AVOID A FEW CUTS AND BRUISES DEFEAT
THEMSELVES. UNDERSTAND FROM THE VERY MINUTE THE FIGHT
BEGINS THAT YOU'RE GOING TO TAKE DAMAGE. ACCEPT IT.
YOU'LL SUFFER FAR WORSE FROM THE IDIOTS AND COWARDS
ON YOUR OWN SIDE.
         —**William Wilde Curringer**, *Unfinished Memoirs*

I t was hot in the Residence kitchen.
   True, the room was air-conditioned, and every appliance within its walls was powered by the Project's catalytic fusion reactor which, with thousands of others scattered across Pallas—small-scale, decentralized, and designed to produce oxygen and water as a by-product—supplemented a pair of huge mylar mirrors in orbit as a source of energy, and helped replenish the asteroid's atmosphere.

The kitchen was the largest room in the building, but it wasn't the sort of homey, hospitable refuge she'd grown up expecting to find at the heart of even the most formal executive residence. The ceiling overhead was very high, supported by stainless steel I-beams with rows of circles cut from them—which had lowered their weight for transport through space—that lent the ambience of an industrial plant and at the same time looked spindly, having been engineered for the low gravity of the asteroid, so that in the back of her mind she kept expecting them to come down on her head at any moment. The roof itself was some sort of translucent fiberglass, and the light it allowed into the room felt clinical to her, although she'd felt that way about skylights back on Earth, as well.

The stainless "motif" was echoed in fixtures and countertops surrounding her, throwing the intolerable heat and a series of smeary reflections from their semipolished surfaces. If she'd leaned forward—and if the table before her hadn't been covered with the preparations for dinner—she'd have seen the image of a tall, slender woman who appeared between five and ten years older than her thirty-four years. The strain marking her face was part of an overall tension which shaped her movements and affected everyone around her. She'd heard someone remark, not knowing she was listening—or maybe knowing perfectly well—that she lit up any room she walked into, but that her light was as discomfiting as that of an oxyacetylene welding torch. To a degree, she'd always been that way, she knew, even as a girl. And the years with Gibson hadn't helped.

She was still reasonably attractive, she thought, for a mother of three who'd gone through everything she had. The most frustrating thing about her marriage was that not one of the women Gibson chased had ever been prettier than she was, or even a fraction as dynamic or intelligent.

They were always younger—sometimes a great deal younger. She'd been quite young herself when they'd first met. And equally, they were—here her thinking hesitated as it invariably did, searching for a phrase she could somehow never remember the next time and had to search for all over again—well, they were less inhibited.

But in the first place, why hadn't Gibson ever managed to take her away from herself and make *her* feel that way? She'd always believed he could have helped her if he'd ever cared enough to try. In some ways that had been the greatest betrayal of all. Or was he a prisoner, too, paralyzed like a seaside souvenir cast in a block of transparent plastic, which was the way she'd felt all her life?

And in the second place, there must be something more to life than sex.

There *had* to be.

Gwen Altman, wife of ex-Senator Gibson Altman, glanced at the servants to make sure neither was watching, then ducked her head and gave her face a quick swipe with the hem of her apron. Neither of the women appeared particularly uncomfortable. Perhaps the unbearable heat was something personal, a sign of premature menopause. Perhaps it was just that every day, no matter how bad the day before might have been, she felt more confused and increasingly unhappy.

She shook self-pity off for the moment—although the heat remained unbelievably oppressive—and returned to her inspection of the stainless tableware and place settings. Tonight's dinner guest was very important—not in and of himself, she corrected herself hastily, what an absurd idea—but to her husband's work here at the Project. And that, of course, made this guest important to her. Gwen was the great-granddaughter, granddaughter, daughter, niece, cousin, and sister to a long, distinguished line of congressmen, senators, and Supreme Court justices. She'd also been resigned since girlhood to practicing the virtues of a patient, pragmatic political spouse.

Thus she'd spent six endless three-hundred-sixty-five-day years—the solar year on Pallas was much longer—with her disgraced husband on this isolated frontier world-let the Party had sent him to, helping him as best she could. Until recently (she wasn't exactly certain when her feelings had begun to change), she'd been as stoic about it all as she'd always believed proper. Sometimes she'd been almost cheerful. She'd always believed—perhaps only because she wanted to—that they were simply waiting out here for Gibson's earlier power and prestige to be restored to him once his public reputation was somehow rehabilitated.

But to Gwen's utter amazement—and helpless revulsion—these past six years seemed to have made him content simply exercising what amounted to life-and-death authority over an unwashed, ignorant rabble of ten thousand Third World peasants.

The best evidence of that was that he no longer drank the way he did in office, nor did he beat her at irregular intervals as he had on Earth before the public ugliness which ruined his brilliant career. (The consummate politician at every turn, he'd made certain never to bruise her anywhere that would show on television or in newspaper or magazine photographs—for her part, she'd been horrified to discover that bearing beneath her clothing the marks he did make on her body was the closest she'd ever come to feeling like a woman.) But worst of all, he seemed to have forgotten all his earlier, grander, and, in her estimation, nobler aspirations which had somehow made it endurable for her.

Maybe even a little enjoyable.

One of the servants, Nansey, asked her a question about the salads which the girl should have been able to answer for herself. Oh well, Gwen sighed inwardly, that's why she had to be out here in the kitchen. Alice, their housekeeper, would have been supervising ordinarily, but with important company coming, she was feeding the children an early dinner in their own suite. In Gwen's opinion, Alice was the only one of these colonial women who had any brains at all.

Gwen wished that her opinion had been asked for in the matter of their exile in deep space, but it hadn't been, neither by her father's old cronies in the Democratic Union Party nor by her own husband. To her, the Greeley Utopian Memorial Project—and along with it, each and every godforsaken square centimeter of this miserable ball of rock they called Pallas—would never be anything but an empty wasteland. She remembered doubting, as a coed, the stories of Walter Prescott Webb about pioneer women living in sod shanties on the Great Plains of North America who were supposed to have died of nothing more than loneliness. She didn't doubt them any more. She hated to contemplate living out the rest of her life—and most of all, trying to raise her children here.

As the casserole was taken from the microwave—an all-vegetarian entrée consisting exclusively and conspicuously of produce grown here at the Project—filling the kitchen with even more heat and steam, Gwen unconsciously moved away, toward the open window.

The United Nations had seen fit to situate its experimental agricultural cooperative in a broad, shallow impact feature—in other words, she thought, a big hole in the ground—a little under a hundred miles in diameter, the Residence and attached workers' compound occupying a low central prominence. Consequently, there was nothing to look at in any direction but a crater-pocked prairie ringed by mountains, their impossibly jagged ridges as yet unsoftened by the weather (a relatively new phenomenon itself on Pallas) or by the stands of forest growth everyone promised would someday put in an appearance.

She admitted to herself that the prairie everywhere she looked was dotted by a thousand deep blue, perfectly circular lakes. Well-managed cultivated fields were finally beginning to supplant the ragged, weed-choked "natural" meadows they'd found here when they arrived. And, thanks to patient gardeners requisitioned from the ranks of the colonists her husband watched over, equally well-tended flower beds bloomed all around the Residence itself in brilliant profusion.

All in all, she supposed, she and her husband and their children lived a life that would have been the envy of any British second son sent to the West Indies to make his fortune, or of any southern American plantation owner of two centuries ago. And what they did here was democratic, progressive, for the benefit of workers whom British and southern aristocrats would merely have exploited like cattle.

But the value of any of it was lost on her, calculated against—just to single out one terrible example—the absolutely shocking rate of suicide and spontaneous abortion occurring among the Project's peasants and (according to what little they heard about the subject through authorized channels) the Pallatian colonists beyond the Rimfence whom everybody in the Project called "Outsiders."

Of course a great many men and women—courageous or foolhardy, depending on who told it—had already perished simply in the tremendous undertaking of terraforming Pallas. It was a frequent topic of discussion at her husband's table. Some had made lethal miscalculations in the deceptively low and surprisingly variable gravity of the asteroid. Others had suffered from the predictable but unavoidable hazards of the bitter cold and vacuum of space. Still others had succumbed, even as they might have back on Earth, to ordinary industrial accidents with high explosives and machinery. In the end, there had been over a thousand such victims, more than one for each kilometer of Pallas's diameter, after whom the first landmarks on its surface had been named. And what had it accomplished?

She remembered the way, on Earth, that elected and appointed officials of various national governments and the UN—conscientious and courageous public servants whom William Wilde Curringer had arrogantly written off as "safety fascists"—began to rage impotently over the mounting death toll on Pallas, while at the same time, despite the most urgent warnings, construction workers from all over the planet had continued to sign up by the thousands to take the places of the fallen.

Little did she know—she'd have been about twenty-two at the time, she guessed, and still preoccupied with trying to make her marriage work—that it was her future home they were all talking about. Otherwise she might have paid better attention.

For the most part, it must have been the obscenely spectacular amounts of money Curringer had offered his workers, along with promised land grants on the asteroid, which attracted them despite the well-publicized dangers—just another example of the kind of exploitation Gibson was determined to stop here. But there were many among the survivors who claimed that they—no more or less than those who had died—were no different from millions of earthbound dam and bridge and tunnel builders who'd come and gone before them. They believed that the accomplishment—or even merely the attempt—was worthy of the risk.

Well, she thought—as she had done a thousand times before—if the Greeley Utopian Memorial Project succeeded, in the future, decisions like that would be made only by the people who were qualified to make them. The idea was a source of comfort to her, and she cherished it.

Gwen was an educated woman and knew that the stress of a new environment was taking its inevitable hideous toll. She understood the principle of natural selection, although like her husband, she was committed to seeing that it remained natural, rather than man-inflicted. But it was like having all these spectacular rainbow-colored sunrises and sunsets—which she felt were highly overrated anyway: what good were they when only one new baby out of every seven or eight conceived survived to enjoy them, as if it were still the Dark Ages?

Pressured—among others by a husband who seemed stimulated only by duty and was otherwise uninterested in her body—to provide a worthy example in what she privately referred to as the "Be Fruitful and Multiply Department," Gwen herself had miscarried more than once. In the final analysis there was, she felt, a fundamental *wrongness* about Pallas which she couldn't adjust to, no matter how she tried.

Lesser examples of that wrongness occupied the shelves and tabletops about her now. Except for rare, expensive imports, everything which would have been made of wood or plastic back home was fabricated here from metal or glass—the cheapest, most convenient materials on a mineral-rich world still poor in organics.

Overhead, the cloud-fleeced sky was blue enough, but of an alien shade. Two suns, the genuine primary—too far away and small—and one of its orbiting mirror-reflected counterfeits, were always visible in the daytime. The nights, thanks to those same orbital mirrors, seemed unnaturally brief, embellished by a natural moon which seemed the right size, but of the wrong color and pattern.

Trees, for the most part seeded by ultralight aircraft during the final stages of terraformation, were all exactly the same height, giving the landscape a contrived look which was appropriate but oppressively surreal, like living in a cartoon. It was estimated that in the low-mass regions of Pallas they might eventually grow to be a thousand yards tall.

Even worse, like the trees, the children who managed to be born alive and healthy were beginning to turn out gangly, attenuated, their growing bodies responding to a feeble pull of gravity which varied, depending on the location and its underlying geology, from just one-tenth of Earth normal to the merest twentieth.

And worst of all, Pallas was dull. Having long ago— and not without sufficient reason, thoroughly and humiliatingly laundered in public—lost interest in the intimate aspect of marriage herself, Gwen felt deprived of the cultural and social benefits to which any Washingtonian of wealth and status becomes accustomed. Her husband had argued that, through recordings and realtime transmissions to the Residence from the home planet, she was free to enjoy any drama, dance, or spectacle that anyone enjoyed on Earth. She'd replied that, while everything he said might be true, no one of any importance could *see* her enjoying them. And this telling if somewhat irrational point had long since settled the argument.

At least for her.

IV
TRAGEDY AND HOPE

FROM 1917, AMERICANS WONDERED WHY THEY AIDED RUSSIA
WITH FOOD SHE COULD NOT GROW HERSELF. THE TRUTH WAS,
THOSE WHO HAD SADDLED THEM WITH A FEDERAL RESERVE
AND INCOME TAX DID MORE THAN JUST KEEP SOVIET MARXISM
GOING, THEY HAD CREATED IT. DURING THE FIRST HALF OF THE
CENTURY, GOVERNMENT GREW *500 TIMES FASTER THAN THE
POPULATION.* COULD THAT HAVE HAPPENED WITHOUT AN ENEMY
TO FRIGHTEN VOTERS AND RELUCTANT TAXPAYERS?
— **Mirelle Stein,** *The Productive Class*

A s it was intended to be, stepping into the official residence of the Chief Administrator was like stepping a
quarter of a billion kilometers, all the way back to Earth.

"Dinner's ready, Senator, and Mr. Brody is at the
gate."

As she always did at this time, Alice Ngu had come to
fetch him in from the verandah. Short, plump, and brown,
wearing a plain dress which failed as a servant's uniform
only because nobody else here wore one like it, she was
second- or third-generation Cambodian or Vietnamese—
Altman could never remember which—and delivered her
English with that lilt Orientals seemed to retain no matter
how many of their ancestors had lived and died in America. Her husband and children had been among those he'd
watched returning from the fields.

As usual, he'd already started in and met her in the
family's private living room. "Thank you, Alice, I'll talk to
the gate. Please tell Mrs. Altman I'll be there shortly."

As she left, closing the double doors behind her, it
struck him all over again how Gwen had made a point of
maintaining things as if they were still living on Earth.

Given certain constraints, the place combined the ambience of the executive mansion she'd grown up in with the self-conscious rusticity of the high-tech hideaway where she'd spent most of her vacations. Altman had to concentrate sometimes, remember to slide his feet along as he did outdoors, avoid lifting them too far from the carpet in a pull of gravity only a tenth as powerful as that of Earth, in order to keep from dashing his brains out on the ceiling beams.

The room appeared pine-paneled. There wasn't a tree on Pallas that could have provided the boards—not that anybody was willing to cut, anyway. The cost of importing the rolls of photoprinted plastic had exceeded what many a family had spent simply getting here, but the paneling— and the chairs and sofas upholstered in dark colors, the yellow incandescent light of the fabric-shaded bulbs in end-table lamps—lent a welcome warmth to this room, and to others Gwen had decorated, which seemed lacking anywhere else on the little planet.

He reached an intercom set into the wall beside the doors and touched a key. Its tiny liquid-crystal screen, until now merely displaying the time, date, and temperature, dissolved into a wide-angle view inside the gatehouse, where an International Peace Corpsman waited to hear from him.

"Altman here."

"Sir! Subject identifies himself as Brody, Aloysius, no middle initial, no real ID."

Before Altman could focus on the well-scrubbed face beneath a baseball cap of sky blue (Earth's sky—Pallas's was tinged with a reddish purple Gwen often complained of), a vast hand engulfed the picture, wrenching it about until it settled on a seamier face he recognized. Annoyance colored the young Corpsman's voice, just as reddish purple colored the sky. It was a common reaction which the

Senator understood perfectly but couldn't train his people out of. Outsiders made a point of *never* carrying documents, and under the Stein Covenant—the agreement they'd all signed before immigrating to Pallas—they couldn't be required to.

Brody grinned into the camera. "A good evenin' to ye, Senator darlin', an' will y'kindly be lettin' me in?" Altman was sure the accent was a phony. Not only did it seem to come and go with the weather and the time of day, but his intelligence sources had told him that Brody had been born in an industrial suburb of Boston.

"Sorry for the wait, Mr. Brody. The corporal will have someone escort you to the Residence."

Altman rang off, savoring the room about him for a final minute. Thanks to Gwen, nothing but the gravity reminded him of the world he stood on. The drapes had been drawn before dark and—a welcome difference from Earth—a fire burned in the hearth. At home, with the dwindling resources and draconian pollution laws of eastern North America, it would have been a hologram. Here there was certainly no scarcity of agricultural waste, nor of hydraulic rams and labor to shape it into "logs," and between the chimney precipitators and a selectively permeable atmospheric envelope, no pollution.

Meanwhile, without a crackle or a grain of "snow," the latest digitalized disinformation from LiteLink in Atlanta, admittedly delayed by never less than fourteen minutes, splashed across a large high-definition room screen as it might have done in any home on Earth, without an audience at the moment to appreciate the technical—if not the journalistic—accomplishment it represented.

On the other walls, Gwen had hung framed prints, young girls in sunlight-dappled gardens, quaint bridges arching over their own reflections in quiet, lily-patterned water. On the piano—small, but representing yet another conspicuous expense—stood a picture of her parents. Never mind that it was an old campaign photo taken just before the Big One murdered them and twenty million other Californians. The truth, which he'd never spoken in his wife's company, was that dear old Dad Hathaway's political posterior—or at least his reputation with posterity—had been rescued by the earthquake everybody had been expecting for decades.

Shaking his head at the remembrance, he dismissed it and made his way to the formal entrance, where Alice was answering the door. "Good evening, sir, may I take your—"

At first glance, there seemed nothing to take. From the way Brody leaned on his cane, he wasn't about to part with that. A head shorter than Altman, he wasn't large but somehow gave a contrary impression. Behind antique rimless glasses, his eyes glittered with good-natured mischief—some cosmic joke he was willing to share with anyone who asked—the lines radiating from their corners making him look like a Coca-Cola Santa Claus. He could have been described as broad. His clothes, and the sweeping gestures that formed a part of his vocabulary, accentuated it.

At least he looked clean. Like all Outsiders, he was dressed and groomed abominably, tonight in faded denim trousers, leather sandals, and an off-white smock dyed in primitive splashes of color. His beard and hair were gray-shot, the latter shoulder-length and parted painstakingly in the middle, held behind his prominent ears with a thong. Altman's sources stated that the man was sixty-two years old and had come to Pallas earlier than most immigrants as a laser operator with the original terraforming crew. Having lost his right leg in a construction accident, he'd apparently decided to stay where the gravity was kinder.

From under the obnoxious shirt, strapped to his left

thigh, hung a big, heavy-looking pistol which the Senator wished he'd had the Corpsman confiscate at the gate. Unfortunately, that would have breached the so-called governing document cooked up by pop-philosopher Mirelle Stein and foisted on the locals by Curringer simply because it had been his billions—along with those of a Japanese consortium he'd had under his thumb—which had financed the entire terraformation.

More to the point, Outsiders could be very touchy about what they'd been led to believe were their rights, and the Project badly needed new markets for what it grew. Much as the proliferation of personal arms on Pallas infuriated Altman—he'd been the Senate's foremost advocate of stripping America clean of that particular evil—he was reluctant to offend any potential customer, especially the widely respected landlord of the Nimrod Saloon & Gambling Emporium, which formed whatever social focus the ramshackle town across the lake laid claim to.

Brody gave Alice a searching look. Winking broadly at Altman, standing a couple of meters behind her, he handed her his cane, unfastened the tie-down above his knee, reached up under his shirt and pulled the rig off, pistol and all, handed it to her, and reclaimed his cane. Arm sagging more under the emotional than the physical mass of the belt, weapon, and spare ammunition, she handled the ensemble as if it were a poisonous snake, but accepted it without comment and hung it on a knob of a coatrack near the door.

Altman led the man to what served as a dining room—there wasn't time for the customary drink and small talk in the parlor Gwen kept for such occasions—where they both sat, only to find themselves on their feet again when she entered from the kitchen.

"Justice Aloysius Brody," the Senator began, "my wife, Gwendolyn Hathaway Altman."

Gwen, who'd been supervising the cooking, removed her small apron, wiped her hands, and extended one to match the paw Brody offered. Altman thought he was going to lean down and kiss it.

"Charmed t'be sure, Mrs. Altman, an' at yer service."

"Please be seated," she answered, *"Justice* Brody?"

Gwen had been a thin, pretty, tightly wound platinum blond of seventeen, nine years younger than himself, when he'd first become enchanted with her at an Inauguration ball in 2012. At the time, he hadn't known that she was the elder daughter of the most powerful individual in his own political party. He was still pleased to recall that his ardor hadn't heated noticeably when he'd found out who she was. It had pleased him somewhat less, after their wedding in 2013—during a period when premarital intimacy was less common than it had been generations earlier—to discover that she brought her innate nervousness to bed with her.

She had been the picture-perfect political wife. Sixteen years had given her fine lines at the corners of her eyes (nothing like the mesh decorating Brody's), put a little flesh on her, and added some premature silver to the platinum.

All the patience he could muster had failed to warm the personal side of their life together. In the end, to her visible relief, he'd sought satisfaction elsewhere. They hadn't slept in the same room since their first child, Gibson Junior, had been conceived; a rare exception had allowed the delighted tabloids to show her, eight months into a second pregnancy, at the height of the scandal which had destroyed him. True to her upbringing—for Gwen life imitated the art of the possible—she blamed him less for extramarital adventuring than for getting caught at it. She monitored her blood chemistry and made appointments with him by the calendar, a monthly chore he relished less and less.

"I thank y'very kindly, ma'am." Cane between his knees, Brody folded his hands atop the crook as she refilled his wineglass. " 'Tis an honorary title, dear lady."

The kitchen door swung aside, temporarily stopping conversation. Once the cook and her helpers, colonists like Alice, had served them and departed, Gwen raised her eyebrows prettily. "You're not really a judge, then, Mr. Brody?"

Altman watched with amusement and sympathy—for Brody. Gwen had lusty instincts for a few things, power being highest on the list. Had she been convinced that Brody was a nobody—were she to become convinced even now—she'd drop out of the conversation and let her husband carry on. He'd seen the same thing happen thousands of times and was convinced she was unaware she did it.

The man grinned, turning up the Santa effect. "I'm after adjudicatin' the occasional dispute. Mostly I'm no more than the humble innkeeper y'see before ye—thank y'kindly, I will have another. Y'wouldn't be related t'Dad Hathaway, now?"

"I'm his daughter." She smiled, her eyes downcast modestly on her plate. Her own enthusiasm tonight for the wine they made themselves here was unusual. Ordinarily she'd let her first glass sit through a meal, hardly condescending to touch it.

Alden "Dad" Hathaway had been the last Democratic governor of California. He'd wanted to be the first President from the newly formed Democratic Union Party, but fate—at 9.5 on the Richter Scale—had intervened. The party, large and diverse as it was, solidly rooted in American political tradition, had so far failed to put a candidate in the White House. There were reasons for that—Altman himself was presently foremost among them—but there were other reasons, as well.

Reluctantly on the couple's part, they talked about it

over dinner. The Outsider seemed more interested in discussing events on Earth, which he hadn't seen for years, than business. In a buyer's market he felt free to antagonize them with his peculiar ideas, whereas they—Gwen was aware of the Project's desperate need for customers—couldn't afford to antagonize him by telling him how peculiar his ideas were.

In the ancient Chinese sense, the opening years of the twenty-first century had proven "interesting." Sweeping changes—welcome and long overdue, in Brody's opinion—had imposed themselves on an increasingly confused and confusing world.

Most notable was a shift in the century-old balance of political and military power. Prodigious, domestically unpopular amounts of American aid had failed to keep the Soviet Empire from crumbling after decades of wildly swinging temperament, liberal reforms alternating with brutal strictures often tightened overnight. Those subsidies, along with a last hysterical flurry of foreign military adventures, had only helped cripple that once-great Western nation's own economy and had eventually destroyed both the Democratic and Republican parties.

"Not t'mention their old management, so proud of their bipartisan aid programs," Brody declared, "at least as far as runnin' under the old labels was concerned."

At about the same time, reacting as it had over two millennia to outside influence, split by linguistic and cultural differences little appreciated in the West, China had divided itself into a dozen conflicting principalities, some independent, some controlled by other governments, and some—it was impossible to tell.

"The Chinese picture still seems to change every day," Altman informed his guest.

"But it's fair t'say that socialism as a force in human history seems finally t'have run its course."

Altman watched Gwen, who'd studied Marxist economics at Berkeley, the one university in the world still offering it, until conversation moved to safer ground. In mostly English-speaking Europe, borders meant less each year. Mirroring America's economic problems, Europe had eliminated trade barriers on that continent, along with internal economic regulation.

"They were desperate," Brody observed, "unlike what's left of the States so far."

"And yet today, their most marketable commodity"— Gwen, too, was trying to prevent raised voices and hard feelings at her table—"seems to be nationalism."

Brody laughed. "Now that nobody gives a damn, whole peoples who lost their identities in the fine print of many an ill-considered treaty after many a great war have reemerged as harmless curiosities. Armenians fight Turks each afternoon for theme-park visitors, with extra shows on Saturday and Sunday!"

Gwen seemed grateful to arrive at what was almost a neutral subject. "Fierce Montenegrins with moustachios a foot long pose for the cameras with absurdly huge revolvers."

"While ads," Altman tried to help, "argue over which parliament, Scottish or Welsh, it's more fun to be Member-for-a-Day in."

"An' they all agree that y'can do it on Visa or Master-Card!"

"The effort hasn't paid off yet," the Senator answered. "Most observers feel it's only a matter of time."

"So," Brody offered, "though everybody's broke, whatever trouble people're losin' sleep over these days, they're enjoyin' the first worldwide cease-fire in a dozen decades." He raised his glass. "Here's t'the War Century, over at long last!"

They raised their glasses. "The War Century," repeated the Senator.

"Over," his wife responded, "at long last!"

It was a sentiment they all could share sincerely.

V

UNAUTHORIZED ENTERPRISE

EVERY SUCCESSFUL REVOLUTION PUTS ON IN TIME THE ROBES
OF THE TYRANT IT HAS DEPOSED.
— Barbara Tuchman

F ourteen-year-old Emerson yawned.

"What has happened so far on Pallas is regrettable,"
declared the Chief Administrator, who made an egalitarian
habit every morning of addressing the assembled colonists.

Emerson yawned. His hair was still wet from the
shower he'd been forced to take, he ached with the stiffness of another night spent lying propped against a damp
concrete wall, his arms and legs trembled with newly restored circulation—all of which had kept him from eating
much breakfast. Again. His stomach growled in protest.
Like the other peasants around him, he'd heard it all
before, what this man was blathering about. As far as he
knew, he was the only one who had never believed any
of it.

"Two Lions Consortium of Siskei claimed this asteroid
as private property thirty years ago, in 2007 . . ." The figure posing at parade-rest high on the Residence verandah—far from the plebeian ranks frozen at attention beneath his gaze—wore a face Emerson's parents seemed to
remember only vaguely from TV or the movies of a previous generation. Emerson, who by now had seen that same

face, closer up and more times than he cared to remember, knew better. ". . . in an arrogant and abusive violation of the universally acclaimed 1999 United Nations Convention rendering all such astronomical bodies the common property of all humanity."

It was the same crap every morning. He resisted an urge to scratch beneath one shoulder blade, knowing from long experience that it would only start him itching in a dozen other places.

"It's more regrettable . . ." Despite his bruises, and the ordeal he knew too well by now still lay ahead of him, Emerson yawned again. Even the compliant morons either side of him in their fresh white denims—adults, but as figuratively wet behind the ears as he was literally himself—had begun shifting from one foot to another. ". . . that neither the United Nations nor other governments on the face of our Depression-ravaged home planet possessed spaceships of its own or the resources necessary to build an atmospheric envelope and develop Pallas."

Because, Emerson finished the thought, there wasn't anybody left to steal them from. At his age—the same as the Chief Administrator's son, he'd heard—born on Earth in the western half of what were still technically the United States, he didn't know the words "precociously cynical." He remembered secondhand his grandparents' tales of dirty Asian politics before, during, and after the war in Vietnam: life had been cheap, liberty a joke, the pursuit of happiness a privilege reserved to politicians and their families who did whatever they wished with ordinary people and then—the only difference democracy had ever made—went through the motions of justifying it afterward. Nor, according to what he'd learned bit by bit from his highly apolitical parents, had it been much different in the gerrymandered satrapies of Los Angeles. And Pallas was only smaller and farther away.

"Instead"—the Chief Administrator's petulance came clearly over the public address system—"Two Lions's ultrareactionary founder, William Wilde Curringer, the infamous South African trillionaire polluter and exploiter, was able to use his obscene wealth to foist Mirelle Stein's socially regressive 'Hyperdemocratic Covenant' on anyone who wished to pioneer this asteroid. As if he hadn't already inflicted enough damage on the fragile biosphere and the political ambience of Earth."

The political ambience of Earth. Seeing his fellow workers in the long white rows around him taking it all in, Emerson shook his head in disbelief. He always felt embarrassed for them, and it wasn't a feeling he liked. His grandparents had been "boat people"—among millions of political and economic refugees who'd escaped from war-shattered, Communist-controlled Southeast Asia in the latter part of the last century. They'd been among the fortunate thousands who'd actually made it to the promised land of opportunity in America—only to find that most avenues to personal betterment they'd looked forward to had been barred decades earlier by a tangle of arbitrary rules and regulations, as well as by long-established attitudes and practices which discriminated against Asians.

Life had been better in California than in Vietnam or Cambodia, or at least more secure, and their standard of living undeniably higher. In the end, they'd swallowed their disappointment and settled down to become the most unquestioning Americans they could. It wasn't always easy. Each day, it seemed, another law was passed to impoverish and diminish them, punishing them for whatever success they achieved and rewarding their less competent and industrious neighbors.

Another wave of itching swept his body. He resisted with inadequate, invisible twitches set to the tune of a growling stomach. One of the laborers beside him smirked.

A generation later, the refugees' American children, Emerson's parents, thrilled by rumors leaking past the biased mass media of an open, market-oriented society being built among the asteroids, had believed the Curringer Trust's advertisements which were saturating TV, radio, newspapers, and magazines—"TO PALLAS, FOR THE OPPORTUNITY OF A LIFETIME! TO PALLAS, FOR A LIFETIME OF OPPORTUNITY!"—embellished by promises and reassurances from thousands of unemployed social workers hired to recruit exclusively for the Greeley Utopian Memorial Project.

The only means of getting there they could afford, however, was under UN sponsorship. Nevertheless, hoping for a better future than their parents had won, they'd taken their two-year-old son and emigrated to Pallas, only to discover, when they'd gotten here after a cramped and arduous two-year voyage, that they'd sentenced themselves and their growing family—all forms of contraception being condemned and unavailable within the Project—to conditions comparable to medieval serfdom. In some ways, he realized, it was like an Outsider's description of the maximum-security prisons many of them had apparently come here to avoid. And there was no way of going home—nobody could afford to. The fact that it was meant as a template for larger societies made him shudder.

But the Chief Administrator was going on: "Outside, beyond the humane influence of our Project, the barbaric notions of that crackpot Mirelle Stein—and those of South African anthropologist Raymond Louis Drake-Tealy, another of the renegade trillionaire's cronies and even more regressive than Stein, if possible—have achieved popular acceptance, diverting life on Pallas from the civilized mainstream."

Now what did the Chief Administrator mean by "the civilized mainstream"? The moonshining, drug-running, vandalism, pilferage, burglary, gang-fighting, assault, and rape threatening to become epidemic among the Project's mostly illiterate second generation, which had begun transforming the Chief Administrator's utopian dream into a nightmare of violence and fear? Or did he refer to his recently augmented security forces, conducting increasingly frequent and intrusive household and personal searches for weapons, stolen goods, addictive substances, and contraceptives—measures permitted in the fine print of the Project's articles—without producing any desirable effect?

One of nature's rebels against authority, Emerson felt that he'd been *born* more politically sophisticated than his parents, and, thanks to his clandestine radio and salvaged books, was better informed. Outside, progress tried to march on. Across Lake Selous, the only radio station in Curringer had yet to acquire competition, despite having offered to divide the frequency to which it had staked a claim under the Hyperdemocratic Covenant and sell slots to other broadcasters. Now it promised to transmit pictures in the distant future. He was determined, somehow, to be among the first to see them.

He'd heard much over his hidden receiver that he didn't understand, but certain points had been clear at once. At the onset of the asteroid's development, the Greeley Utopian Memorial Project had boasted the largest single segment of a total population of about twenty-five thousand. A major purchaser of Outsider goods and services, cheap labor had given it a decisive advantage. There was a ready market for its agricultural produce, and its collective opinion, as expressed by the Chief Administrator, had carried weight all over the asteroid and beyond. However, the Project—for some reason, it came as no surprise to the voices he listened to in secret—had begun to suffer at the same time the Outsider economy began flourishing.

Emerson desperately wanted to flourish with it.

To him the Chief Administrator, famed for his passionate advocacy of Democratic Union tariffs, a tightly regulated economy, and stifled hopes for individuals, was almost indistinguishable from the Khmer Rouge butchers who at least had possessed enough integrity to murder their millions outright in his mother's native Cambodia. It was clear—if only from his aristocratic, patronizing face and voice—that the man regarded himself as little less than their feudal master. For the boy, because he'd come to represent everything that had destroyed his parents' dreams—and his grandparents' before them—the Chief Administrator's many lectures, edicts, and opinions carried no weight. No matter what was done to him, this morning or in time to come, they never would.

But the Chief Administrator was ignorant of the judgment being passed on him. "Today," he informed them, "what was promoted as an equitable, progressive, and pluralistic social order under the Curringer Trust and the Hyperdemocratic Covenant has degenerated into a violent, brutal, dog-eat-dog travesty of a society where the strong prey on the weak and the rich prey on the poor. If you doubt it, you can hear the gunfire for yourself, in the fields near our protective Rimfence."

This time, the effort of not scratching tensed every sore muscle in his body and brought tears to his eyes. Despite his carefully practiced attitude of detached cynicism, he was outraged at the lie the Chief Administrator had just gotten away with. Gunfire was certainly there to be heard, the sound of hunting and target-practice. He'd heard it many times himself, crouched in his cave, listening to the radio. But it had nothing to do—very little, anyway—with the manner in which Outsiders chose to order their affairs. And they certainly held no monopoly on violence, brutality, or predation.

It was true there were rules of a sort. Whatever he was caught at, the United Nations personnel who enforced the whims of the Chief Administrator—Project kids called them "blue goons" whenever they thought grown-ups were out of earshot, although he'd heard the same words on the lips of many an adult—couldn't imprison him. Like the Chief Administrator, most of them were exiles, the dregs of law enforcement in their respective nation-states. Their white-collar superiors were no more than armed social workers, would-be criminal behaviorists he knew from bitter experience would soon capitalize on his battered condition, just as they'd done so many times before, to brutalize him in their own despicable way, violate his mental privacy, his sense of personal dignity, and his individual sovereignty with their intrusive and intensive attempts at "understanding" and "rehabilitating" him. Anyway, the Project had no jail to be construed by visiting observers as inhumane.

Instead, they could leave him lying in a dark rear stall of the communal showers all night on a cold, damp concrete floor, driven nearly to madness by echoes from the rough-surfaced, leaky pipes they'd strapped him to, helpless to prevent small, many-legged creatures from crawling over his face. The only thing that had ever helped him at times like these was filling his mind with fantastic, heartfelt images of someday, somehow flying over the hated Rimfence to freedom.

For identical reasons, United Nations Education and Morale counselors couldn't be issued anything as brutal as handcuffs. That, too, might destroy their sponsors' illusions of a brave new world. But they could cinch him to a water pipe by the neck and bind his wrists and ankles, with plastic zip-ties saved for them in a particular refuse bin over at Central Receiving, that restricted circulation in his hands and feet until he couldn't move or feel anything in them.

Similarly, they couldn't whip him or strike him with fists—and every use of their shock batons was supposedly monitored remotely by their supervisors. What they could do was drub him in shifts, for hours on end, with meter-long sections of concrete reinforcement rod wrapped in plastic foam and duct tape—more largesse from some generous soul at Central Receiving—until he could hardly move for the pain, even if he hadn't been trussed up, and it felt like every bone in his body had been broken, even though he never had a single scratch or bruise to show for it.

And, of course, since the Chief Administrator had recently broadened the communalistic charter to forbid personal possessions of any kind, they invariably relieved him of everything he carried in the little pouch he wore on a string around his neck—like every other colonist he knew—beneath his pocketless Project-issues.

Emerson had long understood with the clarity of a born victim—in this respect his cynicism was genuine—that there was always more the blue goons might have done to him if they'd been inclined, and probably would someday unless he found a way to fulfill his desperate fantasies of flight. For now the worst part, once he'd been taken from the stall, cleaned up, and shoved into the breakfast line before assembly, was that his fatigue and pain were more or less invisible. His stiffness and exhaustion would be interpreted by the Chief Administrator as sullen stupidity. His lack of fear—because he'd already survived far worse—would resemble defiance. And more and more, with every day that passed, the resemblance was appropriate.

Many times before he'd reached his present age—not nearly as often as he'd broken the rules successfully—he'd been brought before the Chief Administrator to receive what was invariably represented as the Judgment of the Community. It had begun years ago when he'd retrieved bruised oranges from the Residence trash, cut out the spoiled parts, squeezed the juice, and was caught trading homemade refreshments to field workers for odd bits they themselves had salvaged elsewhere. That was how he'd gotten the spool-ends of wire for his radio. Luckily, no one had ever summed up what he'd acquired and accused him of the additional infraction of "hoarding."

Yesterday, he'd been caught buying admission chits— scalping tickets—from a few of the more amiably corruptible guards who didn't want them, to a charity performance by a visiting Earthie entertainer a little past her prime and the peak of her fame, but gushingly enthusiastic about the Project. There seemed to be many of that type.

Each time they met this way, face to face in his private office, the Chief Administrator threatened to send him Outside into what he claimed was a jungle where every split second represented a life-or-death struggle for mere subsistence. His embarrassed parents—the Chief Administrator's housekeeper and Emerson's father, called in from the fields—always begged their master for leniency, and their humble pleas were always granted. To their distress, Emerson neither experienced nor expressed gratitude at these reprieves. What they'd never have believed, after all the years of forcing themselves to adapt to their own fate, was that, each time he was caught, the blue goons used the excuse to terrorize and rough him up, sometimes claiming afterward that he'd resisted them.

Somehow he had resisted them all these years, and the

Project's psychovultures as well—partly with his mental images of flying—and survived. He couldn't fight directly, but executed his revenge with cold intelligence. In the beginning, he'd waited until the next spontaneous rash of vandalism to commit his own, better-planned acts of sabotage—bits of hay snipped off flush in building and vehicle locks, blocked and overflowing plumbing in the goons' quarters—damage carefully calculated to equal his losses.

He'd never destroyed anything his parents or their coworkers had labored to produce. He hadn't touched the catalytic fusion reactor—yet. As he matured, he'd eventually given up these nonproductive forays, along with their attendant risks, just as he'd given up childish fantasies about miraculously flying over the Rimfence, vowing to pursue revenge only when he could have it at a profit.

He knew the Chief Administrator would always be kindly and forgiving—in public—but that one day, sooner or later, Emerson's many and varied enterprises were bound to earn the boy a convenient accident at the hands of the blue goons, ridding the Project of an individual the older man must see as a perpetual annoyance. Before that could happen, Emerson vowed, he must escape into what he thought of as the real world.

Someone near him coughed, bringing him back from his reverie. The senior Education and Morale counselors were responsible for continuing the assembly after the Chief Administrator's customary introduction. The first thing they did this morning, after he'd stepped off the verandah, presumably headed for his office, was to call a single individual forward by name and all alone, for judgment and punishment—the idea of any kind of trial would have sent both sides into hysterical laughter—which they were privately aware he'd already received.

"Ngu comma Emerson: unauthorized enterprise!"

He straightened his back and strode through the ranks of his fellow peasants toward the Residence.

Again.

VI
THE RIMFENCE

THE HUMAN RACE DIVIDES POLITICALLY INTO THOSE WHO WANT PEOPLE TO BE CONTROLLED AND THOSE WHO HAVE NO SUCH DESIRE.
—**Robert A. Heinlein,** *The Notebooks of Lazarus Long*

Ready, Senator?"
He hadn't come to admire the fence, but admire it he did. Sixteen meters high, 245 kilometers long, it enclosed just short of two million hectares—1.6 percent of the asteroid's surface—along with ten thousand colonists, their UN sheepdogs, and his family.

He wasn't sure why, but it made him feel secure for the first time in his life. This morning's confrontation with Alice's young son, an otherwise undistinguished youngster about the same age as his own, had left him with a hollow feeling and he needed a little reassurance. The boy's transgression was always the same—unauthorized enterprise—differing in an ominous way from Gibson Junior's pranks and the general run of juvenile delinquency they'd been having so much trouble with recently.

"Senator?"

He turned to the reporter who was his real reason for being here this morning. Her impossibly long eyelashes, moist, full lips, long, clean legs revealed by a pair of tight khaki safari shorts, her narrow waist, slender hips, and assets that strained the buttons of a self-consciously proletarian work shirt all hinted, and not very subtly, that she might be willing to stay for another day or two if the famous sexy Senator could just find something to do with the wife and kiddies.

He'd carefully deafened himself over the years to over-tures like this—from bitter experience traversing the sex-ual minefield that was Washington—deliberately blinded himself, concentrating instead on the Project. It would have taken someone considerably more attractive to him than this shopworn young woman to change that.

Today the youthful-looking Senator wore the same running shoes, faded jeans, and plaid sport shirt open at the neck that a series of relaxed and wildly successful cam-paign spots had made him famous for. His attention—and his best political smile—were on the reporter. The shoul-der-stocked camera her assistant pointed at him looked uncomfortably like a weapon. Then again, he supposed it was more powerful and destructive than any gun. So far the idiot, awkward in low gravity, had spent his time trip-ping over furrows and had already ruined several plants, angering the workers. But it was a small price to pay for publicity friendly to the Project.

"Ready when you are, Martie."

She nodded cheerfully into the camera. "We're here, two hundred fifty million miles from Earth, for the Global Information Gathering Organization. With us is former United States Senator Gibson Altman, Chief Administra-tor of the United Nations' Greeley Utopian Memorial Proj-ect on Pallas—and oh yes, his little son, Gibson Junior."

Altman glanced at the sour-faced child fidgeting beside him, tousled the boy's hair, tried to look paternal—some-thing he'd never been much good at—then up again, more at the reporter than the camera. It was obvious that the boy hadn't been dressed by his nurse. This was Gwen's kind of joke, outfitting her son in Levi's, Kevlar shoes, and a shirt identical to his father's. Having the boy with him was a good idea, given past publicity. Having Gwen, their daughter, and baby son would have been even better, but he didn't want them out here in the fields.

"Pallas," the reporter continued, reading from a smartcard concealed in her palm, "is six hundred eight kilometers in diameter and follows a mildly eccentric orbit in a broad band between Mars and Jupiter containing tens of thousands of such miniature planets. Its surface area is 1,161,820 square kilometers, about the same as Colorado, Utah, Arizona, and New Mexico—the so-called West American 'four corners' states—combined, with maybe a quarter of Wyoming thrown in for good measure."

Martie Mough was unquestionably pretty, tall, blond, voluptuous in the extreme—and utterly sexless. He'd noted this before with female reporters, supposing it must be a professional asset in a trade where half the customers were men, subconsciously (or otherwise) dissatisfied with their domestic arrangement, and the other half women, innately jealous and suspicious. Her name, pronounced "moe," was often mangled, most often by her colleagues, in accordance with her physical assets (and some said her intelligence), to rhyme with "cow" or "moo." Personally, he thought "muff" would have been funnier, but at a little under thirty, he guessed, she was at least ten years too old to interest him that way.

"Second largest of the asteroids, Pallas was the first to be explored and settled, thanks to its unique combination of resources: soil, water, and low gravity. Vesta, next-largest of the so-called Big Five Asteroids, is brighter and more easily seen from Earth, but it's composed of granite, is therefore lifeless, and will probably remain so forever, having none of what Pallas has to offer humanity."

Astronomers had known for a century that Pallas's low reflectivity indicated that it was probably composed of carbonaceous chondrites, rather than meteoric stone or nickel-iron, which meant that somewhere between five and ten percent of its mass could be expected to be water, chemically locked into its substance. As a result, with little effort or expenditure of energy, the hydrocarbon-rich surface could be processed into soil. In some senses, it already was soil.

Pallas's size, however, and its consequent attraction, implied that it was an "accretion body"—the little world had proven to be heavily cratered—which for billions of years had collected smaller asteroids of differing composition. Impacting on its surface, they'd left large, discrete deposits of useful minerals and metals. Moreover, certain twentieth-century astrophysicists had held that petroleum did not stem from biological sources—dinosaurs or Carboniferous plants—as popularly believed, but had been produced by the titanic events in which the solar system had created itself from a swirling cloud of interstellar dust and gases. Their theory had been confirmed when oil was discovered within the structure of a body which presumably had never known life of any kind.

The reporter looked up just in time to catch the Senator's eye and warn him wordlessly that Gibson Junior, who had quietly left his father's side, was just as quietly sifting a handful of fine dirt into the big galvanized tub containing the workers' drinking water. Hoping she'd have the decency to edit this little drama out, he reached for the boy, snagged the neck of his shirt, and dragged him back.

The reporter suppressed a grin.

Maybe she had children of her own.

"But enough of these dry, flavorless statistics. Senator, once one gets past that gorgeous sunrise we stopped to record this morning on the way out here, this doesn't look all that different from, say, Iowa. What makes it worth all the trouble and expense to build a farm community a quarter of a billion miles from Earth?"

The fact was that she and her assistant had staggered out of their guest quarters well after sunrise, almost terminally hung over, and the gorgeous sunrise they'd "recorded" would come from stock footage. They'd arrived the previous evening after an apparently uproarious time spent at Aloysius Brody's sleazy establishment across the lake. This time, however, Altman's smile was completely sincere, and for good reason: from here, countless perfect furrows swept away in beautiful, green concentric circles, following the shape of the meteoric bowl the Project lay in and delaying runoff before it settled into a sort of shallow moat around the vast crater's low central peak—or in one of thousands of lesser astroblemes that also marked the landscape and served as irrigation reservoirs.

The green was broken only by white dots, dwindling in the distance before the eye met the horizon, of colonists silently laboring between the furrows, and by the occasional pale blue of one of their E&M counselors spurring them on in the endless battle against insects and weeds which were never supposed to have been permitted in this controlled environment in the first place, but which had taken to the rich soil and moderate climate in the same wholehearted manner as the crops—just another little phenomenon Curringer and his people hadn't predicted.

Even so, saying before a world audience that the place looked like Iowa was tremendously flattering, and, in addition, she'd handed him a wonderfully open question.

"Well, Martie, as you know, the South African billionaire William Wilde Curringer intended Pallas to be a country club for rugged individualism. Just to be here, its mostly middle- and upper-class settlers all paid an amount far beyond the reach of Earth's underprivileged—on average, about four million New American Dollars."

"About the same, allowing for inflation, as the Mayflower's passengers." The reporter smiled without wrinkling the delicate tissues around her eyes, a long-term media survival tactic he'd first heard about in the revival of an old Broadway play. "And for that price, they were all assigned plots of land by random drawing?"

"In those areas Curringer and his people deemed suitable for immediate habitation, yes."

He had to stop again. Now his fifteen-year-old was following along behind the workers, pulling up young soybean plants the same way he'd seen them pull up the weeds. It appeared that all of the white-clad colonists were afraid to say anything about it.

"And they all vote equal shares"—the reporter diplomatically turned to the camera—"on the rare occasions when they're allowed to vote at all." She turned back to him once he'd dealt with Gibson Junior. "Under a contract requiring the unanimous consent of all the settlers for any significant changes to occur?"

"Any changes at all," he answered. Better and better, he thought. "Fortunately, through an unintentional loophole written into Mirelle Stein's infamous covenant—"

She winked. "Which I understand was closed immediately afterward by its embarrassed author."

"Yes—it's been possible for a more humane form of society to gain something of a foothold here."

"You're referring to cooperative agrarianism, Senator?" At present, the idea was all the rage with a cocktail-party set on Earth who would never be called upon to try it.

Nevertheless, he nodded. "As practiced within the Greeley Utopian Memorial Project—just a minute."

This time, Gibson Junior had taken the biggest armful he could manage of the weeds some of the colonists had pulled up and others had collected, and was lifting them into the air a little at a time, letting them scatter back across the field on the breeze. Concealing what he did with his body, the Senator snatched what was left of them from the boy, and threw them back at the hopper they'd come from.

It was some time before peace and quiet were restored sufficiently to go on with the interview, and Altman vowed he'd never repeat this particular mistake again. From now on, Junior would be kept out of sight.

"Er, can you explain the principles of cooperative agrarianism for our TV audience, Senator?"

Knowing perfectly well that what he was about to say would be edited out or—far more likely—voiced over before it went on the air, he went ahead, hoping that the background he was providing would help her make an accurate summary.

"Sure, Martie. It's based on the concepts of universal brotherhood and appropriate technology, which its academic and political sponsors on Earth believe will inevitably triumph here. Their aim, and my own, is to supersede the exploitive techno-barbarism rampant just outside the Project's benign influence."

He nodded toward the Rimfence. Eight times taller than a man (barely adequate in this gravity), the inward-slanting steel-mesh barrier around the crater rim enclosing the Project also served to absorb and deflect all but authorized communications, filtering out undesirable and confusing political and commercial propaganda.

At that moment, as if in answer to a prayer, the sound of gunshots echoed across the fields, most likely from Outsiders hunting in the wild grassland beyond the Project's boundary.

The reporter started. "Does that happen often?"

"Many times a day, Martie, each day including Sundays." He'd assumed a carefully disgusted expression which he now dropped for a look of dedicated confidence. "That's just another reason I'm determined to pursue the United Nations' benevolent long-range goals here, by voting our own colonists' shares for them, as a bloc."

"And this is possible under the special Project articles all of them signed as a condition of free passage here?"

It was time to smile warmly. "Well, I can see you've done your homework, Martie."

"All part of the job, Senator," she smiled back, a bit regretfully. He braced himself for what he guessed was coming. "Unfortunately, so is asking about a less-than-cordial relationship, initially, with what you people call Outsiders—settlers brought here by the Curringer Trust who didn't come as part of the United Nations program. And wasn't there a rumor going around that the Greeley Utopian Memorial Project was originally meant as a pilot program for future penal colonies?"

Altman and his family had been required—by a leadership anxious to get them under cover and the Curringer Line's tight scheduling for its new cold fusion transport— to leave Earth before that rumor (which happened to be perfectly true at the time) could be squelched. Apparently it had been spread by the increasing number of dissenters and refuseniks who were its likeliest future beneficiaries. He couldn't say that to Martie Mough, but fortunately he'd handled the question many times over the years and knew exactly what he could say.

He grinned and lied. "Personally, Martie, I think it's the Rimfence that started that story. Setting aside its admittedly daunting proportions, which, allowing for gravity, are easily equaled by anything the average Texas ranch offers, there's nothing exotic about it. It's plain old homely chain link, topped with concertina coils of ordinary military razor wire. Like many such fences, it's electrified with fifty thousand volts at—well, I forget how many amperes—mainly to keep high-jumping wild animals out of the crops."

"And of course, Senator, it's those very crops you've come out here to inspect this morning," the reporter suggested, accomplishing an adroit change of subject following the obligatory question which few would notice he hadn't really answered.

"That's right. I'm closing a deal—I hope—with a, er, restaurateur in the nearby town of Curringer, and I wanted to remind myself of what we have to offer."

"Even to somebody who knows absolutely nothing about farming, Senator, it's impressive."

"Yes—I mean thank you, Martie. We've worked hard here. The land is contoured and cultivated according to the latest recommendations of United Nations agricultural specialists—"

"I notice the plants are set closer together than they'd be on Earth, is that right?"

"Yes, that's owing to the unexploited richness of the soil and the amount of labor available. These are soybeans, for which my customer professes to have no use—"

She grinned, shaking her head. "We visited his restaurant in Curringer last night. I heard comments about cattle feed unfit for human consumption. The arrogance of it, making fun of something billions of people back home eat every day!"

Because they hadn't any other choice. Unwilling to pursue the matter because he couldn't stomach soya products himself no matter how fashionably plebeian they happened to be, he went on. "They do serve to give me an idea of how the crops are faring. It looks to me—with only nine years' experience at these matters under my figurative belt—as if they're exceeding our expectations."

"This is Martie Mough on the asteroid Pallas, for

GIGO." She smiled, waving to her assistant to turn his camera off. "If your little boy lets them, you mean?"

"What?" Altman pivoted to see what she was talking about, then groaned with something akin to horror.

Behind him, Gibson Junior was bouncing down a row of soybeans, taking exquisite care to land on the hand of each and every silently suffering worker as he passed.

VII
COLD FISSION

EVERYBODY KNOWS THAT NUCLEAR FUSION CAN ONLY TAKE PLACE AT TREMENDOUSLY HIGH TEMPERATURES AND PRESSURES, IN THE PRESENCE OF BILLIONS OF DOLLARS.
— Mirelle Stein, *The Productive Class*

G ibson Altman believed he still had a few friends back on Earth, but the physical conditions governing communication with them—an endless and unconscionable fourteen-minute lag while radio signals crawled a quarter of a billion kilometers—were better suited for delivering diatribes than for conversation.

He'd seen Martie Mough off within the past hour. In the end, she'd been more perplexed than anything else at his indifference to her unspoken advances and had probably come to the conclusion—although people back home would never believe it after all he'd been through—that he was gay. The Greeley Utopian Memorial Project had been her last stop on a general tour of Pallas for her network. Now she'd be heading for the South Pole to catch a Curringer Liner back to Earth.

As a longtime political foe of the internal combustion engine and the private automobile, even he had to admit

that the celebrated interplanetary correspondent for the
Global Information Gathering Organization—not to mention her equipment-laden technical assistant—had looked
splendidly ridiculous, pedaling off on the pair of rattletrap
bicycles they'd rented in Curringer. That sight alone had
made all the trouble they'd put him to seem worthwhile,
although he wished he'd had a chance to see them on their
way down here from the North Pole, dangling like puppets
from the fragile wing of one of the ultralight aircraft which
were presently the only long-range transport on the asteroid.

Shaking his head with amusement, he'd watched them
wobble off and vanish over a horizon much closer on Pallas than it would have been on Earth. Then he'd abandoned the verandah to go inside, where Alice had been
waiting lunch for him. No sooner had he finished,
blessedly alone in his private study after a thoroughly hell-
ish morning in the fields with Gibson Junior, than she
came to inform him that a personal call from Earth was
coming in on the big screen in the family room.

"Any idea who it is or what it's about?"

"No, sir," Alice replied. "The operator would only tell
me that it's a triple-A priority call from Washington, using
one of the United Nations keycodes."

He arose reluctantly from his paper-cluttered desk
where a hundred more important matters awaited his attention, briefly dabbed at his mouth with a napkin and
threw it on the dinner tray, ran a hand through his hair
even though he wouldn't really be talking to anybody for a
long while yet—if at all—and went to answer the call, feeling put upon and deeply annoyed. Earth seemed very far
away these days, in much more than mere physical distance.

What people really needed, he thought as he settled
into a comfortable chair before the wall-sized screen and

waited for the unscrambling software to finish loading itself, was some kind of faster-than-light radio now, long
before any hypothetical departure of humanity for the
stars. He doubted that would ever happen anyway. Mankind had far too much unfinished business in its own backyard. But faster-than-light communication was supposed
to be impossible.

On the other hand, so had household fusion, and look
at the way that had changed the world. Thinking back, it
seemed obvious. An unexpected natural phenomenon had
been discovered in what everyone else considered an academic backwater—Utah, of all places. Large institutions,
dependent on government grants invested in high-temper-
ature, high-pressure technology, had been unable to repli-
cate these "cold fusion" experiments, while smaller institutions had done so with insulting ease.

It helped that these small institutions had followed the
original design faithfully while those who "knew better"
had modified it to suit outmoded prejudices. One intelligent change, consistent with the newfound principle, had
been made by Israelis who'd eliminated an irrelevant elec-
trolytic process, lowered a rod of palladium into a can of
deuterium gas, and gotten neutrons, heat, and helium.

Power lines had started coming down and gasoline
pumps vanishing from the world's highways. No matter
how authorities tried to laugh it off, how many conservative journals ridiculed it, how many frightened oil, coal,
and natural gas companies hated it, or how many state-run
utilities tried to suppress it, the Fusion Age of cheap, freely
available energy had arrived.

Someday someone working in a basement somewhere,
ignorant or contemptuous of the rules that men—rather
than nature—imposed on science, would find a way to
send a message that took less than fourteen minutes to

travel from Earth to Pallas. The Senator wondered why that idea suddenly made him feel afraid.

"Gibbie!"

Altman realized that his mind had wandered. He hated being called "Gib" or "Gibbie." His name was Gibson. It had a long, distinguished history in his family.

The call, however, was from Senator Elwood Dodd, one of the few friends he had left in public life, a longtime Union Democratic wheelhorse who'd served two terms as governor in Hartford before taking up what now seemed permanent residence in the national legislature. Altman knew that Dodd was responsible for his having been given this post on Pallas rather than something unimaginably worse. The man had such close ties in the United Nations his opponents often charged that he represented Colombo rather than Connecticut.

Altman had to suppress a reflexive impulse to return his old colleague's greeting. Communication across interplanetary distances consisted of a series of monologues. This message had been sent no less than fourteen minutes ago. It would take another fourteen for any answer to get back. Dodd's genially alcoholic features projected from the screen almost as if he were here in the room, although he raised his voice as if it were a bad two-way long-distance connection.

"I thought I'd spend a little of the taxpayers' money to let you know what's going on down here before you see it garbled and distorted by Atlanta! I'm afraid we lost another one, my friend. Daniel Webster will be spinning in his grave! Young Lucero managed to force the bill out of committee because we thought we had enough support on the floor, but the goddamned Conservatives and Libertarians joined forces at the last minute and wiped our asses for us on a roll-call vote!"

So that was it. Another failed attempt, this time in the

Senate, to fill the "vacant" Western seats. For more than ten years there had been constant pressure, mostly from his own party, to accomplish that highly necessary task. They even had historical precedent: exactly the same thing had been done to the South during the nineteenth century. It had been the major issue of his career, responsible for vaulting him to prominence—which was why Dodd was calling him about it—but Altman was surprised now at how little he cared. After nine years in exile, it was difficult remembering how the "Cold Civil War" had started in the first place.

Money, he supposed.

What else would it be?

The Second Great Depression had been brought about by Third World debts amounting to fourteen figures, the widespread and enthusiastic repudiation of which had devastated the American banking system. Of course the bankers had understood from the beginning that the gaggle of dictatorships and people's republics they were showering with credit were bad risks. They'd counted on taxpayers to bail them out—with a little coercive assistance from Congress. And why not? Weren't both parties doing essentially the same thing with their Russian aid program?

And hadn't Congress helpfully destroyed the only competition American banks had ever had, the savings and loan institutions, toward the end of the twentieth century?

Then the economy of California had been destroyed by a long-predicted earthquake which, despite expensive (some said repressive) civil defense measures, had killed twenty million in the Greater Los Angeles area alone, inflicting trillions of Old Dollars' worth of damage. Suddenly the money wasn't there to bail out the banks, even if a new three-sided Congress—composed of Democratic Unionists, Conservatives, and Libertarians rather than Republicans and Democrats—had been willing.

"Something you won't hear about at all—from Atlanta or from anywhere else, with any luck—is that the goddamned Jackelopes apparently took over another nuclear waste facility and they've been mailing that crap, an ounce at a time in foil-lined envelopes, to members of both houses! And still we lost the vote! Sometimes I think I ought to give up politics, Gibbie, and look for honest work like you!"

Altman gasped. This was more important than a lost vote in the Senate, and far more dangerous than the eco-terrorism of the last century because it was part of an incredibly popular movement rooted in respect for individual rights and private property. It was the closest thing so far to a provocation that couldn't be overlooked, and it couldn't have been accomplished without the cooperation of Western postal officials. However, owing to the Great Depression II and countless other stresses (which, to give Aloysius Brody credit, much like the San Andreas Fault had been long overdue for relief), a dramatic—although not yet officially acknowledged—political, economic, social, and geographic reshuffling had followed in North America without respect to offices and titles.

Westerners had often complained bitterly of what they felt amounted to colonial treatment by the Northeast, of three-quarters of their land being perpetually tied up for the sake of a future which somehow never arrived, of their involuntary status as the Northeast's dumping ground, its bottomless food, water, and mineral reserve, its hiding place for the Pentagon's most dangerous toys.

Privately, Altman admitted that there was substance to their complaints. His own party had always taken pains to assure that the West was represented by transplanted easterners—"carpetbaggers," some called them—or by westerners with eastern values. The eastern-based media followed the same policy: for sixty years, there hadn't been a news anchor in Denver, to name one example, who truly spoke for western values, although that never stopped them from claiming otherwise.

Nothing lasts forever, of course. During the same sixty years, American industry had become almost universally decentralized as a result of the fairly recent development of small, relatively inexpensive fusion plants, computer-driven machine tools of tremendous versatility which freed the entrepreneur from union labor, and a remarkable process of ion-impregnation which made it possible to fabricate anything from bottle-cap lifters to fusion-electric locomotives out of easily worked materials which could be hardened afterward to any desired toughness.

With each startling innovation, the stranglehold of America's traditional industrial region and the factions that controlled it was broken a bit more, the vital, energetic West, in effect, gradually seceding economically from the moldering, overpopulated Rust Belt which had dominated its existence for two centuries.

"What I don't understand is what the Libertarians gain from acting as de facto representatives for the West." On the screen before him, Altman watched his old friend squirm uncomfortably. "Times are changing too much, Gibbie. I'm getting too old."

Altman smiled sadly. It wasn't Dodd's age, but the age he'd lived in most of his life. He was a survivor of an era of "broker parties," political entities representing no idea or collection of ideas (although they might pretend otherwise when tactics called for it), but which simply accrued power for its own sake.

In a sense, the Republicans and Democrats had been professional athletic teams, striving mightily to defeat each other for the money, the spectacle, for victory itself, but for nothing else. They might even exchange members, who would be expected to play as hard for their new team as they had for their old.

Straddling the transition between two eras, Altman could understand and sympathize with Dodd, but following the worldwide economic collapse, more had changed than the names of two outdated political parties. Altman knew the Libertarians as ideologues who claimed to value principle above all else, including short-term political gain. In his view, they'd remained consistent enough over the years to contaminate the other parties, which now represented ideologies of their own.

In time, the "Sagebrush States," also known as the "Jackelope Republic"—those west of the ninetieth meridian, popularly called the "Webb Line" after historian Walter Prescott Webb—had no longer bothered sending delegates to Congress. Even worse, the myriad mandates of Washington were increasingly ignored as water, gas, electricity, trash hauling, postal, telephone, and other vital services to government buildings became mysteriously unreliable overnight. Thousands of outraged federal bureaucrats, tax collectors, and law enforcement officials found themselves harassed, disarmed, arrested, even jailed.

Afterward, they invariably received apologies from local authorities for the "terrible mistake."

Others, falling into less temperate hands, simply disappeared, never to be heard from again.

With its brightest Presidential hope attuned to the Age of Ideology and foremost among the advocates of harsher policies toward the West, the Union Democratic Party was willing to reimpose Washington's authority by military means. In light of the location of most of America's missile silos, obsolete fission plants, and radioactive dumps, however, this was seen as provocative by others. The Presidency and both houses of Congress belonged to a coalition of Conservatives (who'd followed Democratic example by changing the name of their party) and Libertarians (who'd established themselves as a permanent feature of American politics following the disaster they'd warned was coming for thirty years).

What Brody had said of international politics was true as far as it went. Although the people of Earth neither fully understood nor entirely trusted the circumstances which had brought it about, the Cold War had ended. Sometimes, however, it seemed as if everyone was waiting around nervously to see what would replace it. Preoccupied with what they perceived as dangerous worldwide instability, and in the continuing absence of any sort of open declaration by the states west of the Webb Line, the ruling coalition, at least for the moment—which had so far lasted more than a decade—refrained from acting against the West.

Meanwhile, in what people and the media everywhere were now calling "West America"—and in "East America," as well—a series of everyday economic and social realignments with the Canadian provinces, which had long suffered many of the same regional divisions manifested to the south, had, for all practical purposes, rotated the international border ninety degrees.

But Dodd was going on. "One more thing. I understand that little bitch Martie Mough is headed out your way and plans to drop by the Project for an interview. She came along a little after your time, Gibbie, so you may not know much about her. The story I get from my media people is that she used to pay lip service to Lyle Latheman over at LiteLink, where she started in the secretarial pool, then switched to GIGO last year for a cool fifty million NADs. Watch her, Gibbie my boy. She'll flap those eyelashes at you and waggle her cute little ass, then fuck you the first chance she gets. And not in a nice way."

Altman chuckled, but wondered what the penalty was for not succumbing to the charms of Martie Mough.

"That's all for now, Mr. Chief Administrator. I know you're doing God's work out there, and doing it damned well. Let me hear from you soon. I'll be looking forward to it."

The screen blanked.

Altman sighed wearily, thought about the unfinished work still lying on his desk in the next room, then sighed again and began composing a reply to his old friend back on Earth.

"Elwood!"

Dodd hated being called by his first name.

VIII

THE WELLS FARGO WAGON

INDIVIDUALS OBTAINED RECOGNITION OF THEIR FREEDOM BY
FIGHTING AND BARGAINING, OR — FAILING IN THIS — THEY
COULD RUN AWAY. THIS RUNNING AWAY WAS POSSIBLE BECAUSE
THEY HAD SOMEWHERE TO GO.
                    —Walter Prescott Webb, *The Great Frontier*

Looking out the window and seeing dust on the horizon made Gwen think of the historian Walter Prescott Webb again, and of the women of the Great Plains who knew in the morning, because the prairie was so flat, that they'd have guests to feed before sundown.

Finally satisfied, more or less, with the state of what was unfortunately and undeniably a rather well-worn carpet, she pulled the vacuum hose from its outlet in the wall, rolled it up, and tucked it behind some boxes on a top shelf of the closet.

She was nervous about meeting Sarah Murdoch.

It wasn't just because the aging actress had once been the brightest star of Hollywood and Broadway. Gwen admired her for many more things than that. It was true she'd started in the chorus line and gone from there to musicals and comedies to become the most celebrated singer, dancer, and comedienne in show business. But Sarah Murdoch hadn't been content merely to remain pretty — although it was wonderful what plastic surgeons could do these days to stave off old age — she'd kept in physical shape, as well. At fifty, she'd been pictured on the cover of a national magazine kicking an exceptionally well-turned leg higher than her head, rehearsing for a revival of one of her most successful shows.

Gwen shut the closet door — with considerable difficulty, as it stood open most of the time — glanced out at the horizon again, then turned her attention to the toys and stuffed animals she'd tossed onto the unmade bed to get them out from underfoot. The toy population had long since outgrown the toy box. She'd anticipated that and brought a large carton from the kitchen, filling it and hiding it in the knee-well behind the ruffled pink skirt of the vanity.

Being pretty had never been enough for Sarah Murdoch. In younger days, she and her actor-producer-director brother had stood bravely on the side of every humanitarian issue that the world around them seemed to be turning away from — higher taxes, nature preservation, aid to distressed and developing countries alike, democratic limitations on scientific research, gun control, nationalized industry, animal welfare, state health and housing programs — and for some reason it had never seemed to hurt their enormous, well-deserved popularity.

Now what to do with all these overly cute pelicans, tigers, leopards, and so forth? For a child without grandparents — her own mother and father were dead and Gibson's parents had all but disowned him during the scandal—this one did surprisingly well, thanks to a number of childless maternal uncles and aunts anxious to make up for the fact of their exile as well as the lack of grandparents. Most— the solid Union Democrats—sent soft, cartoonlike replicas of endangered species, the profits from which went to conserving the originals. There was even an appealing, padded bristlecone pine tree around here somewhere.

Sarah Murdoch was pretty solid herself, now that Gwen considered it. In the wake of the collapse and reorganization of the major American political parties, she'd had the sense to abandon the foolish consistency of long-outmoded liberal values and publicly oppose the repeal of pornography and drug laws, as well as fighting a noble but similarly losing battle against the Curringer Trust's pet resolution in the UN proclaiming a so-called human right to vote with one's feet—in other words, to abandon your homeland simply because you think you'll be better off somewhere else, selfishly depriving your native country of badly needed intelligence and talent which weren't truly yours to begin with, anyway.

Shaking her head, Gwen tried hiding the stuffed animals atop the canopy of the four-poster. Its ruffles, and those of the bedclothes, matched those of the vanity, but the fabric was faded and threadbare from too many washings. And the animals were all too apparent, unfortunately, from the perspective of someone lying on the bed. It looked like a bushel of potatoes was about to fall onto one's face.

Sarah Murdoch had lent her name to the most controversial ideas. Wages for housework, which had fizzled during the last century, she'd raised from the dead almost single-handedly. Later, she'd written best-sellers on near-death experiences, telepathy, astrology, spiritualism, prehistoric astronauts, clairvoyance, telekinesis, the *I Ching*, the Tarot, reflexology, and nonsecular faith healing.

In between, she'd been to London as a guest of the last Marxist state on Earth, to Aspen (where she maintained legal residence) as a duly elected delegate to the Union Democratic Party's first national convention, to the Hague to demand that Interpol spray the world's tobacco fields with paraquat, and to Colombo to badger the General Assembly into funding the Greeley Utopian Memorial Project. And she'd soon be here at the Project itself to entertain the colonists and see for herself what they'd accomplished with what she'd helped them obtain.

Unable to avoid another anxious glance out the window, Gwen found she was humming a song from the classic video *The Music Man*, the one about "The Wells Fargo Wagon." The traveling dustcloud had grown closer all day, heralding the arrival of the star and her performing company—too many and with too much baggage to fly down from the North Pole in those ridiculous, tiny, ultralight aircraft the Outsiders used.

Gibson had tried getting them a cargo helicopter from Colombo, but had failed. They'd settled on a huge-wheeled rollabout intended for a UN Lunar settlement that had never quite worked out—the Swiss-South African investors who had bought that colony out were building highways for private automobiles, of all things! The machine had been disassembled on Earth, shuttled bit by bit onto one of the big Curringer Liners, shipped to Pallas, and reassembled at the North Pole.

Once it returned Miss Murdoch and her entourage to the spaceport, someone would drive it back to the Project, where it would double their present fleet of such vehicles, used for heavy farm chores and hauling produce to the market in Curringer. It represented a generous gift, especially since Miss Murdoch had insisted on buying it from

the contractor herself and paying the freight. Too lightly
built for work in the gravity of Earth, it had been sitting at
a factory in Prague gathering dust and taking up space,
about to be broken up for parts.

None of that made Gwen feel nervous now as she personally straightened, cleaned, and dusted the Residence's
only guest room, hoping Miss Murdoch would be willing
to spend a night in it, although at any other time in her life
it would have been enough. Actually, it was her daughter's
bedroom, and as much as she dreaded putting little
Vanessa in with Gibson Junior these days, if only for a few
hours—even the servants and staff had learned to avoid
him—it was necessary. Nor was it the fact that all of her
own clothing was years out of date. Surely Miss Murdoch
would understand and overlook something like that.

What made her nervous was the personal reason she
wanted Miss Murdoch in this room, especially during
those first few precious minutes after she'd led the woman
here, alone, without Gibson around, and was theoretically
making sure that she was comfortable. What made her
nervous was the favor she meant to ask of a person she
didn't know and had only admired anonymously for most
of her life.

Of the three overland journeys the Lunar rollabout
would be making before its conversion to more mundane
purposes, the trip down from the North Pole, the trip
back, and the final trip to the Project, Gwen was concerned about the middle one.

She wanted to go along.

Her bag was packed only with what she and her three
surviving children would require during the two-week
voyage that would take her back to the home her parents
had left her in Arlington.

Making as little fuss about it as she could manage given
the conditions she was operating under, because like it or

not she would always be the perfect political spouse, she was ready—had been ready for a long time—to leave Pallas, the Project, and a husband who had neither needed nor wanted her for years.

Emerson didn't know how he'd gotten roped into this ceremony, but it was messing up his plans.

Cleared through the security gate in the Rimfence, the rollabout from the North Pole had covered the seventy-eight-kilometer distance to the Residence and compound in forty minutes on what was said to be the only paved road on Pallas. After the rough, lumbering journey here cross-country, it must have seemed like flying.

Anybody might have thought it was Santa Claus's sleigh, the way it had been decorated and the way people were acting. All the servants and their families were on display in bright, fresh uniforms, democratically shoulder to shoulder with the Chief Administrator, his thin, pale, nervous wife, and their three children: evil-eyed Gibson Junior (who appeared to be keeping himself uncharacteristically close beside his father), gentle little Vanessa, and the two-year-old—Emerson could never remember its name or gender—squirming in its mother's arms.

Emerson felt like squirming, too. Standing on the verandah with his own mother and several brothers and sisters—his father assigned the humble task of helping make up the crowd scene below—he gave the machine a critical eye to take his mind off the embarrassment he felt for himself, his family, and his fellow peasants.

It was almost identical to the hauler that already served the colony, a great plastic-lidded aluminum trough five meters wide and thirty long, hanging from—more than resting on—two dozen huge fin-treaded tires twice as tall as he was. Grossly overbuilt for conditions on Pallas, which exerted only about half of Luna's pull, both had come cheaply to the Project through UN sources. The canopy of the Project's vehicle had long since been removed to increase its cargo capacity, the curved, magnesium-strutted sheets of plastic having been set on a foundation of meteoric stone to function as a greenhouse which would probably be expanded now, once this machine was turned over to the Chief Administrator.

Where life support machinery—oxygen, cooling, and heating equipment for the harsh Lunar environment—had once hung between the tires, the racks were now filled with boxes, bales, and trunks. Those same racks, on the machine the colony already used, were an important element in Emerson's plans for tonight.

Standing at attention, their shock batons swinging from their belts, five hundred United Nations Education and Morale counselors—one for every twenty of the Project's unarmed and compliant laborers—formed a kind of human corridor along both edges of the brand-new semicircular driveway in front of the Residence. Their pale blue one-piece uniforms couldn't compete with the blazing splendor of the visiting machine or the circuslike spectacle of its arrival.

To begin with, all thirty meters of its hull had been enameled in the pink equivalent of international safety orange. That much of any color was painful enough to look at, but the words SARAH MURDOCH'S INTERPLANETARY TOUR OF STARS were emblazoned over it in a similar fluorescent blue that made the letters shift and dance in one's tear-filled field of vision. Over that were many layers of transparent finish embedded with both metallic and pearlescent spangles, and strings of hundreds of tiny colored lights winking on and off at random.

The plastic dome comprising the upper half of the hull was brightly lit from within, providing a view of dozens of outlandishly costumed dancers and musicians waving and smiling to the loudly cheering crowd. At first there was no sign of their employer—until the lights dimmed, allowing people to shift their attention, and their clapping and whistling, to a small railed platform high atop the dome in which, lit by a spot hanging from a slender upright behind her, the famous actress stood in a minimal black outfit cut almost to the waist front and back, and upward at the sides, its edges finished in some sparkly material.

Her hair was short, straight, and as red as it had ever been. Emerson, who recognized her now that she was here, could see her famous freckles even where he stood, fifty meters away, on the Residence verandah. Sarah Murdoch grinned and seemed to wave a crookless cane and exaggerated top hat directly at him and him alone.

All at once it was difficult for Emerson to remember what he'd heard of this woman, that she was responsible for his family becoming the property of the Chief Administrator and that she was far worse in terms of what she believed and advocated than even the former Senator. Emerson took a deep breath and straightened his back, determined tonight to keep the promise he'd made to himself. It would be relatively easy, he believed, since nobody except him seemed to think of the Project as a place to escape *from*, or the Outside as a place to escape *to*.

His moment came at last, when the brightly colored rollabout came to a halt directly before the Residence and everyone's attention was distracted by Sarah Murdoch mounting a long metal ladder someone had placed for her and sliding down on the sides of her slippered feet to the verandah steps. People all around him crowded forward. The Chief Administrator's wife extended both hands to her guest.

He had time for one brief moment of disappointment. The woman who had seemed so glamorous and beautiful on her platform above the rollabout looked much older this close up, her thickly layered makeup cracked and chalky, her hair almost a helmet of hard plastic. Even her freckles had been painted on. Her perfume reminded him of the pungent insecticides his father and the others sometimes sprayed on the fields. Emerson quietly stepped back, slipped around a corner of the house, and, squeezing between the porch rails, let himself down easily into the flower bed below.

Except for the front of the Residence, the entire compound appeared to be deserted, although how ten thousand individuals could pack themselves into the space enclosed by the circular driveway—or why they would want to try—he didn't know. Without taking any particular trouble to remain out of sight, he hurried to the shed where the other rollabout was kept, slipped inside, and closed the doors behind him.

The rack beneath this machine had also been stripped of equipment there was no use for on Pallas. It held half a dozen spare tires, lying on their sides, and other odds and ends experience had taught them might be necessary on the long, rough road around the lake. Climbing onto the rack, he pushed himself through the narrow space between one tire and the underside of the hull, concealing himself within the tire, where there was even more room than he'd anticipated. The air he breathed was very rubbery and also smelled of lubricants.

After a great deal of thought, he'd decided against taking anything with him. It would have been too risky, and there was little to take in any case. He'd miss his homemade radio receiver, but doubted he'd have to build another. Someday, perhaps, having fulfilled certain other promises to himself, he'd be in a position to come back and retrieve it, provided that no one had found his little cave first.

Inches above his head, the cargo compartment had already been loaded with produce, mostly potatoes, before it had been put away. He had wondered how he'd manage the many hours before dawn when the rollabout headed for Curringer on its regular delivery route, especially with everyone else having such a terrific, noisy time only a few hundred yards away. But he promptly fell asleep and didn't wake again until the machine hit the coarse gravel roadbed outside the Project gates.

He woke when the many-wheeled rollabout began to bounce on the half-finished road and he alternately struck the top of his head on the hull and the point of his chin on the sidewall of the tire. Shaking his head as briskly as he could to recover consciousness he peeped over the rim at the uncultivated grasslands all around him.

He was free.

IX
FREEDOM'S JUST ANOTHER WORD

LIKE THE HUNTER IN THE ABSOLUTE *OUTSIDE* OF THE
COUNTRYSIDE, THE PHILOSOPHER IS THE ALERT MAN IN THE
ABSOLUTE *INSIDE* OF IDEAS, WHICH ARE ALSO AN
UNCONQUERABLE AND DANGEROUS JUNGLE.
— José Ortega y Gasset, *Meditations on Hunting*

Not a stylish way to travel, she thought, or the most comfortable. She and her children might as well have crawled in among the trunks on the rack beneath the rollabout's hull.

By now, her furtive conference with Sarah Murdoch had begun to seem unreal. The woman had been cordial as long as she'd continued to see Gwen as the wife of the

Chief Administrator of her pet social experiment. Eye contact had been minimal and conversation superficial until Gwen had changed the tone—and her identity as far as the movie star was concerned. In an instant Gwen had transformed herself into the object of a conflict between the public relations value of the Project and Sarah Murdoch's long-standing policy of generous support for Wives who Wanted Out.

In the end the woman agreed, a little grudgingly, to find a place for them aboard the rollabout when it left for the North Pole—in exchange for Gwen's promise to accomplish her disengagement quietly. That suited Gwen. She hadn't planned to tell Gibson she was leaving him until the Curringer Liner had lifted off for Earth.

Now here she was, with Gibson Junior, little Vanessa, and fourteen-month-old Terence, over the first physical and emotional hurdle, and squeezing in among the duffels and other light luggage at the very back of the rollabout where she'd feel well hidden and secure during the hour or so before the wheels began to turn. Gibson Junior, the only one of her three born on Earth, seemed unusually quiet, even for him. She'd come to think of him as her dark child, given to disturbing episodes of cruelty toward small animals, younger siblings, and Project youngsters not in a position to defend themselves. The boy kept peeping over the edge of the window he'd insisted on sitting by, staring at who knew what.

The rollabout began to fill with passengers, themselves rather subdued after a long evening of entertaining the Project's inhabitants and hours afterward of entertaining themselves. Gwen heard an unmistakable hangover groan from several of them. The air in the rollabout began to reek of stale alcohol and too many cigarettes the night before. She hoped the children wouldn't be carsick.

At the same time she heard the whine of motors warming up, she peeked cautiously through the window herself and watched Gibson on the verandah, receiving a kiss on the cheek from Sarah Murdoch. Gibson had an expression of annoyed perplexity on his face. He cast about, probably wondering where his wife was. He bore the movie star's small talk—her gestures were plain even at this distance—stoically, but his mind was elsewhere. Gwen began to have second thoughts.

Then his expression and demeanor changed completely. At his shoulder Walter Ngu, a field foreman and the housekeeper's husband, had a hand raised, pointing at the fields. Gibson looked in that direction, nodded, said something to Sarah Murdoch, and descended the verandah steps with Walter, suddenly purposeful and energetic. With the rest of her retinue safely aboard and the engines ready, Sarah Murdoch climbed on—looking tired, hung over, and a bit miffed at such an unceremonious sendoff—let the door shut behind her, and sat down. The rollabout began to move, and before too many minutes had passed, they were doing two hundred kilometers an hour—once outside the Project, their pace would slow appreciably—over the only paved road on the asteroid.

They paused briefly while a guard opened the Rim-fence gate. There was a small disturbance at the back of the rollabout. Gwen's eldest son suddenly stood up in his seat, looked down at his mother, then climbed over her and out into the aisle.

"Gibbie, sit down before the machine starts moving again!"

He gave her an odd look. He'd always been closed to her, indifferent to anything outside the circle of his whims, and she couldn't read him the way she could her other children.

"When the machine starts moving again, Mother, I won't be on it. I'm staying here, with Father."

"Your father . . ." Gwen, surprised and suspicious at the boy's sudden, inexplicable loyalty, failed to observe that she was having a grown-up argument with a child. "The Chief Administrator is too preoccupied to notice that we're leaving. You think he'll notice that the son he's never had time for is staying?"

"It doesn't matter. Here I can be—whatever. On Earth . . ." He made a face as if the rest of his sentence were self-evident. Without a word, he glided down the aisle, demanded to be let off the rollabout, descended the half-dozen steps in a single bound, and skimmed toward the guard post without looking back. The machine started again, rolled through the gate, and began crunching its way southwest toward the rim of Lake Selous, where it would head north past Curringer.

Inside, Gwen Altman held her baby, put an arm around her daughter, and wept quietly.

Emerson was free.

Even at his age, he knew it would be a long while before he understood exactly what that meant.

He'd never seen a map of the region in which the Project lay—or even one of Pallas in general—for the same reason his family's quarters, unlike the Chief Administrator's Residence, lacked windows. How could maps or windows be of use to an individual whose existence began and ended with the cultivation of the Project's crops?

Thus he was unaware that it occupied the middle and largest of three shallow, slightly overlapping impact features stretching east to west over a quarter of the northern hemisphere in what would have been the temperate zone on Earth. The easternmost was smallest, undeveloped, mostly unexplored. The westernmost was deepest. Having filled with water during terraformation, it was called Lake Selous.

The country north of Lake Selous, which might have offered a direct route to the town of Curringer, sitting perched on a bluff overlooking the shore, was too rough for surface travel, pocked with many small, deep craters whose interlocking ridges formed a complex, mountainous terrain. Southward, at the junctions which the broad bowl of the Project made with similar neighbors, lay another pair of deep features, perhaps thirty miles in diameter, but between them lay an uninterrupted plateau stretching south and curving west with a relatively smooth topography that properly sprung and powered wheels could negotiate.

The rollabout's wheels were properly sprung and powered—for Earth's moon. For so large a vehicle, it was almost silent, running on powerful electric motors in each wheel hub, fed by solar panels making up a section of the domed roof that hadn't been replaced. Within an atmosphere, which reduced available light, they were supplemented by batteries it had taken all night to charge and which would be recharged overnight in Curringer before the return trip.

He had no way of knowing that he'd set out on a journey of three hundred miles without water, provisions, or other amenities. He only knew it seemed to last forever, that there were limits to how much anyone could sleep to kill time, especially in a machine bouncing about in lower gravity than it had been designed for, over roads that were no more than lanes cleared of the biggest boulders—usually by rolling them into the smallest craters—and that, by the time he caught his first glimpse of the lights of Curringer twinkling in the distance, he'd be cold, hungry, dehydrated, blackened by the rubber that concealed his presence, and bruised everywhere from his random, brutal contact with it. By then he'd know the freedom to suffer the consequences of his own bad planning.

At moments when the path was smooth and level and he could peep over the wall of his neoprene fortress without fear of having his eyeballs shaken out, he began to see what Pallas had been like before it had been tamed, as it was inside the Rimfence. Something about the pale sun and flawless blue overhead, the ground gently rolling to the golden line that met it, maybe even the prairie wind swirling invisibly between them, alternately warm and cool, always full of strange scents, was different from anything he'd felt before. The words he knew to describe it *accurately*—"empty," "barren," "deserted," "bleak," "desolate"—were negative and therefore somehow incorrect. At the same time that the prairie made him feel a little afraid, it gave him a soaring sensation so welcome it almost took his breath away. It might have been the open plains all around him, or his first real taste of freedom.

The ground was dry, sparsely covered everywhere to waist height with what his father, seeing it poke through the Rimfence, called buffalo grass, coarser than the carefully trimmed Residence lawn, more yellow-brown than green. By the road lay patches of prickly pear cactus he was familiar with. Mingled in the grass were dozens of different plants, freestanding and in bunches, he couldn't identify as readily, although from some arose a spicy odor like that of a broken bottle of light green powder his mother had once had him clean up in the Residence kitchen. Sage, she'd called it.

Standing over the undergrowth were small clumps of trees hardly taller than himself. He knew nothing about trees—he'd never been to the precious, heavily guarded Project orchards and had only seen trees in books—but he knew the closer ones were different from those he saw marching up the sides of hills two or three miles away from the road. Those nearby had flat, pale leaves, branched stems, and trunks that looked like they'd been painted

white and lightly sanded until brown showed again on the
high spots. Those further away were dark, somewhat
taller, and somehow . . . pointier. Occasionally the breeze
would bring him another exotic aroma which might be
coming from those faraway trees, or might simply be the
smell of freedom.

What fascinated him most, however, were the animals.
Even the flowers, purple and white, yellow, pink, every
other color he had a name for, failed to rivet his attention
the way a long-eared jackrabbit could, startled by the vehicle, bounding across the track in front of it. Once he saw a
fat porcupine—it couldn't have been anything else—lumbering along beside the road, oblivious to the machine and
its passengers, going from one well-chewed tree to another
where the bark was tastier. On another occasion, the rollabout frightened a skunk, which sprayed a terrible warning as it passed. He recognized the black and white stripes
from childhood picture books. For some reason he found
the odor—at least at this distance—a bit exhilarating,
rather than disgusting, and knew he was discovering the
freedom to react differently than expected by others.

There were many birds: tiny quail running in a file behind their mother with her antenna-feather erect, grouse
exploding from the high grass, gobbling and clattering
their wings. Off over the horizon, a predatory bird rode
the updrafts, patrolling for small, furry food. He'd never
seen a meadowlark, but he'd enjoyed their melodious trill-
ing at the edge of the Project where he'd kept his secrets
hidden. He appreciated the company they gave him now as
he always had. Nobody had ever had to explain to him that
demanding freedom often meant being lonely.

For the most part, the vast silence of the uninhabited
prairie was broken only by the crunch of wheels on the
road and the buzzing of insects. For some reason this was
deeper than that of the houseflies that swarmed the refuse

bins at the back of the Residence or gathered around a newly plowed furrow. At one point an eight-inch dragon-fly swept past his face on four shiny, transparent wings — looking like a World War I biplane he recognized from books and magazines he'd salvaged over the years from the same bins — and on essentially the same mission as the bird of prey he'd seen earlier. At another point he jumped, bitten by a mustard-colored fly. He'd remember the pain for the rest of his life, as another taste of freedom.

Toward the end of the afternoon when the light had begun to fail and, although he wasn't aware of it, the roll-about was nearing its destination, a heavy-antlered mule deer, fascinated by the machine's headlamps, froze in its path and wouldn't move until the rollabout had stopped and one of the drivers dismounted, grumbling obscenities as he grunted his way down the ladder to shoo it out of the way.

Emerson had almost forgotten the men operating this machine. To his surprise — not to mention the driver's — the animal stood its ground, raked dirt with a hoof, and ducked its dangerous-looking rack at the man until his colleague blew a blast on the horn, startling their unknown passenger out of his wits and frightening the deer into giving way. The boy's last sight of the animal was of the cottony underside of its tail as it bounded, with an incredible slow-motion grace almost painful to watch, over an enormous rock and was gone. He also saw the reflective, glowing eyes of half a dozen animals like it who'd apparently been waiting, all but invisible in the tall grass.

He finally fell asleep and remained so as long as the prairie continued to roll smoothly beneath the tires of the rollabout. When he awoke again, the countryside was no longer quite as flat and the machine was laboring, running on batteries now, to climb back into what remained of the daylight. As they reached the crest of each hill, the slanting sun rays caught them again and the night would be temporarily put off. Straining around the underpinnings of the vehicle for a look forward, each time he could see a little scattering of lights which must be coming from the town. Then the rollabout—and the night—would descend again. They'd reach the trough between two ridges, ford a shallow stream or cross an untrustworthy-looking bridge, and begin to climb again.

He wasn't sure if it was the altitude or the time of day, but he began to get cold and realized he hadn't brought a coat or blanket. There wouldn't be a next time—he hoped—so the experience didn't have much to teach him, but he filed it away as another result of the freedom he'd sought and even napped briefly again, not knowing the danger that represented. Before the sun had vanished from the mountaintops, when a few of the twinkling lights lay around him rather than in front of him, and before the rollabout reached the market in Curringer where he was certain he'd be discovered and sent back to the Project, he decided, after an agony of indecision, to climb over the tire and jump out. He had to start his new life sometime—that's why he was here—and it might as well be now.

No more willing to hit the ground at twenty-five miles an hour than he had been to remain a slave the rest of his life, he waited until the rollabout had just struggled to the peak of another long, slow climb, then rolled off its equipment rack and watched it disappear over a horizon only yards away. Catching his breath after a soft but prickly landing in one of the aromatic bushes, he picked himself up and followed the rollabout at a cautious interval. It was much faster than he was and quickly began to dwindle in the distance, toward the city lights. The ground here was rough, even on the track, and loose stones in the roadbed hurt his feet through the thin-soled sandals he'd been issued that morning, giving him an opportunity to discover the freedom to endure the agony of sore feet.

The evening wore on and soon the sun was gone from the highest hilltop, which was next after the one where he'd jumped from the rollabout. He never recalled seeing the spectacular sunset that night which was characteristic of Pallas. Other things occupied his mind. A subtle afterglow remained on the horizon to remind him it had occurred. Having trudged for hours, concerned about the increasing darkness, trying not to imagine wild flesh-shredders behind every bush, convinced he'd made a mistake by abandoning his ride too soon, he was astonished to hear scuffing noises behind him, transmitted in the unreal silence through the ground.

At once he realized he was seeing perfectly by the blue-white light of Pallas B. Stepping behind an upthrust boulder which had been blasted in half to clear the road, he turned in time to spy a party of a dozen men and women, each armed with a big, heavy-looking pistol hanging from a broad leather belt. They didn't see him, but laughed as they swaggered his way, as arrogant in their bearing, in his view, as the blue goons who dominated the Project and the lives of everyone in it.

To make things worse, swinging glaze-eyed, gutted and lifeless between them, its once-graceful legs tied to an aluminum pole two of them carried on their shoulders—no burden at all in the minimal Pallatian gravity—was a large, furry animal they'd apparently just killed with those guns. He was astonished and sickened to recognize it as a mule deer—the blood still dripping from its mouth was coal-black in the moonlight—maybe even the deer he'd marveled at earlier.

Like an atheist uncertain of his convictions and alone in a great and gloomy cathedral, he discovered suddenly that he believed the horrible stories he'd been told about Outsiders all his life, whether he wanted to or not. They had guns. They all had guns. They had murdered a help-less, beautiful animal he'd admired.

And they were laughing about it.

Afraid, deep inside, that such a fate awaited any inter-loper who caught these monsters in the middle of their ter-rible deed, he fearfully concealed himself in the all-too-sparse undergrowth beside the road and waited, almost afraid to breathe for fear of being discovered, until the hunting party was safely past.

So this was the freedom, he thought bitterly, to be afraid for his life. Shivering in the darkness, he wondered if that was all there might be to freedom.

X

MRS. SINGH

YOU ARE WHAT YOU EAT—WHICH SORT OF ACCOUNTS FOR
VEGETARIANS, I GUESS.
— Raymond Louis Drake-Tealy, *Hunting and Humanity*

E merson didn't cry.

Shaken by what he'd witnessed, cold, tired, aching, and hungry from his long ride in the rollabout—and what by this time seemed an even longer walk—he stumbled along the rough-surfaced roadbed in the moonlight, terri-fied of accidentally catching up with the deer hunters and trying not to travel too fast. He was too exhausted for it in any case, and had no idea where he was going.

For the first time since he'd left the Project that morn-ing, he thought of his family—of his mother, father, five brothers and sisters—but it wasn't the thinking of a tired, cold, aching, hungry runaway. It never occurred to him to miss them. Miserable as he was, he never wasted a fraction of a second on the idea of going back. It was only that he'd just realized that his family had never been very real to him, and it had suddenly occurred to him to wonder why.

Emerson had no way of knowing, because he had nothing to compare it with, that he'd grown up in a kind of silence as thorough and effective as if he'd been born deaf. Whenever he thought about it—something he'd indulged himself in less and less often as he'd gotten older—he did understand that he hardly knew his father.

Walter Ngu had been a closemouthed, stoic-jawed man to begin with, lean and sinewy, with hard hands and sun-blackened skin. No trace remained of his past life—which, lacking any visible or tangible substance, had assumed the proportions of myth in his eldest son's mind—as a senior accountant with a powerful Los Angeles law firm. On becoming foreman, something Emerson did remember, he'd begun rising even earlier than his fellow workers, laboring all day beside them in the fields—doing what he calculated was his own fair share in addition to the supervising—and returning after dark in a state of wordless exhaustion which left him no choice but to delegate the raising of his children to his wife.

Where Emerson's father was thin, and as tall as any of his people ever got, his mother was soft, and as round as it was in her to become. Alice Ngu considered herself fortunate to have been chosen as the Chief Administrator's housekeeper and would do or say nothing to jeopardize a position she believed offered her family certain advantages—which her idea of personal integrity invariably prevented her from pressing—over the ordinary peasants of the Project. If Walter's strategy for survival consisted of working ten percent harder than anybody else, Alice's was to demand ten percent less than she had a right to expect.

Emerson gathered that they'd been different before coming to Pallas, both of them ambitious and dissatisfied with political and economic circumstances in their home state which were increasingly indistinguishable from those their own parents had fled in Asia. It was said—he couldn't remember who'd told him, certainly not his mother or father—that even before the earthquake which had killed twenty million people along the San Andreas fault, California had become an "absolute democracy," a dictatorship in its own way worse than any eastern European nation had been before the Soviet collapse. Everyday living had been all but impossible, the least activity requiring complicated licensing, expensive permits, or simply being forbidden by politicians and bureaucrats who didn't have to live with the consequences because it always seemed to work out that they themselves weren't subject to the same paralyzing rules and regulations.

A great natural disaster had only made things worse, offering an endless supply of new excuses to extend authoritarian controls until they covered every aspect of every minute of every individual's life. The fact that a majority, one over half of the people—abetted by the only legislature in America more debauched, voracious, and corrupt than Congress itself—had democratically inflicted these atrocities on themselves didn't make them any less obnoxious for the minority, one *under* half of the people, who had to live with them.

On Pallas, once they fully understood what they'd gotten themselves into, Alice and Walter had grimly resigned themselves to accepting without further struggle or protest whatever damage they'd done their own lives, for the sake of making life possible for their children. Apparently it had never occurred to them that their children—one of them, anyway—might not appreciate such a sacrifice. In the eyes of their eldest, they'd simply given up—no other words existed for it—and, far worse, they'd always insisted that he follow their compliant example without even the benefit of having fought a losing battle of his own, all of which had made growing up and establishing himself as an independent individual infinitely more difficult than it might otherwise have been.

Now, not very far away, a coyote howled. Emerson knew that sound. Not even the Rimfence could keep it out. With a kind of despair which matched the unseen animal's plaintive cry, he watched the moon descend to the horizon and drop below it, leaving him in darkness more profound than he'd ever known. In minutes, the inexorable mechanics of weather within the asteroid's atmospheric envelope had ratcheted through another turn and a cold rain began to fall. Before it was over half an hour later, Emerson was soaking wet, chilled to the core, and closer to death by hypothermia than he might have imagined, even as it was happening to him.

It wasn't until years later that he understood how fortunate he was—having simply put one weary foot in front of another, again and again, because no better alternative occurred to him, until he could hardly lift his feet at all—to stumble, in what otherwise might have been his final moment, upon an unlikely-looking structure, the first two-story building he'd ever seen, standing by itself on the rain-soaked prairie, on a low rise overlooking the muddy outskirts of Curringer. Unlike the squat, utilitarian prefabrications of the Project which another century had called Quonset huts, it was a gingerbread fantasy—or nightmare, he wasn't certain which—of pierced and scalloped facings, lathe-turned spindles, elaborate railings with decorative knobs, and slender, spiral-fluted columns, carried to the ridiculous extremes permitted by the low Pallatian gravity.

The yard around the house, which consisted of the "native" buffalo grass trimmed back to a more or less uniform height, was illuminated by a pair of chimneyed outdoor lamps attached to tall posts at its corners. The pools of light they spilled across the road failed to diminish a warm, multicolored glow coming from inside through many oddly shaped stained-glass windows.

There was no fence on either side of the ornately embellished wrought-iron gate which opened onto a broad flagstone walk to the front porch. Above the gate, swinging from a scrolled arch and lit by a small lamp of its own, hung a sign:

MRS. SINGH'S BOARDING HOUSE
Henrietta Singh, Prop.

Somewhere out behind the house, a dog began to add a barking counterpoint to the coyote's wail, utterly destroying any vague resolve Emerson might have been entertaining to risk bartering his labor in exchange for a badly needed meal. He was wearily attempting to muster his energy to move on when the front door, sporting a stained-glass window of its own, banged open abruptly. Onto the broad front porch strode the unmistakable figure, visible only in silhouette, of a small, thin woman wearing coveralls. In one hand she carried some sort of weapon.

"Well, what's it gonna be, youngster? Kinda chilly and wet out here, ain't it? Dark, too, now the moon's down. Planning to go on past or come in where it's warm and dry?"

Almost as abruptly as the front door had slammed open, something inside Emerson folded up. He sat down cross-legged in a puddle he hadn't realized he'd been standing in, put his face in his hands, and tried, without success, not to cry.

Mrs. Singh's house, although it looked like wooden homes Emerson had seen in books, was constructed of local stone, carefully chosen, arranged, and worked so that even the natural striations of the rock were made to resemble woodgrain.

Henrietta Singh, as Emerson first knew her, gave an equally deceptive impression, that of a dried-out, garrulous woman of middle age and uncertain ancestry, hardly taller than himself, who for some reason felt the necessity to apologize, as she introduced herself, that Mr. Singh— Horatio, as she referred to him—was unavailable to greet guests. He was buried in the backyard, the widow explained, having died of something called caisson disease, at the age of forty-four.

"Planted him myself, with these hands," she told the boy, showing him a faded black-and-white photograph of a dark-visaged, hook-nosed man with a huge, curly dark beard. "Poor dear passed away without seeing his only child born, though he allowed as how he welcomed death when it finally came, crippled up like he was, something terrible. Never complained none of what'd happened to him, though. Always maintained that it was well worth it to get a new world started."

Emerson nodded, too cold and tired to pay very close attention. They sat in a room more like those in the Chief Administrator's official residence than the peasants' quarters his family had occupied, the woman on a long couch, he on a matching chair she'd draped with a big lavender towel before handing him another towel exactly like it to dry himself with. They were the first towels Emerson had ever seen that were some shade other than the grayish-white the Project laundry produced. At first he hadn't recognized them for what they were.

Emerson initially found himself repulsed by the woman's outgoing nature and friendly lack of reserve, so different from anything he'd known growing up in the Project, and therefore, somehow, threatening to him. Then it occurred to him that if he listened carefully enough, he might learn something about this alien environment into which he'd launched himself so blindly. Or at least some alien environment somewhere—from the hundreds of books and other memorabilia scattered about her cluttered front parlor, he gathered that the late Horatio Singh had been an amateur historian, interested in the nineteenth-century British Empire.

"Back when it was possible to find a testicle in England," Mrs. Singh confirmed, peering at him closely, as if to see whether he was offended by the expression. She'd lit a fire in a tiny grate set in a nearby wall, and leaned over now to stoke it with the long-handled metal tool he'd earlier taken—more or less correctly—for a weapon. "Least that's how Horatio put it, rest his soul. He had a way of talking, that man. Never said much, just looked at his books and listened to other people talking. When he did speak up, it was to a point."

Emerson nodded again, his mind dull with fatigue. All he knew about the British Empire—and it was knowledge acquired in the last ten minutes—was that it had existed.

"Here, now," Mrs. Singh told him, "you're shivering!" She took another big swatch of colorful fabric from where it lay on the back of the couch and rose to lay it over his shoulders. "Pull this blanket around you and wiggle outa those wet clothes while I go see about something to warm you up inside. Won't be a minute."

He obeyed. "M-Mrs. Singh?"

A woman of quick, determined movements, she already had a hand on what was probably the kitchen door, but stopped at Emerson's voice and turned to face him. "Yes, boy?"

"I'm not a beggar, ma'am. I'm cold and hungry, and I appreciate your help, but I'm also used to hard work and willing to do my share for anything you give me."

She nodded. "I figured as much, which is why I'm headed for the kitchen now. We'll discuss the details once we get you fed, if it's all the same to you. Come to think of it, I'm feeling a mite peckish, myself. Must be the chilly weather."

She began to turn. He held up a hand—and nearly lost his blanket. "One more thing, ma'am. I won't bother you long. I have to get moving because I—"

" 'Cause you refugeed outa that ant farm across the lake and you're afraid they'll be after you in the morning. What makes you think you're the first? I appreciate your honesty, but anybody could tell a mile away what you are by the way you walk, slip-shuffling along like you're ashamed you exist. It's something I hadn't thought to see again since leaving Mother Mud. Nobody out here walks that way, not with independence and one-tenth of a gee putting a spring in their step. Now lemme get us something, will you, before one of us dies of starvation?" She pushed the door into the kitchen, went through, and let it swing behind her, leaving him to think about the swaggering hunters he'd seen earlier.

And wonder.

" 'Sgood!"

Fifteen minutes later, Emerson was gobbling down his second helping of a thick, heavily peppered stew containing more protein—although he wasn't aware of it just yet—than he'd ever been offered at a single sitting in his life. On the long, low table before him sat an aromatic loaf of home-baked bread and a stone crock of butter, neither of which would last much longer at the rate they were being consumed. Mrs. Singh had also brought a pot of hot, strong tea which she served in heavy, hand-thrown mugs, with honey almost as black as the tea.

"Glad to have another satisfied customer." She wielded a tooth-edged knife. "How about more bread?"

To his surprise, given what he'd been told about Outsiders, Mrs. Singh had accepted his diffident proposition and offered to trust him for food and lodging until he could arrange some form of employment more steady and remunerative than the odd jobs she nevertheless promised to find him around her own place.

"And don't you worry none about them dragging you back to the ant farm," she insisted. "That place is a fluke, one worm in an apple. Pallas was made for folks that wanted to be free, and they don't take to anybody being sent back to jail."

"Even a kid like me?"

"Even a kid, Emerson, especially one like you — going on thirty-five as you seem to be."

He laughed, then became sober. "Please forgive me, Mrs. Singh, but if I'm going to be an — I mean if I'm going to live outside the Project myself, I have to know how things work. Why would anybody be so generous to a stranger?"

"You mean a wet, hungry, young stranger on the coldest night we've had so far this year? Maybe I've been away from Earth too long. What else would a body do, boy?"

Having finished his stew and the last slice of bread he could manage, Emerson sipped his tea. "I don't remember anything about Earth, but where I come from, the goons would beat him up, dust their hands off, and throw him outside the Rimfence."

His new landlady shook her head. "So much for political communalism and the milk of human kindness."

Not altogether understanding what she meant, Emerson shrugged.

"Far as any alleged generosity part goes," she added, "and aside from plain good manners on a frontier world where I might need the favor returned tomorrow, it's pretty simple. In the first place, I can use another pair of hands around here at the best of times. And in the second, my other boarders are off into the weyers at the moment and it's getting a bit lonely around here."

Fascinated, he watched her take a small ceramic pipe from a box on an end table, stuff it with crumbly tobacco from the same box, and light it, puffing smoke. She was right: Outsiders could do whatever they wanted. In the Project, just getting caught with tobacco would cost you every other meal for a week.

"The wires?"

"Reminds me, I better tell you that you're free to practice out behind the house anytime you want, long as you watch which way you point yourself and it ain't after bedtime."

He shook his head. He was tired. Somehow he'd assumed that Mrs. Singh had indoor plumbing. But what was that she'd said about *practice?* And why not after bedtime?

"Naturally," she went on, not sensing his confusion, "whatever you contribute'll be deducted from your rent."

"Contribute?"

"That's right. You help me cut my overhead, and I'll cut yours." She indicated the supper dishes with a nod of her pipe. "But no more of this here cottontail for a while, mind you. Everybody says they're getting tired of it, and you can die—or go crazy anyway, from malnutrition—eating too much rabbit."

For the next several minutes, Emerson was preoccupied with trying to control his stomach, which threatened open rebellion. He wanted to tell Mrs. Singh that he hadn't understood a single thing she'd just told him. On the other hand, he was equally horrified at the possibility that he did understand her, after all.

"But what can I be thinking about?" Apparently Mrs. Singh misinterpreted the expression on his face. "You being fresh from that blasted ant farm across the lake and all, I plumb forgot that you probably don't own a gun—or any kind of weapon at all, shocking as it may seem—to practice with, do you, boy?"

Gulping bile, Emerson looked down at his bowl, scraped nearly clean with the spoon that still lay accusingly beside it on the table. First it had been poor Bambi, murdered and mutilated by those gloating savages back on the road. And now it was cute and furry Thumper, here in this very stew he'd found so delicious.

Emerson had never eaten meat before.

What kind of surrealistic nightmare had he escaped to, anyway?

XI

OFF IN THE WEYERS

NOTHING IS WRONG WITH AMERICAN EDUCATION THAT CAN BE CURED, OR EVEN CHANGED, BY TINKERING WITH AMERICAN EDUCATION. ITS PROBLEMS, LIKE SO MANY OTHERS IN THAT COUNTRY, ARISE FROM A FUNDAMENTAL AND LONG-STANDING CONFLICT BETWEEN AMERICAN VALUES AND PRACTICES WHICH, UNRESOLVED, WILL GO ON MAKING THINGS WORSE UNTIL THE EDUCATIONAL SYSTEM COLLAPSES, DRAGGING THE REST OF THE CULTURE DOWN WITH IT.

—Mirelle Stein, *The Productive Class*

Mrs. Singh turned out to be as good as her word. Following their breakfast the next morning, a blessedly vegetarian affair featuring pancakes, hashbrown potatoes, and eggs (which were permitted by the dietary restraints he'd grown up under) fried with sliced mushrooms, she immediately found some work for Emerson to do, washing the previous evening's dishes.

She wound up doing a fair number of them herself, standing beside him at the big double sink, since he'd never washed dishes this way before and had to be shown how. He had seen indoor running water, in the Residence kitchen. Mrs. Singh's was smaller but no less luxuriously appointed and felt friendlier somehow. Pots and pans were handled by a noisy, steam-filled machine under the countertop—something a mildly scandalized Emerson had never even heard of before and the Residence kitchen certainly didn't have—but Mrs. Singh maintained that handwashing cups and plates and silverware constituted a form of meditation.

Emerson had his doubts, and not just about washing dishes. He'd have run screaming last night from what had momentarily seemed a house of horrors if he hadn't been exhausted—and too honest not to acknowledge that he'd enjoyed the rabbit stew before learning what it was. Perhaps he'd even guessed. At any rate, he'd allowed himself to be led upstairs and shown a bedroom larger than the quarters his entire family shared at the Project. Crawling naked between clean sheets under a thick, quilted coverlet, he'd fallen asleep before he knew it.

After dishes were dried and stacked in the cupboards, Mrs. Singh showed him around her home, letting him know what chores she'd like to see done, if she didn't get to them herself, as well as which facilities he was welcome to share and which he should regard as private. Windows needed washing and there were floors to be swept. She had a vacuum cleaner exactly like the one at the Residence and dust precipitators standing in a corner of each room, which the Residence didn't have at all.

"These," she explained, pointing at the surrounding walls, "you can pull down and take to your room, long as your hands are clean and you bring 'em back when you're through."

Emerson was speechless. Books on the nineteenth-century British Empire weren't the only items in Horatio Singh's library. The house was full of books, walls lined to the ceiling with shelves, even the bathrooms—which turned out to be inside, and more modern and comfortable than anything he'd known possible. There were books on every subject listed in the encyclopedia Mrs. Singh showed him how to use, and three more sets of encyclopedias. The second stage of his education had begun.

An authorized education at the Project consisted of one topic—selfless cooperation—with just enough reading, writing, and arithmetic thrown in to support the primary subject. Thanking her for her amazing generosity, Emerson explained to Mrs. Singh that his mother had taught him to read long before any school had gotten around to it. "What kind of schools," he asked, "do they have here on the Outside?"

"No schools at all on Pallas"—she shook her head—"though someone's always threatening to start one up in Curringer." They were in the parlor, sitting at the low table before the couch. The day was rainy and cold like the night before and she'd canceled her plans for outdoor work. Instead, Emerson was trying his first cup of coffee. "Even before I was born, the politicians back on Earth had managed to turn the whole planet into a jail, and most of us came here to get out of it. Who needs to start another jail here?"

The boy's eyes were wide. "But how do children learn—"

She sighed. "How'd you learn to read? Teaching kids is what parents—and nobody else—are for."

"But what if they won't—"

She held up a hand. "If they aren't up to it, then it becomes the kid's responsibility, either in childhood or later on. One of the best American presidents—Andrew Johnson, it was—didn't learn to read till he was grown; his wife taught him. Horatio never finished high school: when he was fourteen he lied about his age and joined the teamsters—that was the jail he came to Pallas to get out of—but he read books every spare moment. I once watched him back a famous historian into a corner at a public lecture and make him admit he was wrong. Education never stops, boy, unless you want it to, and I suspect that's just another way of deciding it's time to lie down and die."

"But—"

"Besides, those schools back on Earth were never anything but breeding grounds for petty criminals, tribal gatherings for passing on the commonly held ignorance, and indoctrination centers for political propaganda—useless when it came to teaching the most elementary skills. And they got worse and worse the more money that was thrown at 'em."

"But, but—"

"You're sounding like an outboard motor, Emerson. I taught my daughter Gretchen to read, and among the skills she learned along the way was how to *evaluate* what she reads. That's the last thing schools want kids to be able to do, but it's a matter of self-defense as important as knowing to focus on the front sight and squeeze rather than jerk the trigger. Turned out pretty well, I think, and now she's educating herself, from the same books you see all around you."

Emerson vaguely recalled mention of a child. How old was this Gretchen? Where was she now?

He astonished himself by asking.

"About your age. She's off in the weyers, like I said last night."

"The wires?"

"That's W-E-Y-E-R-S," Mrs. Singh started to explain, when she was interrupted by a high, chirping noise that seemed to come from all directions at once. "Coffee table!" she told the air in the room. Abruptly, the free-standing three-dimensional image of a strange-looking little man sprang into existence above the tabletop between the over-sized mugs they'd been drinking from. The image couldn't have been more than a quarter-meter tall, and it wasn't in the least transparent. It wore a beard, a loose, color-splashed shirt, and a pistol hanging from under its shirttail. "Why, it's Aloysius Brody! Good morning, Aloysius."

"And a gloomy, miserable mornin' it is." The image glanced around. "I'm at loose ends an' wonderin' if y'can stand a bit of company. No particular reason, just feelin' sociable."

Mrs. Singh nodded. "I've got company already. This is Emerson Ngu, late of the Greeley Utopian Memorial Ant Farm."

"A citizen exercisin' his pedal franchise?"

"He has some questions I think you have better answers to. Still game for a kaffeeklatsch?"

"I'll be right out. You might show him your family album."

"Good idea. I'll do it right away." The image over the table vanished. Mrs. Singh rose, went to a bookshelf, and returned with a bulging ring-binder from which paper and transparent plastic protruded at the edges. "You asked twice about the weyers. I just didn't know the best way to answer. Aloysius is right, this may help—and give you a better idea of what the Outside is about than anything I could say. Horatio took these when he was on the ter-raforming crew."

She opened the book. Despite what she'd said, the first item she showed Emerson was a handful of yellowed newspaper clippings and grainy halftone news photographs of massive space hardware and of an imposing man with bushy white hair and matching handlebar moustache. "S'pose the year 2007 seemed eventful enough already for anybody living in Asia or North America," she began, "but it had plenty of surprises for those on other continents, as well. That was the year William Wilde Curringer began launching his first commercial vehicles toward the asteroids."

From school lectures and endless assemblies Emerson knew the name of the infamous West American robber baron and expatriate plastics trillionaire who'd founded Two Lions Consortium, headquartered in the United Cantons of South Africa. Mrs. Singh turned brittle pages, gazing at headlines growing larger and more outraged as time went on.

"Curringer's enterprises were always profitable as all get-out and this time he had the support of Japanese business interests. What I recall is that his manned and manless survey and freight-carrying machines all used cheap, simple rockets built from off-the-shelf components. You can't tell from the photos, but the structure is seamless oil pipe with an extra heat treat. He even used windshield-wiper motors for fuel pumps, and later on made some innovative uses of solar sails."

The first color photograph, still bright under a protective covering, was of the asteroid itself, taken through a spaceship window. Against a starry backdrop hung gray-brown, crater-scarred Pallas as it had appeared before an atmospheric envelope had masked its color and contours in shades of blue and white and green.

"Curringer's idea was to start a permanent colony here under a unique corporate agreement."

"The Hyperdemocratic Covenant?" It was another thing Emerson had already heard about.

"That's it, 'One man, one veto.' The immigrants'd be

shareholders in the Curringer Trust, which, in turn, would
be governed by a hyperdemocratic principle thought up by
Curringer's old friend—and, the gossips had it, lover—Mirelle Stein the philosopher. I have a picture of her somewhere . . ."

What Emerson saw was another blurry newspaper
photograph, one of a rather grim-faced, firm-jawed
woman. Her dark hair was cut to pageboy length, with severe bangs across the forehead.

"In any case," Mrs. Singh went on, "the Curringer
Trust would own the atmospheric envelope, the largest artificial structure ever undertaken. Still is, far as I know.
Curringer started with a bang—in 'blatant contravention
of international law,' like it says in these here clippings. A
few well-placed nukes—make that 'clean atomic devices'—modified Pallas's natural orbit and rotation.
Horatio, rest his soul, helped plant more than one of those
little bombs, himself."

Pictures supported her claim: men in bulky, helmeted
suits, one stenciled "SINGH, H.H.," bending over mysterious canisters. One photo, enlarged until it took up a
whole page, showed an unbearable light surrounded by
multicolored clouds streaming into space. This, too, was
consistent with what he'd been told. Any application of
atomic power, however peaceful or constructive, was always presented by the UN E&M counselors as an ultimate
evil. Only Mrs. Singh seemed to think it was a good thing.
And perhaps, he thought, it was. It appeared to have
worked. Here they all were, and he'd never heard of any
harm—two-headed babies was the example that popped
into his mind—having come of it.

The next pictures, more of Horatio's snapshots, were
of the same men—or men wearing the same sort of spacesuit—arranging huge sheets of plastic over the barren surface. In some ways it was like pictures the boy had seen of

a circus tent about to be erected, except that this "canvas" was perfectly transparent.

"They carried the terraformation out according to a simple plan, but on a scale so big few folks were capable of visualizing it. What they accomplished was no less than the conversion of an airless, frozen wasteland into a habitable world."

Mrs. Singh flipped pages, showing pictures of one construction site after another. "Ten-mile circles were laid out around each pole, marking locations for tens of thousands of anchors set in the soil with laser bores, explosives, vacuum-hardening concrete, and epoxoids. At the same time, a thin, tough, 'smart' plastic was extruded from the bellies of orbiting factory vessels."

Emerson grinned. "*Smart* plastic?"

"You betcha. Curringer figured meteorites and future gun-toting colonists would present a hazard here, so he made his envelope self-repairing—plastics were his business, you'll recall. It also filtered out excess U.V. and other harmful wavelengths, while passing visible and infrared light to the surface."

She turned a page, to a sequence of a dozen pictures. "Here's Horatio's crew arranging ribbons of extruded plastic on the surface, each of them miles long and hundreds of yards wide. No telling where this is today, could be the back of beyond or the heart of beautiful downtown Curringer! But by the time they'd finished, they'd given this ball of rock a second skin over every inch of its 1,187-mile equator, the 594 miles between there and each pole, and laser-welded the whole shebang at the edges. A job like that—it's still hard to picture in your mind. A lot of brave men and women died in the process, let me tell you."

The next pictures showed a bewildering array of men and machinery. Some background objects looked like spaceships with complex mechanical attachments in odd places. Other scenes reminded Emerson of what he'd read about the building of suspension bridges on Earth. A common feature of each picture was a huge white concrete structure, like a great curved dam sweeping from one horizon to the other, into which metal cleats the size of houses were set at a steep angle.

"Meanwhile," Mrs. Singh continued, "steel cables, spun gleaming from the heart of an iron-nickel asteroid, were woven into a loose net around Pallas and locked into the ring of anchors you see here at the poles. Horatio and his people sealed the edges of the envelope, and that put paid to the mechanical phase of terraformation. The rest was up to biology and chemistry."

She turned a page and it was back to clippings, the paper of a different color and texture. "Here's some typical East American wailing," she observed, running a nail down the collected articles. "These are faxes. In those days, it took years to get a paper delivered out here. What it boils down to is that after the envelope was in place, limp and empty on the surface, an artificial bacterium designed for the environment was introduced beneath it at a number of widespread locations." The next photo was of a pair of spacesuited figures, one large and one small, standing arm in arm on what looked like a plastic dropcloth used for painting a house. "I was on the bio team, and that's how I met Horatio. Thanks to various international statutes prohibiting genetic innovation, the whole thing wasn't a bit less illegal than the atomics used to alter the asteroid's motion, and we were proud of ourselves just for breaking that damn silly law."

Emerson sat up. He'd never heard anyone say something like that before, although he'd thought it many times himself. Right or wrong, he believed abruptly that he understood what the Outside—and the Outsiders—were all about.

Mrs. Singh didn't seem to notice his sudden enlightenment, but went on, warming to her own specialty. "Energized by the greenhouse effect," she told him, "supplemented by big flimsy aluminized mylar mirrors fabricated in space like the envelope and cables and placed in orbit around Pallas, our little customized bug went to work converting carbonaceous chondrite into sterile soil, free water, and a mixture of noxious gases. This primitive, poisonous atmosphere gradually inflated the cable-reinforced plastic envelope until, at the equator, it stood twenty-five thousand feet above the primordial crater-scarred surface."

Emerson shook his head, confused again. "The atmosphere was poisonous?"

"Better believe it, boy. Ate spacesuits pretty handily, too. But this 'reducing' atmosphere was quickly altered by a second microorganism—there went International Law again—an artificial species of algae, into breathable air. Just as we'd planned, the oxygen killed off the first bacterium, leaving behind trillions of tons of nitrogen-rich fertilizer as a residue."

Emerson closed his eyes, trying to imagine what it had been like to build a world, trying to see ideas and feelings that didn't show in Mrs. Singh's old photographs.

"Clouds formed beneath the envelope and rain fell, maybe for the first time here since the birth of the solar system," she mused, lost in her memories. "Gossamer-winged aircraft sowed the surface with the seeds of ground-covering weeds, grasses, fast-growing trees. The gray-brown surface of Pallas began to show some green. We had a spruce, developed by a pulp-and-paper outfit back on Earth named Weyerhauser, that'd grow forty feet in ten years even in standard gravity. Which is why we still refer to the boonies as the weyers."

"The boonies?"

"Meanwhile, here's a couple of orbital pictures of the

asteroid's poles. Look kinda like the tonsure of a monk, don't they? That's because they're *outside* the envelope, where they remain airless and barren—but far from deserted. Having served as construction campsites, they became perfect spots for landing spaceships. Cargo and passengers enter the artificial environment here, through a series of airlocks, and—"

She was going to say more, but a bell rang. "Come in, Aloysius!" she shouted. "It's only a mile and a half. What took you so long?"

XII
WHAT WAS YOUR NAME IN THE STATES?

THE SECOND AMERICAN CIVIL WAR WILL BE FOUGHT OVER THAT LITTLE STRIP OF GROUND IN YOUR FRONT YARD BETWEEN THE SIDEWALK AND THE STREET.
—**Mirelle Stein,** *The Productive Class*

W hen Emerson went to open the door, Brody was still standing on the steps to the front porch, stamping mud off his boots. When he appeared satisfied with their condition, he nodded to the boy, climbed to the porch itself, and paused again to shake accumulated rainwater from the plastic poncho he wore over his clothing.

"I'll be after discussin' this with Weather Control," he grumbled as he entered the house. "They're supposed t'limit this grand enthusiasm of theirs for precipitation t'nighttimes."

"Weather Control?" Emerson asked as the man brushed past him. He was temporarily ignored as Mrs. Singh greeted Brody with a two-handed shake and a peck on the cheek, invited her new guest to remove his poncho and sit himself, and offered him a cup of coffee.

"It'd be greatly appreciated, to be sure," the man answered, shucking out of the poncho. Laying a small bundle he'd been carrying underneath it on the sofa beside him, he nodded with apparent familiarity toward the picture book still lying open on the table. "Ah, I see that y'drug the family album out, after all."

She riffled idly through its pages. "Why, yes I have, Aloysius, and I've just finished telling Emerson here about as much as I can myself about the way we terraformed Pallas."

Emerson sat down in a chair placed at right angles to the couch.

"Emerson Ngu." The Curringer innkeeper squinted his eyes, peering at the boy. "Y'look that familiar t'me. Have we met? I do get out to the ant farm now an' then t'buy produce."

Still full of unanswered questions himself, Emerson shook his head and answered politely, "I don't believe we have, sir. My father, Walter Ngu, is a foreman. My mother, Alice Ngu, is the housekeeper at the Chief Administrator's Residence."

"Indeed she is. I've met them both, then." Brody nodded, grinning. "A strong family resemblance." The man accepted a steaming mug from Mrs. Singh, raised his eyebrows and received a nod, then dug in a shirt pocket to extract a cigar. As he lit it, Mrs. Singh touched something under the edge of the coffee table. After that, Emerson noticed, the smoke was drawn to it and vanished into its surface.

"If ye've gotten as far as the terraformin', then the next thing young Emerson here should know is that soon afterward, Wild Bill Curringer an' his merry band began send-in' the glad tidin's out over TV back on Earth, an' radio, an' compunets — "

Mrs. Singh laughed. "And in print, of every language and format, from Afrikaans to Zuni."

"An' everywhere an' anywhere, from Azerbaijan t'Zimbabwe, to a war-weary, history-jaded planetary population which had long since come t'believe itself beyond astonishment."

" '*To Pallas!*' " Mrs. Singh quoted the well-worn advertising slogan which Emerson had heard over and over from his parents and teachers. " '*For the opportunity of a lifetime!*' "

" '*T'Pallas!*' " Brody finished with another of his broad grins. " '*Fer a lifetime of opportunity!*' "

Both of them fell silent for a moment, remembering. Brody puffed on his big cigar, his gaze concentrated on the cover of the photo album. Mrs. Singh got up with a sigh, went out to the kitchen, and returned with the coffeepot to refill their mugs.

Brody heaved a deep sigh of his own, then spoke to them without looking up. "Pallas, the Curringer Trust's advertisements proclaimed, had enough room for everybody an' anybody."

"Anybody willing to make a two-year interplanetary voyage packed in like sardines," Mrs. Singh agreed, setting the pot aside and seating herself on the couch once more.

"Enough room" — Brody looked directly at Emerson — "for eighty million forty-acre farmsteads."

"Or enough room for twenty thousand cities the size of Manhattan," Mrs. Singh stated, "although both were just the opposite of what Curringer intended doing with the place."

Brody shook his head. "Room for a fresh start an' a chance at a dacent an' rewardin' life."

"Fully transferable land title—" Mrs. Singh began.

"—the exact location t'be determined by a random drawin'—"

"—start-up supplies, and membership in the Curringer Trust were built into the price of the fare."

" 'Twasn't a plan entirely without precedent," Brody told Emerson. " 'Tis more or less the same way the famous James Jerome Hill an' his equally famous Northern Pacific Railroad company developed the northwestern United States in the nineteenth century an' populated it with eager European immigrant families who'd paid for their land, a transatlantic boat ride, a long train ride across the continent, an' sometimes even another boat ride at the end of their arduous journey, all in the same package."

"And the price they paid for coming here," offered Mrs. Singh, "was about the same, allowing for four centuries of inflation, as what the Pilgrims paid to get to Plymouth Rock."

"Although some folks like us were paid t'come out here an' only decided afterward t'stay." Brody turned where he sat to face the boy squarely. "Now what y'may not know, boy, is that everywhere on Earth, every possible sort of religious, political, linguistic, an' cultural resentment had been simmerin', just below the surface, sometimes for millennia. At any given moment, almost anyplace y'care t'name, there was a war already goin' on or another simply waitin' its turn t'happen."

Mrs. Singh nodded, remembering. "But before too long all of the Ainu, Pakistanis, Japanese-Koreans, West Indians, East Indians, and Eurasians were leaving England and Japan—"

"—so pristinely an' prissily pure—" Brody observed.

"—and sublimely race-conscious—" Mrs. Singh wrinkled her nose.

"—seekin' more equitable treatment in an environment they were willin' t'labor t'create for themselves."

"Within a few months of Curringer's announcement," asserted Mrs. Singh, "even the Moros ceased a thousand years of pointless struggle and departed the Philippines for the frontier of space, joining their fellow Moslems from war-ravaged Lebanon, war-ravaged Jordan, war-ravaged Iran, war-ravaged Iraq, and war-ravaged Afghanistan."

"The Walloons willin'ly gave up their hard-won corner of tiny Belgium," Brody declared.

"And they were followed in surprisingly short order," Mrs. Singh commented, "by the Flemish."

"Which began t'set a pattern," Brody laughed, "quickly imitated by the Catalans an' the Basques in Spain—"

"And insurgents on all sides from Angola and Madagascar," noted Mrs. Singh, "even sides nobody else had known existed because the media couldn't be bothered to talk about them."

Brody nodded. "Like the poor Miskito Indians from Nicaragua."

"And the anti-Marxist faction of the Quebecois," added Mrs. Singh, "from the People's Republic of Canada."

"Before we earlier pioneers knew quite what was happening, every racial, ideological, ethnic, an' religious minority was represented on Pallas, exactly as Curringer meant it t'be."

"That's right," Mrs. Singh told him. "If it matters, Emerson, you'll find a good many people like yourself here on the Outside—Vietnamese, Thais, and Cambodians of Chinese ancestry."

"An' plenty of good Irish-Americans like me," added Brody, before Emerson could tell them that it didn't matter to him what color a person was, only what they did, "though the majority of the Irish here are northerners from the auld sod of Catholic an' Protestant persuasion, who just got tired of lobbin' grenades at one another."

Mrs. Singh nodded. "Just as there are Sikhs and other kinds of Indians—and all sorts of Palestinians—formerly mortal enemies living together now, side by side in peace, because they're all newcomers on an equal footing here, and they all have something vastly better to do with themselves than killing one another."

"Indeed," Brody agreed, "Danikil an' the survivors of other decimated tribes from the now uninhabitable wastes of Ethiopia, not t'mention many another ruined part of Africa."

Emerson had been trying, not altogether successfully, to take it all in. "Sikhs," he asked, "is that how your late husband happened to come here, Mrs. Singh, from India?"

Mrs. Singh looked startled, then laughed. "Dear me, no. Horatio was from Butte, Montana. I think his grandparents might have belonged to some kind of religious cult at one time, but the only natural enemies he ever acknowledged were prairie dogs."

"Who haven't made much headway here as yet, I'm afraid," Brody observed. "Somethin' wrong about the soil, I'm given to understand. As t'the rest of the immigrants, one an' all they were warned, long before leavin' Earth, t'forget their ancient arguments."

Mrs. Singh began to pour more coffee and noticed that the pot was empty. "It was pointed out that succeeding generations of their offspring would inevitably mingle their blood and genes."

"An' hard as it may have been for them to imagine it when they arrived, in the fullness of time, all of their old feuds would eventually be irrelevant an' forgotten, anyway."

Mrs. Singh stood up, taking the coffeepot in hand. "So why not go ahead and recognize that now—"

Brody looked up and grinned. "—an' get along together on their new homeworld from the outset?"

They both paused, as if expecting some kind of answer from Emerson. The idea certainly made sense to him—in fact it almost seemed self-evident—and he told them so.

"And to me, as well," Mrs. Singh agreed, "but it's equally true, and we must always remember it, that there were more than simple matters of race, religion, or politics involved."

"Too right, Henrietta. These first early refugees from one kind of war or another were soon joined by a virtual army of goat herders who'd simply gotten tired of herdin' goats—"

"That's right," she said, "and by another army of wheat farmers who'd gotten tired of farming wheat—"

"An' by pipe fitters who'd gotten tired of fittin' pipes—"

"And by truck drivers who'd gotten tired of driving trucks—"

"An'," Brody concluded, "although as with the case of leprechauns an' the like, I must confess that I've never personally known one such meself an' have me doubts, by computer programmers who'd gotten that tired of programmin' computers."

"Yes, and to their numbers you can add the innumerable bankrupts—"

"The countless automobile thieves—"

"The ex-convicts—"

"The draft dodgers—"

"The bill evaders—"

"Ah, Billy Vader, Darth's younger brother an' a good friend of mine. An' don't forget the tax strikers—"

"And the husbands and fathers ducking child support—"

"Not t'mention the curse of alimony."

"In short," observed Mrs. Singh, "the antisocial scum—"

"Or the individualistic cream—"

"Depending on who's telling the story."

"—of the Earth's vast, teemin' population."

Mrs. Singh laughed. "Within a year, that old-time movie ditty 'What Was Your Name in the States?' had become this asteroid's informal anthem. Why, I believe they still start their broadcasting day with it at the radio station in Curringer."

Emerson nodded enthusiastically. He'd heard the song many times and wondered what was behind it.

"Pallas"—Brody was suddenly very serious—"was t'be a place for renewed hope under a system—"

"Mirelle Stein's Hyperdemocratic Principle?" Emerson suggested. That, too, from what he'd been told about it, seemed like a self-evidently good idea to him, although he was still waiting, perhaps a little cynically, to hear more before he said so.

Brody scrutinized the boy, then nodded, "—of mutual tolerance an' free individual enterprise."

"And so the very first place-name to appear on any 'official' map of the asteroid Pallas," declared Emerson, still repeating what he'd learned in school, "was Curringer?"

"Yes," Mrs. Singh told him, "but it wasn't because he was the man who'd made everything possible."

"It wasn't?" That was disappointing and confusing. William Wilde Curringer was rapidly becoming a personal hero to Emerson, the first the boy had ever had.

Mrs. Singh sighed, thinking back again. "No, it wasn't. It was because, in the year 2010, at age seventy-four—"

"Durin' a routine aerial seedin' operation in which the stubborn man insisted on participatin'—"

"—he died there in an ordinary plane crash."

Brody shook his head, as if to clear it of the unpleasant memory. His hand strayed to the parcel he'd brought with him, and it seemed to remind him of something. Not for the last time, Emerson noticed that his accent seemed to fade as he grew more serious.

"All that t'one side, young fellow, it's time y'gave some thought t'what ye'll do now t'keep body an' soul together. You're your own man here on the Outside, just as you'd hoped to be, but the liberty to steer your own course necessarily encompasses the liberty to sit down and starve t'death, or it isn't liberty at all, just the same old contradiction we left back on Earth: an illusion involuntarily subsidized by others—purchased, as it were, at the price of their liberty. There are some as might not mind that, but y'don't look the type t'me."

Emerson became serious, too. "I'm not, Mr. Brody."

Brody smiled. "I'm that tempted to'believe ye, Mr. Ngu."

Mrs. Singh explained the agreement she'd made with the boy, along with the fact that they'd already discussed the need to find him something more permanent and rewarding to do. Her voice and expression were kindly. "Is there anything you're particularly interested in or feel you're especially good at, Emerson?"

"Well," Emerson gave it some thought, "my father said he was going to start me on soil preparation next season," he replied. "That's plowing and mulching and sowing. Everything's organic. No chemicals. I was never very good at weeding or cultivating or insect control or harvesting, but they're all I was ever taught."

Brody frowned. " 'Tis everything an' all that I expected. But for any number of reasons that'll be after makin' themselves clear t'ye soon enough, y'couldn't have picked a less desirable array of skills, me boy. I suppose that's the point, though, in a way. Y'didn't pick 'em, they were after bein' picked for ye."

"Isn't there anything, anything at all?" Mrs. Singh was determinedly undeterred. "There must have been something, Emerson. Don't boys have hobbies any more?"

"There was," Emerson replied, "one other thing . . ." Haltingly at first—until he realized all over again that he was Outside, where an individual was free to do whatever he liked as long as he didn't hurt anybody else—he told them about the little crystal radio receiver he'd built in secret from discarded trash.

Brody whistled and sat back. "Now I am well and truly impressed, given the handicaps y'had t'be operatin' under. Emerson, me boy, I've a friend I'll be after talkin' to tonight—if I'm still talkin' to him at all after the poker game—who runs the only garage in Curringer, meanin' the only garage on the whole asteroid. If ye're interested, he might try ye as an apprentice mechanic. What do y'say?"

"An apprentice mechanic?" Emerson gulped, wondering if it was truly possible that someone would actually be willing to pay him to be turned loose with real tools and things to use them on. He was afraid to ask. "I'll certainly try if he will."

"Before we see to that, Aloysius"—Mrs. Singh astonished Emerson once again, this time by winking broadly at him—"we've got an even more serious problem on our hands. It seems that poor Emerson, here, comes to us socially naked and completely unable to provide for himself in the customary and proper manner. He doesn't have a sidearm of his own, and wouldn't know what to do with it if he had one."

Brody laughed broadly. "Well, of course the boy

doesn't have a gun of his own, medear, comin' from where
he does. The only ones who have 'em out there are the uniformed thugs who run the place—an' they're probably all
locked up in an arsenal t'which the distinguished former
Senator has the only key. The thugs wouldn't mind a bit—
they greatly prefer torturin' unarmed peasants with cattle
prods."

Brody lifted the package and placed it on the table with
a thud that gave Emerson a good idea of how heavy it must
be. "However, I anticipated the young man's social embarrassment, and brought this out with me in case I liked the
looks of him, which apparently I do. You'll recall that
Horatio left it t'me when he passed on, rest his gallant soul.
For the life of me, I can't think of a better use t'put it to."

He painstakingly untied the age-stained string which
held the plasticized paper together and carefully un-
wrapped the contents. Inside the shallow nest formed by
its protective wrapping of oily-looking brown paper lay an
enormous, flat, L-shaped slab of greasy, dull-finished blue-
black steel. At some points the monster was almost as thick
as Emerson's slender wrist and no less than a quarter of a
meter long.

It was the biggest pistol the suddenly terrified boy had
ever imagined possible.

XIII
THE GRIZZLY WIN MAG

I HAVE ALWAYS ASSUMED THAT BEFORE A BOY LEAVES HOME HIS
FATHER MAKES SURE THAT HE HAS BEEN TAUGHT THE ESSENTIAL
SKILLS OF LIFE, FROM PROPER PERSONAL HYGIENE TO DRIVING A
CAR. MARKSMANSHIP IS CERTAINLY ONE OF THOSE SKILLS . . .
— Jeff Cooper, *To Ride, Shoot Straight, and Speak the Truth*

I t weighed a kilogram and a half, unloaded. And the cartridges were the size of his thumb.

Like boys everywhere, and despite the self-consciously
pacific upbringing he'd received at the Project, Emerson
had somehow picked up enough firearms lore that he
knew which end of a gun was which, what part to hold
onto, and in a general way, what the trigger, sights, and
hammer did. Beyond that, he was lost.

He watched with fascination as Brody pushed a stri-
ated button located behind the trigger on the left side of
the thing and a silver box slid from the handle, containing
seven enormous cartridges stacked one on top of another.
Emerson counted them under his breath as, having laid the
heavy pistol in his lap, Brody casually thumbed them off
the top of the magazine into his free hand.

The next thing the man did was more amazing. Taking
the gun in his right hand as if he were about to shoot —
Emerson noticed that he rested his index finger alongside
the squared loop encircling the trigger rather than on the
trigger itself — he seized the top rear where a series of parallel grooves had been cut, and pulled back, thrusting his
other hand forward. To the boy it seemed that the whole
top half of the firearm slid backward and an eighth cartridge which had been inside somewhere popped out of a
big square hole and fell into Brody's lap.

Emerson peered eagerly past Brody's shoulder, noticing how contact with something—probably Horatio Singh's holster—had worn the blue-black off the edges and corners of the metal, creating highlights. On one side, on the moving part Brody told him was the "slide," three interlocking hexagons containing the letters *L.A.R.* had been engraved, along with the inscription *"GRIZZLY WIN MAG."* On the other side, a charging bear was depicted beside the words *"MARK I."* Below, on what Brody called the frame, in smaller letters, Emerson read *"L.A.R. MFG. INC., WEST JORDAN, UT. 84084 U.S.A."* and what he guessed was a serial number.

Brody picked up one of the shiny yellow cylinders and held it between his thumb and forefinger. At one end a groove had been cut to produce a sort of rim. At the other, a copper-colored spheroid was truncated to expose a tip of dull gray lead. The man tipped it over so that Emerson could see the gaping hole in the end.

"I've often thought it odd that in the midst of the twenty-first century we're usin' essentially the same weapons as our ancestors of two centuries ago. The last major invention in the field was the self-contained metallic cartridge, in the 1870s, as I recall."

Mrs. Singh nodded. "Earlier, counting rimfire. Some military outfits use caseless cartridges."

"T'be sure—as they did, for all practical purposes, in the Crimean War. I suppose it's because ye can defeat a laser with a chemical fog or reflective longjohns, an' nobody's ever developed a pocketable source powerful enough for particle beam weapons. Here, of course, firearms're rugged enough not t'require repair too often, an' simple enough that we can do it ourselves if need be."

"This is a .45 magnum," Brody turned to Emerson with a grin, "the world's most powerful handgun cartridge— this world's, anyway, unless me neighbor Nails Osborn, the bold an' darin' plumber, finally sent off for that .454 he always wanted. Lemme see now, y'probably think in the accursed Napoleonic system, so this'll drive a fifteen-gram hollow-pointed bullet, a bit better'n half an ounce, at somethin' like four hundred twenty-seven meters per second — that's some fifteen hundred kilometers an hour, about Mach one and a quarter — generatin' almost half a tonne of energy."

He scooped the cartridges up and poured them into the pocket where he kept his cigars.

Mrs. Singh had been watching with an eye on Emerson. "Aloysius is right. The Grizzly belonged to Horatio, rest his soul, who left it to his best friend because it's too much gat for me." She lifted her apron, revealing a holster — and a smaller pistol — which she'd apparently been wearing all along. "My little 10 Millimeter Lite fills the larder with venison and smaller game well enough to suit me. Horatio wanted the extra power for elk and buffalo — and because he wanted the extra power. He was a man, after all. Men look at things pretty oddly."

Brody laughed. "These are the gentlest loads that'll operate the mechanism. We wouldn't be puttin' a cannon like this in yer hands, me boy, except that it's the spare sidearm available. Each gun on this asteroid had t'be shipped up absent the knowledge, or over the mealy-mouthed objections, of many an Earthside government. We've no firearms manufactory of our own."

What stood out for Emerson were the words "in yer hands." Were they actually going to let him touch it? Suddenly he knew what young Arthur must have felt having drawn the sword from the stone. He reached out and took the gun Brody offered.

Even emptied, and even in the kindly gravity of Pallas, it seemed impossibly heavy. Brody had let the slide travel forward again after drawing out the final cartridge. Somewhere during the process the hammer had been cocked, but he had gently lowered it before handing the Grizzly to the boy. Now Emerson grasped the big, rubber-sheathed handle of the weapon with his right hand and the serrated portion at the rear of the slide with his left and tried to imitate what he'd seen. He wanted to know where that extra cartridge had come from.

"Take a look!" Brody exclaimed. "Nobody has to tell him t'check the chamber t'see whether it's loaded! Cock the hammer, Emerson—keep yer finger off the trigger—it'll make it easier t'get the slide back. Let me do this first, so ye'll know y'did it right."

He inserted the empty magazine in the grip.

Following instructions, Emerson strained at the massive pistol, pushing forward on the frame, as he'd seen Brody do, as he pulled back on the slide. His hands shook, but the slide retreated until he heard a metallic click as it locked back.

"Excellent, me boy! That long lever on the side is to let the slide back down. But hold onto the barrel—" he pointed to the tube exposed at the front of the retracted slide "—an' let it down gently. When there's no cartridge in the top of the magazine t'slow it down, it's kindlier to the sear an' hammer."

Emerson did as he was told, although his thumb had to stretch to reach the lever. The slide went forward smoothly against his fingers as they slid along the barrel. Imitating Brody again, he restrained the hammer with his right thumb and left index finger and pulled the trigger. Nothing happened until Brody reached over, inserted a finger, and depressed what he called the "grip safety." The hammer rolled forward, and Emerson handed the pistol over, grip first, to the man.

Mrs. Singh nodded approval. "What do you say we go out back for the rest of this? I don't want to misjudge

Emerson here, but I remember my first time real well and it's likely to be easier on the walls and furniture in the long run."

"As ye will, Henrietta," Brody agreed. " 'Tis yer home an' castle. But it's still rainin'."

"We can stand on the porch. Horatio used to do that, especially just before he passed away. He had to give up hunting, but he kept his hand and eye sharp until the very end."

"As well I remember."

The two rose and led Emerson, as bewildered as he'd been so far, through the warm, colorful kitchen and out the back door onto the railed porch which ran all the way around the house. Rain obscured the hills in the distance and the eaves dripped noisily. It was a little chilly, he thought, but the air smelled wonderful.

Short steel pegs had been driven into one of the lathe-turned columns on either side of the back porch steps, and hanging on them were a number of objects that looked like the headphones worn by the driver of the rollabout he'd stowed away on. Mrs. Singh took down three pairs, passed two to him and Brody, and put the third one over her ears. Both the older people already wore spectacles. They insisted that Emerson wear a pair of amber safety glasses.

She pointed to a bluff outcropping of soil and crumbling rock across the back of the yard, perhaps twenty meters away. "Take two or three of those plastic milk cartons I threw away this morning, Emerson, and stand them up on the side of that berm, will you? Their yellow color ought to stand out real nice."

Emerson complied enthusiastically, although it was necessary for Mrs. Singh to explain to him that a berm was a long, raised mound of dirt. The rain had fallen off to a mere drizzle and he was hardly wet at all when he returned.

Brody gave him the most serious look his normally jolly face was capable of. "Now before we begin, y'must have Colonel Cooper's Four Rules. Observe 'em and ye'll live a long life an' die in bed. Violate 'em an' ye'll either do yerself in or be done in by a flock of angry bystanders. D'ye understand what I'm sayin'?"

Emerson gulped. "I'm not sure."

Brody shook his head. "He's honest, at least. Very well, Rule One is that y'must always assume that all guns are always loaded. Always. Y'must never assume that one is not. Never."

"All right," Emerson nodded. "That I understand — and I understand the reason, too. If you always assume that all guns are always loaded, then you'll always treat them as if they were loaded, and nobody will ever get hurt."

"Accidentally, anyway." Brody looked up at Mrs. Singh. "A bright boy. I believe we'll let him live. Rule Two is that y'must never let the muzzle point at anything ye're not willing t'destroy. Now, Rule Two-and-a-half — it almost oughta be a rule in itself — y'see this little lever here at the top of the left grip? That's a thumb safety. An' the little swinging widget I showed you earlier in the back of the handle is the grip safety. The good colonel, in his wisdom, entreats us t'place only guarded trust in safeties. They can fail."

Emerson nodded again. "That's a good rule."

"In a universe operatin' on Murphy's Law, it is. Rule Three: keep yer finger off the trigger until yer sights are on the target. Obey that rule itself an' ye'll never come t'grief."

"It's hard to see how you could," Emerson replied. "Why would anyone ever want — "

"Because they're stupid, me boy. An' that sometimes even includes yours truly, who hasn't led an entirely accident-free life." He gave his prosthetic leg a thump. "The Law of Stupidity is the one phenomenon necessary to explain the small part of the universe Murphy doesn't cover. Rule Four: y'must be sure of yer target, as well as what's behind it. Never shoot at a sound, a shadow, or anything y'can't identify positively—not even a presumably hostile gun flash.

"Memorize these rules, Emerson, implant 'em in yer psyche so that only by a painful effort of will can y'force yerself t'violate 'em. Only then will y'be safe with firearms."

"Yes, sir."

"Don't yessir me, just do it. I'll write 'em down an' leave 'em with ye if y'want."

"Yes—I mean, okay, I'd appreciate that, Mr. Brody."

Brody had the Grizzly in his hand and was pointing to the rear sight, a square notch in a small rectangular panel, edged in white enamel. "I'll touch a round or two off so ye'll know what to expect. When it comes yer turn, center the front sight up in the rear notch so they're the same height, put the front blade just beneath whatever ye're shootin' at, like an apple on a post, an' slowly increase the finger pressure on the trigger until it goes off."

"That's right," Mrs. Singh encouraged him. "Squeeze the trigger gently and slowly. Snap it like a light switch, and you'll disturb the sight picture you set up so carefully."

"One more thing," Brody told him. "As silly as it may seem to ye, focus yer aimin' eye on the front sight, rather than the target. Let the target get a bit blurry if y'must, but concentrate on that front sight. Live in it. Be in it."

The man removed the magazine, slipped a single big cartridge into it, replaced it in the weapon, drew the slide back, and let it shoot forward again by itself, under the power of the great spring under the barrel. He raised the weapon in both hands.

"Fire in the hole!"

The Grizzly bellowed in a way that demanded Emerson's whole attention, even with the ear protectors. A ball of pink and blue fire as big as his head blossomed at the muzzle, which lifted with recoil until it pointed upward at an angle. At the end of the yard, one of the plastic milk cartons leaped ten meters into the air amidst a great spout of muddy soil and fell again to roll down the embankment.

Emerson loved it. An empty cartridge casing zinged past his ear, caromed off the porch rail, and rolled to his feet. He picked it up. It was still hot from the chamber.

"Dead center!" Mrs. Singh cried. She'd been watching through a pair of big-ended binoculars she'd picked up on her way through the kitchen. "Let's see you do that again!"

Brody shook his head. "It's time that Emerson here got baptized, don't y'think?"

Emerson wasn't quite as certain about that as Brody seemed to be, but he took the empty magazine the man handed him, and a single cartridge, and managed to get the latter slid under the lips of the former, and the former in the handle of the pistol. Keeping the weapon pointed well away from his new friends, he worked the slide—it seemed easier this time; perhaps he was getting used to it—and lifted the handgun, the tip of his trigger finger resting nervously on the guard. Suddenly, the monster machine seemed heavier than it had back in the living room.

"Both hands, Emerson. This ain't no pretty nineteenth-century duel, but real life. No, wrap the left hand around the right, as if it were the one holdin' the pistol. Take the grip so tight yer hand trembles, then back off the pressure until the tremblin' stops. That's fine. Arms straight, both elbows locked, pull back with the left and push with the right—makes a good, firm triangle, doesn't it? Now take a breath, let it out, an' take another half breath. Then line up the sights an' focus on the one in front like I told ye."

There was so much to remember at once, Emerson didn't quite know how he'd manage. The front sight helped. It had an unnaturally bright scarlet stripe enameled into it, was easy to see and impossible not to focus on. The grip panels screwed to either side of the handle helped, too. They were of some sort of black molded rubber and didn't seem to want to let go of his hand. He took a deep breath, just as Brody had told him to, let it all out, and took another half breath before aligning the sights on one of the cartons which were still standing.

The pistol grew heavier by the second and it seemed to take forever to compress the trigger, but the Grizzly went off all at once, its roar and recoil becoming Emerson's whole universe for an instant. It slammed back against his hands while the muzzle wrenched itself into the air. The handle twisted out of his left hand altogether, but he clung to the weapon with his right. In the virtual absence of gravity, the powerful weapon had lifted him back a step.

It was the most wonderful sensation he'd ever experienced. Somewhere, as if from far away, came the tinkle of the ejected casing. The massive slide had slammed back, locking itself into place, ejection port open and barrel exposed. A thin wisp of smoke drifted from the open breech. He lowered the muzzle, disappointed to see the carton he'd aimed at still standing where he'd put it.

"Dead center!" shouted Mrs. Singh. "Damn thing's glued in the mud. Give him another, Aloysius, I wanna see him do that again!"

Straining his vision in the rain, Emerson could just make out a tiny, fuzzy black dot in the middle of the yellow carton. He'd actually hit it with his first shot!

"I'll give him two an' see if he can hole it three times runnin'." Brody bent over Emerson and talked much louder than was necessary because of his ear protectors. He pointed to the rear portion of the barrel that showed through the ejection port. "Ye'll have t'remember hard, boy, that this time it's still loaded after it's gone off. Take yer time with the second shot. Think ye're up to that?"

"Yes, sir," Emerson nodded breathlessly. "I think so." He accepted the cartridges and loaded them with help from Brody, grateful for the chance to rest his arms. Trying to remember everything he'd been told, he raised the pistol with his hands and arms in the proper position, breathed in and out and in again, aligned the sights and gradually squeezed the trigger until the Grizzly roared once more.

This time, as the empty cartridge case struck the back wall of the porch and rolled away, the plastic carton flopped over on one side with a lower corner torn out.

"Seven o'clock, two inches," Mrs. Singh observed, still peering through her binoculars. "Not too bad, boy, for a beginner, but I'll bet you can do better."

Emerson had lowered the handgun, finger off the trigger. This time he took several breaths before he raised it again. His shoulders had begun to ache and he wasn't sure whether it was from the weight, the recoil, or just nervous concentration.

The Grizzly bellowed and another small, faint hole appeared—this time the spent case hit the ceiling and bounced off his head—to the left of the first hole, overlapping it.

Mrs. Singh was jumping up and down. "He's a natural, Aloysius!"

Still trembling with exhilaration, Emerson looked a question at the man as he handed back the now-empty pistol with its slide locked to the rear on the empty magazine.

Brody nodded. "I've seen it once or twice before. Some have t'learn the hard way, some few never get the hang of it at all. Ye've a lifetime ahead of ye for learnin' the fine points, but ye've the hand and eye of a gunman, Emerson, I truly believe y'do."

"Is that good?" he asked.

Nothing would ever convince Emerson it wasn't.

Brody pushed the Grizzly into his hands. "It's yers, Emerson. Give it back if y'find somethin' ye like better, or pay me a bit at a time when ye have it. Ye'll never go hungry on Pallas. As to the rest, like all things in life, it'll be whatever y'make of it."

Emerson grinned back. That was just the way he'd always figured things himself.

XIV
THE HUNTRESS

THE HUMAN RACE IS A PREDATOR-SPECIES SUFFERING AN EPIDEMIC ATTITUDINAL DISEASE WHICH IS ALMOST CERTAINLY THE SOURCE OF MOST OF ITS OTHER PROBLEMS, SOCIAL, CRIMINAL, POLITICAL, AND OTHERWISE, AND WHICH MAY EVENTUALLY RENDER IT EXTINCT. SOME CALL THIS DISEASE THE "BAMBI SYNDROME." I CALL IT *PREYPITY*.
    —Raymond Louis Drake-Tealy, *Hunting and Humanity*

T he drizzle had stopped.

They were back in the kitchen, Mrs. Singh showing Emerson how to disassemble and clean the Grizzly, wielding screwdriver, toothbrush, brass rod, and bronze bristle brush, while Brody made another pot of coffee and a plate of sandwiches, when a clatter coming from the front door distracted them.

"Mom!"

The kitchen door swung open suddenly, and right behind it came a pretty girl of about Emerson's age looking flushed, excited, and perhaps a little road-worn.

She unbuckled a broad canvas belt she wore about her waist, rebuckled it, and hung it over the back of one of the kitchen chairs, where it swung with the weight of a holstered pistol similar to Mrs. Singh's and a large, curve-bladed knife. She threw her arms around her mother's neck, giving her a loud kiss on the cheek.

"Hi, Mom! Antelope steaks tonight! Aloysius!" She untangled herself from her mother and crossed the kitchen to give Brody the same treatment. He laughed and patted her on the back as she stood on her toes to kiss him. "You have to stay tonight and celebrate with us, Aloysius! After all, it isn't every day that—er . . ."

She stopped suddenly and looked at Emerson, who felt his ears redden and hated himself for it.

Mrs. Singh gave her daughter a proud grin, put the cleaning rod down, screwed the cap back on the little powder solvent bottle whose pungent aroma filled the kitchen, and wiped her oily hands off on an almost equally oily rag.

Brody turned from the countertop where he'd been working to watch the proceedings with his usual broad grin. When the girl's back was turned, he gave Emerson a wink.

"Emerson Ngu," the woman told the girl, "this is my daughter, Gretchen, as you've probably guessed by now. Emerson is our newest boarder, dear. And it's a big day for him, too—he just got done firing a handgun for the first time."

By some miracle, Emerson managed to find his voice. He was surprised. Mrs. Singh's daughter was the most beautiful creature he'd ever seen. "First gun of any kind, actually."

"I'm happy to meet you, Emerson." Gretchen smiled at him and he revised his estimate of her comparative beauty to include every known entity in the universe. "Two firsts today, then. I've brought home a pronghorn, dropped with a single round at a hundred yards. I've never shot anything bigger than a rabbit before."

This time, things happened the way Emerson had expected. He could only grin back at her like an idiot and didn't dare speak for fear of stammering. Only an effort of will kept him looking at her rather than fastening his eyes on the floor.

Along with the heavy pistol belt, she'd tossed a lightweight, hooded poncho over the chairback, subtly mottled and straw-colored to imitate the rolling prairie he could see just outside the kitchen window. Under that, she wore form-fitting blue denim trousers tucked into a pair of low, soft-looking boots, an unpatterned lavender blouse with a wide collar and puffy sleeves, open at the neck, and over that a snug denim vest of a darker, redder purple than the shirt.

He nodded politely and hoped that would do.

The name Gretchen seemed incongruous to him. By rights it should belong to some strapping, blue-eyed blond. Gretchen was fair enough in a well-tanned sort of way, he thought to himself, and had a flawless complexion. But her eyes were a deep, foresty green and her waist-long, straight, glossy hair was of such a dark brown color that it might as well have been black, although it threw off reddish highlights under the bright kitchen fixtures. Her eyes were large over broad cheekbones and her nose was straight and turned up just a little at the end. She had full, expressive lips and her teeth were white and perfect.

Even from where he stood several feet away, she smelled to him of sage and woodsmoke.

Mrs. Singh's straight-backed chair scraped, jolting him out of the warm, comfortable fog that seemed to have formed around him without his quite having noticed it. She stood up, took a deep breath, nodded, and dusted her hands off on her thighs.

"Okay, baby, let's see what you brung home!"

Emerson also hadn't noticed that Mrs. Singh had finished cleaning the Grizzly and reassembled it. He didn't
know whether to pick it up or leave it lying where it was.
Brody set his rubber spatula aside—he'd been spreading
some white, creamy substance on slices of bread prepara-
tory to putting slices of cheese and ham between them—
and wiped his hands off on the absurdly flowered apron
he'd borrowed from his hostess, before removing it and
hanging it on a doorknob.

"Good idea! And maybe we can get a snapshot or two,
this bein' such an historic occasion, an' all! Then we'll feed
this girl some lunch, she looks as if she could use it."

"Amen," Mrs. Singh agreed. "When we get back, I'll
put some soup in the microwave."

A laughing, bouncing Gretchen was already through
the swinging kitchen door, headed for the front of the
house. Brody and her mother were right behind her, almost as animated, with Emerson tagging at their heels,
feeling useless.

As his feet crossed the front doorsill, he stopped,
stunned.

His initial horror and confusion at the violent and barbaric customs of these Outsiders, which had begun to sub-
side a little as he had come to know a couple of them, now
returned with its original full force. He wasn't certain what
he'd expected—and his reaction at this particular moment
didn't make sense, even to him—but it was impossible to
disregard the hideous sight confronting him now.

Hanging from the long eaves of the front porch where
they extended out beyond the railing was a medium-sized
split-hoofed animal with coarse, pale golden fur accented
in a darker brown. Instead of antlers like the deer he'd
seen—was it only the night before?—it wore a pair of odd
protuberances on its head, black, about twenty centime-

ters long and hair-grained like that of a rhinoceros except that there were two of them, each branching to a finlike side-spur only a little smaller than the main point they curved to so gracefully.

Although the animal was still warm, there was no question about its being dead. Half a dozen individuals—it didn't occur to him to count them or to recognize them as anything but moving blobs in his blurred, shock-narrowed field of vision—were dancing around, it seemed to Emerson, making gabbling noises that hurt his head, snapping pictures of each other and urging Gretchen to stand beside the hanging carcass with her pistol in her hand. Afterward, he had a vague memory of her running back into the house to fetch it from the kitchen.

There was very little blood.

The gentle-looking creature—Gretchen had called it an antelope—was suspended upside-down from a steel hook screwed in under the eaves which, from its weathered patina, appeared to be a permanent fixture of the front porch, on a short piece of brightly colored synthetic rope from holes cruelly pierced through the skin of both of its hind legs between the bones, just above the backward-working knee.

Not that the animal was in any condition to care about that or anything else any more.

Its eyes were clouded, almost dry to the touch, and its big purple tongue lolled obscenely from its mouth in a white-frosted muzzle. The poor thing had been cut from somewhere between the back legs—remembering the big knife on Gretchen's belt, Emerson didn't dare look too closely—to its throat, and its insides, which now sat on the front porch step in a transparent plastic bag, removed.

Flies buzzed around the carcass and the plastic bag.

Emerson had made himself walk up to the animal and touch it, but it had used up every ounce of courage he could muster. Now he reached out gingerly again to feel the small, ragged, bloodless hole in its side, just behind the front leg, where it had been shot—where the beautiful Gretchen had shot it—and suddenly withdrew his hand and ran back into the house to the little bathroom just off the kitchen, where he violently emptied his stomach into the washbasin.

Time passed.

It couldn't have been more than ten minutes.

To Emerson it seemed more like an hour.

It was Gretchen who greeted him at the bathroom door with a large, soft towel when he emerged again, having cleaned himself and the sink up as best he could with toilet paper and rinsed his mouth out so that it didn't taste quite as bad as it had.

She looked almost as upset as he felt.

"I'm sorry, Emerson," she told him, sounding as if she really meant it. "I realized where you'd come from the moment I laid eyes on you, and I should have stopped you from going out there on the porch until we got the animal skinned out and cut up for the freezer. I was just too excited, I guess. It's a very important rite of passage in the life of a Pallatian, the first big animal."

Emerson felt his head swim again and squeezed his eyes shut, trying not to think about it.

"Don't feel bad," she added, "You're not the first. That's one reason this little bathroom is here."

He gave her back the towel, unused. What he needed most was a shower and what he really felt like was going straight to bed. The big Grizzly pistol still lay, cold, black, and accusing on the kitchen table where Mrs. Singh had left it. He shuddered now to think how much he'd enjoyed shooting it. At the time he hadn't considered what the act of target shooting was intended to be practice for. His voice was hoarse and he'd missed half of what Gretchen had said.

"What do you mean I'm not the first?"

She smiled sympathetically, a smile that was extremely difficult for him to resist. It was still almost impossible to believe that this pretty, lively thing standing before him had deliberately and cold-bloodedly lined her sights up on another beautiful creature like herself, had had the presence of mind to remember to focus on the front sight, had taken a deep breath and let it out, taken another half breath, squeezed the trigger without jerking it, and enthusiastically—rather than simply without a pang of conscience—snuffed its life out.

"We've had quite a lot of non-Pallatian boarders," she told him, totally unaware of how morally depraved he presently believed she was, "almost all of them short-timers, refugees from that ant farm down the road or newly arrived from Earth."

As Emerson listened to Gretchen, he tried his best to harden his heart toward her, tried to hold the image in his mind of the evil deed she was so proud of. He tried to keep his eyes on the knife and pistol she was wearing once again. However—among other things—her eyelashes were far too long for that.

"The latter are usually the worst," she went on. "Like that television person and her crew who stayed with us that time. They all wear leather shoes every day of the week and buy their steaks and chops at a grocery store meat counter. They never think about where it all comes from. The difference with us Pallatians is that we make a point of providing for ourselves and try hard never to lie, to ourselves or to anybody else, regarding who we are or what life is really all about."

"That's what life is all about?" He raised an angry finger—and noticed that his hand was shaking—to point indignantly through the wall toward the front porch. "That's who you are? Needlessly murdering helpless, innocent animals who feel pain, and breathe, and eat, and sleep, and think, just like you and—"

"We're predators, Emerson, that's who we are. Take it easy, will you?" Gretchen shook her pretty head in exasperation, as if she'd been through this a thousand times before. Her dark hair tossed in silky waves and he caught the scent of woodsmoke again. "And besides, who told you that they think? We're not talking about human beings, here. It's never been proven that their intelligence is in any way—"

Emerson was still shaken and disgusted. There just had to be more to life than simply killing and being killed. "Come on, Miss Singh! I don't know about you, but my compassion for someone isn't limited to my estimate of their intelligence!"

She looked him straight in the eye. "Mine is."

Emerson's dinner that evening was a rather somber, solitary affair of pan-fried cornmeal mush and scrambled eggs which Mrs. Singh prepared for him—although he'd offered to fend for himself or do without—before she and her daughter walked the short distance into town to join the boarders and other well-wishers at the Nimrod Saloon & Gambling Emporium which Brody ran in Curringer.

Emerson became suspicious of her reasons for insisting on fixing his meal before leaving for town when, having set the plate before him, she'd gone to the living room and returned shortly afterward with a well-worn book which she placed on the table beside the Grizzly pistol that was still lying there, untouched.

Of Gretchen he hadn't had so much as a glimpse since their rather one-sided conversation earlier that afternoon. Having said what she'd said, she'd gone upstairs to her room, apparently to bathe and rest before the evening's outing.

"We're outspoken folks here on the Outside, Emerson," Mrs. Singh informed him now. "Plenty of times when we were just getting started here, the plain, undecorated truth—told quickly, without wasting too much time on a buildup—spelled the difference between living and dying, and that habit's hung on with us."

She sighed and sat down in the opposite chair, reflexively swiveling the Grizzly on its side a few inches so that its muzzle pointed at neither of them.

"I know it isn't always that way with other folks in other places. We set considerable store by the truth, like I said, but to others it's a highly overrated commodity, a whole lot less important than feelings, and altogether too easy to come by for comfort. Some people dedicate their lives to avoiding it, or even thinking about it, and there are entire languages—like Japanese, for instance, so I'm told—that consist of nothing but fancified hemming and hawing."

Emerson didn't know what to say, so he said nothing.

Mrs. Singh wasn't through, in any case. "You're a free man now, your own person. Nobody on this asteroid is gonna make you hunt animals or shoot a gun or do anything else you don't want to, including listen to the truth. That's the whole point of being here, after all. But there are reasons, most of them having to do with preserving individual sovereignty and dignity, why hunting and shooting—and speaking the truth—are important to us, just like there are reasons, most of them having to do with gaining and holding onto political power at any cost, why all that sort of thing was so violently discouraged back on Earth."

She put a finger on the cover of the book, *Hunting and Humanity* by Raymond Louis Drake-Tealy. "I don't mean to preach at you, Emerson, and this sure as hell ain't no

Bible, but it might help you understand what I'm talking about."

She stood up, sighed again, patted him on a shoulder, turned, and walked out of the kitchen. In a few minutes he heard muffled female voices, then the front door open and close.

After Mrs. Singh and Gretchen had departed and he'd finished eating, he washed all the dishes carefully, dried them thoroughly, and put them away. Then he went up to his room, taking both the Grizzly Win Mag and Drake-Tealy's book with him, but laying them aside as he sat down on the bed to try sorting things out as he listened to the old familiar voice of the radio station in Curringer.

He tried not to imagine the revelry he was missing at the Nimrod, and the jokes at his expense.

Most of all, he tried not to see Gretchen's lovely image whenever it swam up before him in his mind's eye, or to imagine the scent of sage and woodsmoke in her hair

For dear life, he concentrated on the radio.

It seemed odd to him, hearing it all coming openly through a loudspeaker rather than his handmade earphone. The receiver in his room was large, heavy, and painted with a black crinkly finish which gave it a military look. Its face was covered with knobs and dials. He had a feeling that, if he'd known how, he'd have been able to tune in stations on Earth, but all he'd been shown was how to turn it on in order to receive signals from the only commercial transmitter on the asteroid.

He'd liked to have seen television, but Mrs. Singh wouldn't have one and the radio station was only broadcasting pictures a few minutes a day anyway. Mrs. Singh claimed that television was one of the principal annoyances she'd left Earth to get away from.

In the end, even the radio betrayed him.

"Young Gretchen Singh, lovely daughter of the proprietor of

Mrs. Singh's Boarding House—where many of us, including yours truly, spent our first few weeks on Pallas—has killed her first big game, a buck pronghorn, down in Grennell's Gulch.

"Informants, er, inform us that she did it with a running downhill shot at over two hundred yards, using a ten-millimeter longslide customized by one of our local gunsmiths—who'll have to pay for any further advertising he gets here.

"Congratulations, Gretchen! We'll be joining you ourselves this evening at the Nimrod to raise a glass at Aloysius Brody's expense. That is, if our relief ever gets here. Meantime, here's a number just for you, Tom Lehrer's 'Hunting Song.' "

A scratchy-sounding record began to play, a man accompanied by a piano, singing something about somebody shooting "two game wardens, seven hunters, and a cow."

Emerson arose, snapped the radio off in angry disgust, and flopped back onto the bed. He was utterly mystified by these people who seemed, by turns, so kindly and generous—and then so cruel and arrogant. How could a pretty girl like Gretchen, with merry eyes and small, soft hands, coldly use them to end the existence of another living, breathing creature? How could her mother—and everybody else on the asteroid, apparently—possibly approve of such a thing?

His hand strayed to the book Mrs. Singh had left with him.

Maybe it had some answers.

XV

SHADOW OF A DOUBT

HUNTER-GATHERERS PRACTICED THE MOST SUCCESSFUL AND
LONGEST-LASTING LIFE STYLE IN HUMAN HISTORY . . . IF THE
HISTORY OF THE HUMAN RACE BEGAN AT MIDNIGHT . . . BY A
24-HOUR CLOCK ON WHICH ONE HOUR REPRESENTS 100,000
YEARS OF REAL PAST TIME . . . WE WOULD NOW BE ALMOST AT
THE END OF OUR FIRST DAY. WE LIVED AS HUNTER-GATHERERS
FOR NEARLY THE WHOLE OF THAT DAY, FROM MIDNIGHT
THROUGH DAWN, NOON, AND SUNSET. FINALLY, AT 11:54 P.M.,
WE ADOPTED AGRICULTURE.
   — Jared Diamond, "The Worst Mistake in the History of the
   Human Race," *Discover* Magazine, 1 May 1987

F irst it had been an antelope.
      Now Emerson was witnessing the slaughter of a sa-
cred cow.

   Mankind's highly touted invention of agriculture, in
the view of radical, controversial, and outspoken anthropologist Raymond Louis Drake-Tealy—a principal influence, just as the Greeley Utopian Memorial Project's
Education and Morale staff had maintained, on Pallatian
life outside the Project—was not at all synonymous with
human progress or with the development of genuine civilization.

   According to his book, *Hunting and Humanity*, lying
open now in Emerson's hands, it was far likelier to prove a
catastrophe from which humanity would never recover.

   In a black-and-white photo which took up the whole
back of the worn and faded dustcover, the author was depicted against a backdrop consisting of the front cover
painting—a primitive, hairy, not-quite-human hunter
stalking some sort of protoelephant across the African
veldt while he inserted a spear in his spear-thrower. In the

author's almost equally hairy hand lay a heavy rifle described as a .416 Rigby. Emerson had harvested perfectly healthy carrots smaller than the enormous cartridge Drake-Tealy was pushing into its open bolt-action.

The book was an irresistible mixture of scientific fact and speculation, social, political, and economic argument, and outdoor adventure story. By the time he'd reached the second chapter, Emerson had forgotten his own problems, along with the room around him, the people he'd met, and the sights he'd seen in the last twenty-four hours. It would have been inconceivable, had the thought occurred to him, that at exactly the same time yesterday evening, he'd been trudging along a strange road in the dark and the rain, homeless and with no place to go.

It would have been more inconceivable, had he known more of human nature, that in such a short span of time, there were now people who trusted him alone in their home, people he trusted himself, despite their foreign, sometimes repelling ways.

Before long, he'd lost all track of what time it was. Whatever the truth of Drake-Tealy's propositions, the man had an appealing and persuasive way of expressing them, and Emerson had no trouble staying interested. It wasn't so much that he agreed with everything—or anything—he was reading, but that he was fascinated to have been handed a collection of ideas so different from those he'd grown up with.

He turned another page, adjusted a lampshade, sighed with unconscious contentment, settled back against the pillows on his bed, and crossed his ankles.

For most of human history, according to the traditional kind of thinking, people had supported themselves on a hand-to-mouth basis, precisely as their prehuman ancestors had for uncounted hundreds of thousands of years before them, by killing wild animals and foraging for wild plants, a lifestyle often described by philosophers (Emerson had to take Drake-Tealy's word for that, not knowing any philosophers himself) as "nasty, brutish, and short." Since no food was grown deliberately and very little of it stored, this grim struggle, theoretically, began afresh each day to find something to eat and avoid starving.

Escape from this presumably miserable existence had come only about ten thousand years ago, when people first began to domesticate plants and animals. The resulting "agricultural revolution" gradually spread, until today there were only a few hunter-gatherers surviving in Earth's remotest deserts and jungles.

Emerson had been taught—and to a degree unusual for him, simply assumed it was true—that the adoption of agriculture had been one of the most critically important decisions his species had ever made in the struggle for a better life. What modern observer could possibly disagree with that? People today were infinitely better off, in every imaginable way, than their primitive prefarming ancestors. Everywhere, they enjoyed more varied and abundant food, better clothing and shelter, better tools and other material goods; they led longer, healthier lives, and were completely safe from dangerous predators—all of it due, directly or indirectly, to the invention of agriculture.

What kind of lunatic would advocate trading twenty-first-century life for that of a caveman?

Drake-Tealy had a different perspective.

Go to the mirror, open your mouth, look at your teeth, count out from the center—top or bottom, it won't matter—one, two, three. This isn't the dental hardware of a herd beast, a cud-chewing herbivore, but a carnivore, a predator, a killer-ape, one I'm well satisfied—despite common wisdom—was no pack-harrier, but a solitary hunter.

Borrowing the ideas of earlier thinkers and investigators, he maintained that Stone Age people had been measurably healthier and happier than the early farmers they preceded.

Discoveries made by paleopathologists, scientists who studied signs of disease in the remains of ancient peoples, appeared to back Drake-Tealy up, demonstrating that the hunters had been taller—the average height of hunter-gatherers toward the end of the ice ages was often greater than that of their modern descendants—and lived significantly longer. Furthermore, they'd suffered fewer diseases than those individuals whose remains—betraying unmistakable symptoms of shortened lifespan, disastrous malnutrition, bone-deforming physical labor, and chronic illnesses like tuberculosis, anemia, and leprosy—were contemporary with mankind's tragic romance with agriculture.

Once a person began thinking about it, there wasn't very much mystery to it. Even today, for a variety of reasons, farmers tended to concentrate their efforts on high-carbohydrate crops like wheat, corn, rice, and potatoes. Yet the mixture of wild plants and animal flesh in the diets of early hunter-gatherers had provided more protein and a better overall balance of nutrients than that.

According to Drake-Tealy, the average food intake of Africa's Kalahari Bushmen, who added no less than seventy-five different kinds of plants to whatever meat they managed to bring home—while living on far less productive land and with less abundant game than the earliest human hunters—was nevertheless greater than the daily allowance recommended by the United Nations for people of their size.

And it was unlikely they'd ever die of starvation the way hundreds of thousands of Irish farmers and their families had during the potato famine of the 1840s. A paleolithic hunter's diet offered a broad range of nutrients not available again to humanity as a whole until late in the nineteenth century—and then only achieved at a terrible cost of ten thousand years of progress lost to agriculturalism.

Emerson sat back.

All this talk about food had begun to make him feel hungry, although it seemed to him that he'd just eaten. He tried to ignore the feeling and read on, but when he started receiving urgent messages from his bladder as well as his stomach, he sighed, reluctantly closed the book on a finger, and, taking it with him, visited the bathroom down the hall, then went back downstairs to the kitchen.

The house seemed very empty and quiet.

It was an experience he'd never had before.

As he pushed through the swinging door into the kitchen, an astonished glance at the clock built into the microwave oven control panel—for the first time he noticed that Mrs. Singh didn't keep very many clocks in her house—told him it was past eleven, and that over four hours had gone by since he'd started reading.

He wondered when Gretchen and her mother would be coming back from their celebration in Curringer, and what condition they'd be in. He didn't recall it ever being specifically mentioned, but the general impression he'd received from his Project teachers was that the Outsiders, like all barbarians of song and legend, were given to uproarious, drunken revelries. He had a fleeting vision of a laughing Mrs. Singh, swilling fermented honey and apple juice from a horn-shaped cup and throwing double-bitted axes at her daughter's pigtails, pinned to a great wooden wheel for the purpose. He laughed at himself and shook it off.

Somewhat absently, he went to the refrigerator to prepare a sandwich as he'd been told he could whenever he wished, his eyes still fastened on the pages as he worked, sat down at the kitchen table to eat it, and continued reading.

Drake-Tealy was discussing what he meant by words like "progress" and "genuine civilization." He seemed to associate both concepts, just as Emerson had suspected he might, with the value any culture placed on its individuals. They certainly weren't represented, he maintained, by the establishment of agriculturally based mass societies—from those of Sumeria, Egypt, Rome, ancient Mexico, Peru, and China, straight through the Industrial Revolution—in which a nonproductive ruler was God, above contemplation, let alone reproach, and the common individual's identity and dignity had been all but obliterated.

> Unless, as human beings, we come not only to accept but to openly rejoice in our fundamental and inescapable nature as predators, we condemn ourselves, as individuals and as a species, to unhappy, unnecessarily guilt-haunted lives. If we don't allow ourselves to prey on other creatures, as is our nature, we'll prey on ourselves and each other as we have throughout most of our agricultural history. Perhaps worse, soaked with guilt, however undeserved, we'll continue handing our lives and minds over to any charlatan, however absurd, who offers us expiation, however false, for our sins, however imaginary.

Somewhere outside the kitchen windows, far off on the prairie, a lone coyote howled. For the first time, Emerson regarded the sound as a friendly one.

A hunter's life was as free and varied as his diet. Although he might not always have counted it a blessing, it offered continuous challenge to his mind—along with a surprising amount of leisure. Drake-Tealy's average Bushman devoted only twelve to nineteen hours each week to obtaining food, the Hadza nomads of Tanzania (whoever they were), fourteen hours or less. Yet the harsh necessities of agriculture had transformed the former hunter into an overworked victim of weather and other random, uncontrollable forces—the failure of a single crop, for any one of a thousand reasons, could, and often did, spell disaster for entire civilizations—and condemned him to a life of mind-dulling monotony.

But there was worse news awaiting the early farmer.

Stationary as a barnacle—or, more to the point, his own crops in the ground—the farmer was tied to the land and therefore easy prey for roving bandits who eventually recognized a good thing when they saw it, settled down, and organized themselves into the first governments, dedicated to "protecting" the farmer out of everything he owned. All that the first farmer's wonderful store of surpluses guaranteed him, in the end, was that the individual who'd labored so arduously to produce them would be victimized forever afterward by those who hadn't.

This wasn't Drake-Tealy's idea of progress.

Nor, contemplating the Greeley Utopian Memorial Project and its Chief Administrator, was it Emerson's.

Those early bandit-governments, like every government that followed, systematically encouraged agriculture, perpetuating the farmer's misery and servitude.

Equally, they discouraged hunting, usually reserving it as a recreational monopoly of the self-appointed ruling class. They had a practical reason for doing so: the hunter's tools are deadly weapons, capable not only of feeding him and his family, but of defending his life, liberty, and property against predators and thieves—including tax collectors. Requiring more subtlety and dexterity than raw power, they can be wielded to good effect by women, or even children.

Since a primitive people can rarely afford the investment of effort and time represented by two distinct sets of everyday tools, the farmer's innocuous and clumsy implements, most of which had relied on male muscle until well into the nineteenth century, severely limited his ability to fight back, and at the same time cut his potential defensive forces in half, making him a victim all over again.

Emerson put the book down and shook his head with sudden understanding. No wonder Mrs. Singh and Brody had been in such a hurry to see that he was armed. To them, it must have been as if he'd shown up on her doorstep not only wet and hungry, but naked — hadn't they said something like that? — and helpless as a quadruple amputee, as well.

Thus agriculturalism had systematically selected against individualism — and generated, incidentally, the first sharp divisions between classes and genders — in favor of the genetically characterless and mindlessly compliant. Well-established evolutionary trends which, according to Drake-Tealy, had pointed in the direction of greater and greater individuation for three billion years — and helped to separate humanity from the apes — were suddenly reversed.

But there was more.

Just as hunters had been more independent — and more independent-minded — than their agricultural successors, it was also likely that they'd been smarter.

Smarter?

How could that be? Had he missed something back there somewhere? If so, where? Emerson peered at the page in perplexed annoyance, then decided gamely to push on.

Agricultural surpluses encourage overpopulation (all right, he could see that), while at the same time, any farming society's natural desire for more agricultural labor has exactly the same effect. (Emerson nodded in agreement with a phenomenon he'd witnessed personally.) The inevitable result of both tendencies was teeming masses of undistinguished humanity, sooner or later enduring the nasty, brutish, and short existence expected by philosophers of the hunter-gatherer, where before, many fewer had led much higher-quality lives.

Okay so far.

The productive classes of most ancient civilizations had been exclusively vegetarian, living on a single, bland, staple crop. At the same time, their bone-bending, mind-killing labors supported taller, healthier, longer-lived aristocracies (another of Drake-Tealy's surmises which was supported by paleopathology) identifiable by their continued consumption of animal protein.

In both an evolutionary and an individual sense, the full development of a higher-order nervous system — which marks a basic physiological difference between human beings and lower beasts — depends on the ready availability of complex animal fats and certain vitamins not easily obtainable from vegetable sources, at least in a nonindustrial economy. Thus it came to be that the meat-starved underclasses labored at a permanent mental disadvantage with regard to their "betters," a phenomenon that explained, in Drake-Tealy's opinion, a great deal about human history in general and majoritarian politics in particular.

In his final chapters, Drake-Tealy outlined a daring strategy he'd devised to correct mankind's greatest mistake — among the solar system's asteroids.

The volume Emerson was reading had originally been published in the final decade of the twentieth century, before the terraformation of Pallas. He now turned back to a lengthy introduction he'd only skimmed before, written for this edition published several years later, when, with the financial support of billionaire William Wilde Cur-

ringer and the philosophical backing of novelist Mirelle
Stein—under the governing influence of her own daring
strategy, the Hyperdemocratic Covenant—the Pallatian
Outsiders had returned to a hunting economy after ten
millennia . . . but with a high-tech twist.

> . . . as a result, Pallatians now divide their time between
> hunting hundreds of wild species first brought to the aster-
> oid as frozen embryos and raised on private ranches in the
> absence of intensive farming (anywhere on Pallas but in
> the United Nations' Greeley Utopian Memorial Project),
> and what they themselves term "civilization mainte-
> nance"—the usual variety of twenty-first-century tasks
> performed under a profit-driven system of divided labor
> and laissez-faire capitalism.

Divided labor?
What was that?
Laissez-faire capitalism?
He wasn't sure he wanted to know.

Emerson looked down at the crumbling remains of his
sandwich, containing, among other things, thin, delicious
slices of lightly roasted, heavily spiced meat, probably elk
or venison if he remembered correctly what Mrs. Singh
had told him before she left. He hadn't consciously realized
that he was eating animal flesh again—and enjoying it
thoroughly. And the more answers he acquired to his questions, the more questions he seemed to have as a consequence.

He understood—although he was no more certain
what to make of it—that hunting was more than just something the Outsiders did for its own bloodthirsty, barbaric
sake. Hunting was more than simply how they proved
themselves as a people and as individuals. Hunting was
even more than merely how they fed themselves.

To them, hunting was an act consistent with their evolutionary history, with their nature as predators, and with Nature herself—a consistency which made it all that much easier to defy her, when they wished, in matters, such as crossing the dark reaches of space to build a home on an asteroid.

To them, hunting represented independence and freedom—which Emerson realized intuitively are not the same thing, after all. He knew it was the former which created the latter. He didn't realize, at the time, that it was this all-too-rare intuition—and the fact that they could see it manifested plainly in his character—which was the reason his new friends trusted him so easily.

He did understand, beyond a shadow of a doubt, that hunting—along with everything hunting meant to the Pallatians—was their entire reason for being here.

XVI
OF IRON PIGS AND PIG IRON

THE ONLY PRAYER I'VE EVER FELT THE URGE TO UTTER IS THIS:
"WHATEVER GODS MAY BE, PRESERVE US FROM THE
SELF-RIGHTEOUSLY USELESS, THE MILITANTLY HELPLESS, AND
THE DOGMATICALLY UNCERTAIN."
                    —William Wilde Curringer, *Unfinished Memoirs*

E *merson Ngu, you're on deck!"*
The amplified voice of the match director made him jump, although he'd been waiting nervously to hear it say these words for an hour. Flexing the anxiety-stiffened fingers of his right hand, he glanced down at the odd sight of the Grizzly Win Mag hanging in a holster off his right hip, unloaded, slide locked back. His left hand held a score card and a plastic box containing 45 softpoints, each

nested in its own little hole in ten rows of five, one row having been left empty.

Adjusting his ear protectors, uncomfortable and sweaty no matter what he did and inclined to press the narrow earpieces of his yellow-tinted glasses into his temples, he strode to the line, a strip of concrete four or five feet wide exactly like a sidewalk, that stretched across the entire back of the range. He set his card on the concrete at his feet with the ammunition box to weigh it down.

"Emerson, you'll be taking your five practice shots at the swinger, now. Charlie Jackson, you're on the first string of chickens, is that right? Lenda Jackson, you're shooting pigs. Mark Friedrich, you're on turkeys. Gretchen Singh, you're doing the rams. Okay, shooters, load five rounds and make ready."

On the long lope out to the range with Gretchen, who'd gotten him into this, Emerson had emptied his four magazines of the seven hot-loaded rounds they carried and reloaded them with five match cartridges apiece. Now he drew the Grizzly, careful to direct its cavernous muzzle downrange, and inserted a magazine in the grip. Keeping his finger off the trigger, he depressed the slidestop with his left thumb and let the slide jump forward, feeding the first round to the chamber. Common wisdom and his own experience told him this would be the least accurate shot of the five — the so-called "semiauto effect" — and he was glad it would be at twenty-five yards. He flipped the safety up with the same thumb, took a long, deep breath, and waited for the next command.

"Shooters, at your own pace, fire five rounds!"

Emerson raised the Grizzly and sighted it at the swinger which, with the other chickens, was placed twenty-five yards from the line. Like the other chickens used in this game, it was a simple profile cut from a sheet of five-eighths steel. To Emerson it looked more like a duck. Unlike the other chickens, standing on their own little welded feet like toy soldiers, this hung from a frame on a length of motorcycle chain and didn't need to be set up again after each successful shot. Trying to remember all the elements of marksmanship at once, he thumbed the safety off, focused on the brilliant front sight which he held under the foot of the chicken, took a deep breath and let it out, took half a breath and held it, and began squeezing the trigger. Sometimes it seemed like it took forever.

His right index finger was better educated, after nearly a year of doing this, than the first time he'd fired the Grizzly. There was a now-familiar hesitation perceptible about halfway through the trigger-pull which he'd meant to have a gunsmith look at or do something about himself. After a while, he'd simply gotten used to it. It told him the big autopistol was just about to go off.

There it was. The Grizzly Win Mag roared, even with the reduced loads he used for matches, and slammed into his palm as the muzzle lifted. The chicken didn't move. His first shot of the day was a clear miss, an inch low and to the left.

Emerson sighed. He always did badly with his five practice shots and was undismayed, though he could have used a spotter. Joe Tinkle and Noah Fulmor, fellow workers at the machine shop in Curringer who usually spotted for him (as Emerson did for them), were off in the weyers at the moment, hunting deer. They'd also missed work yesterday. Among Outsiders, hunting was considered a perfectly acceptable reason for skipping a day or leaving work early. The boss merely insisted that someone be available to cover for him when he was off hunting, himself.

Somewhere behind his right shoulder came the metallic tinkle of an empty case. Emerson had learned not to worry where his ejected brass went, although it was expensive and reusable. Club members collected it in plastic buckets between courses of fire, along with everyone else's, as he'd collect the empties when it was his turn. It would be sorted out later, and since he was the only one who shot .45 Winchester Magnum, and it was twice the size of the ten-millimeter cases almost everybody else was using, getting his brass back would be easy.

Emerson's second shot took the chicken in the foot, as it should at this range, the Grizzly being sighted at seventy-five yards for the turkeys. As it swung a few times on its chain, he reminded himself that the trick was to take his time. This wasn't a combat match where speed counted as much as accuracy. He was allowed a glacier-slow two minutes for his five shots, and the point was to lower the pistol between them, breathe, relax, and let the circulation come back into his arms.

His third shot splashed lead on the matte-black surface of the chicken in the same place as his second. He'd learned that the Grizzly was capable of one-inch groups at this range if he was up to it. His fourth shot was a bit high, and his fifth—his arms were getting tired—sprayed dull silver in the dead center of the target. He lowered the massive Grizzly and breathed deeply.

Once on the line, Emerson never heard the sound of other people's gunfire or saw or felt their empty cases zinging at him through the air. His five shots had only taken him forty-five seconds. Not good. He'd have to spread them better and rest in between if he wanted to advance to Class double-A as he'd hoped to this morning.

For Emerson, the last year had passed quickly and, he'd been surprised to discover, happily. Accustomed to backbreaking agricultural labor, here he'd worked at several jobs, all of which were cushy by comparison, beginning with chores around Mrs. Singh's place. As she'd predicted, that had only lasted a few days. In a vehicle repair and refueling station, he'd learned more about mechanics. In a machine shop, he was still attempting to master lathe, mill, and drillpress. In a small foundry, on his own time, he was learning to make use of cheap fusion power and Pallas's most abundant natural resource, metals of every description.

Waiting, as all practice shooters did, until the competitors shot another five-shot string, Emerson finally received the command to make sure his pistol was unloaded, holster it, and move to the next position. On command, once the range was clear, he bounded forward to the six freestanding chickens Charlie Jackson had knocked down and set them up again. The difference between this game and matches like it shot in West America was that it was necessary, at Pallatian gravity, to fasten the silhouettes to their stands with meter lengths of slender steel cable sheathed in transparent plastic, so they'd fall where they'd been shot and wouldn't be blasted yards away by the force of the projectile striking them.

Walking back to the line, Emerson's mind wandered to the past—welcome, since it gave him some relief from match nerves—and the distance he'd come, figuratively speaking, since his first day Outside. It hadn't taken him long to discover that the qualities which had always gotten him into trouble at the Project got him promoted into better-paying jobs with more responsibility on the Outside. His specialty was mechanical improvisation—everything from straightening bent wheel rims to converting engines from one fuel to another—his quick mind generating more profitable solutions to problems than any 50 individuals could ever act on.

During that time, he'd met Mrs. Singh's other boarders, two of whom, the Jacksons, were shooting ahead of him this morning. They had turned out to be perfectly decent, ordinary people who, they were quick to assure him, hardly ever ate little Vietnamese-Cambodian refugee boys for breakfast. Slowly at first, with more than a little help from each of them and from Mrs. Singh and her daughter—not to overlook R.L. Drake-Tealy—he'd started to sort things out.

Life was pleasurable and surprisingly easy here on the Outside, without obstacles—like the taxation and regulation Mrs. Singh and Aloysius Brody, among others, loved to shudder over reminiscently, or the UN goons he knew—standing in the way of personal betterment or social progress. Not that there weren't natural obstacles. The weather was as unpredictable here as anywhere, there were only twenty-four hours in a day and seven days in a week. But unlike most of the Earth's populace—or the hardworking, hopeless inhabitants of the Project—Pallatians actually looked forward to getting up every morning. He came to realize they'd be a wealthy people, once their capital base was fully established.

Already a few prefabricated mansions stood cheek-by-jowl with the first corrugated sheet-steel pioneer shacks in Curringer. Its one bustling street was fronted by a bank, a videochip rental, two general stores, three brothels, the plumbing and machinery shop where he currently worked, four saloons (the Nimrod was one of them), five gunsmithing establishments, a combination doctor's clinic and veterinary office, and a barbershop. An oil well pumped cheerfully away in its middle, around which noisy, bustling foot and vehicle traffic had to detour.

At the same time, having given the matter much thought and unwilling to relish what he didn't provide himself, he'd put his pistol to use while paying Brody a little every week. (It had turned out to be expensive, since Pallas had no weapons industry of its own; he'd been interested to learn this and filed it away for future reference.) He'd soon taught himself as much as he could with informal backyard shooting. To gain more proficiency, he'd allowed Gretchen to bully him into competing at the metallic

silhouette matches held every week on the northern outskirts of town. Even so, he hadn't begun making substantial contributions to Mrs. Singh's larder, preferring to
shoot rabbits, grouse, pheasant, squirrels, and other small
game with reduced loads (reduced for the Grizzly, anyway) to risking a shot at his first big game before he felt he
was ready.

As for Gretchen, he remained as fascinated with her as
he'd been the first day. She seemed to understand him, and
the environment he'd come from, better than anyone else
he'd met.

"Bill Gonzales," proclaimed the voice of the director.
The boy glanced back to where—Al Theroux, his name
was—stood at a card table behind the line with the record
book under his hand and a bullhorn at his mouth. *"You're
on deck: five shots at the swinger. Emerson Ngu, you're on your
first string of chickens. Charlie Jackson, you're doing pigs. Lenda
Jackson, you're shooting turkeys. Mark Friedrich, you're on rams.
Okay, shooters, load five and make ready."*

The unspeakably wonderful perfume of smokeless
powder hung heavy in the air, and Emerson was already
feeling the skin-drying effect of its residue on his hands.
He cleared his mind, ordered his nerves to settle—he'd be
fine once he'd fired the first shot that counted—and centered his attention, as well as his scarlet front sight, on the
leftmost of a row of five freestanding steel chickens,
twenty-five yards away.

As always, it looked like twenty-five kilometers.

"Shooters, at your own pace, fire five rounds!"

Before he was aware of it, the first chicken had fallen to
the Grizzly. "Two inches higher than it should have been,"
a soft female voice to the rear informed him, "and a little to
the left, maybe half an inch. Take your time with the next
one. Remember you've got two whole minutes, forever, really." With the voice had come that elusive but unmistak-

able scent of sagebrush and woodsmoke. Gretchen had finished her course of fire and come back to the line to spot for him. It never failed to surprise him how generous "competitors" could be with one another.

He raised the Grizzly, maneuvered the sights into position, and held on the target for what seemed like an eternity, trying hard to get the sight picture just right. Before he knew it, he'd held the weapon up too long and his hands were beginning to shake. Most people were unaware how painful and wearying it is to hold one's empty hands out at arm's length for as long as two minutes, let alone hands weighed down by three and a half pounds of steel, brass, and lead. Wisely, he decided not to take the shot just then. A more common psychological response was to "get rid" of it, to shoot the shot anyhow, and waste it. Instead he let the Grizzly down and took a couple of deep breaths.

Next time, he pulled the trigger. The second chicken slammed backward into the low mound of earth behind it and was immediately buried under half an inch of crumbly carbonaceous chondrite. The Grizzly was too powerful, really, for twenty-five-yard chickens.

"Dead center, which means you're still shooting high if your sights are adjusted right."

Emerson nodded thanks. With him, consistent high shooting simply meant that he was still nervous. He lowered the gun, took two very deep breaths, held the third, and raised the pistol to eye level again. It seemed to hang there in the air before his face without support, tracking the target almost as if by itself.

That meant he'd found it. The Grizzly roared and a third chicken went down, followed quickly—too quickly, really—by a fourth. He hurried the last shot and missed the fifth by an inch. Groaning inwardly, although he'd actually expected this, he heard the command to clear and holster his pistol, obeyed it, and trudged a few feet to the next position, for the second string of twenty-five-yard chickens. He missed the first, then bore down and forced himself to breathe correctly, take his time, focus on the front sight while holding so that the chickens appeared to be standing on it, and hit all four of those remaining. His shots were hitting now where they were supposed to, rather than too high.

The order came to shift to the next position. He collected his ammo box—Gretchen had taken the scorecard, which he'd planned to mark himself—and moved to the right, in front of the first string of steel pigs standing fifty yards away. "This time," she told him, "remember to aim at the bottom edge of the bellies. And Emerson . . ."

For the first time, he turned to face her, a barbarian maiden with long hair streaming in a gentle breeze, bare arms, many-pocketed shooting vest, and gunbelt slanting across her hips. In both hands she held a huge pair of binoculars. "Yes?"

She grinned. "Remember to take your time. It isn't a race."

He nodded and turned back to the pigs. That was his problem with this game. If he could slow down, let his arms rest, he could double his usual score. The trouble always came within the soft, warm cloud of concentration, when his sense of time altered, and seconds seemed like minutes. But he'd try.

The first pig went down with a ferocious, satisfying clang and a cloud of dust. Patterned after a wild javelina of the West American desert, the pigs were heavier than the chickens, although they still vanished abruptly from their stands when hit. Gretchen told him he'd connected dead center, which at this range was acceptable. The second pig disappeared like the first, another center hit, but he missed the third because he'd hurried it. Now he took two breaths between shots, oxygenating blood, clearing vision and mind, letting his arms rest as the Grizzly hung in front of him. When he raised it again, it seemed to float, as it had before, and seek the target by itself. Wishing the trigger could pull itself, he used every scrap of self-discipline he had, took the pull up gradually, felt the hesitation, then the recoil of the weapon as it reared back and spat hot, copper-jacketed lead in one direction and hot, empty brass in the other.

The fourth pig clanged to the ground as he heard a startled yelp from Gretchen's direction. He didn't dare look, but apparently the hot case had found the open V-shape of her vest. It wasn't the first time it had happened. She never seemed to learn to wear a shirt beneath it. Suppressing a grin which could get him killed—or at least threatened—he aimed at the last pig and knocked it down. With Gretchen's coaching, he cleared all five pigs in the second string.

And now it got difficult. It wasn't that the turkeys, at seventy-five yards, were further away. Rams stood at one hundred and were easier to hit. The turkeys weren't small. Emerson, along with every other silhouette shooter he knew, believed the problem was their shape, a grotesque oval pitched at about forty-five degrees, which bore no relationship to the picture made by his rectangular sights. Like every other silhouette shooter he knew, he'd adjusted his sights so that the bullet would go exactly where he was aiming, at the apparent center of the turkey's irregular mass.

He missed the first one. He missed the second and decided it wasn't the turkeys or his gun. The damned things intimidated him and he'd been thinking about them all week, as he did every week before a match. He took his time—he'd hurried his first shots, probably with the idea of getting the turkeys over with—steadied down with help from Gretchen, took several deep breaths, and reviewed the fundamentals.

He caught the third turkey on the tail. It spun end for end, and for a moment he thought it wasn't going to fall. When it did, he went through the same discipline as with the previous shot, hit the fourth turkey dead center, and dead-centered the fifth. It was the first time he'd hit three turkeys in a row.

In the second string, he hit four turkeys in a row.

At last ten rams confronted him. The mostly rectangular targets standing one hundred yards off seemed more difficult than ever before, perhaps because he was aware of how well he'd done on the turkeys and was now afraid of relaxing the discipline that had taken him this far. Although he wasn't keeping count, he knew he'd shot better, so far, than ever before. Gretchen helped him, reminding him to breathe, focus on his front sight, squeeze the trigger, and follow through—to try, although it was impossible, to maintain the relationship between the sights and the target after the Grizzly had gone off. Over and over she told him, "Remember to take your time. It isn't a race."

Emerson wrapped his right hand around the grip, his index finger on the trigger guard until he was ready to fire. He wrapped his left hand around the right, his right thumb on the safety, his left on the slidestop to locate his hands correctly and against the small chance that either control might operate under the substantial recoil and spoil his shot. The hammer was cocked as a result of chambering his first round. He breathed, raised the Grizzly, and squeezed the trigger. The Grizzly bellowed. The lag between its discharge and the impact was perceptible. The ram seemed to hang in the air a moment before it toppled backward in a cloud of dust. Emerson calmed himself for the next shot.

And missed, and missed again. Even as he missed the third time, Gretchen didn't alter the tone of her voice or anything she said. He understood the principles and it was up to him to follow them. Most weapons, sighted for center hits on the seventy-five-yard turkeys, must be aimed at the uppermost edge of the rams. Emerson's shots, according to his spotter, were high, missing the rams by less than an inch.

He missed the last ram in the string and noticed, as he drew the empty magazine, that his hands were shaking. Scolding himself—it was only a game, after all, and the reward for winning was kept small and symbolic to make sure it stayed a game—he moved to the next position, breathing deeply and trying to relax. He loaded five rounds into the empty magazine. "Concentrate, Emerson," Gretchen whispered. "Don't look at the front sight, *be* in it."

The trouble was, the sight covered the target. He could see when he was shooting low. He couldn't see when he was shooting high, which gave him an idea. This time, as he raised the gun, he let the thinnest possible edge of the ram's back show above the bright red sight. That might make him shoot a trifle low, but it was better than missing altogether. He had to let the gun down without firing and try again, but when he reacquired the sight picture he squeezed the trigger and was rewarded by a clang and the sight of the first ram in the string toppling with a majestic slowness which lent Gretchen's voice a worried tone.

"Okay for windage, Emerson, but that was pretty low in the belly."

For the first time, he replied. "At least I hit it."

Emerson's second shot repeated his first, the concentration, the fine line above the front sight, the pull, the clang, the slow fall, the cloud of dust. What he didn't notice was the small crowd of shooters behind him who'd finished their own courses of fire and were staying to watch. Somebody had been keeping count.

He nearly wasted his third shot keeping that fine black

line consistent with previous shots. Before he put pressure on the trigger, he realized his front sight was blurry. He released the trigger, lowered the gun, breathed before he raised it and fired, knocking over the third ram. He missed the fourth, and the low groan behind him made him aware he had an audience. That, and the fact that he'd never hit the last ram in a string, made him more nervous than ever. In a way, it helped, forced him to relax and follow every step in the discipline.

The fifth ram fell to the Grizzly. Gretchen squealed and her arms were around his neck—a serious breach of range discipline—before the command to cease fire had been given. She turned him around, put her soft, warm mouth on his, and kissed him hard and deeply—he was shocked to discover that you could do that with your tongue—before she finally let him go and stood back.

"Congratulations, Emerson," she told him breathlessly. "You've just tied the range record!"

XVII
SOMETHING WONDERFULLY ABSURD

IF THE AMERICAN PEOPLE EVER DISCOVER THE EXTENT TO WHICH THE BROADCAST MEDIA HAVE LIED TO THEM ABOUT THEIR OWN LIVES AND THE WORLD AROUND THEM, THERE WON'T BE A TELEVISION STUDIO OR NETWORK BUILDING LEFT STANDING ABOVE THE ASHES.
—**Mirelle Stein,** *The Productive Class*

E merson didn't know what to think.
More accurately, he didn't know what to feel.
Naturally, he was pleased with his shooting prowess

this morning. The local club would write it down in their books as a "29x40" — as well, according to the match director, as anyone on Pallas had ever done. Emerson was only getting started as a marksman and perhaps he'd do even better someday. Of course it was equally possible that this was the best he'd ever shoot. But he'd never have another first kiss from Gretchen Singh — or from any other girl — and that's what he'd remember about this day for the rest of his life.

Afterward, at an unhurried pace, he and the girl headed home through the little town lying on the western shore of Lake Selous. At one end of the single unpaved street stood the statue of William Wilde Curringer, larger than life exactly as the man himself had been by all accounts — before he'd screwed his ultralight aircraft into the ground close to this very spot. Otherwise, it was difficult to tell what Curringer had been like from this bronze simulacrum, cast from the same native Pallatian tin and copper Emerson worked with every day in the machine shop where he'd been employed for the last six months.

They waved at a passerby they both knew. Tyr May, Brody's assistant, also worked at his family's general store and taught Tae Kwon Do at the bank after hours in his spare time. May grinned knowingly at them and waved back. Except for occasional evenings when, for some unfathomable female reason, Gretchen insisted on going into town alone, she and Emerson had been together practically their every waking hour.

For a small town with only one street, Curringer was a noisy place, filled with people coming and going from here to there on foot, punctuated by an occasional rare motor vehicle. The town stood on a rounded spit of elevated land which didn't quite qualify as a peninsula, although it was surrounded on three sides by Lake Selous. Seyfried Road, stretching past the shooting range northwest of town to-

ward the southwest fringe where Mrs. Singh lived, curved
around to follow the outline of the small cape everybody
called Point Cooper. Apparently the city's founders had
planned for the statue of Curringer to stand in the center of
things, but it hadn't worked out that way. The southern
half of the town had grown so much faster that the statue
stood at one end, while the other was marked by the oil
well pumping away in the middle of the street. From what
he knew of the man, Emerson thought Curringer would
have liked that.

Curringer had been an individual of substance in more
ways than one—"portly," Emerson's mother would have
called him. His heavily moustached face above a broad ex-
panse of vest, tie, and coat cast its benign gaze directly
through the etched-glass front doors of one of the town's
trio of what Brody referred to as "houses of swell repute."
Neither Emerson's meager budget—he'd begun paying
rent to Mrs. Singh almost immediately, along with pay-
ments he made each week for the Grizzly—nor his own
view of the world afforded him opportunity to discover for
himself whether the Nimrod's proprietor was correct in
that assessment.

Flanking Galena's, the establishment Curringer was
fated to admire in perpetuity, were Doc Sheahan's office,
which offered medical and dental services to both human
and animal clients, and May's Dry Goods, one of two general mercantiles. All were on the western, inshore side of
the street. On the other side of the street stood Baldy's, the
town's only barbershop (most men on Pallas appeared to
prefer beards and those who had hair wore it rather long),
and the White Rose Tattoo, one of Brody's three competitors. A vacant lot lay between them, past which Emerson
and Gretchen looked out over the lake, only half aware
that they were doing so. Emerson was thinking for the first

time in a long while about the Greeley Utopian Memorial Project and of the family he'd left behind there.

"You couldn't see it, Emerson, even if it weren't for the curvature of the asteroid," Gretchen observed gently. "Lake Selous is nearly seventy miles across at this point."

He turned to her and grinned. "Reading my mind again, are you? Well, my fine, feathered telepath, it's ninety-four kilometers, almost another fifty miles, from the Rimfence to the Residential compound, in addition. And much, much further off than that in some ways. I was just wondering what my mother and father would think about this morning." He gave the holstered weapon hanging at his thigh a fond, familiar slap and sighed. "Somehow I doubt that they'd be proud of me."

"Oh." Her feelings sounded a bit hurt. She thought he'd meant the kiss. Emerson glanced up and saw that she'd done it to him again—she was joking with him.

He laughed. "All right, have it your own way, then: that, too. My family—my people—can be extremely prudish in some ways, by your Outsider standards." He hooked a thumb back toward Galena's as they passed its garish false front. "In a million years, they'd never know what to make of a place like that, for instance."

She lifted an eyebrow. "And do you?"

Inwardly, he cringed. She was getting ready to embarrass him again. He ought to know the signs by now. "I think I do. You people on the Outside are completely free—supposed to be, at least—to do whatever you want with your own lives, as long as you don't hurt the other people around you, isn't that it?"

For some reason she looked genuinely hurt this time, although the expression quickly faded. "Well, whatever it lacks in philosophical rigor," she replied blandly, "it makes up for in other ways." Abruptly she asked, "Are you a virgin, Emerson?"

"Unh . . ." Straight to the solar plexus. He stopped walking. Damn it, she'd done it again, even though he'd been braced for it this time. A good deal later, it would occur to him that the proper reply would have been, "Are you?"

They glided on in self-conscious silence, Emerson unaware that Gretchen had embarrassed herself as well as her favorite victim. As they reached the actual middle of the town, following the curve of the street around its sharpest bend, they took in the familiar sight of Aloysius Brody's Nimrod Saloon and Gambling Emporium. Parked directly in front of it, taking up a great deal of space in the narrow road, was one of the rollabouts from the Project, the very machine, in fact, that Emerson had stowed away on to get here. Consulting his mental calendar, he was mildly perplexed. This was Saturday, the wrong day for the vehicle to make its produce delivery to the Nimrod. Although the schedule wasn't written in stone, it usually came around the middle of the week.

"So much for my plan," Gretchen told him, visibly grateful for a reason to change the subject, "to show you off and shout your praises at the Nimrod. Aloysius will be busy, and I'll bet you're not terribly anxious to see anyone from back home."

He shook his head. "One of your father's books says that in the Middle Ages, if a serf ran off and stayed gone a year and a day, he was free. I'm about three weeks past that, but I'm not sure the Chief Administrator respects the custom." He shrugged. "On the other hand, maybe he doesn't give a damn if he loses one troublemaking peasant—maybe nobody does. He's got ten thousand more."

"Let's not take chances," Gretchen replied with a grin, although her tone was serious, almost nervous. "We'll just go straight home and find out later what's going on here."

Emerson, all too willing to oblige in this instance, nodded. They detoured around the solar-powered machine, continued down the street past Osborn's Plumbing & Machine Shop, where he worked, two more saloons, more gunsmiths than cities a hundred times the size of Curringer usually had on Earth, residences ranging from palatial to pathetic, and the videochip rental—Gretchen had a TV of her own—where he often picked up movies to take home after work.

Somewhere after they'd passed the oil well, she took hold of his hand and wouldn't let go of it until they passed through the front gate of her mother's house.

That evening, immediately following dinner, Mrs. Singh asked everyone present to remain seated at the dining room table for just another few minutes.

"We got a little unfinished business to attend to," she explained, if that was the word for it.

Suddenly Gretchen swung through the kitchen door carrying something on a big platter. It was an oddly shaped cake. As she set it down, Emerson saw that it had been cut into the shape of the steel pigs they'd been shooting at that morning. Atop the reddish chocolate frosting lay a big, scalloped-edged figure 5.

At a nod from his hostess, Brody arose to clear his throat impressively. "Emerson, as we're all aware, you tied the Curringer range record today with an enviable score of twenty-nine out of forty. I'm sure a 'mere' seventy-two and a half percent sounds less than impressive to the uninitiated, but it's no inconsiderable feat given your relative newness to the sport and the fact that you were shooting offhand over iron sights. That in itself would be reason enough for celebration, but this is in acknowledgment of another accomplishment on your part which you seem to have overlooked—although you may rest assured that we have not. This morning you downed five javelinas in a row." He beamed at Gretchen. "I believe Miss Singh has a small token of the occasion to present you with."

Gretchen moved to Emerson's side as the boy, face burning, awkwardly levered himself to his feet. Reaching into one of the many small pockets of her shooting vest, under which she was wearing a frilly silk blouse tonight, Gretchen extracted a glittering bit of jewelry and ceremoniously pinned it to his shirt lapel. When he got a better look at it later, he saw that it was a tinier version of the cake, silver-edged and enameled in red, with a figure 5 in its center.

"The first," she declared, "of many."

Now that he thought about it, he'd already noticed several pins just like this, chickens and pigs and turkeys and rams, being worn by Gretchen and some of her shooting friends. He'd wondered idly what they were. Gretchen wasn't wearing hers tonight, possibly out of politeness, because it would make this sole distinction he'd achieved appear as ridiculous by comparison as it probably was.

She stood on her toes, kissed him on the cheek, and they both blushed while Brody, her mother, and the Jacksons laughed and shouted and clapped their hands.

"Emerson?"

Gretchen's voice, as soft as he'd ever heard it, had followed her light tapping on his bedroom door. Nevertheless he started. He'd come to his room as quickly as he could after cutting the cake and eating a polite portion to read from another borrowed history book, listen to the radio, and try to think. The feeling of this morning's kiss and the odd discomfort of this evening's honor were burned into his brain. He'd sat on the bed fully dressed, staring at the wall, seeing mental pictures of Gretchen that now made him feel more than a little self-conscious.

"Er, come in." As a hasty afterthought, he swung his legs over the edge of the bed and stood up.

She did as she was told and quietly closed the door behind her, giving him a smile with downcast eyes that was partly bold and partly shy. A half-conscious glance at the clock standing beside the radio told Emerson that it was later than he'd thought. Brody would be gone. The other inhabitants of the house, including Mrs. Singh, would have been in their beds by now for at least an hour.

Ordinarily, so would Gretchen, he assumed.

She was certainly dressed for it in a lightweight and translucent, vaguely robelike thing with who-knew-what on underneath. Inexplicably, he felt guilty just for noticing how the light came through it, outlining her body. He tried, unsuccessfully, to look away. More accustomed to seeing her in rough denim outdoor clothing that concealed, he was astonished at the way the form-fitting fabric she wore was pushed in and out, here and there, as she moved.

As she breathed.

It was a lot like the first day he'd met her. He swallowed and tried to talk, but couldn't think of anything particularly intelligent to say. His breath came to him raggedly, his hands shook, and his legs felt like warm jelly. At the same time there was a feeling throughout his body as if it were held together by fine, hot wires which had been pulled too tight and might tear through his flesh any minute if they didn't burn their way out first. He had a suspicion, one he hardly dared to recognize, let alone hope was correct, that Gretchen had come to his bedroom for something more than a kiss.

Looking more than a little self-conscious herself, she glided toward him, pausing to turn out the desk lamp as she passed it, which left only the small reading light mounted on the headboard of his bed, and the softly glowing dial of the radio—where something gentle and, well, seductive was being played, a classic from the middle of the previous century. She didn't stop advancing until she stood as close to him as possible without touching, every contour of her body within millimeters of his own. It may have been an illusion of some kind, but Emerson believed he caught the faint whiff of sagebrush and woodsmoke he'd noticed about her from the first day they'd met, a sensation he'd always associate with her.

She smiled and this time looked him in the eye, although her breathing, he observed, was no less uneven than his own. "Aren't you going to ask me to sit down?"

He swallowed again and nodded toward the chair across the room, instantly hating himself for his stupidity and bashfulness. "Would you like to sit down?"

"Why yes, thank you, I would."

She took his hand and sat down on the bed, pulling him down to sit close beside her.

She cleared her throat.

"I didn't come in here to make you nervous, Emerson, and I don't really care whether you're a virgin or not. I'm very sorry I said that this morning. It was a stupid thing to say. I'm nervous, too, in case you wondered, which is why I'm talking so much. I wish to hell you'd say something so I could shut up."

"Unh . . ."

He rolled his eyes, mindless and totally lost to panic, torn between taking this beautiful creature in his arms and kissing her or jumping out of the window. He hadn't wondered why she was talking so much—he hadn't even noticed. If anything, he was grateful. For one horrifying instant he did wonder what Mrs. Singh would say—or do; she was a better shot than Gretchen—if she were to walk in on them. Then he realized suddenly that he didn't care.

There were worse ways to die.

He put both arms around her and kissed her. She did

smell of sagebrush and woodsmoke. She moaned quietly, as if she'd waited for this a long time. He felt a sort of shudder run through her body and the wet warmth of tears on her cheeks. After a long while, he sat back from her a little, lifted her chin with gentle fingertips, and asked, "Is this also because I won the match this morning?"

A million other girls might have been insulted by that question, or pretended to be. Gretchen wiped her eyes and laughed, her long, glossy hair shimmering with each movement of her head. "No, Emerson, it isn't. That was going to be my excuse, but I've been thinking about doing this for months, almost since the minute I met you—although I don't suppose I should admit that. It did help me get my courage up, having an excuse. And you certainly weren't going to do anything on your own, were you? Don't answer that—you couldn't, on account of where you're from and maybe what you think Mom might think."

"I was wondering, kind of—"

She laid her hands atop his. "There's nothing to wonder about, Emerson. On Pallas—what you call the Outside—you're a free man, I'm a free woman, and that's all there is to it. It doesn't matter if my mother, or anybody else, disapproves—although she likes you very much and I'll bet she's actually been wondering if we'd ever get around to it. If she did, the worst she could do is throw us out of her house, but that wouldn't be the mother I know. As long as you pull your own mass and take responsibility when it's yours to take, nobody has anything to say about what you do. That was settled quite a while back on this asteroid—and my mom and I settled it long ago between ourselves."

She squeezed his hands beneath hers. "Besides," she whispered, "Mom's busy. You left so quickly after dinner. I'll bet you think Aloysius went back to town, don't you?"

He opened his mouth. "I—"

"I think that's enough talk." She placed a gentle hand on his chest, pushed him back onto his pillow, and fumbled briefly with the copper buttons of his Levi's. "Mmmhmm, I thought so. I wouldn't take the initiative, but we'll have to do something about that if this is going to turn out right for both of us."

She worked the zipper, and, with his stunned and somewhat frightened cooperation, pushed his pants down until they bunched at his knees. Still sitting, she bent over him—her dark, soft hair brushed and tickled his thighs—and began doing something wonderfully absurd which kept them both from talking for a while.

At some point—he was never quite certain when it happened, but the time required was all too short—every muscle in his body tensed and suddenly released. A low, involuntary shout wrenched itself from his throat and his mind exploded with a white light mystics talk about and look for in all the wrong places.

Afterward, as shocked disbelief and the memory of unspeakable pleasure sang through his veins—he'd never heard of people doing anything like what had just happened but was afraid to ask about it because he didn't want her to know it was his first time—they lay together, her head on his shoulder and his arms around her.

He started to say something.

She put a finger to his lips. "Don't you dare thank me for that. Believe me, it was pure self-interest, the most practical application of capitalist theory I know." She giggled. "Postponing present gratification—you can't really say consumption, can you?—in order to guarantee future satisfaction."

They didn't speak after that. He kissed her eyelids, the bridge of her nose, her cheeks, her mouth, her chin. She kissed his fingertips. Without more prompting than that, he pulled at the slender, silky ribbons of what she wore and opened her clothing, gazing down at her in the soft light of the room, touching her everywhere, unlocking the secrets of her body and claiming it for his own, inhaling her warm scent and marveling at her firm, smooth fullness.

Nor did she lie passively beneath his hands.

And in due course, Gretchen discovered that the most reliable miracle in the universe had occurred, that he was ready for her once again, and that she was now ready for him.

"Remember to take your time," she advised him with a grin as she swung a leg over his and rose to place herself atop him. "It isn't a race, you know."

Somewhat awkwardly at first, Emerson followed Gretchen's advice precisely as he had that morning at the range, and indeed, this time it turned out right for both of them.

And the third time was even better.

XVIII

CONFRONTATION

McCOY: You offer us only well-being . . .
SCOTT: Food and drink and happiness mean nothing to us. We must be about our job . . .
McCOY: Suffering in torment and pain, laboring without end . . .
SCOTT: Dying and crying and lamenting over our burdens . . .
BOTH: Only in this way can we be happy!
            —Stephen Kandel, "I, Mudd," *Star Trek*

Emerson woke late the next morning, happier than he'd known was possible. And from the sight, indescribably, almost painfully beautiful to him, of Gretchen's still-sleeping face against his pillow, he believed that she was, as well.

The radio was still playing softly. He traced the graceful, delicate line of her jaw with a gentle finger. She smiled and snuggled further into the blankets.

It must have been obvious that last night had been his only experience with a woman. Apparently—miraculously—she hadn't seemed to care. For the first time, he wondered whether it might have been her first with—dare he call himself a man? From what she knew and how she did it, he doubted that she'd been a virgin when she came to his bed. What he felt about that—not knowing that it would have seemed no less miraculous to her—was undiluted gratitude. He did find he preferred never to know who the other fellow—fellows?—had been.

He sighed contentedly and looked around the room, remembering. The place would never seem the same, and here was a day that was truly new. Outdoors, the morning sun seemed to be hammering at his window, demanding to be let in. Grinning to himself, Emerson arose, careful not to disturb the girl. He strode across the small room, trying not to swagger, and pulled the curtain back. His grin vanished when he saw what waited in the road just beyond Mrs. Singh's gate.

It was probably what had awakened him.

Suddenly the hammering was real, at his door instead of at the window. Gretchen sat up, gorgeous and completely unself-conscious in her nakedness, blinking with disorientation at the disturbance. Before the boy could wrench his eyes away and grab his pants to put them on, Mrs. Singh was shouting at them from the hall.

"Emerson! Gretchen! Wake up and get out here in a hurry! Looks like we've got company!"

The door opened to a four-inch crack and Mrs. Singh's heavily veined hand appeared, holding her daughter's

Levi's, vest, and gunbelt. She tossed them on the bed without looking in, closed the door, and they could hear her
footsteps almost immediately, clattering down the stairs.
Without a word, with hardly a look between them except
for the briefest possible brush of her lips across his, both of
the younger people dressed hurriedly, strapped on their
weapons, and followed after her.

The air downstairs smelled pleasantly of frying bacon.
Mrs. Singh must have been interrupted in the middle of
preparing breakfast. Outside, through a screen of privacy
offered by the sheer curtains of the living room windows,
the three of them watched former United States Senator
Gibson Altman clamber down from the electric Project vehicle Emerson and Gretchen had seen in Curringer the
previous afternoon and, flanked by a pair of thick-necked,
uniformed security men, their shock batons in hand, stamp
up the walk to the steps of the front porch.

"That's close enough, boys!" Mrs. Singh opened her
front door all the way, leaving the outer screen hooked.
From a large apron pocket she pulled a 10 millimeter pistol
almost identical to Gretchen's, although she held it at her
waist behind her back. Her voice was high but firm. "This
don't look like no friendly visit to me. State your business
or get off my property!"

The Chief Administrator of the Greeley Utopian Memorial Project, just about to start up the porch steps ahead
of him, stopped with one foot in the air. As he put it down,
the pair of toughs behind him each took a sideways step,
spreading out defensively, their batons held menacingly
across their chests.

Altman wasn't wearing a hat, but somehow gave the
impression of politely taking one off before he spoke. In
one hand he held a sheaf of official-looking forms. "Good
morning, madam—Mrs. Henrietta Singh, I believe. My
name is Gibson Altman. I'm here because I have reason to

believe you're harboring a fugitive—unknowingly, of course. Is there an Emerson Ngu on the premises?"

"I know exactly who you are, Senator," Mrs. Singh informed him. "What if there was?"

"He's a minor child, madam, an illegal runaway from my jurisdiction, and his parents want him back." He spread a modest hand across his chest, then indicated the official-looking bundle in his other hand. "I'm only here to help them."

The woman tossed a quick glance first at Emerson, then at her daughter, then at Emerson again. For the first time Emerson realized—and was utterly astonished—that Gretchen's mother seemed to know of their relationship and approve. There was a good reason for that, although Emerson, as yet, was unaware of it.

She turned her attention back to the man on the front walk. "He may have been a minor when he escaped your jurisdiction, Senator, but he ain't no more. Now unless Emerson wants to bother with you—which I can see he don't—you can run along and peddle your papers someplace else. I got things I gotta do this morning."

Altman gave Mrs. Singh his warmest and sincerest smile, but his words had an ominous ring. "Now you know, madam, that I can't do that. We've come a long way for this child, over bad roads. The summons and other authorizations I brought with me are fully in order. His parents are here, waiting for him in the rollabout. We have every right to take him by force, if necessary, and we outnumber you."

She snorted, looking from one of the intruders to the next. "You three poor pitiful things?"

"And additional personnel aboard the rollabout"—Altman lifted and spread his hand toward the vehicle in a graceful television gesture—"sufficient to the task, madam."

"Not if all your side brought with 'em is those little electric toad-ticklers." Taking the pistol from behind her back and pointing it at the Senator's chest, Mrs. Singh recited: " 'In days of old when knights was bold an' someone hadda feed 'em, they did require a local squire to scare the serfs an' bleed 'em.'

"Only the Middle Ages're over, Squire Altman, in case you weren't aware of it, an' we ain't none of the disarmed and cowering peasantry you're used to bullying."

Emerson had stood half-frozen in the middle of the living room until this moment. "Well," he turned to Gretchen, "I guess the Chief Administrator gave a damn after all. Nice to be wanted." He left her side—the girl almost extended a hand to stop him, then thought better of it—to join his landlady at the door. "I'll talk to him, Mrs. Singh. I don't want anyone to get hurt over—"

"Over a sacred principle." Mrs. Singh turned and looked him hard in the eye. "Don't you forget that for a minute, son. There's a deal more happening here than just the business of the moment. And you'd better not go out there without that weapon of yours drawn and the hammer at full cock, you hear me?" She lowered her voice, almost to a whisper. "Gretchen'll be right behind you, Emerson. Bein' the mistrusting and suspicious type I am, I'm gonna watch the back door!"

Emerson glanced down briefly at the Grizzly, which suddenly seemed to hang twice as heavy in its holster as it usually did. Although the blue goons only had their electronic shock batons, he knew from previous experience that they could be very fast with them. Once they so much as touched him with them he'd be completely incapacitated. If he had to draw, it would take him forever to get the big autopistol into action. He'd only been using it for what amounted to target practice anyway, not combat exercises, and he now appreciated the utter folly of employing the hammer-down, so-called "Ahern carry" for safety's sake.

He regretted even more the fact that he'd never reloaded the weapon after the previous day's match.

Not realizing that she'd left an unarmed boy behind, Mrs. Singh headed for the kitchen, on her way to the back door. Gretchen glanced after her, came to what she may have known was the decision of a lifetime, and remained where she was. When Emerson unhooked the screen and stepped out onto the porch, leaving the massive autoloader in its holster where, he believed, it already looked impressive and intimidating enough, Gretchen—who knew his habits and may have been aware of the condition of the Grizzly—was not behind him, but beside him.

"Well," the Chief Administrator managed to get in the first word, "I see that you've picked up a couple of bad habits, living among these barbarians." He tossed a sneering glance, first at Gretchen, then at the gun on Emerson's hip. "Take that filthy thing off, little man, and get into the car. I'm not entirely certain why, but your parents are anxious to see you. I only hope for their sake that you haven't already killed somebody or acquired some kind of disease."

As often happens in an emotional and potentially violent confrontation, the boy never heard or understood those ugly words until afterward. Emerson could see both his parents aboard the Project vehicle, surrounded by goons. For some reason, Altman had brought his son, Gibson Junior, along, as well. Alice Ngu's face pressed against the plastic of the canopy, staring out at her son. His father kept his eyes ahead, stoically refusing to look his way. It all seemed to bother Emerson less than he'd expected. He'd made his choice more than a year ago.

"I'd like to see them, too," he replied, nevertheless. "Let them out of that thing and we'll talk here."

The Chief Administrator shook his head, apparently more in sorrow than in anger. "I'm afraid it isn't as simple as that, child. You know your own people and their beliefs, better than I do. This is a matter of 'face.' They feel disgraced by what you've done, by the ingratitude to me and to the Project that it represents. They will refuse to have anything to do with you again unless and until you return willingly and accept whatever penalty the law sees fit to impose on you."

"Sounds to me like a blank check if ever I heard of one." Suddenly aware that he'd unconsciously imitated Mrs. Singh's West American accent, Emerson gave him a humorless grin. "Return willingly and accept whatever penalty the law sees fit to impose? And you're the person I'm supposed to make it out to? You're the law?"

"You know perfectly well that I am, according to the charter of the United Nations"—the Senator shrugged and gave him a generous, self-deprecatory smile—"as well as the government of the United States of America. Now I'm getting quite weary of your nonsense. Tell me truthfully, aren't you, just a little bit, as well? Let's avoid any further unpleasantness. Take off that . . . that *thing*, tell that little slut of yours good-bye, and come with us. *Immediately!*"

Across the road, high in the air above an empty and uncultivated field, a circling hawk suddenly spied something small and furry moving in the buffalo grass below. It stooped and struck. The victim squealed briefly and fell silent. For the first time in his life, having witnessed this sort of thing often in the Project fields, the boy felt no pity for the rabbit being lifted and carried away in the claws of the raptor, but understood and shared the exultation of the predator.

"I believe . . ." Emerson drew the giant Grizzly and thumbed the hammer back as if there were a round in the chamber and seven more in the magazine. He aligned the colorful front sight precisely on the center of Altman's torso as if he were a seventy-five-yard turkey. The two thugs flanking the Senator tensed, but they were basically powerless to do anything about it and they knew it. At the same time, Emerson heard the sweet whispery ring of steel on wet-formed leather as the girl standing beside him followed his example. ". . . I'll decline your offer."

"Your call, Emerson," came Gretchen's voice, gentle but determined. He half expected her to remind him to take a breath, focus on the front sight, and squeeze. Unlike the boy, she hadn't missed the Chief Administrator's unpleasant insinuations. "I've got the others covered—don't think I can trust myself with Altman."

The Chief Administrator gave her an odd, evaluating look, as if he knew her already but at the same time was meeting her all over again. Emerson nodded without looking back at her, keeping his gun level, wondering why he didn't feel afraid.

"In effect," he told the man, "there isn't any US government any more, although you manage to keep the fact from most of your slaves. And the UN has nothing to say about what goes on outside the Rimfence. This is Pallas we're standing on and I'm a free man. I'm not your servant or my parents' property, and I won't go back to be beaten up or buggered by your trained animals. Now get out of here or I'll kill you where you stand." He wished he hadn't cocked the Grizzly quite so soon. Psychologically, this would have been a better time.

The Senator swallowed, but stood his ground. Emerson suddenly understood, in a manner rare even among grown-ups, that the man may have been a lot of evil things, but he wasn't a coward. "You'd actually shoot another human being, child, and an unarmed one at that, over an abstract philosophical concept so alien to your upbringing that you can't possibly understand it, let alone believe it?"

"I'd shoot a politician, Senator," the boy told him, convinced, at least for the moment, that he was speaking the plain truth. "It isn't the same thing at all."

"No," Gretchen agreed cheerfully, "it isn't."

Emerson had been glaring at the Senator, all his attention focused on the man while he trusted Gretchen to keep an eye on the pair of thugs he'd brought with him. Now he was distracted for an instant as, out of the corner of his eye, he caught sight of a small cloud of dust coming up the road from the nearby town. At the base of that cloud strode Aloysius Brody, cane in one hand, pistol in the other, followed by at least two dozen well-armed, angry-looking men and women.

Beside Emerson, Gretchen smiled, nodded to herself, and released what must have been a very deep breath, although she kept her own weapon ready in her hand.

"Chief . . ." One of the Senator's toughs tried to warn him that something new was happening. It was a noisy crowd coming up the road and Altman had already turned to see what the racket was about. So did his men, their confrontation with Emerson and Gretchen momentarily forgotten. As the people from Curringer approached Mrs. Singh's front gate, another pair of goons alighted from the rollabout, handling their shock batons uneasily and looking to the Senator for some indication of his wishes.

Altman didn't seem to notice.

"Gretchen!" the innkeeper shouted when he was near enough. "Your mother called t'say you could use some moral support. Stand yer ground, Emerson! Now what's this all about, Senator darlin'?"

Emerson was mildly confused, although he realized it was irrelevant at the moment. From what Gretchen had said, he'd thought Brody had stayed at the house last night.

He had a brief, ridiculous mental flash of the man sneaking out the back door, pants in hand.

Equally taken by surprise, Altman snarled. "Stay out of this! It's Project business!"

Brody raised a hand, telling his companions to remain in the road. He came through the gate himself, making a ceremony of letting his pistol pivot around his finger by the trigger guard, rolling it backward in his hand until he held it by the slide with its handle reversed, and dropping the weapon into his holster with a twist at the last moment so that it settled with the handle in a normal position. "I can scarcely believe that haulin' Curringer's new champion silhouette shooter off t'durance vile is legitimate Project business. Like all Pallatians, this young fellow's a free man. He's got rights which must be respected."

Behind Emerson, the screen door creaked as Mrs. Singh joined him and her daughter on the porch. She'd either decided it was safe to leave the back door unguarded or simply couldn't resist finding out what was going on here at the front of the house. Uncharacteristically, she remained silent, waiting for others to talk.

The Senator shook his head, obviously relieved that they were all still talking. He visibly began to relax. Emerson knew that this sort of thing was what he was best at. "Judge Brody, the boy is a minor, a legal ward of the Greeley Utopian Memorial Project, of which I happen to be Chief Administrator. I have a duty which I cannot neglect, to his parents and the community as a whole—"

"I'm glad to see we share the same opinion of your *community!*" Mrs. Singh put in. For the first time, Emerson noticed that she'd acquired another gun from somewhere in the house. She held both of them at her waist now, leveled on Altman.

Brody's expression was pained. "Now, let's try not to complicate things more than they hafta be." He eyed the muzzles of Mrs. Singh's pistols, then turned to Altman. "Senator, y'must know I've a duty of me own t'discharge, one I take no less seriously than you do yours, for all that it's a bit on the informal side." He turned to the porch again. "Emerson, me boy, would y'be objectin' to a hearin' t'settle this matter once an' for all, over to the Nimrod?"

Brody's proposition caught Emerson by surprise. He supposed he'd been expecting his new friends simply to run Altman and company off, back to where they'd come from. In his life at the Project, he'd never had any reason to trust adults before, and he was suddenly filled now with an odd foreboding, a premonition of betrayal. "I don't know, Mr. Brody. I don't see why I should have to—"

Brody shook his head. "Y'don't hafta do anything, son, but this'd settle it publicly an' permanently, to everybody's satisfaction. Or at least their mutual an' equal dissatisfaction. Y'know these lawyer types, me boy, sneaky an' persistent bastards that they be. Y'don't wanna go through this malarkey every few months, do ye?"

The boy shook his head. "No, sir, I don't."

"Best t'get it done, then. An' don't 'sir' me, Emerson."

"Yes, s—I mean, Mr. Brody."

The older man looked him over carefully, tossed the briefest possible glance at Gretchen, then scrutinized Emerson again. "Time y'started callin' me Aloysius, me boy."

"Yes, Mr.—Aloysius."

"An' how about yerself, Senator darlin'?" Brody had turned to Altman. "If ye're dead set on the due process of law, let's see where that leads us. Y'may be the HMFWIC where ye're from, but, as y'know, it's me that's the magistrate here."

Emerson wondered what an HMFWIC was. For some reason Altman seemed even more dubious about the idea than the boy himself. Nevertheless, after some thought, he

nodded. "Very well, Judge Brody. I'll go along with you —
provisionally."

"Done." Brody clapped his hands together once, then
looked at his watch. "We'll all meet at the Nimrod in two
hours. That'll just give me an' mine a chance to tidy up a
bit."

He winked at Emerson.

Emerson suddenly felt very cold.

XIX
A PLANETFUL OF LAWYERS

FOR ANY TWENTIETH-CENTURY AMERICAN WHO'D BEEN PAYING
ATTENTION AT ALL, THE PHRASE "CRIMINAL JUSTICE SYSTEM"
SHOULD HAVE BEEN WARNING ENOUGH.
— William Wilde Curringer, *Unfinished Memoirs*

They took his gun at the door.

The Senator and his enforcers had climbed back
aboard their rollabout after reaching an agreement with
Brody and returned to Curringer. When the time arrived,
two hours later, Emerson and Gretchen, along with her
mother and the other boarders, had walked into town,
fully armed and in their best clothes. Emerson wore a stiff
woolen suit of Horatio Singh's which the widow had been
threatening to cut down for him.

It was clear that news of Emerson's plight and the
Chief Administrator's mission had spread by word of
mouth; there had been nothing said about it on the radio
Emerson had listened to while he'd waited. Altman and his
party weren't popular. People had gathered in knots along
both sides of the street, muttering to each other and watching the rollabout. For his part, the Senator, perhaps wisely

considering how well armed these hostile observers happened to be, had kept himself and his own people securely buttoned up inside the vehicle.

Emerson wasn't certain how fair and impartial this hearing would be, but decided, pragmatically, that since Pallas in general and its magistrate in particular appeared to be siding with him, he didn't care. Fair and impartial were one thing, admirable in themselves as far as that went. What was *right* was something altogether different. As he and his companions passed through the middle of Curringer—gathering well-wishers and spectators along the way—Brody, who'd apparently been off somewhere on an errand of his own, met them on his way back to the Nimrod, escorted them inside, and helped them dispose of their guns.

"Hand 'em over t'young Tyr," he grinned. "They'll be taken care of."

There was something much like sawdust on the floor. The building's construction of long, narrow, folded strips of plastic-coated sheet steel gave an impression of wooden planks. Mrs. Singh mumbled under her breath but complied, glaring at Brody's assistant as he hung her gunbelt on the tines of a set of elk antlers which had frightened and disgusted Emerson the first time he'd set foot in the Nimrod. Now they merely seemed a part of the wall, along with a boar's head, a stuffed trout, a jackelope—the product of some whimsical Wyoming taxidermist, he'd been told—and other trophies of the hunt.

Only then did he and Gretchen follow her example, and in no better humor—which was expected and allowed for. Outside the Project, Pallatians would tolerate a demand that they disarm themselves only in saloons and courtrooms, which, in Curringer, happened to be the same. Many maintained that even this was too much restraint on the rights of the individual and therefore set a dangerous precedent.

Although the bar itself was closed in anticipation of the hearing, the room was half full of customers, as it always seemed to be whether liquor was being served or not. Several of the girls from Galena's had taken a table toward the back of the room and sat around it in their working clothes—consisting mostly of brief swatches of bright colors and satiny finishes—laughing, giggling, and commenting in loud whispers on the scene about them. As he squeezed past their table, one of them, a little blond hardly older than himself, eyed him speculatively. Her golden hair was frothy, he thought, rather than curly, and hovered about her head like a pale cloud. She winked at him.

He averted his eyes and blushed.

The Nimrod happened to be the principal social gathering-spot in Curringer only indirectly because it was a bar. Many theories had been offered over the years to explain it, but no one knew why the personal use of alcohol—another of agriculture's dubious gifts—had been diminishing on the asteroid almost since terraformation. Possibly the requirement that they do their drinking in a state most regarded as nakedness had something to do with it, although that failed to account for those seated here with softdrinks before them, their guns hanging on the wall with Emerson's and Gretchen's and Mrs. Singh's.

The widow maintained that there was no mystery to it at all. Before the fall of the Soviet Empire, she pointed out, the alcoholism rate in Moscow had been estimated at sixty percent, and liver disease had been a principal cause of death in European welfare states from Sweden to France. Deprive a people of what they worked so hard to earn and you deprive them of hope. Deprive them of hope and almost automatically they look to the bottle. In the old United States, where the IRS Code had supplanted the

Bill of Rights to become the highest law of the land and Americans were intimidated into forking over half of what they earned, drunk drivers killed the population equivalent of a medium-sized town every year.

In the absence of any more acceptable explanation, the proprietors of establishments like the Nimrod had been compelled to diversify the number and variety of services they offered the public. One saloon, the Surly Snail, served as the town's post office. Another, His Master's Voice, centered on the radio station Emerson had listened to clandestinely in his cavelet at the Project. And the Nimrod, of course, was the bailiwick of His Honor, Aloysius Brody.

Just because Emerson's weapon was no longer on his hip didn't necessarily mean it had to be out of sight; in fact, some special measures had been taken to assure it wasn't. As he'd entered the Nimrod and surrendered his belt, he watched it being hung on a back wall behind a waist-high rail along with those handed over by all who had preceded and followed him in. With Mrs. Singh and her daughter, he took a table in the center of the room where he could keep an eye on his gun. New as he was to the Outside, he was suddenly aware that he agreed with the cranky, rugged individualists, most of them being among the oldest, earliest arrivals on the asteroid, who complained about this custom. Whatever he did, calm or angry, drunk or sober (in fact he had never had an alcoholic drink, in this place or any other), was his own responsibility, and that—his responsibility—was what he suddenly felt deprived of.

He didn't like it.

The Altman party, including the Senator's hostile-faced, evil-eyed son and Emerson's mother and father—both looking very subdued (whether it was Altman's presence, the current circumstances, or they'd always been that way and he'd never noticed it before, he couldn't guess and didn't want to—entered the room and sat down well toward the back, where he had to look past them as well as the little blond from Galena's, to check on his weapon.

He liked that even less.

"Very well," Brody announced to the room, taking his place at a corner table where he customarily held forth whether court was in session or not. "Let's be after startin' this proper. We've strangers among us who don't know how we do things, so if nobody objects, or even if they do, I'll be takin' time to explain as we go along."

He produced a battered gavel from somewhere on his person and rapped on a tabletop much scarred from such abuse. "First off, the Curringer Trust, in which all Pallatians are shareholders under provisions of the Hyperdemocratic Covenant, is all the government Pallas has or wants or needs. Its only responsibility is t'maintain the atmospheric envelope over our heads. Every manner of dispute, even those held elsewhere t'be of a criminal nature— providin', of course, the criminal has survived the initial encounter—are settled by professional intermediaries like meself as civil procedures, where the idea of restitution, rather than punishment or 'rehabilitation,' is the accepted custom."

Brody glanced around the room.

"That understood, we're here today in the matter of Gibson Altman, Chief Administrator of the Greeley Utopian Memorial Project, an inhabitant of the asteroid Pallas within the meanin' of the Hyperdemocratic Covenant, versus Emerson Ngu, also an inhabitant of Pallas within the meanin' of the Covenant. It's me duty to inform y'both that the arbiter, meanin' meself, may be supplemented, should either party insist, by a jury of individuals fully informed as to their thousand-year-old obligation t'weigh the law itself, as well as the facts of the case."

He paused, as if formally awaiting an answer from each of them. Emerson didn't know what was customary or expected of him. He got along with most of the people of Curringer comfortably enough, and they seemed to like him, as well, but he didn't believe that his fate could be in better hands than it already was.

Before he could compose an answer, the Senator arose and spoke from the back of the room. "Your Honor, I'm somewhat concerned that any jury we choose—as well as you yourself, Your Honor—will necessarily be personally acquainted with this child, who, in any case, is legally disqualified by his age to be a party in any proceeding such as this. Naturally, I intend no offense."

Brody smiled. "An' none taken, considerin' that there's no alternative in a town this size. As t'Mr. Ngu's age an' qualifications, that remains t'be settled."

Altman nodded amiably. "I'm sure we can rely on you, Your Honor, to do what's right in this affair. It's an open and shut matter, really, once you understand that—"

Brody raised both hands to make erasing motions with them as he shook his head. "And we'll be after makin' it all clear soon enough, Senator darlin'. In the meantime, I must hear from the other party, as well." He shifted his gaze to the middle of the room and to Emerson. "How about it, Mr. Ngu, d'ye want me t'judge this case, or do ye want a jury of twelve good men an' women tried an' true?"

Emerson swallowed and rose. "I'd prefer that you be the judge, Mr. Brody."

"I thank y'both very kindly for yer confidence in me. Now y'may state your case, Senator Altman. I understand that y'want this young fellow handed over t'be returned to the Ant—I mean, the Greeley Utopian Memorial Project, is that correct?"

Like most of the other people in the now-crowded room, Emerson had to strain his neck in order to turn and

watch as the Senator, still standing, replied. Aware of the
attention and not entirely comfortable with it, Altman
cleared his throat.

"Your Honor, the truth is that I'm here primarily to
represent this child's parents, who—"

"We'll get to them directly," Brody interrupted, betraying a trace of irritation. "An' I suggest fer best results
that y'try representin' yerself, Senator, an' nobody else,
since, one way or another, most of the people on this asteroid came here in the first place to escape a planetful of lawyers an' their bloody handiwork. In the meantime, have I
not stated what y'want correctly?"

The Senator was obviously suppressing annoyance
himself. "Essentially, Your Honor."

Brody nodded. "Now that we understand each other a
little better, will y'kindly be after explainin' why I should
allow such a thing when it's clearly against his will?"

"For two reasons, actually, Your Honor," replied Altman, "either of which ought to be sufficient in itself, since
they're both inarguably true and speak to long and well-
established precedents under the law. In the first place,
this child is well under the legal age traditionally pre-
scribed for personal autonomy."

A low, grumbling noise arose among the onlookers.
Emerson couldn't tell whether it represented disapproval
of Altman's claims, and therefore the public support he'd
expected, or whether the people around him were now re-
considering their position.

"In the second place, whatever his age, he had no right
to opt out of the Greeley Utopian Memorial Project in violation of the binding and perpetual articles his parents
signed on his behalf years ago under the United Nations
Charter."

Now there was no mistaking the reaction of the audience. Emerson hadn't met an Outsider who wouldn't have

enthusiastically razed every UN building in Sri Lanka so that "not one stone was left standing on another, and salt sown on the ruins." The words had been those of Aloysius Brody, quoting William Wilde Curringer.

"I see," Brody replied in what Emerson knew was his most noncommittal tone. "And now will y'kindly be satisfyin' me personal curiosity as t'why y'waited so long t'come after Emerson? It's been a trifle more than a year, as I recollect."

"Well, until recently, Your Honor, we didn't know for certain where he was, and while it's true that the number of places he could have been on this asteroid was limited, I'm an extremely busy man with no administrative staff to speak of. You see, there are over ten thousand other lives at the Project—and numerous other important tasks—for which the United Nations holds me personally responsible. Also, Emerson's parents persuaded me to wait, hoping his experiences here would help him develop sense enough to return where he belongs on his own."

"I do see," Brody replied, "indeed. And how did y'happen t'find out where he was?"

Altman cleared his throat again, embarrassed color visible in his face. It was clear he'd rather have not been asked this question. "Er . . . from my son, Your Honor, Gibson Altman, Junior, who learned of it from a casual remark made by a girl in town he happens to have been, er . . . dating. That's her over at that table, isn't it, Junior? Gretchen Singh, I believe she calls herself."

Gibson Junior nodded, but his eyes were on Emerson, who felt a sudden unpleasant tightness spread through his body. It wasn't fear, of the Altman boy or of anybody else. Inexperienced and self-conscious, he'd completely failed to notice that Gretchen had been trying to resolve a personal dilemma. He wasn't altogether aware of it, even now. All he knew was uncertainty and a bitter feeling of betrayal.

What did it mean, *dating?*

Were he and Gretchen *dating* now, too?

Ignoring the personal implications of what the Senator had said, Brody turned to the principal subject of the conversation. "And what have ye got t'say fer yerself in this, young fella? Can y'give me one good reason why I shouldn't simply hand ye over t'this man—actin' fer yer parents as he is an' all?"

With difficulty, Emerson wrenched his mind back to the matter at hand. Naturally, he'd thought a great deal over the past two hours about what he intended to say at this point. He hadn't discussed it with Gretchen or her mother. It was his life that was up for grabs. Nor did he want to talk about what was likely to happen if he did go back—Brody knew about that, in any case. In the end, knowing what he knew about the Outsiders, he settled on the simplest truth possible.

"Yes, sir. I don't want to go."

Brody turned back to the Senator and sighed, his customary brogue all but inaudible as he spoke. "Chief Administrator Altman, although it may not meet the eye at first, I happen t'be a man of no small number of responsibilities, meself. One of 'em is operatin' in a manner consistent with Mirelle Stein's Hyperdemocratic Covenant, under the terms of which, I'm happy t'point out, the notion of a 'legal age' is a fallacious concept which the Pallatians wisely left behind on Earth."

The table Brody was sitting at may have been worse for the wear, but it contained a number of surprises. The arbiter lifted a section immediately before him and punched a number of keys. Instantly the wall behind him became a communications screen displaying a body of text prominently labeled at the top. Brody gave his hidden control board a few more keystrokes and the display scrolled down to the section he was looking for, which he blocked off and highlighted.

"As y'can see, Emerson Ngu's autonomy is fully established by the fact that he's self-supportin'. It has nothing whatever t'do with where or when he happened t'be born."

Outrage on his face, Altman opened his mouth to speak.

Brody stopped him with an upraised hand.

"Moreover, Senator, I vehemently deny the legal or moral power of anyone to bind their children, their heirs, their posterity, to any sort of contract, business, social, or otherwise, in perpetuity—and so does this agreement, which, unlike the benighted and downtrodden denizens of your domain, fer whom a tragic misinterpretation of the terms allowed ye t'sign collectively, each of us 'Outsiders' signs on his own hook as soon as he or she feels responsible enough t'do so.

"I might add, somewhat parenthetically, that I don't believe for a minute the reasons y'had t'give me fer waitin' so long t'come after Emerson. I suspect it's because things are goin' badly for ye inside the Project and you wanna arm these goons of yours with real weapons, usin' us Outsiders as an excuse."

He slammed the gavel on the tabletop.

"But that's irrelevant an' immaterial. I hereby rule meself outa order an' warn me not t'let it happen again. In the meantime, Senator darlin', I support the right of this individual to've refugeed outa your Greeley Utopian Memorial Ant Farm and t'remain on the Outside or anyplace else fer as long as he wishes."

The gavel came down again.

"Case dismissed. Emerson wins."

"*Just a minute!*" The Senator, still on his feet, somehow appeared to have just stood up. "I want you—all of you— to understand clearly the implications of what this man

Brody has just done, the consequences he and his support-
ers may have to pay for failing to send Emerson Ngu back
to his family."

He turned a threatening expression on the entire room.

"I tried a peaceful, orderly approach to this matter. Legally I could have sent my entire force of United Nations
Education and Morale counselors Outside and seized
Emerson Ngu, wreaking God only knows what havoc in
the process. But I gave you people an opportunity, and
now I've been rewarded for my restraint."

Brody shrugged. "Well, Chief Administrator, if
y'should happen t'change yer mind, I cordially invite ye
not just t'send yer goons, but t'come out an' play yerself.
It's only fair t'remind ye, though, that I don't know a soul
in Curringer or anyplace on this rock excepting yer own
stompin' grounds who doesn't own a gun an' know how
t'use it. Even young Mr. Ngu here," he observed, "seems
to've become a pretty fair shot, an' I plan t'be right beside
him with both hammers back and both index fingers on the
triggers. I'll also point out that UN blue's a mighty conspicuous color against the brown-green background of
Pallas."

A low fire burned behind the Senator's eyes as he
curtly signaled his party to get up and follow him out.
From their expressions Emerson couldn't tell what his parents were thinking.

"I'll keep that in mind," Altman replied. "Rest assured,
Your *Honor*, that the next time I appear in Curringer, I'll
have the requisite resources to make good *any* claim."

Across the room, Junior caught Emerson's eye again,
grinned maliciously, and made a throat-cutting gesture
with his thumb. Then he turned and followed his father
out. Emerson turned for a glance at Gretchen, only to discover that she was gone.

Unfortunately, the dramatic exit Altman had appar-

ently intended was about to be spoiled by the fact that he
and his companions would be spending another uncomfortable night in town, crowded together in the rollabout,
waiting for their "solar" vehicle's batteries to recharge for
the long trip back to the Project.

XX
DAY BEFORE YESTERDAY

... WHEN RENE RELAXED HIS GRIP UPON HER—OR WHEN SHE
IMAGINED HE HAD—WHEN HE SEEMED DISTRACTED, WHEN HE
LEFT HER IN A MOOD WHICH SHE TOOK TO BE INDIFFERENCE OR
LET SOME TIME GO BY WITHOUT SEEING HER OR REPLYING TO
HER LETTERS AND SHE ASSUMED THAT HE NO LONGER CARED TO
SEE HER AND WAS ON THE VERGE OF CEASING TO LOVE HER,
THEN EVERYTHING WAS CHOKED AND SMOTHERED WITHIN HER.
THE GRASS TURNED BLACK, DAY WAS NO LONGER DAY NOR
NIGHT ANY LONGER NIGHT, BUT BOTH MERELY ... PART OF HER
TORTURE ... SHE FELT AS THOUGH SHE WERE A STATUE OF
ASHES—BITTER, USELESS, DAMNED ...
—**Pauline Reage,** *Story of O*

For as long as he lived, the remainder of that afternoon
and most of the next day were nothing more than a
blur to him, filled with indistinguishable noises echoing as
if in a tunnel and the inexpressible pain of betrayal. Even
the stuffed game animals mounted on the walls around him
seemed to be leering.

Before Emerson knew what was happening, people all
around were on their feet and heading toward him. In
other circumstances it might have been a frightening experience for the boy. Those already close were laughing,
cheering, clapping him on the back. None of their congratulations meant a thing.

All he knew or felt was a loss he couldn't quite define.

For a few sweet hours he'd believed, without ever consciously realizing he believed it, that Gretchen had given herself to him. Now, suddenly, he was learning, and in the hardest way possible, the second-hardest lesson prerequisite to growing up—that no one ever truly belongs to anybody else. He'd long since learned the hardest lesson, and far less painfully, that other people were as real as he was.

As if in a nightmare, he looked around for Gretchen, every muscle in his body straining with an anguish that was more than physical, trying to see over and between the people mobbing him. She had disappeared and was nowhere to be seen. Preoccupied, he didn't notice the way Mrs. Singh was watching him, half analytically, half in sympathy, understanding at least a part of what he was going through.

"Whatya say we get the hell outa this riot?" she shouted over the noise, directly into his ear, and seized him by one arm. "I suspect we got a lotta talking to do!"

Several members of the unruly crowd of well-wishers pushing in upon them began to protest. Almost anything constituted a good excuse for a party among this frontier community, especially at the Nimrod, and Emerson's victory, although it had come as no surprise to any of them, was a better excuse than most. They didn't intend to let such an opportunity slip through their fingers.

Emerson never knew why he shook his head at his well-meaning landlady and gave in to the demands of those around him. Probably he dreaded hearing from her more unpleasant truths that should have been plain to him if only he'd opened his eyes. In any case, he shook her hand off and let himself be buried in the crowd.

The last thing he remembered clearly—after that it only came in bits and pieces—was being hauled by both wrists to the table where he'd seen that little blond and the other professionals from Galena's. Come to think of it, it was the little blond who'd done the hauling, aided by a dark-haired girl with freckles and startlingly blue eyes. Now that the tension of the hearing had begun to dissipate, and despite his personal concerns, he was noticing more about those around him, and one thing he noticed right away was that the girls all smelled strongly of perfume, a dozen varieties competing violently with one another.

Under the circumstances, especially in a hot, crowded, smoky room and wearing a hot, uncomfortable woolen suit, it was almost enough to make him sick.

It didn't help that they were all laughing and talking noisily and seemed to be making jokes at his expense. Although he thought they were speaking English, for some reason he couldn't understand a fraction of what they were saying. Perhaps it wasn't English. There appeared to be as much variety in the colors of their skin, and therefore possibly their nationalities, as in their costumes. The former occupied considerably more surface area than the latter. Only a couple of the girls were like the little blond and her blue-eyed friend. A couple more were black. Others were of various shades between the extremes. One had the same almond-shaped eyes he did and her skin was the same color as his own, but it was the little blond who seemed fascinated with him.

Maybe she thought he had some money.

If so, she had been misinformed.

Someone, the little blond again—why couldn't he remember her name?—shoved a long-stemmed glass under his nose, filled with something fizzy like a pale golden softdrink. Preoccupied with the sight of what seemed to be acres of half-clothed flesh all around him, he gulped it down. It tasted like a softdrink, too, its flavor somewhere between that of green grapes and fresh apples.

And it only made him thirstier.

He thought—although the actual memory was only a vague impression—that he drank a lot more of it. All he could hear in the background, above the babble of what seemed like thousands of other people in the room, was Aloysius Brody's mechanical piano, the one with thumb-tacks set in the felt of hammers driven by heavy punched-paper rolls, playing "Old-Fashioned Rock and Roll." At least the taxidermized animal heads seemed to be enjoying the music.

They were smiling at him now.

Emerson's next memory was of lying on a squeaky white cloud with a golden lining, still slightly sick to his stomach, having just been bathed by someone in a way—and at an anatomical location—that he hadn't ever been before by anybody but his mother. There was an angel looking over his shoulder—she was deeply tanned and there seemed to be something wrong about her feet—and another perched on his legs. There seemed to be something wrong about her robes. The sky above his head was pink and filled with floating purple orchids. Whenever he made the mistake of closing his eyes, the cloud whirled around and around.

He strained against the aching in his head and became aware, after a fashion, that the cloud was actually an over-stuffed mattress and quilt on a spindly brass bedframe with squeaky springs and that the sky was garishly printed wallpaper. The angel at his shoulder was a small bronze statue of a mermaid, sitting on a night table beside the bed. The someone who'd bathed him—only in one critical spot—and now sat on top of him, straddling his ankles, was the ubiquitous little blond. Somehow—he had no memory of the intervening period—she'd gotten him to her room on one of the upper floors of Galena's.

And now she was wearing only long mesh stockings and a bright red, satiny, corsetlike thing which was apparently designed to hold her stockings up but in the process left her round, firm breasts—and almost everything below her navel—exposed.

"Good morning, Sunshine!" She grinned down at him, nodding toward a window somewhere behind him. "Actually, it's only about one o'clock, and the night is young."

He tried to struggle up to his elbows, but she was too heavy and the bed was too soft. Also, his head hurt too much. He thought it must have been all the perfume. "I don't have any money." His voice came in a croak but he was quite sincere about what he said next, especially from the waist down, where—unlike from his neck up—everything still seemed to be working. "I'm terribly sorry."

"You keep on saying that," she replied with a momentary frown, then brightened. "If I cared about that, silly, we'd be in one of the cribs downstairs instead of here in my own room. We're gonna have fun. Pallas is a small world, and we can make the round trip as many times as you're up to it—and I can be a lotta help in that department, believe me. I liked you the first time I laid eyes on you, and I wanna help you celebrate how your hearing came out. Besides, who knows? You might turn out to be a steady customer someday."

"I, er . . ."

She frowned again, perplexed. "You know, you may be a grown man legally, Emerson Ngu, but you still smell just like a little boy. You don't smoke, do you?"

"Uh, no—" He was relieved. He'd thought she'd been about to ask if he were a virgin, and the only clever comeback he'd ever thought of to that question scarcely applied.

"Or drink coffee?"

"A little. Not really. I—"

"I thought so. Well, it's nice doing somebody who smells clean for a change." She grinned, then leaned forward so that he could only see the top of her head.

To his relief and disappointment—he'd never been aware before that a person could feel both of those emotions at once—everything went black again after that.

"Jealousy's a perfectly proper emotion, Emerson, don't let anybody tell you otherwise."

He shook his head, which still hurt, but didn't disagree with Mrs. Singh, although what she said was the opposite of what he'd been told all his life. In a utopian community where everybody was supposed to love everybody else—something told him that something may have been wrong with the terminology and that he wasn't dealing with the same kind of love in this instance—jealousy was at the top of a long list of unforgivably individualistic sins. Nor did it occur to him to question her assumption that jealousy was what he was feeling.

It was morning again, the day after the hearing at the Nimrod. He'd managed to stagger to the boardinghouse from Galena's an hour after sunrise, hung over (although he didn't know it) and aching severely from just below his navel to just above his knees. The worst was that he felt as though someone had punched a huge, hard, hairy fist into his bladder. The little blond—he still didn't know her name; after their third or fourth ultimate intimacy, he'd been too embarrassed to ask her—had been as good as her word about helping him.

She'd been a lot of help.

Probably too much, from the way the insides of his thighs chafed whenever he took a step.

She'd also been kind enough to let him shower at her place, help him to restore his suit to some semblance of decency, and even feed him a lavish breakfast. She'd have kept him even longer, she'd informed him sometime during the half hour she'd taken to kiss him good-bye, if she hadn't needed her "beauty sleep" for the long work night ahead. Something deep inside told him that he ought to have skulked back to Mrs. Singh's much earlier, in the dark, shamefaced and laden down with guilt, but, among other things, he was far too tired for that. And he'd had altogether too good a time—parts of him had, at least.

And Gretchen wasn't back yet, herself.

Mrs. Singh didn't know where she was.

In some ways, it was like that first day he'd come to this house. Mrs. Singh, who seemed to be as worried about him as she was about her own her daughter—perhaps even more so; he suspected she thought Gretchen better able to take care of herself—had made hot chocolate and they sat together now in her living room. Only the lighting was different. He'd arrived at night, in a rainstorm. Now the only dark clouds and freezing drizzle were inside of him.

"It's a species survival trait," she was going on, "which, among other functions, protects the home, the family, and insures the healthiest offspring possible."

He nodded dutifully, suspecting that the woman took some comfort from discussing this matter theoretically, abstractly. So did he, when it came to that. He didn't enjoy having to think about yesterday, or worrying about where Gretchen might be now. He enjoyed thinking about tomorrow even less.

Mrs. Singh finished her cup of chocolate and immediately poured herself another from the pot on the coffee table. He'd seen people at the Nimrod go through the same motions with a bottle of liquor. There was an open pack of cigarettes lying on the table beside the pot. Although she wasn't smoking now, the ashtray was full of burnt and crushed-out ends, many of them only partly consumed, apparently from the night before. Emerson had never had any idea that she smoked.

"Now you just imagine a bull elk, if you can, having

survived an entire season of the kind of antler-bashing that serves his species as natural selection—"

For once Emerson knew exactly what Mrs. Singh was talking about. As a sort of student hunter, he'd recently watched the ritual from a blind in a deep-woods game preserve, only a few yards away from the animals—with Gretchen.

"—then catching one of the second-rate males he's already bested, trying to beat his time with one of his cows." She snorted, reached out to the pack of cigarettes, evidently thought better of it, and pulled her hand back. "Now can you imagine that elk saying to himself that jealousy's just an immature emotional reaction resulting from his own insecurity and lack of self-confidence?"

Despite the way he felt, he laughed, spontaneously seeing, in his mind's eye, the ridiculous image of a gigantic bull elk lying on a psychiatrist's couch.

"Emerson." Mrs. Singh put a hand over his own where it rested on his knee. It was the first time she'd ever touched him that way, and he didn't know how to react, since neither his mother nor his father had been physically affectionate. He noticed that, exactly like Aloysius Brody, she tended to shed her folksy accent under stress. "Only humans are foolish enough to convince themselves they don't go through a selection process just as brutal in its own way, or that their homes and families and gene pool don't need protecting."

He nodded, not knowing what to say.

Mrs. Singh lifted her hand and sighed. "Lookie here, Emerson, I'm real sorry that Gretchen didn't see fit to tell you she had another suitor. We've had quite a number of set-tos about her privacy, me and that girl, which she won fair and square because she was dead right and made me see it. I sure as hell didn't figure it was my place to let you know which way the wind was blowing."

This time he patted her hand. So they'd finally come to it. "I don't blame you for anything, Mrs. Singh. You took me in when I didn't have anything, and trusted me when you hadn't any reason to. But why didn't she tell me? How long—"

She took the empty cup from his hand and poured from the pot, carefully not looking at him. "I expect young Altman's been making visits into town to see her, on an increasingly frequent basis, for about the last year. That's only a few weeks longer than you've been with us, isn't it? Since his old man kept referring to you as a child—unless that was all lawyer's horsehockey, intended for the politics of the moment—he was probably sneaking rides with the rollabout drivers under Daddy's nose. That could account for some of the hostility on Gibson Senior's part. I never knew what she saw in the boy—maybe he was the only face around here she hadn't grown up with—nor how far the whole thing went."

"But why—" Emerson stopped, realizing he didn't know what it was he'd meant to ask.

She shrugged. "And then you came along. But from Gretchen's viewpoint you were a tough nut to crack. I watched her try. I honestly believe, from something she said to me early on, that she thought you were gay. Pallatians are a pretty direct, outspoken folk, and she'd never seen anybody as bashful and reserved as you are. But it kept her interested, and once she figured it out, well . . ."

He kept his eyes on the carpet. "It wasn't that long ago. Only day before yesterday."

"I know," she nodded. "I thought she was never gonna get through to you, and I was glad to see it happen. But it did mean that, without either of you knowing it, you and young Gibson Ant-farm Junior were courting the same girl. I saw that coming and hoped you'd turn out to be the best man. My bet's that she made a decision in your favor

quite a while before day before yesterday and told him—
that's her idea of fair play—and that's why he ratted you
out to his father."

Before Emerson could say anything, the phone began
to chirp. Mrs. Singh answered it at the coffee table, where
the flat plane of a two-dimensional image formed in the air
above the surface. Even at his angle, which foreshortened
the image, Emerson could see it was Gretchen—apparently the phone she was calling from was more primitive
than those in Curringer—and his heart, possibly encouraged by what her mother had just told him, gave a leap in
his chest.

"Gretchen, baby!" the woman cried, delighted to see
her daughter. "Honey, all you all—"

*"This is a recording, Mother, because I don't want to argue
with you—or anybody else. I'm calling from the Residence at the
Greeley Utopian Memorial Project."*

Mrs. Singh gave him an uninterpretable look and
somehow turned the image so that he could see, too.

*"Gibson Junior proposed to me day before yesterday when he
was in town and I accepted. I came back with him yesterday and we
were married last night by his father."*

Even over his own feelings, which seemed to have deserted him for the moment, Emerson would remember the
stricken look in Mrs. Singh's eyes for as long as he lived.

Gretchen's expression appealed for understanding.
She appeared to have been doing a great deal of crying.
*"Mama, I'm trying my best to do what's right. Please tell Emer-
son . . . tell Emerson I hope he can forgive me. He'll meet other
girls. There's a little blond at Galena's who's had her eye on him
and really worried me for a while.*

"Anyway, I'll see you soon. Be well. I love you."

The image above the tabletop dissolved.

Emerson sat where he was on the couch, too stunned
at first to move or even think. The first thought that

managed to filter into his mind was that even though she was likely be residing with the Chief Administrator's family, it was a bizarre reversal.

Gretchen had taken his place at the Project.

And he would mourn the loss for the rest of his life.

XXI
THE PLUMP BROWN BANK

ALL THAT IS NEEDED TO GIVE RISE TO A MIGHTY NATION, GENERATE A WAVE OF PERPETUAL PROGRESS AND PROSPERITY WITHIN IT, EVEN REVIVE A DYING CIVILIZATION, IS A SIMPLE, IRREVOCABLE GUARANTEE THAT INDIVIDUAL MEMBERS OF THE PRODUCTIVE CLASS BE PERMITTED TO KEEP WHATEVER THEY CREATE. THAT IS WHAT AMERICA WAS SUPPOSED TO HAVE BEEN ABOUT; ITS PREEMINENCE IN THE WORLD IS A DIRECT RESULT. LIKEWISE, EACH OF ITS FAILURES ULTIMATELY STEMS FROM THE GRADUAL BUT UNRELENTING ABROGATION OF THAT GUARANTEE.
—**Mirelle Stein,** *The Productive Class*

W hat've you got there, Emerson?"
"Nails" Osborn, Emerson's employer and proprietor of Osborn's Plumbing & Machine Shop, leaned over the boy's shoulder to examine a number of oddly shaped metal plates laid out neatly on the bench. He was a big-shouldered, bearded man, closer to seven feet than six, with a clear tenor voice that usually took strangers by surprise. It was an hour after closing, and for the first time that month, Osborn had stayed at the shop after hours to catch up on the accounts.

Although it still smelled agreeably of heated cutting lubricant and other odors which are like a rare perfume to those who love machinery, the shop was darkened, the heavy equipment on the floor looming as ominous, bulky shadows against a back-lit latticework of skeletal supply shelves, except for a pilot glowing here and there, the glassed-in office cubicle where Osborn had been laboring, and the pool of light spilling onto Emerson's bench from a floodlamp clamped to its edge.

"An idea I've been working on for a few weeks." Emerson didn't look up, but instead applied a fine-surfaced file to an edge of one of the plates until he was satisfied with the way it felt under his work-blackened thumb. Peering critically at a small hole which had been drilled in it—the polished steel threw reflections of the lamplight onto his face—he set it aside and began inspecting the next plate.

Stainless could be tricky sometimes, and any burred edges on these pieces would spoil everything.

As an afterthought, he added, "In my spare time."

"I see." Osborn tapped a bent, flattened cigarette from the pack he made a habit of carrying in the left hip pocket of his greasy overalls, applied a lighter he'd constructed at this same bench, and exhaled smoke. "Not during working hours, I trust."

"I said in my spare time, didn't I?" The boy set down the plate he was examining and picked up the next. There were more than a dozen of them lying on the bench before him and he was only halfway finished with them. He'd almost run out of time because Mrs. Singh didn't like him skipping dinner. Also, although he didn't say so, he hated it when people watched what he was doing over his shoulder.

Surprised at the reaction, Osborn raised his eyebrows. "No need to get testy, Emerson. I'm the boss. I'm expected to say things like that. What the hell is it, anyway? It's kind of large for a surrealist's notion of a padlock." The largest of the plates would have just spanned his outstretched fingertips.

Emerson grinned, turned on the metal stool he occupied, straightened his back to relieve the ache that came from hunching over the bench, and pushed the magnifying glasses he was wearing back onto his forehead. When he looked up at Osborn, there were dark circles below his eyes where the frames had gathered oily sweat and working grime. "Pretty good guess. I got the idea from one of those laminated padlocks, made up of several layers of steel, riveted together."

Osborn nodded understanding. Locks were reasonably rare on the Outside, where people tended to trust one another—possibly because burglars seldom survived their initial foray into the field—but what locks there were had usually been sold, installed, or repaired by his shop. Emerson, of course, had seen plenty of locks in the Project, where, despite the goon patrols—or possibly because of them—almost every door and window required some sort of mechanical security.

For his curious employer's benefit, Emerson stacked the finished plates together with the unfinished ones until they began to assume a recognizable form. It was still very difficult for him to think about that terrible Sunday morning, almost a year ago now, when Gretchen Singh had disappeared forever from his life after changing it beyond recognition, but there were some less emotionally painful aspects of it to which he'd given considerable thought. One of them was that Senator Altman and his thugs would have had no trouble dragging him back to the Project against his will if he and the women hadn't had the means to deter them.

Sometimes he almost wished they had. He could always have escaped again. Junior wouldn't have had the opportunity, right after the hearing at the Nimrod, he assumed, to propose to Gretchen. And Gretchen . . . he shook off the thought, telling himself for perhaps the millionth time that it was pointless.

By now, he almost believed it.

"I'll be damned." Osborn shook his head, patted Emerson on the shoulder, and grinned down admiringly at the inch-high stack of stainless steel plates. "It's a pistol!"

"As far as I know it's the first to be manufactured on Pallas," Emerson told him, "or will be once it's finished. It's simple: straight blowback and double action only. Not counting springs, it'll only have four moving parts: slide, trigger, trigger bar—this part here—and striker. I knew Pallas doesn't have the industrial facilities to mass-produce guns or anything else by forging, machining, or casting, and I don't like ordinary stampings, so I chose lamination. The whole thing can be bolted together with four Allen screws."

Perhaps attracted by the warmth of the worklight, BCH, the "company cat," chose that moment to hop up on the bench and begin sniffing at the parts Emerson had there. Osborn took the animal in his arms and stroked its head until it laid its ears back and began to purr. Both humans fell silent for a long moment.

"And by unskilled labor," Osborn nodded at last, appreciating the boy's genius all over again. "But straight blowback, Emerson—no breech-locking system, just the inertia of the slide and the power of the recoil spring—that's an antique method only suited to obsolete pocket-pistol cartridges. You don't even have a hammer and mainspring to fall back on. You'll never sell a little popgun like that to Pallatians, especially the deer and elk hunters."

Emerson laughed and shook his head. "It's designed to be a fully powered 10 millimeter, Nails—since that seems about the most popular cartridge on this asteroid—with dual recoil springs so powerful that even you couldn't pull the slide back by hand. But you won't ever need to. See how the barrel tips up, like a break-action shotgun, so that you can slip the first round into the chamber?"

"Like an old .25 caliber Beretta," Osborn chuckled. "Well, any patents ever issued on that one ought to have expired by now. Who else did you steal ideas from?"

"Aside from Master Lock, you mean, and Astra, who made full-power straight blowbacks in the twentieth century? I think the trigger bar is my own idea. I think. See how it acts as its own trip-release and disconnector, camming on the frame?"

"And once you have a working model . . ." Osborn looked thoughtful. He'd acquired his nickname, and built what fortune he could lay claim to, by being the first individual to manufacture anything on Pallas—nails, badly needed by the early colonists, from heavy wire left by the terraformation crews. He gently set BCH down on the floor and began laying the parts out on the bench again the way Emerson had originally arranged them. ". . . what do you plan on doing with it?"

Emerson grinned, but without the slightest trace of humor. "I'm going to recruit some of that unskilled labor you mentioned and make a lot more just like it."

Her name, as it had turned out, was Cherry.

And she was much more than just one of the girls at Galena's. Among other things, she was the second-largest depositor at the First Pallatian Bank of Curringer.

The largest depositor was Aloysius Brody.

The late afternoon sun blasted through the plate-glass window and beat directly on his wool-covered belly and thighs. Emerson felt as uncomfortable as ever in the suit he hadn't worn since the first day he'd met Cherry, but Nails and Mrs. Singh had insisted it was important. They were with him now, in the office of the president of the bank, sitting across a genuine dark mahogany desk from that esteemed institution's first and second most important customers.

The banker himself was little more than a master of ceremonies.

"So that's your business plan, is it?" Brody asked rhetorically. "Well, me boy, it has the virtue of simplicity, and seems to cover the contingencies. Now for the fun part." He picked up the gleaming silvery object lying in the center of the banker's desk blotter. "I've seen this already, medear, and even fired it several times. There isn't any safety, and you can't pull the slide back. I can't, anyway. Remove the magazine and operate the barrel catch, like this." The rear of the barrel popped up. "You see, the chamber's empty."

"Why, thank you kindly, Aloysius." The little blond took the pistol, closed the chamber, and sighted it expertly at the shiny round seal of one of the bank president's certificates of civic virtue on the wall. She then bent down to get her bag from where it lay on the floor beside her chair, extracted an elderly-looking .45 automatic, and, having likewise emptied it, held it beside Emerson's invention, hefting each, then swapping them in her hands and hefting them again.

"It's quite a bit lighter than mine," she observed, "and a lot shorter. It feels better in my hand. 10 millimeter — won't that kick pretty hard, Emerson?"

"No harder than that .45 you have there, Cherry." He resisted the urge to shove a couple of fingers in his shirt collar and wrench it a few inches looser. Neckties, he was certain, must have been invented by the Spanish Inquisition. He wondered whom he had to confess his heresies to in order to get his neck out of this one. "There's an integral muzzle brake at the end of the barrel, and the middle of the backstrap, in the grip, is spring-loaded to absorb recoil, as well."

At least Cherry didn't make him feel nervous, the way some girls did. She smiled her most radiant nonprofessional smile and nodded. "I always knew you were smart, Emerson. I always knew that you'd amount to something big, and here you are. I like this little gun, I like you, and I'm going to invest in both of you."

Nails grinned broadly at Emerson and gave him a brotherly punch on the shoulder. As he was recovering, Aloysius and Mrs. Singh beamed approvingly at him, as well.

"Now, little lady—" the banker made throat-clearing noises and raised a plump brown hand to advise her from behind his desk "—that's no basis at all on which to make business decisions. I think it wisest not to be too hasty in this matter. After all, weapons are controversial in many quarters, and their manufacture somewhat questionable, ethically. At least we should begin with a series of market surveys."

He was a plump brown man all around, the boy thought to himself, in his plump brown suit, sitting here on his plump brown bottom behind his plump brown desk in his plump brown bank. At the moment, Emerson couldn't remember the man's name and didn't know where he'd come from—wherever lawyers and bankers and ministers always come from, he guessed, just when everybody else has things arranged the way they like it.

He certainly wasn't the Pallatian type.

Like me? he asked himself.

Like me, he decided. No matter how many of these little guns he made, he planned to go on carrying the Grizzly which hung heavily next to his right thigh where the braided tie-down bunched his trousers and put a wrinkle across the crease. *It's a new low,* he thought, *when you're getting revenge on a three-piece suit.*

Cherry frowned. "Now you just hush your mouth up, Glea Thomas," she insisted. "It's my money we're discussing here, and I think a little more respect is called for—for

the money, if not for myself." She smiled sweetly. "Otherwise, I'll just take it all to another bank—or maybe start
one of my own."

The banker blanched—and hushed. In a community
where fractional reserve banking—the lending of more
money by a bank than it holds in the form of deposits—
was considered an act of criminal fraud, banks often ran
out of spare cash of their own and had to court their customers into making loans. His once mighty profession had
been reduced to that of financial matchmaker.

Emerson could see Aloysius and Nails each stifling a
grin. Both were aware, as was Emerson himself and anyone else in town who frequented Galena's or the Nimrod,
that Thomas would like to have been one of *Cherry's* best
customers, but that she was too choosy and had declined
the offer on several occasions.

Emerson couldn't afford Cherry professionally, and
he'd had too much self-respect over the past year to presume on her charitable hospitality again, although they
often enjoyed each other's chance companionship at
Brody's establishment. She was the only Monopoly player
there who beat him regularly.

"I believe I'll second the lady's motion," Brody told
them all, taking the gun from Cherry and admiring it all
over again. "Cut me in for a third of the action."

"Make it a quarter, Aloysius, if we're going equal
shares." Mrs. Singh, being an expatriate American and a
bit old-fashioned about such things, was inclined to disap-
prove of Cherry on principle, owing to her profession, but
always warmed to the little blond after a few minutes' reac-
quaintance. "One for the young lady, one for you, one for
me, and one for Emerson for having invented the damned
thing. Don't get ahead of yourself, there's enough here for
everybody."

"Then let's make it a fifth, Mrs. Singh." Nails leaned in

to lay a huge, grimy hand on the banker's otherwise pris-
tine desk. After insisting that Emerson go home early and
put on his suit, he'd come straight from the shop wearing
his greasy work clothes. Emerson's suspicion that it was a
deliberate slight was immediately confirmed. "I managed
to scrape a little bit of money together at the last minute.
No thanks to you," he added, glaring at the banker.

The banker sighed and rolled his eyes, obviously dissatisfied with the barbaric way these colonials conducted
their affairs. Bankers didn't usually last long on Pallas,
Emerson knew. This one was the third in the last year, and
probably wouldn't last another quarter. They'd end up flying him back to one of the poles for transshipment to Earth
in a straitjacket. The last one had gone native, quit his job,
and was now a lone surveyor somewhere out in the weyers.

Come to think of it, it didn't sound like a bad life at
that.

"Then it's all settled except for the paperwork," the
banker announced, gamely enough, Emerson conceded. It
was the only way the man was going to make money on
this deal.

"That's right," Nails agreed. "It's all settled. And now
we're all going to get rich!"

"No," corrected Cherry, generating a look of extreme
pain on the banker's face. "I'm going to get richer."

Aloysius laughed and clapped his knees. "Medear, I
was about to say exactly the same thing!"

When Emerson and Mrs. Singh arrived back at the boardinghouse that afternoon, ready to prepare a festive dinner
for their old friends and new business partners, they found
a small inset green light glowing from one of the few items
of furniture set against the wall in her living room that was
not a bookcase.

"Looks like we got us some mail," his landlady observed. Like the boy, she was laden down with supplies they'd purchased on their way home. "Why don't you take a peek, Emerson, while I get these here groceries into the icebox."

More and more, since Gretchen had left them, Mrs. Singh had treated Emerson like a son. He was the only boarder she'd have asked to take a look at her mail. Emerson set down the bags he was carrying on the coffee table, gratefully removed his necktie and shoved it into a jacket pocket, and began unfastening the tie-down of his gunbelt. His three-piece suit had never been designed for such an accessory, and the weight of the weapon around his waist had grown increasingly uncomfortable throughout the long, unseasonably hot afternoon.

Or perhaps it was just having spent two hours of that afternoon with Cherry—and anticipating another couple of hours with her this evening—whom he was beginning to consider approaching on a personal, rather than professional, basis. Thinking pleasant thoughts of a kind he hadn't for many months, he went to the elaborately decorated cabinet, half again as tall as he was, and opened the double doors to inspect the output of the printer it contained. It was this device which the present message had sought out and found.

The physical delivery of mail was something of a hit-or-miss proposition on Pallas, as it had become in many places on Earth most people would have regarded as civilized.

Partly this was a consequence of unreliable state monopolies on letter delivery, made worse in recent decades by the gradual collapse of government institutions in general. Partly, however, it was simply a result of technical progress. Three-quarters of the mail sent and received in the twentieth century needn't have been sent at all, and most of the remaining quarter would have traveled faster and more cheaply—and with a greater guarantee of privacy—electronically.

The message was from Gretchen, the first they'd received since her recorded phone call of more than a year ago. Not knowing precisely what he was feeling—he supposed he should have known that this was inevitable—he tore it from the printer and reluctantly took it to the kitchen. It was from this moment on, he realized many years later, that he first began thinking of Mrs. Singh— because from this moment she'd begun acting that way— as an old woman.

> *Mr. and Mrs. Gibson Altman, Jr.*
> *are pleased to announce*
> *the birth of their daughter*
> *Gwendolyn Rosalie*

XXII
LUNCHBOX SPECIALS

. . . DESIGNED TO BE DROPPED INTO ENEMY-OCCUPIED ALLIED COUNTRIES. THE IDEA . . . ORIGINATED WITH THE JOINT PSYCHOLOGICAL COMMITTEE. THE ORDNANCE DEPARTMENT MADE UP . . . SKETCHES OF A [SINGLE-SHOT] WEAPON . . . MADE OF STAMPINGS WITH A . . . SMOOTHBORE BARREL MADE OF SEAMLESS STEEL TUBING . . . GUIDE LAMP DIVISION OF GENERAL MOTORS MANUFACTURED ONE MILLION OF THESE PISTOLS BY 21 AUGUST 1942 AT A COST OF SLIGHTLY OVER $1.71 EACH.
W.H.B. Smith, *Book of Pistols and Revolvers*

T he first hundred "Ngu Departure" semiautomatic pistols were manufactured in a flimsy annex, no more than a shed, hastily thrown up behind Osborn's Plumbing & Machine Shop.

While Emerson cut stainless plates on a bandsaw and Nails drilled them for the connecting bolts—as well as the crosspins that would hold the parts inside the assembled frames—Aloysius wielded a chambering reamer on the barrel blanks which the two machinists had already cut and turned to the correct outside dimensions.

Cherry, doing the job Nails had interrupted the night Emerson first discussed the idea with him, made certain all components were properly finished.

Mrs. Singh took the completed parts and turned them into pistols.

They all took turns proof- and function-testing the finished product through the back door of the shed, which let out onto nothing but empty prairie behind the town.

Toward the end, when they'd already begun receiving prepaid orders, all the partners stayed up late into the night, laboring to make sure the orders were filled on time. Sometimes Emerson wondered if the profit would cover all the coffee they consumed. The whole process taught him and his friends a great deal that they'd thought they already knew about mass production. As one consequence, a brief interval followed during which the partners actually refused to take anybody else's money until they all felt they were truly ready.

The second hundred pistols, along with every other weapon Emerson and his little company ever made, were completed six months later in a modest factory building erected—neither by accident nor coincidence—on an unclaimed plot of land just five miles outside the gate of the Greeley Utopian Memorial Project. The consequences of that decision would reverberate for almost a century afterward.

Exactly as Emerson intended.

Although he kept his principal motive to himself at the time, Emerson had already learned something from his many jobs and everything that had happened to him since he'd run away from the Project. Arguing one strangely idle night in the Nimrod—shortly after the first run of pistols had been completed (and sold out within just a few hours of KCUF's public announcement of their availability)— with those friends of his who'd been willing to take a risk with him against the possibility of a profit (and then added their sweat to his to raise that possibility to a probability), he emphasized the point that the manufacturing business they'd started together was completely dependent on hand assembly.

"Yes," he replied impatiently to someone's objection, "I know exactly how far away it is. Didn't I ride the whole way in the cargo rack of a rollabout where I could count every last corrugation in a road consisting of nothing but washboard? Didn't I measure every desolate mile—every yard—between there and here? But it's also where the cheapest available labor on the asteroid happens to be—"

Aloysius laughed heartily. "Not to mention ten thousand potential new customers!"

One of their "old" customers chose that moment to pass by their table, drink in hand, patting Aloysius and Emerson on the back by turns and pointing happily to a worn and weather-stained pistol belt hanging on the elk rack at the back of the bar with a brand-new, shiny Ngu Departure pistol resting in its holster.

"There is that," Emerson acknowledged, once these congratulations were over with. His attention had strayed momentarily to the fans hanging from the ceiling overhead. He'd always liked them for some reason he couldn't quite get hold of. They'd been imported from Earth, originally. Aloysius had once told him that he'd been required to step down the speed of their motors in order to keep them from blowing drinks off the tables—not to mention his clientele off their chairs—in the low Pallatian gravity.

Tonight, looking up at them made him think about his secret boyhood dream of flying over the Rimfence to freedom.

"Steady down now, boys," advised Cherry. "We've got a lot more planning to do before we choose a manufacturing site. In the first place, the good Senator—"

"The good *former* Senator," Nails corrected her.

"I'd say the only good Senator is a former Senator," Mrs. Singh observed smugly. She peered down into her coffee cup and frowned at the reflection she saw there.

Cherry ignored them. "—will never let his people go to work for us. In the second place, even if he did by some miracle, he'd never, ever let them have guns. Sometimes I think that was the whole point of the Project in the first place. And in the third place, how could any of them possibly afford to buy one?"

"I think you had two first places in there somewhere," Nails told her quietly. Emerson had always privately suspected that he was a little bit afraid of her.

Mrs. Singh shook her head. "Lookie here: when automobiles were first produced, they cost a couple of thousand dollars apiece. That's old American dollars, at about thirty-five to the ounce of gold. Which was way more than anybody but rich people could afford back then—not that I remember it personally, mind you.

"Then along came Henry Ford, with a mind to put the whole damn country on wheels, and car pricing was never the same afterward. He charged a flat eight hundred dollars, and when his higher-priced competitors came around to whine about it, he explained that if the average individual who worked in his car factory couldn't afford to buy one of his cars, there wasn't any point to making them."

"I stand corrected," Cherry replied. "I guess. I've never been in a business before where anyone gained anything by economy of scale and volume pricing."

Aloysius laughed again.

Emerson grinned, too. "For as long as anyone remembers, gunshops around here have been demanding three gold ounces—at about a thousand New American Dollars per—for anything that'll shoot. And they're the same old clunkers, recycled and recirculated, that have been here since they were first brought up from Earth by all of you people. Meanwhile, the gunshop owners complain constantly that business is flat."

"We asked half an ounce for ours," Aloysius agreed, "and sold a hundred on the same day."

The partners were interrupted again when the Jacksons, Mrs. Singh's other steady boarders, stopped by to ask Emerson a technical question about the pair of consecutively numbered pistols they'd just taken delivery on. In Lenda's hand were two delicate glasses and a bottle of the Nimrod's most expensive wine, which they'd bought to celebrate the occasion. Emerson noticed the gaze of her husband Charlie straying to the Grizzly hanging in its heavy belt on the back wall. Aloysius and the others had argued that it was bad business for the boy not to be carrying one of the guns he'd designed. Emerson had answered that the Ngu Departure was for people who didn't already have weapons they were satisfied with.

"We could have sold twice as many," Nails added when the Jacksons had left, "at twice the price. I knew this guy, one time, who hand-made the best five-string banjos in the solar system. But he damn near starved to death because his prices were so low it looked suspicious, like he was selling junk or something. Nobody bought from him until he doubled what he'd been asking for them."

Emerson nodded. "Except that we won't. You once asked me, Nails, what else I'd stolen from the old Earthside gun outfits when I showed you my first prototype, remember?"

Nails gave him a dubious look. "Yeah, I remember."

"Well, Mrs. Singh's house is full of history books," he explained, "and I've read as many of them as I had time for. There's a good deal more in the past that any halfway intelligent entrepreneur can use than just simple design features. Whether we ever state it publicly or not, Nails, I've adopted the motto from the old Iver Johnson Arms & Cycle Works: 'Honest Goods at Honest Prices.' "

"Honest goods at honest prices," Cherry remarked brightly. "Now that's something I *do* understand."

Emerson turned to the little blond. "The Chief Administrator may not have any choice much longer about what he lets his workers do, Cherry. I think there's something going terribly wrong out there. We've all noticed how the quality of the produce the rollabouts bring to Curringer seems to get worse every week."

"Something odd must be going on," she agreed, "because the drivers don't spend any time at Galena's any more while their machines are recharging overnight."

Emerson remembered that driving produce deliveries had been a privilege individual workers competed for. The temporary freedom of the town must have been a major inducement in obtaining volunteers for the long trip from the Project and back.

"More to the point, perhaps," suggested Aloysius, "they're not spending any money, not at Galena's, not here at the Nimrod, nor any other place here about."

Emerson went on. "I keep hearing rumors of all kinds. What they boil down to is that there's a rampage of violence and petty crime going on out there, basically because orders are dropping off and Altman's people have less and less to do."

"And you plan to give them work." Cherry nodded. "I saw that coming. It's one reason I invested in the company. It's something you can do to help your parents and your little brothers and sisters, even though they all still refuse to talk to you or see you. I knew there was a good reason I like you, Emerson."

Inwardly, Emerson cringed at Cherry's words. He was all too well aware that Cherry liked him, and that she was almost as beautiful as Gretchen had been. But with the best will in the world on both their parts, she wasn't Gretchen, she could never be Gretchen, and they both knew that nothing would ever change that.

What bothered him now was that, given what she did for a living, she was far too trusting, and he didn't have the heart to disillusion her. What he'd been seeking to accomplish with this plan of his was something a good deal more like revenge than charity. At a healthy profit, of course—remembering his fantasy of flight had awakened another memory. He wouldn't cheat his partners.

But why was it that whenever he looked up at those damned ceiling fans, he thought about the Rimfence?

Aloysius, who knew Emerson—in the present context, at least—far better than Cherry ever would, spoke up. "I hear me share of rumors, too, me boy."

"Such as?" inquired Mrs. Singh. Something about Emerson was beginning to worry her.

"Such as the Project security stooges are now arming themselves not only with those so-called 'shock batons' they were issued at first and which once constituted their only armament, but with light automatic assault rifles—'bullpups,' they call 'em—recently sent from Earth in answer to the risin' unrest inside the cooperative."

That got Emerson's attention off the ceiling.

Nails grinned admiringly. "Where in God's name do you manage to hear these things, Aloysius?"

"A crystal ball he keeps behind the bar," Cherry suggested.

"To go with his wooden leg?" Nails asked sweetly.

Mrs. Singh shook her head. "No, Cherry, he's got a Tarot deck up his sleeve, tucked in with the regular aces." It was the first joke she'd ever made with the girl.

"Now in truth, were I a good journalist, I'd be after wantin' t'protect me sources." The innkeeper shrugged. "But since, unlike former senators an' suchlike, the only good journalist is a dead journalist, in this instance I had it from a cargo handler at the North Pole to whom I send an occasional case of Irish cheer in exchange for tidbits exactly like this. The weapons in question are 2.8 millimeter hypersonics—.11 caliber, if y'can imagine it—individually safety-keyed t'special coded magnetic rings which the goons wear, and which must be destroyed before they can be removed from their cold, dead fingers."

"Well," observed Mrs. Singh, "so much for that idea."

"Some tidbit." Nails shook his head. "What idea?"

Brody nodded. "There's more. What's worse—for them, not for us—is that a radio control link prevents their bein' fired without the electronic consent of their regimental muckety-muck, safe in his command post behind the lines."

Emerson nodded understanding. The arrangement his friend was describing was idiotic and suicidal—and thoroughly consistent with the way he'd been brought up.

Cherry sat back and sighed. "Gee, it must be a comfort to the men out in the field who need to shoot in a hurry and can't get their little guns to work because their boss has gone to the powder room. What *do* these things shoot, anyway, death rays?"

"They use self-consuming caseless cartridges," Brody explained, "designed not t'be picked up an' reused by the subject population—an' ultravelocity Lexan bullets. Both weapons and ammunition are shipped out to the Project in sealed containers, inventoried at both ends in an attempt t'keep 'em out of undesirable hands."

Nails nodded. "Then that was a pretty good guess you made at Emerson's hearing about Altman's real reasons for having dared to venture out among us barbarians."

"Either that," suggested Mrs. Singh, "or Hizzoner, here, gave him the bright idea there and then." Occasional mention of the hearing was as close as any of them ever got to discussing what had become of Gretchen. Her name was never spoken among them, not because they were angry, but because her absence was too painful.

Cherry hadn't known Gretchen, but respected her friends' grief and obeyed the custom.

Aloysius gave Mrs. Singh a sour look.

"I don't believe the poor man's capable of having one all by himself," she went on, "or they wouldn't have stuck him out here in the back of beyond with all of us."

Wrenching his attention back to the conversation and away from the ceiling fans, Emerson shook his head. "That wasn't my hearing, Mrs. Singh, it was the Chief Administrator's. And I think it's extremely dangerous to underestimate the man. They do say he could have been President of the United States, after all."

"I rest my case," declared Mrs. Singh. Puzzled at Emerson's behavior, she peered up at the ceiling, following his example, but she didn't see what he'd begun to see.

"Emerson's right on both counts," Aloysius insisted. "It was no guess. The only human factor that never changes is the blind instinct of those who've obtained power t'maintain it. It was your own husband who said that—or was it Bertrand de Jouvenel? Anyway, it was the only thing that made sense under the circumstances."

He leaned forward, across the table. "In many ways, Emerson, those guns are the exact opposite, philosophically speakin', of the ones we're makin'. There's nothin' like a quick-firin' high-capacity assault rifle for defendin' life, liberty, an' the pursuit of property, but these things're designed specifically to oppress the individual rather than allow him to liberate himself."

There were murmurs of agreement from everyone around the table.

Emerson believed that Aloysius was correct. In startling contrast to what he'd just heard described, he'd revived an older, simpler technology made economical once again by the metal-rich Pallatian geology. His large-caliber semiautomatic pistols employed reloadable brass cases, molded lead bullets, and the same smokeless propellant powder now manufactured and widely used on the asteroid for construction and demolition. His weapons may have been old-fashioned—although they were of an improved, compact design featuring more sophisticated alloys and many fewer moving parts—but they were cheap and reliable.

In short, he explained, they were precisely what was needed by colonists with such a long, expensive supply line back to their mother planet. What's more, he informed Cherry, from the standpoint of their affordability by the impoverished Project peasants, he planned to allow easy credit. And hadn't Henry Ford also nearly doubled the going wage for automobile workers, he asked Mrs. Singh, for exactly the same reason that he'd cut the going price for automobiles?

"Oh, pshaw, as people of my age are supposed to say now and again—though I was never quite sure how to pronounce it—I hate it when you're right, boy." Her expression, almost that of a proud mother, gave the opposite impression.

Arms *and* cycles. Henry Ford putting "the whole damn country on wheels." The ceiling fans and the Rimfence. Why did it all seem like it should mean something?

One thing Emerson didn't tell his friends that evening was that he was also counting secretly on at least some of his cottage hand-assemblers to create "lunchbox specials" from pilfered parts—and take no serious steps to prevent it. In fact, his production scheme was designed specifically to encourage it.

The whole thing reminded him of an old drawn-out Russian joke he'd once heard about smuggling wheelbarrows, but ultimately it would mean that peasant families like his own would no longer be bullied by United Nations goons, however impressively armed. People, he had learned since coming to Curringer and living among free individuals, defend themselves with character, not with technology.

The latter was only one means among many; the former was indispensable.

It was a lesson many leaders of technically advanced nations back on Earth had either never learned or had forgotten as soon as it was forcibly impressed upon them. Emerson intended to remind at least one of them all over again.

But first, he had to get back to the shop.

He'd just had an idea he wanted to try out.

XXIII
THE WINGS OF EMERSON

I'VE ALWAYS BELIEVED IT SAYS SOMETHING SIGNIFICANT ABOUT
HUMANITY THAT IN THE SEVEN OR EIGHT MILLENNIA WE'VE
BEEN FIGHTING WARS, WE HAVEN'T MADE A TINY FRACTION OF
THE TECHNICAL PROGRESS WE'VE MADE IN THE MERE CENTURY,
FROM KITTY HAWK TO THE ASTEROIDS, THAT WE'VE BEEN
FLYING. PEOPLE FLY MUCH BETTER THAN THEY FIGHT. NICE
THOUGHT, ISN'T IT?
> —**William Wilde Curringer,** *Unfinished Memoirs*

It was a crude-looking lash-up.

As soon as he was able to make excuses, Emerson had left his friends at the Nimrod and hurried back to the machine shop. Seyfried Road, the main—and basically only—street of the town, was all but deserted, and the stars twinkled fiercely through the atmospheric envelope.

Nails was accustomed to taking on almost any sort of job, especially since he'd hired Emerson to assist him, which people thought they couldn't do for themselves. In the tavern, the boy had suddenly remembered the pair of big electric office fans that some customer had left sitting on their front counter near the door. Their heavy cast-iron bases, it seemed, weren't quite heavy enough, in Pallas's minimal gravity, to keep them wherever they were put. Propelled partly by their own blades, partly by the vibration of their motors, they tended to drift along a surface until they found an edge and fell off onto the floor.

Nails had purposed fixing them in two ways. First, their bases would be replaced with screw-adjustable spring clamps like those he used to mount flood lamps on the edges of working surfaces throughout his own shop. Since the fans also tended to blow everything downwind of their blades into the air—and apparently their customer's cat was getting tired of being thrown against the nearest wall in the middle of a nap—Nails would step the motors down electrically, exactly as he'd done a few years ago with the overhead fans at Brody's place.

The job still wasn't done.

With all of the hurry, recently, to complete the first run of pistols—"crawl" might have been a more appropriate word—Nails hadn't gotten around to modifying the office fans yet, and neither had Emerson. Their customer hadn't complained, not very energetically, anyway, because he was on the Ngu Departure waiting list.

Taking what might be his last appreciative look at the starry sky and the darkened storefronts of Curringer for quite a time—there was no telling in advance how long he'd labor over this crazy idea he'd had (or that had him) before he even ate or slept again—the boy let himself into the machine shop. Reflexively, he reached up to silence the bell tinkling above the doorframe and greeted BCH, the cat, who'd come to investigate this uncustomary intrusion.

Switching on a light, he saw that the fans, complete with work order and claim tags, were still gathering dust on the front counter where they'd been left weeks ago.

For a moment, as BCH stropped happily at his shins, he allowed himself to stop and admire the fans. They were perfect for his experiment, with 16 inch blades mounted in lightweight wire cages, driven by big 45 watt motors. Then, in an instant, he had a screwdriver in his hand and the heavy bases off. In another, he'd duct-taped the two machines to either end of a four-foot piece of scrap electrical conduit, their cords running to the head of a switching extension cord he'd attached to the center of the conduit at a point convenient to his thumb.

With mounting excitement, as he gathered up the free end of the extension cord and maneuvered this unlikely collection of parts into the assembly shed, which had more overhead, he considered the one and only time he'd ever given swimming a try—at Gretchen's insistence—in a perfectly circular swimming pool with natural glass sides and bottom, the remnant of a primordial meteor strike between what, millions of years later, would become the town site and the lake.

Fed by a tiny sun-warmed trickle of a stream momentarily delayed on its journey downhill to Lake Selous, the water had been surprisingly clear, fresh—from time to time the local volunteer fire company washed the algae out with their high-pressure hoses—and not too cold. Nor had it turned out quite as deep as he'd expected. Among a number of other silly things, he'd attempted standing up, with his feet planted none too firmly either side of a discarded inner tube, and very nearly gotten away with it in the low Pallatian gravity, but wound up, instead, standing on his head for an instant at the bottom of the pool.

Which was how he'd learned about mouth-to-mouth resuscitation—also at Gretchen's insistence—and eventually decided, reluctantly, not to count it as a kiss.

Such a memory—of his tawny, emerald-eyed Gretchen at her happiest, her beautiful, long-legged swimsuit-clad body wet and sparkling in the sunlight—should have been painful, but in this instance it was instructive, which for Emerson, at least, made all the difference. The fans would have to be above him, where his weight would hang below and balance naturally. Accordingly, he moved the extension head, with its neon-lit rocker switch, to a shorter piece of conduit which he hung a foot beneath the longer piece like the rung of a rope ladder, using a pair of multilayered straps of duct tape. He plugged the cord in across the room, near the back door of the shop, at what had once been an all-weather outlet.

Only mildly curious—because he hadn't been ordered

to stay away—BCH sniffed at the cord where it was plugged in, then hurried back across the room after Emerson, anxious to reassume his feline responsibility to be underfoot whenever possible.

Emerson, meanwhile, laid the longer piece of conduit across the narrow gap between two of the firearms-assembly tables, so that each of the fans rested facedown on a separate surface. He made sure that the oscillator clutches built into the fan housings were disengaged and that the rotary switches on the motors were turned all the way up. Unable to think of any more preliminaries, he sat down on the floor between the tables, removed the cat from his lap several times, took a deep breath, and grasped the hanging rung with both hands.

"Well," he informed BCH, unconsciously imitating Mrs. Singh, "here goes nothin'!"

"Brrow?" replied the cat.

Emerson thumbed the rocker switch.

Before he knew what was happening, both his arms were yanked almost out of their sockets. His feet were wrenched from his shoes. He and his electric contrivance smashed violently against the ceiling. Without thinking, he let go of the bar and fell—more gently than he might have on Earth—to the concrete floor again, hitting a worktable apiece with his hips and shoulders on the way down. Ignoring his impact-damaged posterior, he huddled on the floor between the tables, arms over his head, waiting for the fans to fall and crush his skull.

BCH had teleported from the room.

To the boy's surprise, the infernal machine was still overhead, bobbing and clanging against the corrugated metal ceiling like a maddened bumblebee suicidally determined to break through a pane of glass. The resulting noise was dreadful—and absolutely wonderful. Only Emerson Ngu and perhaps a few other pioneering spirits would have said what he did as, making sure that all of his body parts were still in the right places, he clambered painfully to his feet.

"It works!"

"What works?"

He turned, too excited with his success—and numb from his bruises—to be startled. "Oh. Hi, there, Cherry. When I ask, will you please unplug that extension cord from the wall over there? Wait a minute, let me get up on this table first."

BCH was in the girl's arms, trying frantically to bury his head between her breasts. She looked dubious, as people often did when asked to deal with Emerson's ideas, but—also as they often did—obeyed him. Overhead, the clanging noise abruptly stopped. The whirring of the fan blades descended in pitch rapidly until they, too, fell silent. The young inventor easily fielded his primitive flying machine as it dropped. Assuring himself that it was essentially undamaged, he carefully laid it on the table and hopped down to the floor.

"I was on my way home from the Nimrod," Cherry told him, sounding apologetic. "I saw the lights as I walked past, so I came in. I hope it's not—"

"It's terrific." He brushed grit from the shop floor out of his hair, wondering what a cast for both a broken hip and shoulder blade would look like. "I'm grateful you were here to help me, Cherry. Otherwise I'd have had to unplug it myself and let the whole thing fall wherever it wanted— and they're not my fans."

Setting the cat down on its feet on one of the tables, she came close and helped him brush at his clothes. "Maybe not, but I certainly am—here, you've cut yourself."

The short sleeve of his shirt was torn. There was also a long shallow scratch along his upper arm, from one of the tabletops, but it had already stopped bleeding.

"Uh, Cherry . . ." For the first time this evening, he noticed how she was dressed, in pink velvet shorts with a matching top that left her midriff bare—unlike most Pallatians, she wasn't wearing a pistol belt; these days she carried a Ngu Departure in a compartment between the halves of her handbag—and demonstrated beyond the shadow of a doubt that she was a female mammal. She wore no makeup and there was the faintest scattering of freckles across her nose. For some time, he realized, she'd been using a great deal less perfume than when he'd met her.

Possibly none at all.

"Sorry." She backed away. "You'll never know how sorry." She muttered under her breath and changed the subject. "What in the world are you doing here, anyway?" She glanced at the lashed-together fans lying on the table, BCH giving them a cautious going-over. "Is this another invention? What's it supposed to do?"

Emerson grinned. "It's supposed to fly. And take me with it. And—for a moment—it did."

Cherry gave a delighted squeal and clapped her hands. "You weren't yourself at all tonight back there at the Nimrod. I knew you had something on your mind!"

"You bet I did," he told her excitedly. "I still do. I think I know what I did wrong, and how to fix it. You want to come to the office with me for a minute?"

She looked puzzled. "Sure. How come?"

"Because there's something in there I need."

With BCH trailing along in front of them, as cats will, Cherry followed Emerson to the glassed-in office cubicle, where, in a matter of moments, he had a chair upside-down on the floor and was attacking it with a screwdriver. The upper part of the chair, consisting of the seat, arms, and railed back, was wooden, the lower part, with its swivel base and casters, mostly made of steel.

"Isn't that the antique oak swivel chair that Nails brought with him personally from Earth?" Cherry asked. "I seem to recall his saying that it belonged to his great-grandfather. And please don't try to tell me he'll never miss it."

"Don't worry," the boy replied, pulling the last screw out of the underside of the seat. He stood and seized the top of the chairback in one hand. "I'll put it back exactly the way it was as just as soon as I'm through with it. Besides, if he were here, Nails would be the first one to suggest using it."

He pushed past her through the door.

"Okay, don't mind me," she warned him as she followed him back to the assembly shed. BCH sniffed curiously at the truncated and abandoned chair base, complained vocally about it, and then hurried to catch up with them. "It's your funeral."

This time, trying to guess where the center of gravity would be when someone was sitting in the seat, Emerson duct-taped a fan to each arm of the chair where he could easily reach the three-speed controls, and turned both knobs to the lowest settings. He attached the rocker switch to the right arm, and, feeling a bit silly sitting on the floor in a legless chair, turned to Cherry, who was looking more uncertain about the whole thing with every minute that passed.

"Speaking of funerals," he grinned at her, putting the cat off his lap, "would you care to come and get this animal and then plug in the extension cord again?"

She shrugged and complied.

He depressed the rocker switch.

This time, Emerson's ascent to the ceiling was less spectacular. The lowest setting wasn't enough to lift his weight and that of the heavy chair. Careful to make both adjustments simultaneously, he turned the knobs to the middle speed and began to rise, swinging his legs back and forth to balance the load.

He reached up gently and touched the ceiling. "This is great, Cherry! You should try it!"

"After they work the bugs out." She laughed nervously. "Don't run out of extension cord!"

Emerson had pushed, tilting the motor housings a few degrees, and began to move forward. With Cherry's advice in mind, he pulled on the housings and returned to his original position. Pushing and pulling at the same time allowed him to pivot. He pulled and pushed, reversing the process, and turned the other way.

This time, BCH had stayed to watch.

"Now it really is a swivel chair!"

Cherry had been keeping a cautious eye on the outlet. Now she turned her face up and looked at him. "Yeah, but how do you get down—besides the one obvious way?"

"Simple—I think." Emerson turned the speed-control knobs—almost losing his balance in the process and tumbling out of the chair—to the lowest setting and descended smoothly to the floor. He switched the fans off and, feeling slightly weak in the knees, stood up. BCH stropped his ankles and buzzed at him.

"You're right, though, there are a few bugs to work out. For one thing, having a seat in this chair only complicates things. All it needs is a back and a pair of arms. I can easily carry my own weight on my forearms—we're only talking about twelve pounds, after all—and let my legs dangle as a counterweight, like the tail of a kite."

"Swell."

"For another, if this thing is going to be any use as transportation, I'm going to have to figure out another power source besides plugging it into the wall outlet."

"Transportation," she murmured, beginning to see the possibilities. "Do you realize that this could change everything, transform the face of Pallas almost as drastically as terraformation? Emerson, we could have other towns—more customers! Count me in for another fifth! When do we start making these things?"

It was Emerson's turn for a dubious look. Even with all the talk about Henry Ford at the Nimrod tonight, it had never occurred to him that they might manufacture and sell something like this contraption.

But Cherry was right; it could change everything.

Everybody he knew had always been dissatisfied with the clumsy, expensive, inappropriate surface transport available on Pallas, which only had one road—if that was the word for it—from the North Pole to the South Pole via Curringer, with a side spur to the Greeley Utopian Memorial Project. Most Pallatians hated it so much that they traveled, when they had to, by the same ultralight aircraft—hardly more than underpowered gliders, really—that had been used to seed the little planet after it had been terraformed, and which had won William Wilde Curringer his monument out there in the street.

According to Mrs. Singh and her husband's books, Henry Ford had put an entire nation on wheels.

Maybe Emerson Ngu was going to send the population of a whole world into the sky.

His dubious look turned into a grin, then broke out in laughter. Cherry threw her arms around his neck and he whirled her around and around before he put her down. By that time, of course, the cat had given up and vanished all over again. Cherry seized the moment and locked her mouth on his until they both ran out of breath.

She let him go reluctantly.

"I wasn't exactly telling the truth about why I came in," she told him with her eyes on the floor. Her arms were still around his neck—she was perhaps half an inch taller than he was—and if she was wearing any perfume, he couldn't detect it. He realized that his hands were resting on the bare flesh of her waist.

He swallowed hard and cleared his throat. "I kind of wondered why I didn't hear the bell."

"I didn't let it ring." She kept her eyes down and spoke softly. "I was sort of sneaking up on you. You've been avoiding it, but I was going to be real insistent this time. I'm tired of looking at you across a Monopoly board, Emerson. If I see one more little green plastic house or red hotel, I'm going to scream. You won't get out of jail free this time. I'm taking the next couple of days off and I'm going to drag you back home to my place and cheer you up!"

He nodded, not knowing exactly what he was feeling, only that a certain heated tautness throughout his body, which he'd only felt once before, was coming back whether he wanted it to or not. "But I don't need cheering up, Cherry."

She looked up and dazzled him with her smile. The harsh lights of the shop made her hair glow like a golden cloud. "I know. Now you need to celebrate! *Please?*"

"I don't deserve you, Cherry." He reached up, took her arms from around his neck — then put his arms around her. An individual, he realized, could only withstand so much mourning, so much self-denial. He may even have known that a healthy young man can only withstand so much celibacy, especially under the pleasant onslaught of someone like Cherry. "But I'll go home with you. How can I resist?"

"Good!" She gave him a rough kiss on the cheek, stood back from him abruptly, clapped her hands with joy, then seized one of his hands and pulled him toward the door. "We'll have fun. You don't remember asking me about the little mermaid on my dressing table, do you? And I know damn well that you don't remember how I answered you.

This time, Emerson Ngu, I swear you'll remember everything!"

He didn't know whether to take that as a promise or a threat.

But he took it.

XXIV

REVENGE AT A PROFIT

BUT THE GROWING OF THE MOUSTACHE IS AN ART, HASTINGS. I
HAVE SYMPATHY WITH ALL WHO ATTEMPT IT.
—Hercule Poirot in *Double Sin*, **Agatha Christie**

Emerson plummeted like a stone.

The wind screamed past his ears, whipping at his long silk scarf and forcing his cheeks into a frightful grin beneath the lower rims of his goggles. He could feel it riffling the sparse hairs he was encouraging to grow along his upper lip.

He'd have been grinning even without the wind's help. He had just reached up and touched the sky, fulfilling in every detail his boyhood dream of flight.

He remembered it perfectly.

It hadn't been that long ago, after all.

The plastic atmospheric envelope beneath his fingers had felt exactly as he'd expected. In fact, it had been *above* his fingers, and he'd almost lost his balance and tipped over into an unplanned dive when he'd reached up to touch it.

It had even gone *blimp!* when he'd flicked it.

The one thing he'd missed, which would have made it perfect, would have been to surprise one of the spacesuited maintenance contractors on the other side of the transparent "smart" material that sheltered the asteroid and gave it such spectacular sunsets, but the odds had been against it. Repair crews from the North and South Poles had a lot of territory to cover in their never-ending rounds.

In the end, he'd been satisfied just to look up at the stars, visible in broad daylight this close to the envelope, to regard the miniaturized features of the surface beneath his swinging heels, and to surprise the occasional passing bird. All too soon, the battery-level indicator under the palm of his right hand told him he had just enough power left to return safely to the ground, five miles down.

Five miles.

Far beneath him lay the not-quite-finished Ngu Departure weapons factory, surrounded by stacks of plastic-covered construction material and piles of leftover scrap. It was a flat-roofed, single-story L-shaped building, built from the same folded sheet-steel strips as Brody's tavern, as long and wide as the asteroid's only rolling mill could manage. The larger of the two wings served as the factory proper. The smaller afforded ample space for storage, the boss's — Emerson's — office, and three small apartments for himself and overnight stays by his partners, who still lived most of the time in Curringer. Whenever Cherry came out to the plant, which wasn't often, she stayed with him and helped make endurable the few nonworking hours he allowed himself.

Four miles.

He could even make out the gleaming tubular structure of Mrs. Singh's "tricycle," standing by itself in the unpaved, work-churned ground they all optimistically called the "parking lot." Around the factory, houses had begun to spring up, soon to be followed, Emerson was certain, by stores and bars and other amenities.

Three miles.

Progress was on the march here on the prairie.

Two miles.

In a long, slanting swoop, he aimed for the factory rooftop, which at the moment looked much smaller than any postage stamp. Unanticipated crosswinds had blown him several miles from the vertical during his ascent and he hadn't cared to waste power by correcting for them. To save weight, he wasn't even carrying a weapon.

It would have been different, of course, if he'd been carried unarmed over the Rimfence into Project airspace. The front gate of his former home lay only five miles from the Ngu Departure site, and in that case, he'd have aborted his climb and waited for better conditions. Even now, the idea of falling back into the hands of Gibson Altman and his blue goons made him shudder.

One mile.

Flying free as he was, however, no negative mood could last very long. Two-thirds of the way along this long diagonal flightpath, Emerson took a sudden tumble and fell a thousand vertical feet before he regained control only a few hundred yards above the ground. Intently focused on the rapidly dwindling figures in his power display, he'd been caught off-guard by another phenomenon of nature on Pallas, having flown over an unmapped "mascon," a hidden deposit of material, probably nickel-iron, denser than the average mass of the asteroid.

Pallas was, after all, an "accretion body," the accumulated result of millions of collisions, over billions of years, between whirling worldlets of dissimilar composition, three-quarters of them carbonaceous chondrite (nobody knew why it should be that particular ratio) and the remaining quarter mostly granite of one type or another or a cosmic, naturally occurring high-grade steel alloy.

Five hundred feet.

Drying his sweaty palms, one after another, on the opposite shoulders of his work shirt, he made a mental note to mention the location of this near-fatal mishap to Mrs. Singh, who was attempting to chart the mascons in the Curringer-Project area, not only for the benefit of future purchasers of the "Ngu Departure Flying Yoke" but as possible revenue-enhancing claimstakes for mining operations. Over the past several months, Emerson's latest invention had evolved radically from the crude assembly of duct tape and purloined components he'd begun with into a sleek, efficient means of individual transportation.

This morning, in addition to fulfilling fantasies, he'd been trying to find out *how* efficient.

Gone were the electrical conduit and the temporarily dismembered office chair, replaced now with a two-foot hoop of hollow, glass-reinforced plastic tubing just large enough to be filled, around most of its circumference, with rechargeable batteries. A short nylon strap attached at the front and back, passing between his legs, kept him from falling through, while a panel of rudimentary instruments showed the status of a pair of small, powerful, ducted fan motors located outboard at the ten and two o'clock positions. Their speed and pitch were controlled by two joysticks, slaved to one another, on either side of the panel.

To supplement the batteries, which Emerson was unhappy with, he was presently considering a modest photovoltaic collector where the backrest of a chair would have been, but he wanted to keep the whole contrivance light and hand-portable, and his experience with solar power made him dubious about its value, in any case.

Fifty feet.

The graveled rooftop of the factory building expanded beneath his soles just as a flock of startled pigeons arose all around him. Ignoring the birds, he alighted with practiced ease, shut the power off—the display read straight zeroes anyway—and stepped out of the yoke, carrying it in one hand like the tire of a bicycle.

Pushing through a steel door which led to a short stair-well, he was met by Mrs. Singh carrying his pistol belt.

"Well, how'd it go, Junior Birdman?" Tipping her head down toward him, she ran a hand through her hair. "See any new gray ones? I swear I could feel 'em sprouting one by one. I sure wish you'd taken some kind of walkie-talkie with you."

"It would have to be a 'flyie-cryie,' or something like that, wouldn't it?" He grinned at her affectionately, set the hoop against a wall, strapped on his Grizzly, checked both magazine and chamber beneath her approving gaze, picked up his flying yoke again, and started down the stairs. "Anyway, I couldn't afford the extra weight. I made it, though—just barely—and I found another mascon on the way down. Let's go to the office and I'll show you on the map."

Almost everyone knew that the gravity of Pallas varied from spot to spot, from a tenth of the pull of Earth to about a twentieth, due to its varying geological composition. A big man like Aloysius Brody "weighed" somewhere between ten and twenty pounds, depending on where he was standing. Emerson wasn't a big man himself and never would be, "weighing" somewhere between five and ten pounds.

He was willing to bet the map they needed had already been made long ago, probably from orbit during an initial survey, and was sitting in some filing cabinet or computer memory back on Earth, inaccesible because it had been lost and ultimately forgotten in the bureaucratic jumble generated by any large organization, even a relatively benign one like Curringer's Two Lions Corporation.

As they reached the ground floor, Mrs. Singh shook her head. "I'm afraid it'll have to wait, Emerson. I heard from Aloysius just before you landed, and he's still on the line, waiting to confer with you. It seems our friendly neighborhood dictator's raising hell about your plan to hire people from the Project."

Emerson laughed.

He'd been expecting this. It was only the latest development in what was turning out to be a prolonged conflict. This particular phase had begun with his campaign to "persuade" the reluctant operators of KCUF—principally by threatening to start his own radio station—to dramatically increase their broadcast range. Despite their frequent, grandiose promises of improvement, they'd been content for years with a low-power transmitter and an antenna mast that was no more than a bit of heavy-gauge copper wire thrust up a few feet above the roof of His Master's Voice, the bar in which their studio was located. He was still surprised that he'd been able to receive their signal almost seventy miles away, probably because most of it was across the open space over Lake Selous.

As usual, Emerson had a public reason and a personal reason for what he'd done. Publicly, he'd wanted his workers to be able to keep in touch with the radio voice of Curringer at his new factory site and along the road running to it, where he anticipated that development and population were now likely to expand. Also, a higher antenna could be used for private communications over the same distance.

Personally, never having forgotten his principle of revenge-only-at-a-profit, he'd been experimenting lately with a prototype receiver even simpler than his first hand-made crystal set, a tiny, unpowered device permanently tuned to one frequency, designed to be manufactured almost for nothing, which could be given away at a minimal loss, greatly enlarging the listenership of KCUF all over this hemisphere of Pallas, especially among the peasants at the Project, who, one way or another, would be the very first recipients of his free radios.

He still hadn't figured out how to persuade somebody—he had the owners of KCUF in mind again, but that would have to wait until they'd gotten over being annoyed with him about the mile-high antenna he'd "inspired" them to build—to back the manufacture of his little receivers. It was certain that he couldn't afford to do it himself, not with every spare ounce of gold his little company was earning from making and selling guns going to pay for the factory building or being plowed back into development and eventual production of flying yokes. It often frightened him how much Cherry, Mrs. Singh, Nails, and Aloysius trusted him.

Nor had he figured out how to get his radios efficiently distributed to the inhabitants of the Project, but he'd already done a fair amount of damage by giving away dozens of semiproduction prototypes to the rollabout drivers who made weekly deliveries to Curringer. Doubtless, since Emerson went to a great deal of trouble to make the supply of free receivers seem endless, they bartered them away inside the Project for food or sexual favors or something else.

And naturally, from the first day the new antenna had been operational, the Ngu Departure Company had run advertisements offering jobs to anyone—but especially to Project peasants—willing to train and work hard for an honest day's payment in cold, hard cash. All they had to do was find a way out the front gate (or some other convenient exit) and down the five miles of road—at an average of one-tenth of a gravity, that was practically next door—separating the two establishments. Transportation would eventually be provided, in the form of even more "lunchbox specials," but Emerson didn't advertise that.

Nor did he add that permanent defections would be rewarded as his own had been, with warmth and friendship and as much help as possible toward starting a new life on the Outside.

It wasn't a plan that could be concealed for very long,

nor had it been calculated to please the Chief Administrator of the Greeley Utopian Memorial Project, which was why Emerson wasn't surprised to be hearing, just about now, from Aloysius. It seemed a long time since he'd struggled so hard to understand that, in a free world anyway, kindness and good business amounted to the same thing. It was natural for any Outsider to sympathize with the Project's victims, to cheer when they broke free, and to welcome them as new neighbors. New neighbors, of course, were new customers, as well, as long as they became self-sufficient (and if they didn't, they wouldn't last long, but would have to whimper their way back into the Senator's good graces). For the most part, everybody won—if not a full-fledged example of Adam Smith's "invisible hand" at work, it was, at least, a sign from one of its friendlier fingers.

With Mrs. Singh behind him, he pushed through the open door of his tiny, cluttered office, leaned his flying yoke against a bookcase, and sat down at his desk.

Aloysius and the Senator were already there, in electronic spirit, manifesting themselves in the middle of his blotter as a pair of six-inch leprechauns.

"What can I do you for, Aloysius?"

A tiny, not-quite-transparent three-dimensional replica of Emerson stood at the center of Brody's corner table in the Nimrod. Bent over it were Brody himself and Gibson Altman, both of whom were similarly displayed to Emerson, three hundred miles away, thanks to the equivalent electronics at his end of the conversation. Brody suspected that his old friend Henrietta was there, too, somewhere in the background, but the narrowly focused device wasn't picking up her image.

"Not a thing fer me, but fer the Senator here, me boy." The tavern keeper turned over a broad, hairy hand, indicating Altman. He was trying hard not to appear to be taking sides, but it was difficult. "I'm afraid he's after suin' ye agin."

Emerson's miniature image turned, as if he'd been occupied with other matters until just this moment and was only giving them his full attention now. Perhaps Henrietta had said something to him. He looked the Senator in the eye and smiled, his unshaven upper lip making him look even younger than he was.

"What for this time?"

"I have just traveled four hundred miserable kilometers, young man," Altman complained, "in a good-faith attempt to accomplish things in the manner you people seem to regard as customary. The least you can do is to expend an equal effort. I expect — no, I *demand* — to see you here in this . . . er, courtroom, immediately."

Emerson smiled again. The picture of Gibson Altman being stuck overnight in a town he hated, among people he hated, with the prospect of an equally arduous return voyage ahead of him — all for nothing, if it could possibly be arranged — appealed to the boy. "Now let me get this straight, Senator: you actually believe that wasting your time and energy in a stupid gesture that was entirely your own idea creates some sort of obligation on my part to — "

"A moment, if y'please."

Brody had held up a hand, interrupting Emerson before things went too far. He turned to Altman.

"It's a long way indeed from there to here, Senator darlin', as ye yerself can attest. It's also possible that this matter can be resolved here an' now. Young Mr. Ngu could give up without a fight, simply t'save himself the inconvenience. Why don't y'let me read him this here bill of particulars that y'brought along with ye, and we'll see what's what before we formally summon him."

Both parties knew that Brody, as an adjudicator under

the Stein Covenant, had no power to coerce. He was not like an Earthside magistrate in that respect. But among Pallatians, in a dispute of real substance, the failure to appear in court to answer a charge could result in lost business, even in ostracism.

Altman nodded grudgingly. "Very well, but if—"

"Now let's just look . . ." Brody settled his glasses on the end of his nose and held Altman's sheaf of paper up before them at arm's length, shuffling through the many pages. "Ah, here it is. Emerson, the good Senator here wants ye t'stop all radio broadcastin' into the Greeley Utopian Memorial Project, as he asserts that this violates the privacy of the inhabitants therein."

Emerson said nothing. The assertion and the accusation were so absurd that he probably didn't know what to say. Brody didn't either, at first. Finally, he turned again to the other man, squinting at him over his spectacle rims. "Now it seems t'me that ye'll be needin' t'take that up with the proprietors of KCUF, Senator darlin'. But we'll let it pass fer the moment an' get on."

All three knew what the station owners would have to say to Altman, if he were foolish enough to confront them. The Stein Covenant strictly forbade any interference with the right to free speech, and, unlike the native country of all three, on Pallas that right extended to broadcast media, which required no license to operate. Altman had nothing either to offer them or threaten them with.

To Emerson: "He also wants ye t'stop transmittin' private or commercial messages to the Project inhabitants intended, as it says here, to incite their disaffection."

The tiny simulacrum shrugged. "I haven't broadcast any personal messages yet—although it's a good idea and I'll certainly give it due consideration. Anything else, Aloysius?"

"Indeed." Brody sighed and shook his head. "He demands that ye refrain immediately an' henceforward from employin' the inhabitants of the Greeley Utopian Memorial Project at occupations unauthorized by said Project's Chief Administrator . . ."

Emerson grinned.

"Particularly," the innkeeper continued, "manufacturin' by what he calls the exploitive, wasteful, an' ecologically irresponsible process of mass production . . ."

Emerson chuckled.

"An' *most* particularly," Brody plowed onward, "the manufacturin' of clandestine communications devices, personal vehicles, an' deadly weapons intended fer individual use."

Emerson laughed out loud.

Brody sighed, feeling the mounting fury and frustration of the man beside him as a tangible force. "He further demands that ye refrain from sellin', givin' away, or allowin' the Project's inhabitants t'steal any an' all such manufactured goods."

"Excuse me, Your Honor," interjected Altman. The man was barely under control, speaking between clenched teeth. "That's a bit more general than I intended. For the time being, I only ask that he keep these things out of the hands of my people."

"There y'have it," Brody finished.

"I see," Emerson replied.

XXV
OLD BUSINESS

SHALL WE DEBATE IT, DOES A GIRL HAVE TO BE STIRRED BEFORE
SHE'LL LET A MAN TAKE HER? OF COURSE NOT. SOME OF THEM
ARE, BUT ONLY A MINORITY; MOST OF THEM LET THE APRON UP
BECAUSE THEY'VE BEEN CURIOUS ABOUT IT SO LONG . . . CURIOSITY
IS OFTEN SO STRONG THAT NO MAN OR WOMAN CAN RESIST IT.
—**Rex Stout,** *Death of a Dude*

What," asked Emerson, "am I supposed to do now,
Alo—Your Honor?"

Brody massaged his beard in thought. "Well, I told the
Senator here y'might be willin' t'give in without botherin'
t'travel all the long two hundred miles—pardon me, three
hundred sixty kilometers—t'Curringer. Otherwise, he
wants a public hearin' like before."

Emerson laughed and shook his head. Brody had
watched the boy mature and become increasingly self-pos-
sessed since the Ngu Departure Company had been created, but something else was elevating his spirit today.
"Not *exactly* like before, I'll bet."

Altman waved Brody aside. "See here, young man, this
is a serious business. I demand that you treat it—and me—
with the respect it deserves!"

"You're just full of demands, aren't you, Senator?"
Emerson shrugged. "But that's what I'm doing, believe
me, giving this business—and you—all the respect they
deserve."

"Talk to him, Brody!" Altman's hands shook and he
sprayed little gobbets of spit as he hissed the words between his teeth. *Another half hour of this,* Brody calculated,
*and Emerson won't have any legal problems because the plaintiff
will have keeled over.*

Before he could intervene, Emerson asked, "What's the matter, has KCUF's antenna made it wasteful and ecologically irresponsible to jam their signals the way you did when I was one of your serfs?"

Altman was stiff with fury. Idly watching a vein pulse on the man's forehead, Brody decided that Henrietta must have left the room, forcing Emerson to fend for himself. He'd never known her to remain quiet when an argument was going on.

"I've been doing some reading," Emerson told Altman, visibly dizzying the man with the change of subject. "Reading you'd never have authorized. We could argue all day over freedom of communication, or the individual right to the means of self-defense, but I doubt it would get us anywhere. So let's discuss something else."

"Such as?" The Senator was wary. Brody had watched him recover in only a few seconds and was impressed. The cost would be high—blood pressure, gastric problems, perhaps ultimately cancer—but it was nothing short of miraculous. No wonder he'd been successful, up to a point, in politics. The tavern keeper remained silent. This was not a formal hearing, and if it came to that, Altman was going to accuse him again of conflict of interest. It was true enough, his interests were in conflict. And this time, as a principal investor and director of Emerson's company, he doubted whether he could shrug it off—or wanted to.

He was aware that, to one degree or another, everything Emerson did these days was motivated by a long-held, deeply felt desire for retribution. On the other hand, the boy was within his rights and if anyone ever deserved to exact retribution . . . The Senator wasn't just wrong in each of his nasty little authoritarian demands, he was wrongheaded—all of which, naturally enough, disqualified Brody as an impartial adjudicator. Perhaps the best thing was to let them talk it out.

"Such as the flying yoke you seem to resent so much, even before it's on the market, and the fact that your former country and mine started with the most efficient mass-transport system in history—the private automobile—which took the individual from precisely where he happened to be to precisely where he wanted to go, at precisely any time he wished, in comfort, privacy, and comparative safety."

Altman started to reply, but Emerson didn't let him.

"That didn't suit people like you, Senator, politicians and planners who nurture a profound, unwavering hatred for private transportation because they see individual comfort and privacy as a threat—and personal safety as a lamentable lack of opportunity. It didn't give you the control you wanted and needed so badly."

That hadn't sounded like Emerson at all. The phrasing and vocabulary were wrong. Brody suspected that Henrietta was still beside him after all, silently coaching him.

"What can you possibly know about it?" the Senator demanded. "You were only a child—you're still only a child! The nation wanted and needed public transportation! The people voted for it time and time again! The private automobile was selfish, wasteful, dirty—and the highways were falling apart!"

"Eventually you believed your own propaganda." Emerson shook his head. "And the results of the endless referenda you rigged so carefully. So you spent billions, maybe even trillions, of tax-extorted dollars on expensive, complicated, failure-prone systems that only shifted power consumption and pollution somewhere else—"

"It's not true!"

Now Brody was certain Henrietta was helping, probably scribbling notes as fast as her fingers could fly. He'd heard her on this subject too many times to doubt it.

"Systems," Emerson was saying, "that ran mostly

empty because they were inconvenient, uncomfortable, and dangerous in terms of the crime they bred and the fact that hundreds, maybe even thousands, of innocents died whenever some bureaucrat, usually safe in his office or control booth, screwed up. The fact that it would actually have been cheaper to give everyone a car never told you that *you* were screwing up. Nor did it ever occur to you to use it to keep the roads repaired—or hand them over to private parties willing and able to do it."

Altman clenched his fists on the table, fighting for calm. "What has any of this got to do—"

Emerson anticipated him. "Because I know the Project was formed, among other things, to explore the forcible elimination of private transport back on Earth. It's in your basic documentation, grant applications, print media that were sympathetic at the time. Which is why it especially galls you that your slaves may begin helping me to manufacture personal vehicles, despoiling your utopian dream altogether."

That sounded more like Emerson. Altman didn't reply, although he seemed more relaxed, sitting with his shoulders slumped, which made Brody guess that Emerson's accusation was true.

But the boy wasn't finished with him: "Now I have a question, Mr. Chief Administrator. Did you even bother to *read* the Stein Covenant before you signed it for ten thousand other human beings? It's only one page, you know, seven little paragraphs."

"I—"

"Paragraph Two presupposes the right of each individual to listen to what he likes. If you don't want KCUF, don't tune it in. The same clause implies that people can go anywhere, any way they wish, and that you haven't got a thing to say about it. Paragraph Three asserts the right of self-defense, I quote, by 'whatever means prove necessary'—meaning fists, knives, guns, thermonuclear hand grenades—as long as it doesn't violate any other provisions of the Covenant."

"You're not a lawyer, you're hardly qualified—"

"Beggin' yer pardon, Senator darlin', neither am I." He heard Henrietta chuckle in the background.

"The Covenant belongs to those who've signed it," Emerson continued, "and to nobody else. Mirelle Stein put it in plain language expressly to eliminate the argument you just made."

"But that's *anarchy!*"

"*Organized* anarchy." Emerson nodded. "Now: we can fight this out in a public hearing, Senator, but if you insist on it, this time I'll counter that the very *existence* of the Project violates the fourth, fifth, and sixth paragraphs of the Covenant."

"And as the only local arbiter available, Senator darlin'," Brody warned the man, "prejudiced or otherwise, I'd have no choice but t'rule that, under established hyperdemocratic doctrine, ye may not prohibit Project inhabitants either from acceptin' outside work in their off hours—even in the privacy of their own homes—or from ownin' radios, flyin' machines, or weapons of self-defense."

Emerson nodded agreement. "I don't believe anyone on this asteroid has a desire to move in and shut you down, but that could change. There's always the chance that I can recruit enough of your own victims to accomplish it from the inside."

"You're threatening me?"

"Senator, I'm only telling you what might happen as a result of a public hearing on the charges you've made. Now—and I mean this literally—you want to try me?"

❀   ❀   ❀

"Shit!"

Emerson threw his stylus down in disgust, blacking the display he was so tired of looking at.

He rubbed his weary eyes. He had to face it: the flying yoke worked, in its own crude fashion, but there was no way to get more altitude or speed out of it. The motors were as powerful as mass and energy-storage considerations allowed. Solar panels would make things worse. He was already using the lightest, strongest materials available and his impellers were as efficient as the laws of physics and his manufacturing techniques permitted. The problem was the batteries, enormously heavy and neither very powerful nor long-lasting. There hadn't been an advance in that area for decades, and he wasn't the one to make it.

Would his potential customers be content with a top speed of fifty miles an hour, a range of four hundred miles, a maximum safe altitude (as opposed to what he'd tried this morning) of twenty-five hundred feet, and a carrying capacity of no more than three hundred Earth pounds? Or would they simply laugh him and his useless toy out of business?

He sat up from the hunched position he'd unconsciously assumed for hours, felt his back complain, and rubbed his eyes again. Ten o'clock—where had the time gone? He'd meant to call it a day after finishing with Aloysius and Altman, but there'd been one or two little things he'd wanted to look at first.

Now here he was, tired and sore and hungry, all for nothing.

And alone.

The few workers he'd already recruited had gone to their homes on the surrounding prairie. Through his window he saw lights twinkling sparsely in the distance. Mrs. Singh had returned to Curringer in the conveyance she'd driven here—her visit had been a surprise to show it off—a lightweight alloy frame suspended from what looked like three six-foot bicycle wheels, pushed by an even bigger propeller mounted in a cage behind the driver's seat. With the huge wheels to smooth the road, the contraption, built to her design by Nails and Tyr May, could cover the distance from here to Curringer in under four hours.

He chuckled to himself. He could still see her slashing away with a felt pen at long sheets of leftover printer paper, silently arguing for him with Altman. She—

Before he knew why, he glanced up. Someone was tapping on his window and had been for some time. Pulling the Grizzly from its holster where it lay beside his keyboard and thumbing the hammer—he snapped the safety up and kept his finger off the trigger—he turned the desk light toward the glass, pulled up the blinds, and nearly dropped the weapon.

He did drop his jaw.

On the other side of the dusty pane Gretchen Singh— no, Gretchen Singh Altman—was gesturing like a lost soul.

Heart hammering in his chest, he signaled her to a side door down the hall. He set his gun on the desk and went to meet her, hands shaking and wobbly-kneed as he pushed the panic bar to open the steel door with a thump that seemed impossibly loud in the stillness of the deserted factory. His mouth was dry and there was an odd, clamped feeling in his throat.

She stood on the walk outside, illuminated by a single bulb over the door. Her hair, once waist-length, straight, and of a glossy dark reddish-brown, was chopped off severely at the shoulder. There were circles under her eyes and fine lines showing at their corners and at the corners of her mouth. She wore a peasant's denims. For him, the bulb over the door might as well have been a halo. She was still indescribably, painfully, the most beautiful creature he'd ever seen. They looked at each other for a long time, both uncertain what to say or do. Then, with a sob breaking from her throat, she threw herself into his arms.

"I promised myself I wouldn't cry!"

Feeling many things at once, he discovered in that moment that he was angrier with her than he'd let himself realize and loved her more than he'd known. He was so happy to see her he had no way of expressing it. Tears were streaking his face, too, when he gently lifted her away from his chest and ushered her inside.

"Five miles is further than I remembered," she told him once he'd gotten her to a chair under the window—he'd had to shove books and papers onto the floor—and started a pot of coffee. "I'm out of condition." She took the paper towel he gave her, wiped her eyes and blew her nose, and glanced around the office. "Ngu Departure—I'm impressed, Emerson. I knew you'd amount to something important someday."

The thought of the last person who'd said that to him— Cherry—made him more tongue-tied than ever. He thought of something to say, inane as it was, and stammered it out. "You just missed your mother . . ." Then he looked at the wall clock again—he'd never gotten used to wearing a watch. Actually, it had been a good many hours since Mrs. Singh had returned to Curringer.

"I don't know if I could take the two of you at once." She shrugged, her eyes still moist and threatening to brim over again. "It's so *good* to see you, Emerson. I just—I had to get out and, well, I don't know exactly how to put this . . ."

"That makes two of us." He resolutely turned his attention to the coffee machine, which wasn't finished dribbling and making groaning noises. With the feelings of someone about to go over a ski jump, he swallowed. "Let me make it easy. Whatever you need, count on me."

For an instant, both of them thought she was going to burst into tears again. Then: "I don't need much—a word of comfort and advice from the best friend I ever had."

He nodded, wanting more than anything to ask the one-word question that had tortured him since their last day together, but unable to, partly because she'd been un-available to answer it for so long that there hadn't been any point and he'd tried to shut it out, now because he'd prom-ised unconditionally to help her. As usual, she knew what he was thinking. "But you need to know why I ran off and got married."

"Yeah." He didn't trust himself to say more.

"He used to sneak into Curringer every few weeks by bribing the rollabout crew," she told him. "I met him at the Nimrod. I didn't like him much, but he was extremely per-sistent, and very different from anybody else I knew. The other boys in town were afraid of me, probably because of Aloysius or Mother. And"—she smiled and for an instant was the Gretchen he remembered—"I hadn't met you at the time, of course." She sighed raggedly. "Is there a ciga-rette around somewhere?"

Like mother like daughter. Mildly surprised, he rum-maged in a drawer, found a pack Mrs. Singh had left, handed it to her, and poured them each a cup of coffee. She lit a cigarette, inhaled and exhaled with an ecstatic look, and took the cup he offered. She swallowed, tilted her head back, and closed her eyes.

"God," she sighed again, "it's been a long time."

He wasn't at all surprised at how well he'd remem-bered every feature of her lovely face, its tanned, amazing smoothness, flawed now only by transitory marks of stress and fatigue. Her eyes were the deep, luminous green he recalled, still impossibly large over her broad cheekbones. Her eyelashes were still too long to be believed. Her nose was straight, turned up a little at the end, and her full, ex-

pressive lips parted to reveal teeth that were white and
perfect. Whatever else she'd been through, she'd grown
up, and it looked good on her. He sat down with his own
cup in the antique swivel chair Nails had given him the day
the factory had opened and with a nod, encouraged her to
go on.

"Emerson . . ." She hesitated. "Jesus, this is difficult
. . . I only . . . I had this confession all planned out, and now
it's falling apart. You probably won't believe me, after everything that's happened, but Junior didn't mean a thing
to me. He was just—well, girls can be pretty damned mer-
ciless when they're curious about certain aspects of life, especially when they grow up in a small town where everybody knows them and everything they do gets back to
their family."

He smiled at her, thinking of his own family, and of
Cherry. "No more than boys, I suppose."

"Thanks for the thought. You can't say I slept with
him. I never spent a night with him or even went to bed
with him. I fucked him in the goddamned rollabout, Emerson, while the crew were busy spending his money at
Galena's. Pretty cheap, right? But I learned what I
thought I wanted to know—not as much as I'd already
learned by reading my father's books. Junior didn't know
anything except getting a hard-on, getting it off, and . . .
hurting—although that came later."

He tried to ignore the stab of pain he suddenly felt, for
himself, for her, for both of them.

"Anyway," she went on, "I met you and everything
changed. From you I learned what I'd really wanted to
know all along, months before you ever touched me. I
thought you'd never touch me, and I wanted you to. But
finally you did, and by then I'd told Junior I wouldn't be
seeing him any more. He got real mad and . . . well, that
doesn't matter, he found out how far that got him. I never

told him about you or even that there was somebody else, but he found that out, too, somehow. It probably wasn't hard. And he got his father to come for you."

He and her mother had figured that much out. "But I won, Gretchen."

"You won at the Nimrod," she objected. "Junior took me aside that morning and told me—well, probably the only true thing he ever said to me. He said he'd recruited a cadre of E&O goons personally loyal to him. I don't know how, even now, but it's true. I've seen them. He said they'd beat you to death when you were taken back.

"And if his father lost, he'd send them out to kill you."

XXVI
Thin White Scars

PEOPLE MAY DIE FOR LOVE, BUT THEY SELDOM KILL FOR IT. BY THE TIME THEY'RE READY, IT'S USUALLY TURNED INTO SOMETHING ELSE.
— **Nathaniel H. Blackburn,** *The WarDove*

S o you—"
No one had ever had the knack of rendering Emerson speechless the way Gretchen had. Without being told, he knew the rest of the story, and it stunned him.

She nodded. "I . . . I told him I'd go with him if he let you be. To tell the truth, I was surprised when that meant becoming Mrs. Gibson Altman, Jr. I'd expected . . . well, never mind what I'd expected. His father insisted on the marriage and performed the ceremony himself. I proposed the bargain, and I've been trying my best to keep it . . ." She almost broke down again, but struggled and regained control. "For two long, miserable years. But I don't think I can any more, not with that . . . Junior, and not in that socialist hellhole. Not even for you. There are limits to what anybody can take. Can you forgive me?"

Her words had left him openmouthed and speechless, but she didn't look up. "For what it's worth, I haven't been with Junior since my daughter was conceived. It was hard to manage at first, but it seems to suit him now as much as it does me, although his father is always pressing me to get pregnant again as an example to the colonists. I don't know what Junior does. I don't want to know."

She hesitated, then pressed on. "I don't expect that things can ever be the same between you and me. If you don't have another girl by now, I'll be disappointed with you. But I love you, and I need to know that you don't hate me, that you won't hate my little Gwen-Rose when you see her. It's been left to me to raise her. I doubt Junior's looked at her a dozen times, and every time he does, it scares me. It's not her fault who her father is, she's really very . . ."

Before she could finish, he was across the room and had taken her in his arms. "I've never loved anyone but you," he told her, "and I don't believe I ever will."

"How can you love me?" she demanded. "How can you trust me after what I've done?" She wrapped her arms around his shoulders as he knelt beside her, burying her face beside his neck. Her fingers dug into him as her shoulders shook, although she didn't make a sound, and in a few moments that side of his shirt was soaked.

He stroked her hair. He'd been deeply angered at what she'd told him, but he was no longer angry with her. How could he be? He was completely overwhelmed by the love her sacrifice represented and wanted—needed—to prove himself worthy of it. What made him angry now was that she had felt it necessary—that somebody had *made* it necessary—and he knew precisely whom to blame for that.

"What have you done?" he asked her softly. Somewhere, beneath the odor of fear and the harsh Project soap she'd been using for two endless years, she still smelled of sage and woodsmoke. Without his being entirely aware of it, his hand had crept inside her tunic and he felt her naked breast, warm and softer than he recalled. If she noticed that his hand was surer at this sort of thing than it had been, she said nothing about it, but only made a little noise halfway between a moan and a sigh. She shuddered in that grateful way women sometimes have. "You were saving my life," he observed, pausing to kiss her and brush the tear-dampened hair from her eyes, "and apparently it worked. So now it's my turn. Where's your little girl right now? Who's taking care of her?"

She spoke into his shoulder. "I had to find out how hard it was to get past the Rimfence before I could risk taking her out with me. I left her at the Residence." She sat up, keeping her hands on him as if afraid he might disappear. "She's being watched by—oh, Emerson, it's your mother taking care of her!"

It made sense, he thought, but it was strange. "Does she—my mother—know where you are?"

She shook her head, crushing out her almost-forgotten cigarette in the ashtray on his desk after taking a final drag. "I don't know what she knows, or how much she'd tell or to whom. I've never been able to read her. I'm afraid I didn't think this through very well. I meant to get back, this time at least, before anyone noticed I was gone. The trouble is, I avoided the road as much as I could—it's rough country—and I've already been gone longer than I'd planned."

He disengaged himself from her arms, stood, and nodded. "That's okay. I think I can get you back in about six minutes." It was true; a part of his mind, operating independently, had just solved most of his problems with the flying yoke. "We'll use the time to get you something to eat. I know what food can be like at the Project, even at the Residence. I have an apartment here, with a kitchen."

"God, could we? Something with red meat in it?" She stood up. "And maybe a shower? You wouldn't believe — but of course you would. You grew up there."

He shook his head. "No, my love, I wasn't even born there, and I grew up out here, on the Outside. The next trip you make out — tomorrow night, if possible — will be your last. You have to bring your baby daughter out so she can grow up free. You mustn't leave her with the Senator's servants, whoever they happen to be related to. They're willing slaves and they can't be trusted."

"I know," she told him. "But it won't be tomorrow. I'm going in for Gwen-Rose and coming back out tonight. I'd have been here sooner — I decided to leave weeks ago and start life over again, no matter the cost, no matter where I had to go — but it had to wait until the Senator made one of his rare trips to Curringer. Junior uses the opportunity to get drunk and spend the night in the colonist compound."

He laughed. "Then I'm the reason you're here, and I'm going in with you. Altman went to town to make trouble and got his nose bloodied again." He put his arms around her. "You don't have to go anywhere to start over. You're already where you belong."

Tears escaped her tightly shut eyelids as she held him as hard as she knew she could. At last he led her by the hand to the apartment he was using, where he fried her a steak while she showered. The little suite was fully suited for human habitation, but the food in the refrigerator was the only thing personal he kept there. Everything else, including a change of clothes, was in his office.

He realized, sooner or later, that he was going to have to tell her about Cherry. And Cherry about her, which was going to be more difficult.

She emerged from the little prefabricated bathroom unit wearing a big cotton towel wrapped around her body and another wrapped around her head. Their bleached institutional whiteness contrasted strikingly with the natural color of her skin.

"I forgot to tell you." She inhaled the aroma of the cooking food and gave him the same look as when she'd lit the cigarette. It was the same look, he remembered now, that she'd had on her face that first time when, straddling his hips, she'd —

He shook the thought off. "What did you forget to tell me?" He flipped the contents of the pan — African Cape buffalo steak, wild onions chopped with wild garlic and mushrooms — onto a plate and added hash browns he'd fried in a separate pan.

She sat on a stool at a counter which was the apartment's only table — he'd forgotten how long her legs were — pulled the towel from her head, massaged her shortened hair with it, and laid it across her lap, giving her other towel a strategic tug that did more damage than it had been meant to repair. She lit another cigarette, inhaled, and exhaled. "I've been to your secret cave."

"What?"

"The little hollow in the crater wall under the Rimfence where you built your crystal radio? It's the only time I ever felt safe out there, a stolen minute hidden among things you'd made with your own hands. It's still there, artfully concealed by sagebrush, and so are all your treasures. I wish I could have brought them with me."

He grinned, slid the steaming plate toward her across the counter, poured her a cup of coffee from the fresh pot he'd just made, and began to dish a plate up for himself.

"Believe me, you did."

As she smiled back and reached for her cup, her towel gave in and fell gracefully to her waist in the Pallatian gravity. She looked up at him, over the rim of her cup, from beneath her impossibly long eyelashes. "You know," she observed quietly, not looking up from her plate, "if I'm coming back out tonight, I should wait until about three, when Junior's passed out thoroughly and the goons are cooping. We've got a couple of hours—think we can find some way to use them?" He looked straight back at her, enjoying what he was seeing, and nodded.

She forgot the towel and finished the meal as she was.

Afterward, he could never remember having tasted his own food.

In the end, Gretchen's self-deprecatory remarks about her physical shape proved to be exaggerated. Free of her bulky denims, she was just as beautiful as he'd remembered, and his memory was good. Five miles had seemed like more because she'd walked across country in slippers meant for sidewalks and soft soil. The same kind of slippers he'd escaped in. She had the same blisters on her feet.

To him, her shoulders and collarbones and the flawless skin that lay over them were still the same fine work of sculpture. The graceful intersecting curves of her breasts made them seem larger than they were. He didn't know how to tell if she'd fed a baby with them. Her belly was flat, exactly as it had been before, descending in a breathtaking but inviting rush past many another scenic feature, and her hips, while narrow, were also unmistakably female.

This time, it was she who seemed to appreciate what he knew, although, like him, she never asked how he knew it. She knew how he knew. Again they made love several times, each better than the one before. In between, at odd moments, she was able to tell him something of the conditions under which she'd been living. The rumors they'd been hearing on the Outside were true, as far as they went. The details were worse than even he had imagined. What

he remembered as a steady but negligible trickle of vandalism, petty crime, and violence had become a deluge. No
one was immune anywhere, at any time of the day. In the
two years she'd been there, the security contingent had
been doubled, redoubled, and doubled again, and it only
seemed to make things worse. The personnel being sent up
from Earth each time were more corrupt and brutal than
their predecessors.

But they weren't the only source of brutality. Low on
her back above her right hip, he was horrified to discover
half a dozen thin, white parallel scars, each perhaps five
inches long and no more than an eighth of an inch wide.

"Oh, those," she answered. "I got them the same night
I got Gwen-Rose, along with a lot of fairly nasty bruises.
He had the cuffs on me before I knew it, fastened through
the bed frame. The whip was made of some kind of wire.
Good thing we make such flimsy furniture on this planet —
he just had time to do this before I ripped the bed apart,
blackened both his eyes and broke his nose. I would have
had his dick out by the roots, too, but he hit me with a
lamp — you can't see that one, it's hidden in my hair — and
your mother was at the door, which interrupted anything
else he planned to do after that. I can't say it was the end of
a beautiful friendship, but it was the end of something."

He felt like vomiting, sickened that she'd had to go
through something like this — for his sake.

"Don't look that way," she told him gently, brushing
his cheek with her fingertips. "It's over now, and I got off
easy. His father's had to smooth over several messes with
colonist girls. There's a rumor that he killed one of them.
Besides — " she glanced up at him from beneath her long
eyelashes " — some of it — the handcuffs, not the whip —
might have been fun with the right person."

For the next half hour, she showed him what she
meant.

And then it was time to go.

When she was ready, he carried his yoke, along with a spare prototype, out to the parking lot, cross-connected their control panels the way he'd suddenly thought of earlier, and assured himself that they operated in the manner he'd anticipated. Duct-taping the yokes together, he switched their impellers on without taking his place within either machine. Obedient to the adjustments he'd made, they rose three feet into the air above the unpaved surface and stayed there.

Giving her a reassuring smile, he helped her step into one yoke, then stepped into the other himself. She weighed about the same as he did, and he had no plans more ambitious than ferrying her back to the Project at a modest altitude and speed, so they shouldn't have any power problems like he'd experienced earlier, despite the added weight of the Grizzly on his thigh.

Keeping her hands off the panel of her machine, she donned the goggles he handed her, checked the chamber of the pistol he'd found for her in his office—his first Ngu Departure—and nodded. He advanced a lever. Together they rose, side by side, into the night sky. At rooftop height, he oriented himself, turned carefully, and they began to move ahead at about thirty miles an hour.

"Wonderful!" she shouted. "I want to learn to do it myself!"

"That should take you about thirty seconds!" He grinned as the night-black prairie slipped beneath their dangling feet, proud that something he'd built made her so happy. "How about tomorrow night?"

"It's a date!" She grinned back, then turned to peer through her goggles at the country ahead. The breeze made conversation difficult. Before they realized it, they were more than halfway to a destination neither really wanted to reach. Abruptly, she spoke again. "What are those green lights down there?"

Just as abruptly, he felt something slap his face, as if he'd collided with a large, fast-flying insect. A cold, stinging sensation at his hairline above his right eye was followed by a warm liquid trickle—sweat, he thought at first—running into his eye, momentarily blinding him. He brushed at it and his fingers came away blackened in the silvery moonlight, smelling of salt and iron.

A sharp crack followed, and another. He was aware she'd drawn the pistol he'd given her. One of their impellers began to disintegrate in its housing. He realized he was hearing—and feeling—the effect of supersonic bullets as they passed close by. He leaned on a joystick, spiraling them down out of the moonlit sky and leftward, away from whoever was shooting at them. He'd seen no flashes, heard no gunfire from the ground, only the noise of the passing projectiles.

They hit with a muffled crash in chest-high sagebrush. Gretchen stifled a scream. In a shallow bowl, in the moonshadow of a low hill, they were less visible than before, but it was hard to see what they were doing. Beside him, she was already struggling to disentangle herself from the complaining flying yokes—which he shut off—and sit up. He was blind again in his right eye, and this time he didn't think it was the blood from his scalp wound but the wound itself.

"Damn!" she whispered, "I've either sprained my knee or broken it!"

"I wouldn't advise standing up, anyway," he told her just as quietly. He slid from the yoke and drew the Grizzly. His head had begun to hurt. Worse than that, a broken string of bobbing green lights had come over the hilltop and was starting down in their direction.

"Goons!" they both hissed at the same time.

He added, "What are they doing here? We didn't fly over the Rimfence. We're two miles from the gate."

"Junior's thugs," she replied. "He's sent them after me." Moaning under her breath from the pain of her knee as she ground it against the turf, she leveled her pistol and fired. One of the lights fell into the sagebrush and went out.

Someone hollered, "There he is!" Someone else yelled, "Grease the sonofabitch!" A dozen other voices shouted in anger and confusion, then all the lights went out.

"Correction," she whispered, "they're after you!" Hearing muffled curses as the men stumbled over unfamiliar ground, they crawled quickly from where they'd landed, their position given away by Gretchen's shot, and waited.

The noise grew louder. The setting moon was no help. He couldn't tell whether he was really blind in his right eye or it was just the darkness. He listened to his heartbeat— he could almost hear hers as they arranged themselves back to back, pistols leveled across their knees—and the amazing clamor of the advancing thugs.

Finally there came a footfall in front of him, no more than three yards away. Raising his gun, he pulled the trigger. The Grizzly bellowed and illuminated the night. The sights had been centered on the torso of a man wearing a pale blue uniform and carrying an awkward-looking rifle. The forms of three or four more, crowding up behind him, had been visible for an instant just before Emerson was truly blinded by his own muzzle flash. He fired at where he thought they were—knowing he was breaking a cardinal gunman's rule—and fired again.

Gretchen, too, had begun shooting. Beyond knowing that, everything else was confusion. He heard and felt the hypersonic bullets zipping past his head, heard the screaming of the men he'd shot or of those who were trying to shoot him. For that matter, it might have been his own screaming.

He fired three more shots in quick succession, then became aware that she'd stood up behind him. As he rose and turned, the muzzle of his weapon hit something yielding which grunted. Pressing it further, he pulled the trigger and watched its muzzle-flash light up a man's face—just before his head exploded. Something hot and cold hit him in the hip and he was down again, flailing, as three or four men yelled and started to kick him in the back, the ribs, and the head.

She screamed, but it was choked off. He was aware that somebody turned him over with a toe and stepped on his throat. A sickly green light flared briefly.

"Yeah, this is the guy!" growled a voice. "Nasty little slope with a Fu Manchu. This way we won't have to slog it over to the factory. Junior may have been shitfaced, but he isn't stupid. He said finish him quick, nothing fancy. We gotta get these hot-wired weapons back to the armory and into legal config before they're missed."

Somebody mumbled. Emerson didn't understand. It was followed by the laughter of several men.

"Yes, asswipe, I do know who the cunt is! Who gives a shit? She's his girlfriend, an Outsider whore. Do whatever the fuck you want with her, the whole squad of you. Just do it fast and make goddamn sure you finish her off afterward."

The last thing Emerson remembered was hearing Gretchen struggle. One man stumbled back from her, howling like a gutted animal, fell atop him, scrambled off, and collapsed.

Emerson hardly felt it. He never felt the muzzle jam against his temple and slide, just as it went off.

XXVII
THE POCKS

"I'M GOING TO PUT THE SHIP ABOUT, MR. CARGILL," HE SAID
... HE FELT THE TENSION, HE FELT THE BEATING OF HIS HEART,
AND NOTICED WITH MOMENTARY ASTONISHMENT THAT HE WAS
ENJOYING THIS MOMENT OF DANGER ... THE HANDS WERE AT
THEIR STATIONS; EVERY EYE WAS ON HIM. THE GALE SHRIEKED
PAST HIS EARS AS HE ... WATCHED THE APPROACHING SEAS ...
DESPONDENCY FOR THE SAKE OF DESPONDENCY IRRITATED
HORNBLOWER ... HE KNEW TOO MUCH ABOUT IT.
　　　　　　　—C. S. Forester, *Hornblower and the Hotspur,*

Hello the house!"
The meadowlarks and pine buntings fell silent, but
the squirrels began to chitter. The old man set down the
stainless steel bucket he'd been about to carry to the spring
and picked up the heavy rifle he'd just leaned against the
high end of a short ramp leading up to the cabin's porch.
The turnbolt of the weapon, its hollow knob polished by
decades of use, worked smoothly under his practiced
hand, sliding one of the huge brass cylinders from the magazine into the chamber.

"Hullo, yourself!"

He raised the rifle to his shoulder.

It wasn't the friendliest of greetings he knew, but experience had proven it necessary. Perhaps this was merely
the pilot of the ultralight which had just dropped them
their supplies for the month. Although he'd spoken to them
many times, he'd yet to see one of them in the flesh. Perhaps the unfortunate chap had suffered some aviator's mishap and required assistance. The old man knew all about
those little aircraft and was astonished, now that he gave it
thought, that accidents hadn't happened many times
before over the last thirty years.

Then again, it might well be the vanguard of a maraud-
ing band of runaways from the never-to-be-sufficiently regretted Greeley Utopian Memorial Project settlement a
thousand miles to the northwest. The asteroid's low gravity made travel relatively easy, and sometimes the miserable wretches got this far. They usually didn't last long, but
they could be a lot of trouble before the wild country ate
them up.

Whoever this fellow was, he appeared inhumanly
steadfast—or simply too damned stupid to live. The average individual showed a trifle more reaction at having the
gaping business-end of a .416 Rigby Magnum leveled on
his solar plexus. By no means the most powerful of the
classic African hunting rifle cartridges ever developed, it
was merely the best. The softpointed 410-grain projectiles,
traveling at something exceeding twice the speed of sound,
gave up over two and a half tons of kinetic energy at close
range—rather more than sufficient for any organism that
had ever evolved on Earth—and could tear a big man in
half.

This wasn't any big man centered over the rifle's express sights, but a young, wiry, rather sinister-looking Ori-
ental with a thin, scruffy beard and a black fabric patch
covering his right eye. Off his left hip, low-slung and floor-
plate forward, hung an enormous black semiautomatic pistol. Over his shoulders he carried the limp, antlered carcass of a mule deer very nearly as big as he was.

In answer to the challenge, the stranger merely smiled.
He'd appeared as if by magic out of the dense cover of
evergreens surrounding the cabin on all sides, and stood
now on the opposite bank of the rocky-bottomed creek
whose nearby source was the cold, clear little spring the
old man had been headed for with his bucket.

"I'm not hiding out," the stranger declared quietly,

"and I'm not running away from anybody—except maybe from myself a little. I haven't come to hurt anybody."

"Too bloody right you haven't," replied the old man. "Keep your hands where I can see them."

Before he received an answer, there came the all-too-familiar clatter of worn wheel bearings from the cabin behind him. "Raymond, what the hell is going on out there?"

The old man didn't need to look back over his shoulder to know that the old woman had appeared in the cabin door, erect and proper in her wheelchair, its chromium parts gleaming from the relative darkness of the interior. His ancient .455 Webley Mark VI—quite possibly the only revolver on Pallas—would be lying in her lap. He could even hear its lanyard ring tinkling as she moved. He wondered idly what the young stranger made of that. It must be a bit like having a flintlock pointed at him, no less deadly for all that it was ridiculous.

He answered without turning, never taking his eye from the front sight. "It seems that we have a visitor, Miri. We're in the process of discovering what he's here for."

"I'm just a traveler," the young stranger told them, apparently unable to take his good eye off the cabin. Likely he'd been born on Pallas and never seen anything like it. The end walls and chimney were constructed entirely of unshaped stones epoxied together, as were the front and back walls up to about shoulder height. In all likelihood it was the only building on the asteroid made even partially of wood—whole logs with the bark spokeshaven off, laid in the traditional West American manner under a shake-shingled peak—having been erected atop their original dugout as stones were gathered and the trees around it had grown large enough to harvest. "I'm only looking for a chance to spend the night under a real roof for the first time in six months. I brought this deer to make up for any trouble I might be, but if I'm imposing I'll move on.

"My name is Emerson Ngu," he added.

The old man frowned to himself. The name seemed familiar somehow, and for some reason that eluded him, he associated it with good things. Perhaps he'd heard it over the wireless which, aside from monthly grocery deliveries, was his only link with civilization out here in the Pocks. Half expecting to regret it, he decided to take a chance, thumbed the safety backward, and lowered his rifle.

"Come on over, son," he answered. "My name, as you heard, is Raymond—Drake-Tealy. Most people call me Digger. The lady on the porch is my wife, Miri—Mirelle Stein."

For a moment, the youthful stranger who'd faced the muzzle of an elephant gun so casually—Drake-Tealy could see now that he was no more than a boy—stood rooted where he was, as if in shock, eyebrows up, mouth open. It took them like that sometimes. Having become a legend—one that a majority of people were surprised to discover still living—was, for the most part, a pain in the posterior. Then the young man seemed to accept what he'd been told and crossed the stream using stepping stones which had been placed there for the purpose.

Drake-Tealy set his rifle aside again and helped him hang the mule deer from a hook set under the eaves of the porch. It was a handsome buck, large enough to feed a sizable family for a month, indicating some patience and selectivity behind the sighting eye and trigger finger. Young Ngu began to field-dress the animal immediately using a big curved knife he carried on his trouser belt rather than his gunbelt—a survival-wise practice the old man heartily approved and which further raised the young fellow in his estimation. He started into the house before he remembered what he'd been about before the stranger put in his appearance.

He took the bucket to the spring and filled it.

By the time he'd carried the water and his rifle through the screen door, his wife had vanished toward the back of the cabin, where he could hear her stirring up a fire, never allowed to die out altogether, in the old-fashioned stove he'd constructed out of boyhood memories and salvaged materials from the terraforming operation. She rolled over to him, ball bearings clicking, took the bucket from his hand, set it on the stone-flagged kitchen counter, filled the big copper kettle they'd expensively imported from Harrod's many years ago as one of the few genuine extravagances they'd allowed themselves, and placed it on the stove.

"Thank you." Her face was set in an expression of grim determination. Company of any sort, under any circumstances, was a tremendous ordeal for her. No one could possibly loathe being crippled, and in her view helpless, more than the popular novelist who'd created a worldwide political movement out of her own personal philosophy of self-sufficiency. Theirs was not, perhaps, the happiest of marriages — they were not the happiest of individuals — but they had seldom been deliberately cruel to one another and she knew what occasional contact with the outside world meant to her husband. "Ask whether he prefers coffee or tea."

Drake-Tealy nodded wordlessly and went back out onto the porch. The afternoon sun sparkled along the broken surface of the creek, and iridescent hummingbirds hovered and flitted about the feeder hanging at the opposite end of the porch. He was always glad he'd insisted on introducing hummingbirds to Pallas. He leaned against a rough-hewn pillar, shoved his hands into the upper pockets of his bush pants, and watched the newcomer expertly wielding his knife, taking much the same pleasure from it as he did from watching his hummingbirds.

"You're quite welcome to spend the night with us, Mr.

Ngu," he declared, "provided that you don't mind dossing
down in what we laughingly refer to as the parlor—which
is to say our combination kitchen and front room. We were
about to have tea when you arrived, and supper will be
perhaps another hour. The lady of the house wishes to
know whether you'll actually have tea or would rather
have coffee."

The sentence had come out awkwardly. It wasn't the
first time he'd noticed that sort of thing, which he at-
tributed to insufficient practice at relating to his fellow
human beings. It didn't help that he and Miri didn't talk
much any more. For the space of a few heartbeats, he and
his guest listened to the hammering of a woodpecker, hollow in the distance, looking for its own supper.

"Whatever's easy," the young man began, then he
turned and grinned. "To tell the truth, sir, it's Emerson—
and I'd give just about anything for a real cup of coffee."
He wiped a bloodstained hand off on a rag he'd brought
with him, then fished carefully in his shirt pocket and extracted a pair of long, thin cigars.

"I don't mind if I do, Emerson," responded Drake-
Tealy, accepting one of the cigars. He was a pipe smoker
by habit, but any change was welcome, and no one was
more sensitive than the anthropologist to the necessities of
human ceremony. He fished about in a pocket of his
jacket, extracted his lighter, and lit both cigars. For another few heartbeats they stood savoring the tobacco
smoke and the moment; then Emerson turned back to his
grisly task, filling a plastic bag with the deer's viscera. "Is
there anything I can help you with?"

"I left all my gear in the trees over there," Emerson replied without looking away from the gleaming edge of his
knife. He'd finished the field dressing and begun the skinning process. "There isn't much of it, if you wouldn't
mind—Digger."

"Not at all." Drake-Tealy was secretly grateful to be asked. People he met these days, and they were few enough, were all considerably younger than he was. They took one look at his thick shock of snow-white hair and walrus moustache, the latter stained like antique ivory from the pipe smoke streaming past it, and tried to do things for him, whether he wanted them done or not. It was one reason — not the major one, by any means — that he and his wife lived in seclusion here in the center of an area set aside by the Curringer Trust for future growth.

Leaving Emerson to finish with his work, he stepped across the creek and followed a trail of freshly trod grass into the trees. Beside one of them, within easy sight of the cabin, lay a peculiar object consisting of two hoops, each almost a yard in diameter, hinged together at one edge and presently folded, lying parallel to one another. At the edges opposite the hinge, two pairs of louvered football-sized pods appeared to contain electric motors with short-bladed propellers. One of the hoops held a harness in which the pilot — that much was a guess — presumably sat. The other was rigged to carry a large rucksack.

When he picked the contraption up, he was astonished at how light it was, not much heavier, in truth, than a pair of ordinary bicycle wheels lashed together. He also suddenly remembered in what connection he'd heard the name Emerson Ngu. So this, then, was the brilliant young inventor, originally a penniless refugee from that blasted Greeley commune, if Drake-Tealy recalled correctly, who'd been manufacturing pistols for the past several years, half a world away.

Admittedly, it was a rather small world.

But there had been something else, as well, hadn't there? Some harrowing tale of jealousy and bloodshed in which this young fellow had been a victim — but then Drake-Tealy made a point of never paying attention to such things and couldn't remember the details. Nor did he attempt to do so now. Instead, he lugged the peculiar device back across the stream and set it down beside the wheelchair ramp.

"Flying machine?" he asked.

Emerson nodded again without looking up. He'd finished the skinning and was sitting at the top of the ramp, resharpening his knife against the edges of a pair of long brown triangular stones set at an angle to one another in a plastic base. As the youngster tested the results of his effort against a thumbnail, the older man caught a glimpse of sheet-gold initials—*GS*, not *EN*—inlaid in the dark, hardwood handle of the knife. "You're looking at the first production model of the Ngu Departure Flying Yoke, with room for cargo or a second passenger."

"A motorcycle with a sidecar," Drake-Tealy observed amiably, "or a bicycle built for two."

For some reason Emerson didn't reply, but concentrated harder on what he was doing. The whole story suddenly came back to Drake-Tealy and instantly he regretted what he'd said.

There'd been a girl.

About a year ago, it must have been.

Even at the time, he'd thought it was like something out of an old Jack London story. They—he still couldn't remember who "they" happened to have been—had found this poor chap lying in the middle of the spur road which, as he recalled, looped around Lake Selous from Curringer to the damned Greeley Project (he'd named that lake himself, which was why the territory remained relatively fresh in his memory), shot to pieces, half bled out, and very close to death.

Beside him lay the broken body of a young girl, already dead for several hours, which he'd either carried or dragged the two miles over rough country from where their flying machine—he'd automatically assumed it to be an ultralight—had been shot down by UN security hooligans acting outside their jurisdiction.

The girl had been connected with the Greeley Project somehow, not as one of its clients or whatever euphemism they were currently employing where the word "slave" stated the case much better. He was hazy on many of the details, or perhaps they'd never been clear to begin with. One thing was hideously clear: she'd been gang-raped and beaten to death, not necessarily—or exclusively—in that order. In its own way, it was a perfect example of the sort of phenomenon most individuals had come to Pallas in the first place to get away from.

Nor could Drake-Tealy recall anything coming of the semiofficial inquiry afterward. The weak point of the vaunted Stein Covenant, in his opinion—which he'd gone to some lengths to express during the early days on Pallas—was that it failed to specify an adjudicative structure. Miri, with Wild Bill Curringer to back her up, had always argued that the Covenant shouldn't limit any future arrangements which might prove better than anything she'd been able to think of at the time. In the end, of course, exactly as he'd predicted, the struggle for survival on a new world had claimed every bit of the time and energy which immigrants and pioneers might otherwise have expended coming up with something better.

This travesty had been inevitable.

At any rate, the UN guards had claimed that they'd been lost in rough country, shooting at what they'd innocently believed was a trespasser in the dark, and stuck to their story tenaciously—as what rapists and murderers wouldn't? The sole survivor wasn't available for comment, having remained in a deep coma for weeks.

So this was what had become of him.

It certainly accounted for the eye patch and the limp he'd observed.

Still feeling apologetic for his offhand remark, Drake-Tealy shuddered and forced himself to speak. "Would it be possible to try a spin, perhaps sometime tomorrow? I've heard a great deal about these things of yours and been fascinated."

The truth was that he hadn't flown since the accidental collision of two tiny, fragile aircraft out of three flying together which had killed his best friend and crippled the woman he loved, and furthermore, he had no desire to. Yet he often felt that there was nothing left of him any more but a garrulous old man, half starved for company. Moreover, he still needed to atone for the careless wagging of his tongue, in order to reclaim something of his self-esteem.

Apparently it worked. Emerson looked up from what he was doing and smiled. "Sure, Digger. I'd be happy to take you for a ride. Your lady, too, if she wants."

Drake-Tealy smiled back, pretending to an enthusiasm he didn't feel.

Or perhaps he did, after all.

And for the first time in years—but not the last for a long while—it suddenly occurred to him that their lives, his and Miri's, were about to change forever.

It was about bloody time.

XXVIII
DAYMARES

ALL MEN TELL THEMSELVES LIES IN ORDER TO MAKE THEIR
LIVES TOLERABLE, WHETHER IT HAPPENS TO BE BIG LIES LIKE
BEING LOVED BY AN ALL-SEEING, ALL-POWERFUL, ALL-MERCIFUL
GOD, OR LITTLE ONES LIKE BEING SIX FEET TALL INSTEAD OF
FIVE ELEVEN AND A HALF. TO LIVE WITHOUT THOSE LIES IS TO
WALK NAKED THROUGH A HAILSTORM, BUT IT'S ALSO TO WALK
FREE.
                        —William Wilde Curringer, *Unfinished Memoirs*

G *retchen screamed.*
  *Machine guns hammered at him in the blackness of the
night, tearing away his flesh.*

*He struggled to draw the Grizzly, but there was no feeling
left in his fingers. He was forced to look down helplessly as the
ultravelocity bullets splashed through him, stripping first the
skin, then the muscle from his body, pecking out his organs shred
by shred, leaving nothing behind but gleaming, bullet-riddled
bones.*

Gretchen screamed.

And suddenly it was daylight.

Emerson awoke with a start, his hair soaked and his
face bathed in a cold sweat. His back ached from the impression of rough bark being made on it through his shirt,
and he prickled from contact with the dry bed of brown
pine needles he was sitting on. Although for the past few
weeks, and especially the past few days, he'd generally felt
better, physically, than he had for more than a year, there
were, even yet, these unpredictable occasions of weakness
and fatigue when his body betrayed him—as it apparently
had half an hour ago, by his watch—and he was compelled
to realize all over again that he was still in the process of

recovering from wounds which by all rights ought to have been fatal.

For a long while he'd wished they had.

He discovered that he was sitting against the base of a tree a couple of miles from the cabin he'd been staying at for a week. The idea this morning had been to repay the kindness of his hosts with something that would relieve the monotony of venison. In his hands he still held the lighter and an unlit cigar he'd meant to smoke when he'd suddenly felt the need to sit and rest for a few minutes.

Instead, he'd nodded off and here he was.

Looking at the dry needles beneath and all around him, he was glad he hadn't lit the cigar.

It wasn't the first time this had happened to him, by any means. He'd come terrifyingly close to screwing his flying yoke into some unseen hillside more than once on his way across the face of the asteroid, which had been a factor in his decision to stop for a while. It wasn't the first time he'd had a dream like this, either, and he understood with a shuddering certainty that it wouldn't be the last. They seldom recalled anything that had literally occurred during the gunfight they inevitably concerned, but that didn't make them easier to take.

The machine-gun hammering continued off somewhere to his left. He knew it now for what it was, some variety of woodpecker happily drilling away at a hollow tree trunk.

With a deep sigh, he lit his cigar at last and leaned back again against the tree, drawing the Grizzly from its holster and keeping it in his lap, hammer cocked and safety on, his eye upwind on the muddy little wash where he and Digger had seen tracks yesterday. There were fierce pigs who came down to water here, where the evergreens thinned into deciduous woodland. No more than a dozen yards away, less than twenty feet uphill, he could still hear the mustard-colored flies buzzing around the big yellow blossoms of prickly pear cactus. But down here in what some of the Project peasants he'd grown up with would have called a wadi, the ground just beneath the forest litter, a hodgepodge of brown leaves and red-brown needles, was damp, and the air had a mushroom odor.

Digger—Emerson still found it hard to accept that his new friend was really the legendary anthropologist and adventurer Raymond Louis Drake-Tealy—had promised to churn up some sort of special barbecue sauce if Emerson could bag one of the pigs. The old man's easy confidence in his ability was touching. He was somewhere up the hill and downwind at this very moment, gathering the wild onions and garlic that grew in profusion everywhere on Pallas. He was well equipped to make good on his promise. They raised sweet Italian tomatoes in a tiny sheet-plastic greenhouse behind the cabin, and kept other supplies stashed away in a "root cellar," carved from the soft native carbonaceous chondrite, where they'd hung the deer a week ago. A bank of thermocouples powered by a gallium arsenide array on the cabin roof helped maintain an almost freezing temperature in the underground larder.

Now if only Emerson could reciprocate.

If only Emerson could stay awake.

Only Emerson could have wondered why he continued having dreams like this. There were impressive pseudoscientific words for what he was going through, as well as words well established in the common idiom—posttraumatic stress syndrome, flashbacks, shell shock, combat fatigue—but at best they only labeled the phenomenon. They failed utterly to explain it or make it easier to live with.

He knew it wasn't a matter of guilt over not having given an honorable account of himself during the attack outside the Project. Although the UN contingent had car-

ried away their own dead and wounded, professional
trackers hired by Aloysius had told him afterward that he
and Gretchen had been set upon by no fewer than a dozen
of Junior's uniformed hatchetmen, of whom he and the
girl—dazed and injured as they'd been by having been
shot down and by the subsequent crash landing—had
killed four and possibly as many as six (although there was
some reason to believe that more than one had died from
overly enthusiastic "friendly" fire).

For that matter, it wasn't any kind of guilt at all. The
only thing he felt about having killed a human being, possibly more than one—and he'd never been in doubt about
this from the moment he'd regained consciousness—was a
fervently held regret that he hadn't managed to kill many
more of them that night.

Nor was it simply a matter of missing his beloved
Gretchen or regretting her death. No words were adequate to express how he felt about that. He wasn't sure
there were any adequate feelings for it, either. He might
never come to terms with it, nor with the circumstances
connected with it. In some respects he'd been ashamed to
realize in the months that followed the event, during which
he'd had very little to do but think about it, that he still
clung to sanity only because he'd given her up for dead
when she'd married Junior, and the one brief night they'd
had together afterward seemed unreal. But if that was
what was bothering him now, why did he never dream of
her except to hear her screaming like a fighting banshee?

God knew that he could see her clearly enough in his
waking mind's eye and remember every intimate moment
they'd had, as well as every intimacy, in happier times.

The thing he ought to be having nightmares—or day-
mares—about was what had happened afterward. Emerson had been a long while recovering from his wounds,
longer than he'd known was possible. He'd spent weeks in

a coma, so they'd told him, many weeks more when he was
too weak to speak more than a couple of words or even
raise his head from his pillow, and months in which sitting
up, standing, taking three steps across the room—or simply lying motionless and enduring the pain inflicted on him
by a shattered body and what came very close to being a
shattered mind—had exhausted him for the rest of the day.

There had been surprises, all of them unpleasant. He'd
never suffered a prolonged illness before and never realized that a person could actually be too sick to read. He'd
lacked whatever it took to concentrate or care, and the
words on the page had simply slid by the eye he still had
left without imparting any meaning to him.

There had been other things he'd been too weak for.
He'd first awakened in Curringer, in Cherry's squeaky
brass bed in her room upstairs at Galena's, during a
fiercely whispered argument the girl seemed to be having
with Mrs. Singh. Apparently he'd come out of his coma a
day or two earlier, although he had no memory of that, and
had been sleeping more normally off and on since then. Believing he was still asleep, the two women had almost come
to blows over where he was going to finish recuperating
and who would be taking care of him.

He'd pretended to sleep until they were gone.

That afternoon, without their knowing it, he'd persuaded Doc Sheahan, the husky blond veterinarian who
was Curringer's only physician—and who might well have
been named Gretchen if her name hadn't already been
Heidi—to tell both of them that he couldn't be moved after
all. It wasn't that he preferred staying at Cherry's place—
although, of course, in some respects he did—but he was
already here, and to some degree Mrs. Singh must be used
to that fact. Being the cause of fighting between the two
living souls he cared most about was a burden he wasn't

strong enough to shoulder and possibly never would be again.

In time they'd both accepted the status quo and, free of some of their worries over him, had returned to the amicable if guarded relationship they'd had before the disaster. At this moment, along with Nails and Aloysius, they were running the Ngu Departure plant together, Mrs. Singh as chief of quality control, Cherry keeping the books.

He'd also been too weak for a long time to benefit from—or even to appreciate much—certain unique notions his volunteer nurse cherished with regard to convalescent care. Even now, to some extent, the reliable miracle wasn't all that reliable, and what surprised him most— even more than his disconcerting problem with reading— was that it was every bit as difficult to finish the process as to begin. It was as if his status as an organism fit for survival—and on that account for passing on his genes—had been ruled probationary.

But even that wasn't the worst.

Nobody but Junior (and evidently his father, sometime after the fact) had ever known who it was that had raped and murdered Gretchen and left him for dead. They might as well have been nameless, faceless automata, and would likely remain unidentified forever. There'd been a sudden rotation of the Project's UN personnel back to Earth, and the men who'd accomplished Junior's dirty work for him were probably beyond reach, one way or another, since the UN, safely tucked away beyond freedom of the press, and therefore criticism, in its Third World enclave, tended to be more direct in its methods than previously these days, and even more inclined than those among Doc Sheahan's profession to bury its mistakes.

Strangely enough, Emerson had found that he didn't care about the goons themselves. Every day he'd vowed to get up out of Cherry's soft, luxurious bed and go after the person who was really responsible for everything that had happened. More than anything he wanted to hunt down the murderous son of a bitch like the dog he was, and to kill him as slowly and painfully as possible. When he'd been able to read again, he'd made a serious study of the subject, summoning the electronic versions of books on the limits of human endurance and the history of torture, only to realize, with a pang of regret, that he was too civilized and that he'd have to be satisfied with making sure that Junior was dead.

But when he'd gotten on his feet, he discovered he'd been cheated out of even that much satisfaction. Gibson Altman Junior had fled rather than face him. Apparently he'd left Pallas altogether, bound for where, not even his own father knew—or so the man had claimed when confronted; it was difficult to be sure over the phone and, ironically, there was no possibility now that Emerson would be admitted onto Project property to confront him in the flesh.

The Senator, it seemed, was afraid of Emerson.

As well he might be.

Junior was probably on Earth; there weren't that many other places to go. Earth's moon (the distinction had to be made since Pallatians were likely to refer to Pallas B as "the moon," as well), once almost exclusively reserved to scientists and the military, had become a ghost world with the outbreak of the second Great Depression. Mars, a good deal less hospitable than Antarctica to everyone but incurable romantics, had defeated one attempt at conquest after another until the would-be conquerors had given up and gone home, at least for this century. Only William Wilde Curringer's unique vision of human beings populating the asteroids had proven viable so far, and even that

viability was limited, for the time being, to mining operations scattered throughout the Belt, although there was always talk of colonizing Ceres.

There was always talk of colonizing Ceres.

For a while, with those mining settlements in mind, and
with the help of Aloysius's business and political connec-
tions at both Pallatian poles, Emerson had employed his
convalescent period and the phone to become familiar with
spaceships, schedules, and spaceport characters in an attempt to track Junior down. He'd met a lot of odd and colorful individuals that way, but with one exception, nothing
had ever come of it. He had learned that Gretchen's little
daughter, Gwen-Rose, had been shipped Earthside by a
grandfather unable or unwilling to care for her.

Junior himself had vanished.

A sudden noise, the rustling of dried leaves in the undergrowth, brought Emerson back to the present. There,
by the wash, stood a feral pig—a sow by the look of her,
despite her enormous size—about to bend her head to take
a drink.

Emerson forced himself to breathe.

Although she minced with exaggerated delicacy on her
tiny hooves, there was nothing cute and pink about this
great, shaggy beast, nor was there an ounce of piggish fat
on her long, broad, heavily muscled frame. She looked as if
she were put together from bridge cable and fiberglass,
covered with steel lathe-chips. Emerson had knocked
down thousands of metallic silhouettes patterned after
creatures like this without understanding at a gut level that
they represented a wild and hardy animal big enough and
powerful enough—and, more importantly, determined
enough—to maim or kill him if he missed this shot.

She'd caught him much worse than flat-footed. He'd almost been napping, sitting with his legs folded under him.

Slowly he raised the Grizzly in his right hand, cocking

his head over on his shoulder to get his good left eye behind the sights. By now he'd trained himself to shoot left-handed, but in this primal moment it never occurred to him to try.

At the last instant, as he thumbed the safety off with a faint click, the sow heard him and pivoted on her front feet. Before she'd finished her turn, she was rocketing toward him, a brownish-yellow blur of animal fury preceded by four wicked, side-thrusting yellow tusks well capable of hamstringing and disemboweling him.

It was a very different experience from shooting at an iron cutout. Dust motes seemed to hang frozen where they were caught in shafts of sunlight streaming through the treetops all around him, and the smell of moist earth and leaf mold was all but overwhelming. He could watch the fetid steam blasting from the sow's flared nostrils, hear her frenzied breathing, see the fury in her eyes and the cruel ridges on the roof of her mouth between her razor-edged molars.

While he was preoccupied with these observations, his front sight seemed to rise of its own accord—he was completely unaware of his rear sight, exactly as he should have been—and as the scarlet inlay found the center of her chest, just below her blunt chin, the trigger seemed to pull itself. He never felt the Grizzly recoil in his hands or heard the blast that shook leaves from the trees.

It did seem to him that she should have stopped, or at least stumbled, under the appalling impact of half a ton of kinetic energy, but she didn't even hesitate as the bullet struck—he watched the dust explode from her coarse fur as it did—but continued straight for him until her forelegs collapsed beneath her and she slid the remaining two feet, motionless and dead, her wet snout pushing up a ridge of soil before coming to rest against his folded knee, leaving a small damp spot to darken the worn and faded denim.

Emerson remembered to breathe again.

"*Olé!*" It was Drake-Tealy, rising from a crouch in the woods behind him. "You've got a cool hand, Emerson Ngu. When she charged, I'd have climbed that tree behind you, backwards!"

Emerson, too, got to his feet, forcing his reluctant limbs to cooperate. He had to lock his knees to keep them from folding under him again. Prodding the sow with a cautious toe, he flipped the Grizzly's safety upward, switched to a full magazine, holstered the weapon, and laughed. "I hate to disillusion you, Digger, but I was too scared to move!" He was astonished to realize that he felt alive again for the first time in almost a year, although he was going to have to think long and hard about why that should be—why the death of one entity should bring life to another—before he understood it without shrinking from it.

Drake-Tealy joined him in laughter. "Fortunately, your trigger finger suffered no such affliction. Let's get her back to the house." He indicated the wicker basket hanging on his arm. "I've got what I came for—dangerous vegetables. We ought to hang this old lady for a day or two, but my mouth is set on barbecue tonight."

Emerson nodded, regretting that he hadn't brought his flying yoke and wondering if he ought to fetch it from the cabin. They didn't have far to go, however, and the pig, although she weighed twice what he did, wouldn't be much of a burden.

He took hold of her back legs to let her bleed through the chest wound along the way, and perhaps to avoid those tusks which even now gave him the shudders. Dragging the animal behind, he followed Drake-Tealy up the hill onto drier ground and back through the woods. His mouth was set, as well, although he didn't know on what. His ancestors may have invented it, but he'd never tasted barbecued pork before.

He also realized, as he came in sight of the porch and of the hook screwed into its ceiling beam, that he'd never dressed or skinned a pig before, either.

XXIX
PROPHETS IN THE WILDERNESS

I DISTRUST PROFESSIONAL SKEPTICS WHO SPEND A DISPROPORTIONATE AMOUNT OF ENERGY DENOUNCING DUMB BUT RELATIVELY HARMLESS ENDEAVORS LIKE ASTROLOGY AND UFOLOGY, WHILE PARTICIPATING IN MORE AMBITIOUS HOAXES THEMSELVES, SUCH AS GLOBAL WARMING, OZONE DEPLETION, CENTRAL ECONOMIC PLANNING, AND ORGANIZED RELIGION.
— Mirelle Stein, *The Productive Class*

M en—ridiculous!"
Mirelle Stein was obviously unused to sitting, watching others cooking and serving in her own home. Looking at her now, she seemed liable to fly apart any moment.

Nevertheless, with Emerson to assist him, that was just what Digger had insisted on. He'd grown increasingly impatient watching his young friend attempting to butcher an unfamiliar carcass. To begin with he had taken over that task, carefully washing and stropping Gretchen's knife afterward before returning it, giving it excellent marks— praise from the solar system's foremost expert on primitive weapons—for its beauty and practicability, characteristics which, Emerson felt, merely reflected similar virtues in its original owner.

Then the old man had run both Emerson and his wife out of the kitchen (simply a matter of insisting that they remain on the other side of the room) while he cooked.

Emerson was supposed to amuse and divert the lady of

the house, no easy task for him because, somehow, Stein (he'd never have thought to call her by her first name or its diminutive, and "Mrs. Drake-Tealy" didn't seem to work either) intimidated Emerson.

For a while, he'd tried to escape his awkward assignment by pretending to reexamine the great fireplace which occupied almost one whole end of the high-ceilinged living room, constructed of native stone as varied and colorful in composition—thanks to the massive prehistoric bombardment by meteoric material which had given this area of Pallas its name—as the exterior of the house.

Naturally, he paid more attention to Digger's rifle, which was almost as impressive, a laboriously reworked Pattern 14 Enfield, whatever that meant, originally overbuilt for a much less powerful military cartridge. Obviously enjoying the gleaming blue-black steel and the dull sheen of dark, polished hardwood all over again through Emerson's eye, the anthropologist had told him, shortly after he'd arrived, that it might be the only full-powered long-barreled weapon on the asteroid. The colonists, who'd virtually paid by the ounce for their passage here, preferred handguns, and the assault carbines now being issued to Project security didn't count, since they employed cartridges hardly more powerful than pistol fodder, depending on what Drake-Tealy had called "trick bullets" and a high rate of fire rather than the energy of each shot.

More than anything else, however, Emerson was fascinated with what Stein referred to with mocking gravity as "Drake-Tealy Objects," almost a hundred of them, laid out along the mantelpiece.

Named, with whatever sincerity, after their discoverer, they'd been found when the foundations of the house and the root cellar had been excavated and had apparently remained on the mantel for years as simple curiosities. It was possible, in Drake-Tealy's view, that the weather-worn,

time-distorted Objects were artificial, remnants of an unimaginably ancient, nonhuman intelligence. It was equally
possible, he conceded at his wife's scornful insistence, that
they were no more than peculiar vacuum extrusions of volcanic stone and metal, like the pillow lava on Earth's ocean
floors, left over from the natural formation of the asteroid.

None was larger than Emerson's fist.

Some were simple shapes: cubes, rhomboids, parallelo-
grams, cylinders, half-cylinders, ovoids, triangular and
pentagonal solids, oddities with six, seven, eight, or nine
sides. It was difficult to see how such perfect forms could
have been natural, but Emerson knew little about crystal-
line minerals. He had to admit that he'd seen naturally occurring shapes somewhat like this before. The trouble was,
all of these appeared to be made of the same dense, dark
bronze—later he would learn it wasn't bronze, but a semi-
conducting material considerably harder than steel—and
didn't a crystal's shape depend on what it was made of?

And if they were truly crystals, why were a few of them
shaped like short T-handled spoons, spools or spindles,
gears with strangely cupped teeth, even vaguely threaded
bolts, complete with hexagonal nuts screwed onto them
halfway up the shaft?

"Let me see, now: dried tamarinds, black pepper, mo-
lasses . . ." For a while, with his back toward them, Digger
kept up a commentary as he collected his spices, then
washed and cut up the produce he'd brought in from forest
and greenhouse. "You know, when you first showed up on
our doorstep, I thought you were a Project runaway."

"I know," Emerson replied. "I am, in a way."

"So you've informed us, although it sounds like you've
made quite a place for yourself since then in the real
world—Outside, as you call it. We've seen such runaways
more and more frequently over the years, even as far away
as we are. I guess Wild Bill was right: when we found, to

our dismay, that we had no choice but to let them in, he held that sooner or later the Project would collapse anyway. Nine-tenths of the people on Pallas are one kind of refugee or another, from various calamities on Earth. It wouldn't make that much difference, in the end, if some of them turned out to be refugees from a local calamity, as well."

"It's a calamity, all right." Emerson reflected on how much easier it was to talk with the old man than with his wife. "I can personally testify to that. And it does seem to be collapsing; at least that's the impression we get two hundred miles away in Curringer."

"Or five miles away at the Ngu Departure factory?" asked Stein, raising her eyebrows.

Emerson turned to her, no less intimidated than before, but unashamed and unapologetic. "Yes, ma'am, I'm helping it to collapse—doing my very best, anyway."

Stein opened her mouth to reply, but was interrupted.

"But here's the real reason," declared Digger, "that the Greeley Utopian Memorial Project is inexorably doomed." He turned to them with a peeled onion in one hand and a freshly trimmed radish from the greenhouse in the other. "These tears you see upon my countenance are not for the demise of socialism on this planetoid, but on account of the onion. The wild ones are always stronger."

"Mustard seeds from one prophet," Stein stated enigmatically, "onions from another."

Whatever it meant, Digger ignored it. "When we planned this undertaking, my esteemed partners and I, we unwittingly made certain that the ground was prepared, as it were, with all that was required for the Project's ultimate dissolution. Not only do Pallatians eat several times the meat enjoyed by the average inhabitant of Earth, and consequently have less use for vegetation as a bulk food, but there's always an abundance of hardy wild produce available for the gathering."

Emerson nodded understanding. In the Lake Selous region, both game and wild crops were taken from private land, sometimes for a fee, if that was the business the landowner happened to be in. Most Outsiders picked mushrooms, berries, or whatever else was in season, sometimes making a community occasion of it. But they often did it even while they hunted. Although he'd read Drake-Tealy's book several times, he hadn't realized that this reflected a deliberate policy.

"What we didn't foresee," Digger went on, "was the popularity gardening would enjoy among the immigrants. I suppose it could be that old agricultural habits die hard— I've often believed that's why the Yanks and Brits are so maniacal about their bloody lawns—or simply that it's dead easy to grow things on this fresh new world. Nor did we anticipate that gardening would fill the rest of the grocery bill as well as it does, given a bit of bartering amongst the gardeners. The better established our uniquely designed culture on this little asteroid becomes, the less need there is for something like the Project."

Emerson shook his head. "Which means that ten thousand agricultural workers—"

"Will be absorbed by a more modern, more efficient economy," Drake-Tealy interrupted him, "as they trickle out of the Project, exactly as you were, old chap—those that aren't eaten first by wild predators or blunderbussed by irate householders."

The older man turned and fell silent as he concentrated on sautéing the ingredients of his barbecue sauce. At last, Emerson was forced to converse—or make a stab at it; he was afraid of creating as big a mess as he had of the hog— with the woman many felt was the solar system's foremost expert on ethical philosophy.

That he was afraid of her, he'd already admitted to himself. There was nothing warm about the woman, nothing kind, almost nothing human. Instead, there was an injured belligerence, even when she seemed to be relaxing. He felt that he was being continuously judged—and convicted—merely for the crime of existing.

Her appearance didn't help much. Beneath a dark cloaklike garment which she usually kept across her knees, but which could also double as a cape on chilly evenings, she seemed to be wearing her husband's faded work clothes. In a long, ivory-tipped ebony holder, she chain-smoked one smoldering cigarette after another, consuming more tobacco every day than her husband and Emerson combined.

Her hair, worn in a style he didn't know was called a pageboy, with bangs across her forehead that might have been cut against the edge of a ruler (and may very well have been, if the methodical Drake-Tealy did the cutting), had once been dark, but was now heavily streaked with gray. Her face below the bangs was a tortured network of fine lines, more the product of constant pain than age.

That much Emerson could understand. He'd recently experienced that kind of pain himself.

Her eyes were brown and very large, like those of the children he'd seen in some overly sentimental postcard portraits Horatio or Mrs. Singh had tucked into one of their books on fine art and apparently forgotten. Even more than those of the children, Stein's were lost eyes, orphaned eyes, eyes starving for something.

Emerson wasn't certain for what; he was certain he didn't want to know.

"They were talking about you on the wireless while you were off hunting, young man."

Her words came in a heavy, often almost incomprehensible eastern European accent, although Emerson had

thought her an American. Digger looked even more surprised at the news than Emerson, who'd gathered from
several things he'd heard over the last week that the old
man hadn't known his wife ever listened to the radio on
her own initiative. They were out here in the Pocks, Digger had told him in so many words and more than once,
because of her insistence on seclusion. She hated being a
cripple and hated even more for people to see her that way.

Most of all, according to him, she hated being reminded that other people existed.

"They speak of a brilliant young fellow who mysteriously disappears after a tragic incident, leaving behind all
of his friends, his various business enterprises in their
trustworthy and capable hands, and, taking advantage of
his most recent invention, travels across the unexplored
and undeveloped reaches of Pallas."

"As you know, ma'am," Emerson, sitting on the rustic
sofa where he'd slept for the last six nights, nodded to the
wheelchair-bound woman, "that's essentially the truth."

When he'd discovered what he had to do, he'd most
dreaded leaving Cherry behind—or rather telling her he
had to go—but he needn't have worried. Of all the people
he'd known and cared for in the little town of Curringer,
she'd understood him with the least explanation. Although
she loved him in her own peculiar way—or possibly *because*
she loved him—she'd encouraged him to go.

Their last night together had been full of miracles.

About now, looking into the lost eyes of this old woman
who was Cherry's precise opposite in so many ways (or
Gretchen's, although the two girls couldn't have been
more different from one another), and although he sensed
that he was far from finished with his wanderings, he'd
have given anything to be with the little blond.

"Yes," Stein told him. "I know."

Know what? Emerson had to struggle to remember

what he'd just said to her. He suddenly realized that she
was opening up to him this way (if that was what was happening) because she identified his temporary need to be
away from civilization with her own, more permanent affliction. Perhaps she was justified in that. In his own way,
at the moment, he was just as crippled as she was.

"And now stories filter back of this brilliant young fellow's exploits and discoveries. He is in danger, it appears,
of becoming another Daniel Crockett or David Boone—"

"That's Daniel Boone and Davy Crockett," Digger
corrected her from the kitchen. Although his words were
bantering, there was something ominous in his tone that
Emerson hadn't heard before. He had no idea who these
people were talking about, Boone and Crockett, old
friends of theirs? Nevertheless, with each moment that
passed, he felt more and more that he was about to be
trapped—and pulped—between the unstoppable gears of
some massive piece of ancient machinery.

"Another Pierre Radisson, then," she went on, "although a certain former United States Senator, who seems
to blame this brilliant young fellow for every failure in his
own life, attempts to ridicule these stories in the media he
influences, and demands that the brilliant young fellow be
tracked down and dragged back, possibly even to Earth, to
be tried on charges which he somehow always avoids
specifying."

Emerson's eye widened and his blood raced at the
mention of Altman. Was the Chief Administrator blaming
him for what had happened? Of course he was, don't be
silly. But Stein had raised so many other questions that he
didn't know where to begin asking them.

What exploits and discoveries?

He'd done nothing and seen practically nobody since
he'd headed for the wilderness months ago. Pallas had
about thirty thousand people living on it, a third of them

concentrated in the Project, a few thousand more on the opposite shore of Lake Selous, the rest scattered over the asteroid's surface, usually in larger groups—but only slightly larger—than typified by Digger and his wife.

Maybe the media were talking about that pack of feral dogs he'd helped drive away from a tiny settlement at the foot of Mount Jack O'Connor, but if so, they were exaggerating horribly. It had needed doing and he'd done it. Nothing heroic about that.

And what media?

Had KCUF suddenly taken to interviewing their worst enemy?

"It is said"—and now Stein watched her husband, whose back was turned as he worked at the counter, while she continued to address Emerson—"that in his wanderings, this brilliant young fellow has encountered the legendary R.L. Drake-Tealy himself—"

Stirring utensil in hand, Digger turned abruptly. "Miri—"

"—long rumored," Stein went on relentlessly, "to have died or departed Pallas years earlier. Instead, he is living in seclusion in the 'Pocks,' an empty, heavily cratered wasteland far to the southeast of Curringer, with the woman he married—"

"Miri, stop it!"

"Growing in detail and drama as alleged eyewitnesses from the asteroid's pioneer days are discovered, the story has it that she was seriously injured in the same aviation accident that killed William Wilde Curringer. For all these decades she has been confined to a wheelchair, cared for by the selfless anthropologist, who somehow escaped the same aerial mishap without so much as a scratch."

Shoulders bowed, Digger turned back to the counter, resting both hands on its edge. Whether he was trying to control his temper or his tears, Emerson couldn't tell.

Mostly, it just looked to Emerson as though he were exhausted right down to his bones.

"Will the legendary founding couple return to human ken, the media want to know, now that this brilliant young fellow—*damn him!*" Momentarily, she whirled on Emerson with hatred burning in her eyes. "—has ferreted them out? Is that what you truly wish for, Raymond, the adulation you deserve and never received?"

By now Emerson was more than confused, he was utterly lost and deeply embarrassed. What was happening here? Why were his new friends turning on each other this way? Were they always like this when they were alone, and had they merely run out of company manners in a week's time? If so, how had they survived all these years?

If Mirelle Stein hated Raymond Louis Drake-Tealy as much as she seemed to at this moment, why did she stay with him?

And how much of what she'd said about the radio had been true?

Suddenly he felt very tired, himself.

XXX

THE GOSSAMER GOONEY-BIRD

PEOPLE—PARDON ME, JOURNALISTS AND POLITICIANS—HAVE
OFTEN ACCUSED ME OF BELIEVING THAT I'M ABOVE THE LAW.
AND YET, WHO ISN'T? EVERYWHERE YOU PROD IT, EVEN WITH
THE SHORTEST STICK, THE ESTABLISHED SYSTEM ISN'T SIMPLY
CORRUPT, IT'S UNEQUIVOCALLY PUTRESCENT. THE LAW IS
CREATED BY DEMONSTRABLE CRIMINALS, ENFORCED BY
DEMONSTRABLE CRIMINALS, INTERPRETED BY DEMONSTRABLE
CRIMINALS, ALL FOR DEMONSTRABLY CRIMINAL PURPOSES. OF
COURSE I'M ABOVE THE LAW. AND SO ARE YOU.
      —**William Wilde Curringer,** *Unfinished Memoirs*

D igger?"
  "Shh!"
  Emerson shook his head with exasperation. The old
man hadn't turned, but had continued to sit on his poncho
on the creek bank at a spot where a beaver dam lower
down had widened the little stream into a pond. He was
holding a fishing pole, line hanging limply into still water.
A wicker creel sat open beside him, empty so far.

Across his back were the straps of a shoulder holster in
which he carried his Webley Mark VI. They'd seen what
he'd identified as African leopard sign in the neighborhood
yesterday afternoon, and it never paid, the anthropologist
had warned, to be blasé about mankind's ancient enemy.
He had proprietary feelings toward the beast since it had
been he, over the strenuous objections of some of the other
planners, who'd insisted on bringing large, dangerous
predators to Pallas.

They were about a mile from the cabin, and Emerson
was feeling impatient. His work had been stopped—and
his concentration broken—for lack of the simplest of tools.

"Digger, I'm sorry, but do you have a three-eighths-inch hex wrench I could borrow?"

Drake-Tealy sighed and began to reel his line in. He set his pole aside and turned to face Emerson. "D'you mean an Allen key? I've a nine-and-a-half millimeter that'll serve. I thought you carried a tool kit in that velocipede of yours. What are you about, anyway? Why don't you give up on mechanics this afternoon and come fishing? I've another pole—Miri's, actually, but she never uses it."

"Digger, you're an exceptionally kind host." Emerson grinned down at this man who'd wanted him to hush up. "But if I wanted fish, I'd jump in and shoot them rather than dangle a string from a stick, hoping some animal you can't see will be dumb enough to get pulled in. I can't think of a less intelligent or productive way to waste time."

Drake-Tealy got slowly to his feet. "That's only because you've never seen golf." Grunting a little, he bent to pick up pole, poncho, and creel. "Besides, what's the point of wasting time, if you do it intelligently and productively?"

Emerson laughed. "I guess I never looked at it that way before. I do have a tool kit, Digger, but only for emergency repairs. I never anticipated what I'm doing now."

"Which is what?" With an eye out for dangerous predators, they began walking back toward the cabin. Emerson had to admit that it did add a certain zest to life, something like having to watch for the goons when he listened to his clandestine radio—except that he could admire a leopard at the same time he was wary of it.

"Separating the two halves of my flying yoke by pulling them apart at the hinge. The wrench is for the hinge pin. Which reminds me . . ." Emerson hesitated, uncertain how to continue. "It might be best—I mean, it might be a good idea . . ."

The old man answered with a low chuckle, not altogether humorous in character, "If I made myself scarce when you're ready to try out whatever scheme you're working on? Emerson, if you're up to what I think you are, I couldn't agree more."

Emerson was surprised—and relieved. "I'm sorry—"

"No need to be. It's certainly no fault of yours." Drake-Tealy shook his shaggy head. "Miri and I made our bed—an unfortunate turn of phrase if ever there was one—thirty years before you were born, and we've been lying in it ever since."

Emerson didn't know what to say. Digger and his wife hadn't repeated their strange fight, if that's what it had been, in the five weeks following that uncomfortable evening. Dinner had probably been magnificent, but none of them had really tasted it.

Perhaps millions of young people would have been completely disillusioned to discover that their heroes were human, that they suffered human feelings and made human mistakes. Emerson had never assumed otherwise. It made Stein, Curringer, and Drake-Tealy no less heroic in his eye, rather the contrary. Individuals who were never afraid, who never felt fatigue and despair, were automata or lunatics, not heroes. Individuals who were moved by all of those considerations and managed to forge ahead in spite of them—those were Emerson's heroes.

Five weeks—six altogether. He hadn't meant to stay this long. In fact, he'd been determined to trudge on the next morning, toward the South Pole, the destination he'd always had in mind. But the old man had persuaded him to give them a second chance. Even his wife had thawed sufficiently to argue that he was less than well and needed the kind of shelter, food, and rest he could get with them. Both of them had promised—in so many words, and when the other wasn't around—that they wouldn't tear into one another in his presence again.

The whole affair made him feel vaguely ridiculous whenever he gave it any thought, like a parent being successfully wheedled by two elderly children who'd misbehaved. It was their own business if they wanted to disembowel each other verbally. He simply didn't want to be an unwilling witness or referee. But he'd had to admit that Stein was right. His recent practice of dozing off while flying mountain passes or hunting wild boar was not exactly conducive to survival.

But now, he was beginning to feel embarrassed again. "Look, Digger, it isn't any of my—"

"Half a minute." Drake-Tealy stopped walking, turned to face him, and put up a free hand. They weren't quite within sight of the house. "As difficult as it may prove, I've a mind to clear the air now, before this goes another step further, because I believe I know what you intend doing this afternoon, and I approve, very, very much. We needed you to come along, Emerson, quite desperately. We could have used someone like you ten years ago—no, make that twenty years ago."

Feeling a peculiar panic rising within him, Emerson put up both of his hands. "Digger, you don't have to—"

Drake-Tealy was firm. "Yes, Emerson, I'm afraid I do. You see, even old fossils like Miri and I, with one foot in the mortuary metaphor and the other on a tropical cliché, have our passions—or at least our memories of them. And, as I'm certain you've already discovered for yourself, sometimes memories can be a burden."

Emerson had never thought of Digger and his wife as fossils, any more than he had ever thought it of Aloysius or Mrs. Singh. Most of his Outsider friends, it seemed, had gray hair and ages closer to three figures than to one. But this didn't appear to be the time to protest that aspect of what Drake-Tealy had said. And yes, he acknowledged inwardly, he knew burdensome memories all too well.

"All right." He looked the old man in the eye. "Say what you have to say, Digger. I'll listen."

"Good on you." There was relief in Drake-Tealy's expression. "Miri's burden, all these years, and it's weighed as heavily on her as her injuries, is that she was engaged to Wild Bill Curringer in the old days. They were to be married in a splashy public ceremony—the first wedding on Pallas—when the immigrant ships began arriving from Earth. But by the time we'd done with the terraforming and had begun seeding the planet with the life you see all around you now, things had changed. She'd fallen in love with Curringer's best friend."

"You."

"Guilty." Drake-Tealy shrugged. "It happens. We'd been planning to have a talk with Bill about it after we'd finished seeding operations around what's now called Lake Selous, but a thing like that is rather hard to hide, and he must have had some idea of what was going on, possibly even before we did ourselves."

Both of them began walking again, although at a slower pace. "Bill was the sort of chap who simply had to have his hands in anything he was connected with," Digger explained, "and Miri and I couldn't be satisfied unless we were right there beside him, up to our own elbows in the muck, as well. Each of us was flying a little ultralight that day—the professional horticulture crew, quite understandably, had tried to talk us out of it. We were spreading our precious consignment over the landscape, soil molds, buffalo grasses, and earthworm eggs, each particle with a special protein coating to assure that the timing would work out right."

Emerson shook his head. He knew, of course, how this story was going to turn out. He'd examined Curringer's statue and read the inscription on the base too many times

to forget. But it was the first time he'd heard it from someone who'd been there.

"You know what a World War I biplane looked like?"
Drake-Tealy asked him. "Well, these were rather like that,
our little aeroplanes, only smaller, with transparent wings,
and a deal more fragile. Bill snapped a wingspar, the gods
alone know how, and plummeted like any bird with a broken wing. Most likely he'd have survived a fall, given what
we've got for gravity hereabouts, but by the time he hit the
ground, headed in under full power, he was doing almost
two hundred miles an hour."

Drake-Tealy stopped again, just within sight of the
cabin.

"Miri came to believe afterward that it couldn't have
been an accident. I've never been convinced one way or
the other, altogether. It is a difficult mishap to explain, but
I find it endlessly more difficult to believe that Bill committed suicide."

"Could it have been murder?" Emerson asked.

"I've given it some thought. Wild Bill was by no means
the most popular fellow in the solar system. One fact is in-
controvertible: it was a bitterly unhappy man at the controls that day, and we were the ones who'd made him that
way. At the time, Miri followed him down, desperately trying to catch him up and get his nose up or nudge him into
the lake. Instead, they packed it in together as I circled,
watching helplessly. Truth to tell, old chap, neither of us
has ever learned how to live with the guilt we still feel
every day over what happened."

"So instead," Emerson suggested, glad to get the words
out, "you've spent the past several decades together, hating yourselves and making each other miserable."

"You're very wise for one so young, my boy," Drake-
Tealy replied. "I may let you live, anyway."

❊   ❊   ❊

They found the wrench Emerson needed in the toolshed, actually more of an outdoor closet, that comprised one end of the greenhouse. Digger, complying with Emerson's earlier request, ducked inside the house briefly for his rifle and immediately hurried off on an errand of his own. He didn't intend doing anything about the African leopard, he explained, but he wanted very much to see it.

"What's life," he grinned as he turned to march back into the forest, "without a little danger?"

"A whole lot easier on the cardiovascular system," his young friend replied automatically, but he didn't really mean it, and the old man didn't hear him, anyway.

Emerson sighed and went to the front porch, where he sat cross-legged for over an hour, carefully dismantling his flying yoke and reassembling it just as carefully as a pair of the independent machines he'd first invented. Each half of the device would now suffer from the same range, speed, and altitude limitations which had frustrated him during the process of development, but that was irrelevant at the moment.

It wasn't a set of wings he was building, but a set of legs.

Then came the really hard part.

Taking one of the machines with him, he went through the front door and into the living room, where Stein was sitting with a book processor in her lap, reading. Unaware that it was rude, he looked over her shoulder and saw that she was leafing through the *Unfinished Memoirs* of William Wilde Curringer, the only thing the man had ever written, published shortly after his untimely death.

Emerson had read it, too, but from paper pages, bound between plastic covers.

Why do I suspect that if all the money spent on ramps, bus elevators, and the like in an attempt to make the world

"wheelchair accessible" had been dedicated to neurologi-
cal research, no one would need ramps and elevators?
Why do I suspect that, if it had, the lawyers would have
stopped it on behalf of clients who prefer being crippled
and helpless to losing their government benefits?

As his shadow fell across her shoulders, Stein cleared
the screen, folded the laptop, and set it aside.

She looked up at him. "It is an amusing paragraph, is it
not, prophetic and pathetic at the same time?"

How was he supposed to answer that?

"Poor William never guessed that these words would
ever be published. He was so misunderstood—willfully so
by politicians and the media—that it was something Raymond and I thought must be done for him after he passed
away. Raymond calls it history's longest epitaph. Writing
casually, for his own benefit, William conducted no research and did not know that such a lawsuit had been filed
already back in the nineties, for precisely the depraved and
disgusting reason he specified. Nor did he realize that
what he wrote would ever apply to anyone he knew personally. He was an engineer. He simply hated the waste."

Emerson nodded, still not knowing what to say. This
was too much like an extension of the conversation he'd
just had with Drake-Tealy. These two old people might
not be happy together, but they were very much alike, and
he was aware that there can sometimes be too much mutual understanding. He was reminded of something he'd
read in one of Horatio Singh's books—was it Shaw or
Churchill?—about the British and Americans being two
peoples separated by a common language.

Her eyes suddenly brightened and he could see a trace
of what once must have been great beauty. "What have
you been working on out there all morning, young man? Is
that it, there in your hand? Is it what I think it is? If it is, I

believe I shall surprise you. I know that I can be rather forbidding at times, but you need not dread the necessity of arguing me, of all people, into something new."

Emerson felt a wave of excitement. "Then you'll—"

"I would very much like to try your invention, if I may. I have wanted to since you first arrived. These wheels—" she slapped a palm down on the armrest of her chair "—were not made for the wilderness, nor the wilderness for them."

Emerson nodded again. One of the things he'd feared most during his recovery was that he might end up in a chair just like hers on an undeveloped frontier world.

"And now," asked the foremost ethical philosopher in the solar system, throwing her lap blanket aside and grinning up at him like a child, "what do I have to do?"

He looked her over. She was wearing trousers on her withered legs. Her arms, as he'd observed long before this, were surprisingly muscular. Emerson had arranged the nylon support straps so that they could be unfastened easily from the rim of the flying yoke. Under the kindly gravity of Pallas, it was relatively easy, even as awkward as he felt doing it, to move her from the chair to the floor, slide those straps beneath her, and refasten them where they belonged.

She now sat, as he had on the porch, with her legs crossed, the flying yoke around her waist. He showed her the controls and cautioned her to keep the motors running slowly.

Then he stepped out of the way.

Motors thrumming, the yoke lifted itself, hesitated, then lifted Stein until her lifeless toes just touched the handwoven rug underfoot. Her face was frozen in a valiant attempt not to betray too much emotion, but an amused and powerful intelligence still twinkled behind her eyes as she advanced the lever which took her, very slowly at first, then more rapidly, across the living room.

She stood, and that was almost the right word for it, looking down at the kitchen counter. When she turned back, there was a smile on her face and tears coursing down her cheeks at the realization that with his flying yoke she might regain some portion of her mobility—and perhaps even mastery over her own life. Emerson knew all the signs.

"Can we try it outside?"

He opened the screen and stood aside. "Careful on the steps."

XXXI
A MESSAGE FROM VESTA

ALL ARGUMENTS IN FAVOR OF COERCIVE GOVERNMENT
INVARIABLY REDUCE TO AN ASSERTION THAT PEOPLE ARE
IRRESPONSIBLE CHILDREN WHO NEED TO BE WATCHED AND
TAKEN CARE OF. THERE IS PROBABLY SUBSTANCE IN THIS CLAIM.
KEEP ANYONE IN THE NURSERY LONG ENOUGH, SAY UNTIL HE'S
SIXTY-FIVE, AND HIS BEHAVIOR WILL BE, AT THE LEAST,
SOMEWHAT ERRATIC.
—**Mirelle Stein,** *The Productive Class*

D*ear Emerson,*
Bet you're surprised to hear from me! Nails is a better typist, but when your order came, via the South Pole of all places, he said it should have the woman's touch. Not a woman's touch, he told me to emphasize. He was trying to be nice. Aloysius and Henrietta will see if they want to add anything, so it won't be very personal. I'll run spelling and grammar when I'm done so you won't be ashamed of me.

Everything at the plant is running fine and we're making piles of money. We all miss you very much—add an extra "very" for me, although the style program hates it. The experimental barrels you ordered from Czechoslovakia before you left finally came and they work just like you said they would, 15% higher velocity with peak pressure actually lower than a conventional barrel. I understand how progressive twist, graduated groove diameter, and polygonal rifling work together to achieve the effect, but how do you think of these things in the first place? Nails says we'll have to make them ourselves, as supply and quality are unreliable and the freight is too high. He says to tell you he's working on it.

Now for the part I've been avoiding until now. They've just had word in Curringer of Gibson Altman, Junior, from, of all places (another tussle with the stupid style program, insisting I shouldn't say that twice, but why not?), Vesta. Aloysius (who's right here peeking over my shoulder and making me generate typos you'll never see) says it looks like Junior lit out for Berkeley when he left here.

Anyway, on account of recent economic and political events back on Earth, where our Pallatian-style Hyperdemocracy is threatening to catch on, 50 or 60 young "socialist reactionaries" (Aloysius wanted to be sure I used this term, which seems to amuse him no end for some reason) have "seized" what Aloysius calls the bleakest and least-likely-to-ever-be-inhabited of the asteroids, for all that it's the third largest, and are "holding" it. From what or whom I've no idea, since nobody has ever claimed that rock or ever wanted to as far as I know before this.

We found out about this because the TV at the Nimrod, which sometimes gets broadcasts from Earth, picked up a press conference relayed from Vesta where Junior and his Berkeley friends announced they're establishing a "People's Economic Democracy." Mrs. Singh said it looked like they were mostly liberal arts professors and their more gullible students, innocent, she said, of any technical or survival skills. Even I could see, once Aloysius pointed it out, that all they had was flimsy recreational gear, camping stuff, and tourist-grade spacesuits.

Unlike Pallas (Mrs. Singh is dictating this), a water-rich carbonaceous chondrite containing all the essential elements and compounds necessary to existence. Vesta is barren granitic rock, incapable of sustaining human life even given current technology. When their air and other supplies run out, this ill-conceived and badly equipped expedition is going to run into exactly the kind of trouble anyone besides a bunch of academics could have predicted before it left Earth.

I guess that means (me again) that you don't have to worry about looking for Junior any more.

Enclosed please find (which is a stupid expression, considering) the two complete flying yoke units you ordered, plus a supply of spare parts. I hope they're okay when they get to you. They have a long way to travel by not very reliable means.

We all hope you're well and happy and staying warm and getting enough to eat, and that we can see you soon. I hope you're getting well inside and out and that you find what you're looking for. Nails is here with the crate now—he says you're going to be surprised because these are the new, improved model with better batteries and more efficient motors—so I guess I'd better close this.

All my love,
Cherry

Hands shaking with rage, Emerson threw the letter to the floor—then carefully picked it up again, folded it, and tucked it away in an inside jacket pocket. It had been neatly laser-printed on gold-embossed stationery from Galena's, subtly perfumed and well intended. The fact was, he hadn't been surprised to get it.

He was sitting on a rustic plank-and-pole bench on the front porch of the Drake-Tealy cabin. The heavily built plastic crate Cherry had mentioned lay directly under his gaze, the top pried up and plastic bubble-wrap draped over its edges. After the story Digger had told him, he was glad he hadn't had to fly it here, slung beneath an ultralight aircraft. The flying yokes it had contained were gone. Digger and his wife were already up in a meadow above the house, giving them a try.

Now, he told himself, it was really time to go.

Somehow, another six weeks had mysteriously slipped by. Granted, they'd been a great deal more pleasant than the first six he'd spent here, since he'd gotten to know his hostess better and she'd spent every spare minute she had practicing with his modified flying yoke. The monthly ultralight could pick up mail as well as deliver it, thanks to a hook it carried and an arrangement near the cabin like a clothesline strung on a pair of fifty-foot poles. He'd meant the new machines he'd ordered as a sort of bread-and-butter present, anyway.

In addition to the letter from Cherry, he'd even received a present of sorts himself. Nails had very thoughtfully included a full complement of batteries of the new type, significantly lighter in weight and much longer lasting, and a pair of improved motors for retrofitting to his old flying yoke. It appeared to Emerson that they might take half a day to install, calibrate, and test.

And then he must be gone.

He was determined not to be cheated again by Junior's lack of character. First it had been his adversary's cowardice, now it was incredible stupidity. A comparatively easy death by starvation, freezing, asphyxiation, or even explosive decompression would never do. Junior had to know who was killing him and why.

He was not going to get away this time.

The complicated double thrumming noise of two pairs of counter-rotating impellers came to Emerson at about the same time he looked up from his tightly clenched fists and watched Drake-Tealy and his wife drift like autumn leaves around the corner of the cabin in their new flying yokes, their faces flushed with excitement.

"Tallyho!" hollered the anthropologist.

"I actually chased a deer!" Stein exclaimed, almost looking like a girl again. "I lost him in the trees, but for almost a kilometer, I stayed right on his tail. I could not have done that *before!* Emerson, what you have accomplished is amazing!"

With an expression communicating that he agreed, although in a different context, Digger let his motors die on the pathway to the porch, settled to his feet, and eyed Emerson closely. "Here, now, my fine young miracle worker, was there bad news in that letter? You look as though your best friend had just died." There was concern in Stein's eyes, as well. Perhaps he *was* a miracle worker.

"My worst enemy." Emerson shook his head, as if to clear his mind of an unthinkable idea. "Digger, tell me something. Doesn't that receiver of yours transmit, as well?" Despite his early experiences, he knew nothing about radio.

"I'd have thought you'd noticed that already." The old man stepped out of his flying yoke and folded it. Stein remained suspended in hers, her motor speed reduced, and appeared almost to be standing beside him. He draped an arm over her shoulder. "As long as someone at the other end is listening. There's a regular schedule for that at the South Pole—a contract dispatch office where we pay them to look after all of us Outbackers at least once a week— and an emergency frequency, besides. I established the system myself, many years ago."

"Good." Emerson stood, resettled his gunbelt about his waist, extracted a cigar, and lit it. "Is there any way they can relay a message to somebody in Curringer?"

Drake-Tealy shrugged. "None that I know of specifically, but I'm sure it can be arranged, one way or another. What's this all about, Emerson, if you don't mind my ask-

ing? Your worst enemy—that'd be the former Senator Altman, wouldn't it?"

"His son, who seems to have turned up again. And
that's all I want to say about it now, Digger. You and . . .
Miri have been kind to me. I don't want to have to argue
with you about what I'm planning to do. I need to try sending that message to Curringer, and then I have to go. I
have to go, in any event."

"As you will, then." Drake-Tealy nodded, striding up
the now-needless ramp and onto the porch, where he left
his flying yoke leaning against a wall. "By all means, let's
see what can be done. I'm a bit curious myself. I'll crank up
the wireless."

"And I'll make us a nice cup of tea," declared Miri.

Both males stared after her as she wafted through the
screen door and into the kitchen.

"This is Jean-Luc Picard, calling Starfleet Command. Picard to Starfleet Command. How do you read me? Over."

It was only the work of a few minutes, seated before
Digger's big, black, complicated-looking radio—United
Cantons of South Africa Defense Forces surplus, he informed Emerson—to establish contact with the dispatcher
on duty at the South Pole, who was employed by a company similar in purpose and structure to the several which
maintained the atmospheric envelope around the asteroid.

*"Doctor Drake-Tealy—Digger—this is South Polar Central
Dispatch. Janet speaking. What can we do for you? You're not
scheduled for regular contact until next Tuesday. And could you
please be persuaded to use proper radio procedure? Over."*

Drake-Tealy had explained that while there were
probably more convenient communications systems in
use—computer-enhanced cellular telephones like those
employed in Curringer, for example—none was simpler or

less failure-prone than the old-fashioned shortwave he'd first seen in everyday use in Australia.

He grinned at his unseen listener who had likely identified him by his voiceprint. "Probably not, my dear. You're new, aren't you? Ask the others. But before you do that, we've a favor to ask of you, if we may. Over."

On Pallas, the frequency band had been chosen specifically to bounce off the atmospheric envelope—Emerson remembered that KCUF used the same idea, which was why it could be heard now, even out here in the Pocks— and it was theoretically as easy to talk to someone anywhere on the surface as to someone at the South Pole.

It turned out that it was just as easy for the dispatcher to "patch" them into the Curringer system. Apparently it was an everyday procedure which Drake-Tealy didn't know about because, living in deliberate isolation as they had for so long, they didn't know anyone in Curringer and had never had reason to ask before this.

"Aloysius?" Emerson couldn't help shouting, although the connection was perfectly clear. He could even make out the normal background noises of the Nimrod.

"Well, speak of the devil! Emerson, me boy, how have ye been? We were just talkin' about ye. It's a shame this isn't a visual hookup. I'd like t'see how yer beard's—"

"I'm sorry, Aloysius," Emerson interrupted impatiently, "I need to ask you a big favor—"

Drake-Tealy tapped him on the shoulder. "He's still talking and can't hear you. You both need to say 'over' when you're through talking. Tell him that when you get a chance."

Emerson nodded.

"—comin' along. We're all here, Nails, Henrietta, an' meself—not t'forget the lovely Miss Cherry. I assume ye have a reason for callin' us up. What can we do?"

Drake-Tealy nodded toward the microphone on its

stand in front of the knob-and-dial-cluttered radio. For such a small object, it suddenly looked rather intimidating.

Emerson leaned forward. "We have to say 'over' when we're done talking, Aloysius, since this is a one-way-at-a-time system. I need that list of names you once gave me of people you know at the South Pole, connected with asteroid mining. Or anybody else who can rent me a spaceship. I'll also need a letter of credit from the bank."

He waited for a reply.

And waited.

"Over," he finally remembered to add.

"Rent ye a spaceship, is it? Bound fer Vesta, I presume. Well, I'll waste no airtime tryin' t'talk ye out of it, although there's others here who might give it a try. I know ye too well, me hot-blooded young friend. Look up a fella name of Fritz Marshall. He owns Advocate Minin' an' Salvage an' might be after takin' ye where ye hafta go. I'll transmit a letter of credit to ye direct t'his bank. It'll be there in the mornin' or we'll sue the bejabbers out of 'em. Over."

Drake-Tealy whispered that South Polar Central Dispatch could handle a letter of credit. Emerson nodded, leaned forward again, and passed the word to Aloysius. "I may not be there in the morning. I'm still up in the Pocks with . . ." He paused at the sudden, apprehensive look on Miri's face, reflected on Digger's, as well. "With some new friends I hope you'll get to meet someday. The flying yokes were for them. I'll get down to the Pole as quickly as I can. Over."

This time Miri and her husband showed him a pair of grateful expressions. Apparently they weren't quite ready yet to rejoin the world. He'd hoped to help them more in this regard than he'd done with his gift of flight, but now there wouldn't be time.

It wasn't his only regret, as he soon discovered.

Aloysius had a lot more to say, and Emerson spoke briefly in turn with Mrs. Singh, Nails, and Cherry. He found that he missed Cherry more than he'd realized, an empty aching that wasn't quite love, perhaps, but an empty aching all the same. There wasn't much they could say in public, on the radio, and that made it worse. Finally, just as he thought the conversation was over, Aloysius was back on again.

"One more thing ye'll need t'know, Emerson. Junior's little band of adventurers are into the deep shit already, accordin' t'Lite-Link an' GIGO, who concern themselves with such things. Their air an' power are about gone. By the time ye arrive, he may be in no condition to appreciate what y'plan doin' to him. Over."

Emerson shook his head violently, but what he said was, "I understand, Aloysius, and thank you. You might call your friend Marshall and have him make preparations while I'm on the way. I'm leaving as soon as we're finished talking. Over."

"Roger that, as the vernacular has it. Personally, I'd as soon the bugger were already dead. I don't know whose jurisdiction Vesta falls under. Certainly not me own. I'd hate t'see y'tried for the murder of such as Junior Altman. On the other hand, I promised I wouldn't give ye a hard time. Good luck. Over."

Emerson grinned, trying to ignore the welling tears. "Thanks again, Aloysius, and good-bye."

"I believe the customary phrase is 'over an' out.' Good-bye. Come back to us well an' whole."

"I'll do my best. Over and out." Emerson sat back from the microphone, desperately fighting what he regarded as inappropriate sentimentality and already planning the details of reassembling his flying yoke and packing his few belongings. Although it was past noon, he wanted to leave today, before dark, and said so to his hosts.

There was a long pause.

Digger looked to his wife, and then nodded. "We thought you'd feel that way, but we'd appreciate it if you stayed until morning. We can leave before sunup if you like, but that way we can fix some decent food and get a good night's rest."

There was an even longer pause.

"We?" Emerson frowned.

"We," Miri repeated. "We discussed this on the way back from the meadow, because we knew you were about to leave, even before you got that letter from your friends. Raymond knows some people at the South Pole who can help you, and we both think it is high time that we took a little break from our lifelong vacation."

" 'Struth," agreed Drake-Tealy. "If you don't mind, we'd like very much to go with you."

"Only if you promise to bring that with you," Emerson nodded at the heavy rifle hanging over the mantelpiece. "There's African leopards out there, you know."

Digger grinned. "And lions and tigers and bears."

"Oh, my!" Miri added.

XXXII

AT THE SOUTH POLE

UNIVERSALLY, INSTINCTIVELY, INDIVIDUALS HATE AND FEAR
THE STATE. THE STAUNCHEST, MOST PATERNALISTIC
CONSERVATIVE, THE MOST INTRUSIVELY MATERNALISTIC
LIBERAL, EACH BLANCHES AT A PHONE CALL FROM THE
GOVERNMENT'S COLLECTION AGENCY AND PALPITATES FOR
HOURS AFTERWARD, NO MATTER HOW SINCERELY HE
ADVOCATES COERCIVE POLITICS AT OTHER TIMES OR TRIES TO
COMPLY WITH THE LETTER AND THE SPIRIT OF THE LAW.
SHOULD EITHER EVER ACQUIRE THE INTEGRITY TO RECOGNIZE
WHAT THAT MEANS, AND THE COURAGE TO DO SOMETHING
ABOUT IT, THE WORLD WILL CHANGE MATERIALLY FOR THE
BETTER.
— Raymond Louis Drake-Tealy, *Hunting and Humanity*

Do we knock, or what?"
The plaque set over the tunnel entrance, if that was
the proper word for a monumental, ribbonlike slab of foot-
thick native blue-black steel affixed with thirty-six equally
thick stainless-steel characters at least six feet high, read:

PORT AMUNDSEN AIRLOCK NUMBER TWENTY-NINE

The thing had been visible—easily legible—for the
past half hour of their flight down here. Even though he
knew perfectly well that the permanent population hereabouts was actually smaller than that of Curringer, Emerson felt like a rustic on his first excursion to the big city.
He looked from one of his two older companions to the
other, suddenly very glad they'd insisted on coming along.

Perhaps they knew what to do now.

And perhaps the gracefully curving six-lane concrete
highway that emerged from the shade-blackened maw in

the side of the partly artificial mountain standing before them would someday do more than simply peter out a few hundred yards away from the entrance, lost abruptly to the trackless, crater-broken landscape surrounding the asteroid's South Pole. For the time being, however, anything even remotely resembling genuine civilization in this particular neighborhood of Pallas lay within those titanic, multistory metal doors they were about to enter.

Naturally, Emerson hesitated.

Outside, in the sunlight, this was a region of scrub oak and palmetto. Even from the air, they'd spotted the tracks of wild pigs and other large animals all along the way, and at the moment he could hear the twittering of birds, the buzzing of insects. He didn't know exactly what he'd expected—penguins, maybe?—but it was no colder down here than it had been hundreds of miles further north. The total volume of the atmosphere of Pallas was small compared to that of the Earth, and its circulation around the little globe was many times more efficient.

From this close to the mountainside, it seemed to Emerson that the slope soaring steeply before him touched the sky—which, in a manner of speaking, was precisely what it did. Along the top of the escarpment, actually the circular rim of a deep crater ten miles in diameter chosen especially for this purpose, were set tens of thousands of anchors for the asteroid's atmospheric envelope, too far back from the lip to be seen from this angle. But it was here, and at the North Pole six hundred miles away, that the envelope reached the ground, leaving twin ten-mile circles enclosed within impact-created walls, exposed to the harsh vacuum and the bitter cold of the interplanetary void.

The facility at the North Pole was called Port Peary.

Spaceships landed here!

Emerson hesitated. It was the massively inhuman scale

of the architecture, of course, which bothered him, a humbling effect imposed here entirely by an accident of engineering necessity—but which had been used deliberately against the individual for thousands of years by governments and organized religions on Earth. He wasn't aware that this was why Pallatian trials were conducted in places like the Nimrod and there were no public buildings, but his two companions certainly were.

They'd planned it that way.

"As I recall," Digger told him, visibly trying to stretch his memory back over thirty years to matters which had never directly concerned him anyway, "there's a smaller, people-sized door set into the side over there, and you just go in."

The old man's powerful .416 Rigby Magnum rifle lay across the hoop of his flying yoke, secured by its sling and ready for whatever it was called upon to do. He'd had no use for it so far, but all the way down here he'd grumbled about how awkward the customized Enfield was to fly with, and was currently threatening to retire his ancient .455 Webley to the cabin mantelpiece as well, replacing both weapons, for most everyday purposes, with a pair of Ngu Departure 10 millimeter semiautomatic pistols, provided they were available at Port Amundsen.

When Emerson had offered to present him with two of his factory's popular handguns, one for the anthropologist himself and one for his wife, he'd become extremely angry, or at least put on a convincingly intimidating demonstration of it, and stubbornly insisted that it was his fundamental Pallatian right to buy them.

Emerson had understood and shut up.

The huge metal doors presently looming before them in the tunnel shadows, Drake-Tealy had already explained, were not so much for future use—Pallas was never supposed to grow the way Earth had, or at least not in the same directions—as for bringing in massive earth-moving machinery and megatons of raw materials which had been employed in the original terraformation process. Similarly, the "highway" they were standing on at the moment had served mostly as an airstrip for the hundreds of ultralights which had bestowed life on the little planet.

"Of course," Digger offered an afterthought, "it's been rather a long while since we were last down here, and procedures may have changed a trifle over the years."

"He is right," Miri agreed. "Now you simply walk up, hammer on the door, and demand to see Jabba the Hutt." Despite her words, her voice sounded weak and shaky to Emerson. He knew she was tired and nervous. This was her first trip—almost her first excursion outside her own cabin door—in something like three decades. She was sunburned and exhausted from what must have been to her an ordeal. Moreover, in all that time, she hadn't seen another human being besides Digger and the occasional—sometimes hostile—passerby, and never more than two or three other individuals at the same time. Now she was about to see hundreds.

"Well," Digger sighed, apparently suffering trepidations of his own, "there's no time like the present."

Miri seemed to blink back tears and nod.

Emerson swallowed.

Together, they lifted gently from the concrete underfoot and drifted on their flying yokes toward the daunting tunnel entrance. Just as Digger had predicted, there was a much smaller door, with a much smaller sign welcoming the traveler to the South Pole of Pallas. To nobody's astonishment, there was also a dusty tangle of leaf-littered brush and old spider webbing around and over the door which Miri insisted must be cleared away before they could enter. For Emerson, the whole thing greatly resembled stumbling upon a lost civilization.

At last he turned a spoked metal wheel, threw his weight against the door, and practically fell in, discovering, as he did, a clean, well-lit chamber roughly the size of a small bedroom, in which they were compelled to close the outer door before the inner door, cleverly set at right angles to it, was physically free to open.

"That's Wild Bill's engineering touch, all right," the anthropologist observed, trying to manage his flying yoke and the long-barreled rifle at the same time. His voice echoed oddly from the smooth, hard walls around them. "Mud-simple, dirt-cheap, and foolproof. It takes an advanced degree to fuck things up well and truly."

Both he and his wife, of course, had PhDs.

They emerged into a quiet, apparently little-used corridor which was also well lit and featured a large, colorful, liquid-crystal signboard on the wall opposite the miniature airlock. A series of animated arrows pointed toward Main Airlock Twenty-Nine, immediately to their left, as well as to Main Airlock Twenty-Eight, a mile around the circumference of the hollow mountain, to their right. There were also directions for getting to South Polar Central Dispatch, Spaceflight Traffic Control, something called "Freight Routing," Port Amundsen Security, and several bars, hotels, and restaurants with names Emerson recognized.

A flickering line at the bottom of the sign showed yesterday as the last time it had been updated.

"The bright lights at last!" Digger grinned at his wife, offering her an arm which she took for a moment and held tightly. "Let us partake of the fleshpots, my dear!"

Emerson didn't know what fleshpots were and wasn't sure he wanted to find out. He knew about restaurants, hotels, and bars, many with the same names being advertised on the sign across the corridor, from the movies he'd seen, and was curious to learn more about them, but he was also on a tight schedule. His intended victim might be dead already and beyond reach of the justice he planned to dispense.

"Well," he told the elderly couple, suddenly very reluctant to see the last of them, "I guess I'm headed for Spaceflight Traffic Control. That's where I'm supposed to meet this guy, Fritz Marshall. Try and have a good time, you two."

Miri smiled. "We will see you at least as far as that, Emerson. We are in no hurry, are we, Raymond?"

"Indeed not, my beloved, after a mere thirty years of abstemious self-mortification." If Emerson hadn't known better, he'd have suspected that Digger was already a bit drunk. "Let's see how these Buck Rogers flying belts work indoors, shall we?"

His wife nodded.

Motors thrumming, they skimmed off down the corridor in the direction given by the sign.

"Okay, where are we now?"

Emerson and his friends soon discovered that the mountain they'd entered was moth-eaten rather than hollowed out. Otherwise, it might have lacked the structural strength required to withstand the enormous stresses imposed on it by the constant pull of thousands of steel cables, each of them hundreds of miles long, which were lifted by the atmospheric envelope and held it in place.

Port Amundsen was a maze, but it was a maze that made sense. Each level within the massive ring-mountain consisted of a series of tunnels or corridors arranged in concentric circles, connected by radiating spokelike passageways. The crater wall, naturally, was broadest at its base where it contained there the greatest number of circular corridors. (There appeared to be no subsurface levels, which surprised Emerson, as that was the way he would have chosen to service ships and load and unload cargo.) Every level above it—reachable by gently sloping ramps rather than stairs or elevators—had fewer corridors and shorter spokes.

The directions on the wall screen, and others they found along the way, led them deeper into the mountain and higher at the same time. They had to go inward, toward the crater's center, the equivalent of fifty city blocks, and up more than a hundred stories, each section, horizontal as well as vertical, separated by hundreds of feet of steel- and concrete-reinforced rock as solid as ever it got on Pallas.

Emerson couldn't imagine how anyone got around this establishment without something like his flying yoke—until he and his companions finally began to encounter people, more and more of them on upper and inner levels, hurrying purposefully from one place to another with wheels attached to the bottoms of their feet.

"Roller skates!"

He'd recognized what he was seeing from various books and movies he'd enjoyed. Individuals skimming past them down the corridors nodded and smiled pleasantly, some of them sparing a curious glance at the flying yokes.

"Roller blades," Digger corrected. "Fore-and-aft instead of square-rigged, if you follow my meaning. Much more pleasant and efficient—and blessedly quiet. I used to be pretty good with them myself, once upon a time."

Emerson laughed at a peculiar momentary vision he had of Drake-Tealy as a small boy—complete with ivory handlebar moustache, for some reason—wheeling across the African veldt, flushing startled antelope, wildebeests, and hyenas.

Even with their flying yokes, mostly because they were unfamiliar with the territory, it took them over an hour to find what they were looking for, wandering up and down the clean and cheerful passageways and sometimes—asking passersby for directions only seemed to confuse things more—doubling back. At long last, within a few levels of the summit, they found a number of offices labeled:

ADVOCATE MINING AND SALVAGE
FRITZ MARSHALL, PROP.

"This is it!"

Taking a deep breath, Emerson stepped out of his yoke, folded it, and walked through the open door, where he was greeted by a female receptionist sitting behind a desk. It was a long moment before he could give her his full attention, however, for behind her was a wall-sized window, opening—only in a manner of speaking, of course—onto the unterraformed crater floor several thousand feet below. Outside, he knew, there was no air. The temperature would be either close to absolute zero or hot enough to boil the blood in his veins, depending on sun and shade.

From where he stood, well back from the window, he couldn't see any spaceships.

"Excuse me," repeated an insistent voice. "I said, may I help you with something?"

He looked down at the receptionist, a tidy-looking elderly woman of about Miri's age, dressed, he assumed, in what was the latest fashion on Earth. In his opinion, the plaids and stripes did nothing for each other, especially in fluorescent colors. "I'm sorry, ma'am," he told her, "that's quite a view you've got there. I'm Emerson Ngu, and these are my friends . . . er, Digger and Miri."

Recognition lit her features. "Good afternoon, Mr. Ngu." She nodded politely at Drake-Tealy and his wife. "Mr. Marshall is expecting you. You may go right in."

Emerson moved in the direction indicated until he came to a door which opened before he reached it. A big, broad-faced man, also wearing fluorescent stripes and plaid, stood just inside with his hand on the knob, but Emerson hardly noticed him at first. Further inside the office, seated before another spectacular window with a mug in one hand and a cigar in the other, was a familiar figure.

"Aloysius!" He rushed in and seized the innkeeper's hand.

"Surprise!" Aloysius answered. "Only the surprise is after bein' on me, it seems. Fritz," he addressed the man who'd opened the door. "Allow me to introduce me old friend Emerson Ngu, and me even older friend, Raymond Louis Drake-Tealy—'Digger' to his intimates—an' his lovely spouse, Mirelle Stein."

Marshall blinked. "You mean, the—"

"The *the*, themselves," Aloysius replied, "t'quote the funniest movie ever made. Emerson, yer a sight fer sore eyes—but who wants sore eyes? Come an' sit down. Pour yerself some of Fritz's hand-imported coffee. Why did ye not tell me it was these two ye were stayin' with out in the Pocks? Why, I've known 'em since—"

"Since you dug me out of the wreckage"—Miri wafted forward to take his hand—"and sat with Raymond for three days while they patched me together. Aloysius Brody, of all the faces I might see for the first time after thirty years, I would want it to be yours!"

The man actually blushed. "Mrs. Drake-Tealy, we've got to stop meeting like this."

Emerson shook his head with exasperation. "Aloysius, what are you doing here? And how did you get down here before we did? It's twice as far from Curringer as it is—"

Aloysius waved it off. "Henrietta's overgrown dune buggy will do twice the speed of one of your hula hoops as long as you can keep it on the road. As to why I'm here, I presume ye want t'be charterin' the fastest asteroid minin' ship available on this rock, one of the new fusion/ion-driven craft, perhaps. Well, I've come t'make sure this sharpy here don't take ye to the cleaners."

Marshall only laughed.

"But why—" insisted Emerson.

"Because, me boy, I'm goin' with ye."

XXXIII
Utopia on Ice

HE WHO LOVES SHOULD LIVE, HE WHO KNOWS NOT HOW TO
LOVE SHOULD DIE, AND HE WHO OBSTRUCTS LOVE SHOULD DIE
TWICE.
                                        —Pompeiian wall inscription

T he red banner, printed on some lightweight synthetic already beginning to deteriorate under the onslaught of hard vacuum and unfiltered ultraviolet light, read: "Personkind Has Matured Beyond the Need to Accumulate Material Goods."

Like oxygen, Emerson thought. Like food, water, or electricity, since these would-be People's Economic Democrats disdained use of the cold-fusion reactors on which the rest of civilization seemed content to run. Below the banner's six-inch letters, he could just make out another motto, "Fraternity, Equality, Political Responsibility." Clearly they'd identified and dispensed with that part of the old French Revolutionary triad which had caused all the difficulties.

"Sure, an' wasn't it Lenin himself who said that freedom is precious—so precious it must be rationed?"

For some reason, Aloysius had been in what Emerson always thought of as his literary mode ever since they'd taken off from Port Amundsen. The man's voice came clearly to him now over his spacesuit helmet radio. At the moment, in fact, it was the only thing to be heard above the constant low background hiss of a hundred billion stars gleaming down coldly on them as they trudged across the unbearably bright but utterly lifeless basalt surface of the asteroid Vesta.

Just within the camp perimeter as they were, they should have heard other voices long before now. They'd been calling from time to time since Marshall had lowered them on a slender cable from synchronous orbit. They'd even tried calling earlier, from the ship.

No one had answered.

That didn't keep Emerson from wishing he had his Grizzly strapped around his waist. Unfortunately, fire-arms were an iffy proposition in circumstances like these. For one thing, it was possible for the cartridges to "cook off"—discharge spontaneously—simply from the heat of the sun, unabated by an atmosphere.

With the constant boost of catalytic fusion to speed them on their way, the journey here had lasted a hundred hours, a little over four days. Nearly all asteroids had eccentric orbits, Pallas's a bit more than most, Vesta's a bit less. Pallas had been chosen for colonization in the first place because, among other things, its path swept through so much of the Belt, offering developers an accretion of highly varied materials as well as a convenient jump-off to a great many more resources relatively nearby. There were times when the orbits of Pallas and Vesta overlapped deeply, but this wasn't one of them. Murphy's, Emerson had learned long ago, was the fundamental law of the universe.

He recalled looking through Marshall's office window, across the broad, mountain-ringed crater plain of Port Amundsen, at the *Darling Clementine,* the little mining ship he'd offered them. She'd rested on the airless surface like a gnat on a serving platter—there had been no access tunnels under the surface, Emerson had discovered, because this South Polar crater, like many of its neighbors, was filled with a titanic dust-covered glacier ten miles across and a couple of miles deep—and he'd expected the voyage ahead to be cramped and boring.

But he'd been wrong on both counts. Prospectors and miners like Marshall and his employees often spent months in space, and provided themselves with every luxury they could afford. The comfortable apartments at his own Ngu Departure factory were a good deal less luxurious and well-appointed than this little ship, which had turned out considerably bigger than she had looked at first.

Basically a short, fat cylinder sitting on mechanical legs, with work-blackened ion drivers protruding from her flat underside, and instruments, antennas, and folded ore manipulators sticking out of her top, she carried whatever cargo she happened to acquire behind her—there'd be none on this trip, at least on the outbound portion of it—in fine-meshed nets at the ends of long cables.

Inboard, elbow room was at a premium only with respect to the oxygen and other breathing gases it had to be filled with. And since three-quarters of all asteroids—the carbonaceous chondrites—were made up of six to ten percent water, and a third of that was oxygen, and the electrical power to extract it was plentiful if not practically free, that seldom represented a serious problem.

Darling Clementine "flew" with her upper surface forward. Inside, she was divided into three decks or levels with a utility core running down the center. The lowermost level contained the engine and all the machinery and equipment which made asteroid mining possible. It looked rather like Nails's plumbing shop in Curringer.

The middle level was cut into wedges, with a little com-

332   L. NEIL SMITH +>══

panionway running around the outside of the utility core, providing private sleeping spaces (the cabin Emerson was shown to was larger than his room at Mrs. Singh's), places to wash up, prepare food, do laundry, and the hundred other little chores required to maintain life.

The uppermost level served as a sort of lounge or living room, and its many windows and mostly transparent ceiling allowed sunbeams and starlight to fall across several overstuffed chairs and sofas sitting on a plushly carpeted deck. It featured a bar, as well as expensive and powerful communications and entertainment gear.

Marshall himself acted as captain and pilot.

During the first few minutes of their voyage, another few when they'd been halfway to their destination, and the last few when they'd arrived, he'd left his recliner and swung up into a control chair at the uppermost end of the utility core, cut at this level with windows so that he could continue to converse with his guests. Like any other constant-boost spaceship, they'd accelerated all the way out to the halfway point. At turnover, when the ship would go on doing precisely what it had been doing so far—only with its thrusters pointed in the direction they were headed— he'd invited Emerson to occupy the copilot's seat.

Trying to conceal his excitement, Emerson had climbed the four ladder rungs required to take him from the living room floor to the controls of the *Darling Clementine*. Aloysius, on a sofa below with a seatbelt loosely across his lap, had a drink in his hand, by which he said he planned to judge Marshall's piloting skills. Emerson had strapped himself in and looked over the panel of instruments. There were plenty of those, but where he'd expected to see a steering yoke and thruster levers, all that presented itself was a computer keyboard.

"We're really here more to kibitz than to do any flying ourselves," his host had informed him. "I had my company mainframe write this navigating program for *Clementine* before we left, and I'm just making certain now that it's running right. Look over there, Emerson. Displayed in blue on that screen is our projected course, overlaid in red with the route we've already followed. On this screen here, *Clementine*'s counting down the seconds before we turn over. We're not supposed to feel a thing, but you can look out the window and see it happen."

And that was how it had gone.

The numbers on the second screen had dwindled until they were a long line of zeroes divided by a colon and a decimal point. Something began to beep and there was a faint hissing audible throughout the ship as attitude thrusters operated briefly.

Emerson already had his eye on the stars, which whirled overhead in a complex, dizzying pattern. When they were steady again and both the hissing and the beeping had stopped, he looked down at Aloysius, sitting with his drink undisturbed.

"Nary a drop spilled," he observed. "Do I congratulate the pilot, the *Clementine*, or yer company mainframe?"

Marshall ignored him to punch a few more keys, then unfastened his own lap belt and sat up. "So much for this exercise in spacemanship." He grinned at Emerson. "Let's inspect the refrigerator and see what we can microwave for dinner. Baked potatoes, that goes without saying. And I had my assistant lay in a carton of American bison steaks. All of this drudgery has given me an appetite."

Emerson followed him down the ladder.

Aloysius joined them as they descended through a hole in the carpet to the middle deck.

In one respect, Emerson's first experience with space travel had been a trifle disappointing. He'd secretly looked forward to being free of gravity, to squatting cross-legged in midair like a levitating yogi or bouncing off the walls as he'd seen people do in science fiction movies and old NASA films. Yet, owing to her internal architecture and the fact that *Darling Clementime* accelerated (and later on, decelerated) at a constant rate throughout their entire voyage, he might as well have stayed at home. His feet seemed to exert the same amount of pressure on her carpeted deck as they would have on a floor on Pallas.

Much of his time aboard *Darling Clementine* had been occupied with what he came to think of as "spacesuit practice," and that, too, had turned out rather differently than he'd anticipated. Most of what he'd read about the subject was apparently obsolete. Where he'd expected complicated equipment and long checklists to assure its proper operation, he discovered instead the deceptive simplicity — another age had called it "user friendliness" — of a mature technology.

The spacesuits carried aboard *Darling Clementine* were "menu-driven" from a "heads-up" display inside the visor. That meant that whenever he put the helmet on — and that was always the first item of business with this kind of suit — he saw, floating before his face and superimposed on the real world outside, a series of computer-generated questions which he could answer either by looking directly at the selection he desired and blinking hard or by pushing buttons on either of the miniature keyboards on the forearms of his sleeves. The system "walked" him through the process of putting the suit on, powering it up, making sure it was properly sealed and completely functional, and adapting it both to his own body dimensions and the environment in which he planned to operate.

It had even asked about and allowed for his missing right eye.

Lacking any better facilities for the exercise — it would have been impossibly dangerous even for a professional to work outside the ship under acceleration — Marshall had evacuated a small compartment on the lower deck for Emerson to practice in. Aloysius joined him in these maneuvers. They'd reluctantly decided to limit their expedition to three people because of the room which would be required for rescuees aboard the *Darling Clementine* if the effort were successful. He was certainly no amateur when it came to using a spacesuit. He'd spent most of his time wearing one a lot more primitive than these, he informed Emerson, during the terraformation of Pallas. On the other hand, that meant that he was long out of practice and needed updating on the latest technology.

Together, they practiced getting in and out of the equipment, climbing up and down, dealing with various types of emergencies, even engaging in some hand-to-hand sparring.

Now, standing on the unforgivingly rugged and sterile rock of which Vesta was composed. Death by freezing lurked in the shadows, with the faraway but cruel sun beating down on his armored head and shoulders. Emerson was grateful that he'd spent all those hours, essentially locked in a closet, getting to know his equipment. No technology was perfect. Whenever he looked away from the sun, into the profound blackness that only an airless world engenders, incredibly lacy crystals began to form at the bottom edge of his visor until it became necessary to prompt the tiny computer and get the helmet blower working.

"This is Darling Clementine, *gentlemen, with a regular time-check."* Marshall was calling from where he orbited a few miles over their heads. *"It says here you've got two more hours of air left. Sounds awful quiet down there to me. Come back."*

"Hello, *Darling Clementine,*" Emerson answered. "We're quiet because there isn't much to say. How do you describe an airless ball of sunbaked frozen rock, and why would you want to try? We've found signs of what we're looking for—signs literally, I mean—but no indication of life so far, which is another reason it's quiet down here. We're just inside the front gate, in a manner of speaking, and there's some sort of formless heap about fifty yards ahead. Over."

"Probably all that remains of their airtent after a couple of months of micrometeorite bombardment," Aloysius guessed. *"Cheap equipment, but we knew that, did we not?"*

"We're going to check it out," Emerson added, not feeling enthusiastic at the prospect.

"Roger that," Marshall replied. *"I can see you in my little spyglass, now that you're out of the shadows."* Not certain how they'd be greeted if there were any survivors, they'd dropped to the surface in slightly rougher country than this, a mile or so from the camp. *"Try and keep in touch a little better. Over."*

"We'll do it," Emerson told him. He looked back to make sure Aloysius was following him—he worried a little about the man's age and the fact that one of his legs was a prosthetic. Then he reluctantly made his way toward the object he and his older companion had described, knowing long before they reached it what they were about to find.

"As an anonymous urban guerrilla once put it," observed Aloysius, drawing beside him and looking down at the heap of rubbish before them, *"y'can't dig a foxhole in a side-walk."*

Marshall's guess had been correct. What they were looking at appeared to be the remains of a plastic airtent suitable only for the briefest use by people like tourists. It was exactly the kind of thing, according to Aloysius, that some of the less scrupulous concessionaires rented to visitors at Port Amundsen and Port Peary. Its brilliant toy colors had already faded and it was in worse shape than the banner they'd seen earlier. Emerson was sure that most of the meteorite holes in the thing were microscopic and that there were likely to be millions of them. Naturally, that hadn't stopped the air from leaking out, and it had given the destructive effect of ultraviolet light that much more surface area to work on.

What he didn't really want to investigate more closely, or even think about very much—although he would force himself to the task, since it was the reason they were here on Vesta—were the two dozen or more motionless lumps lying beneath the flattened plastic. Emerson gulped, suddenly very conscious of what it would be like to lose control of his stomach inside a spacesuit.

With every nerve screaming at him not to, he bent down to lift one corner of the collapsed plastic tent. He'd never seen a dead human body before—at least he had no conscious memory of it—and he deeply dreaded having to see one now. It was possible that the bitter cold of the shadows had preserved these lumps of once-human flesh, if that was what they were. That would be bad enough. It was equally possible that the sunlight and heat had gotten to them through the cheap material, allowing them to slow-cook inside their sealed spacesuits.

That would be infinitely worse.

Emerson gulped again.

In the end, it proved necessary to rip the plastic corner to get into it and, with Aloysius's uncharacteristically quiet assistance, to spread it out over the adjacent rock. There, huddled facedown in suits of about the same quality as the tent, were all that was left of the People's Economic Democracy of Vesta.

Emerson glanced up at Aloysius. The man's face couldn't be seen through his sun-darkened visor, but his theatrical shrug was visible even through the bulk of his suit. *"Sure, an' yer the glorious leader of this expedition, me boy. 'Twas all yer idea—an' yer privilege t'turn over the first corpse."*

"Thanks a billion, Aloysius." Emerson grimaced, bent over against the resistance of his suit, put his hand on the shoulder of the nearest body, and rolled it over.

To his relief, the tent had apparently retained its insulative properties and the body was frozen, having probably died of oxygen deprivation. He went to the next body and turned it over, and the next. Aloysius began to help, as well.

Before they were through, he and Aloysius counted twenty-seven dead in all, of all races and both sexes, ranging in age from about eighteen to somewhere in the region of sixty.

Junior was easily identifiable. He lay where he'd died, clutching an empty air cylinder to his chest.

Emerson was glad to see him.

And not a bit sorry he was dead.

"*My God,*" Marshall exclaimed, still watching them from orbit. His voice coming suddenly that way startled Emerson. "*It's like Scott's Antarctic expedition!*"

"*My ass,*" Aloysius retorted angrily. "*It's a hell of a lot more like Jonestown!*"

Emerson didn't know what the two men were talking about, and he didn't particularly care. What he could see most plainly was that, in a gesture completely typical of him, Gibson Altman Junior had thrown his life away on a venture which anyone else could have seen was obviously doomed from the outset.

" '*Do every man equal justice,*' " Aloysius quoted. " '*Let no innocent man suffer, let no guilty man escape.' Wise words of a nineteenth century predecessor of mine, Isaac Charles Parker of Fort Smith, Arkansas, otherwise known as the 'Hanging Judge'.*"

Equal justice, Emerson thought. The three of them had arrived at the lifeless rock which was Vesta, too late to do anything but bring back frozen bodies to their families.

To the Senator.

XXXIV
THE RABBIT PEOPLE

A WISE MAN ONCE POINTED OUT THAT THE AMERICAN EAGLE
EATS CARRION, NEVER PICKS ON ANYTHING ITS OWN SIZE, AND
WILL SOON BE EXTINCT. THAT BEING SO, PERHAPS AMERICANS
OUGHT TO SELECT A SYMBOL MORE IN KEEPING WITH THEIR
CURRENT CONDITION, LIKE A MILKED COW, A SHEARED SHEEP, A
PLUCKED CHICKEN, OR A SLAUGHTERED STEER.
— William Wilde Curringer, *Unfinished Memoirs*

Former Senator Gibson Altman took his first sip of coffee and sat back, bifocals temporarily folded. The elm tree he'd planted with his own two hands over Gibson Junior's grave — had it really been ten years ago? — cast a pleasant shade on this end of the verandah, and the breeze coming off the fields was warm.

As he had each morning for the last twenty-five years or so, since he'd first been appointed Chief Administrator of the Greeley Utopian Memorial Project, Altman was reading the overnight mail relayed electronically from Earth. He took another sip of coffee before he began again, yawned, and stretched.

If you're over a certain age, the thought ran through his mind, not for the first time, *and you wake up in the morning and nothing hurts, then you're probably dead.*

It was an excellent quotation, and he'd been tempted to use it publicly, perhaps as a humorous opening remark to one of his speeches (not about Social Security, of course), until his research staff discovered that it had first appeared in the writings of some twentieth-century right-wing crank, a retired Marine colonel who had apparently hated everything Altman's predecessors stood for — public health and safety, social responsibility, ecological sanity, rever-

ence for life and for the Earth in general—and had called
them the "rabbit people."

In any event, the quotation didn't seem to apply here,
in the kindly gravity of Pallas. In fact, one of the items in
this morning's mail was another of the scientific reports
he'd been receiving recently from the UN on the positive
effects of advancing technology—and, in a footnote which
was the reason he was included on the mailing list, of the
asteroid's undemanding gravity—on human longevity.

He didn't know if that was the reason he felt so good
this morning, but he wouldn't be suspicious of the feeling if
he could avoid it. Perhaps it was because this was his
birthday, although birthdays were usually far more likely
to depress him. Thinking about Social Security, he was—
he realized with a little start similar to the one his elm tree
always gave him—sixty-five years old today.

Most of the time lately, he conceded, he felt lousy. To
begin with, he was alone in life and less prepared to deal
with it than many other people he knew. He'd always been
suspicious of those who preferred solitude. For most of his
sixty-five years he'd never been able to stand being by
himself for more than five minutes at a time.

But here he was, ironically enough, far more pro-
foundly alone than most of those who wanted to be. His
wife, Gwendolyn—often he had to struggle for an instant
to remember her name, and her face had been an indistinct
blur in his memory for a long while—had left him years
ago, taking two of their children with her. What had transformed her from a near-perfect political wife into a petu-
lant, selfish, useless . . . *individualist,* he never knew. He'd
never seen or heard from them again, or tried to.

His elder son, who'd loyally remained with him, had
gotten mixed up with that wild colonial girl. Then she'd
been killed. And then he'd been killed. And neither calamity would have happened if it hadn't been for Emerson

Ngu, still disgustingly alive and well—and obscenely wealthy—after all these years. After all the trouble and heartache he'd inflicted on everyone around him. That seemed to be the way it always worked, didn't it?

Their baby daughter, Junior's and—what had her name been, now, Ingrid, or Hilda, something like that? — who could never have been anything to her once-famous grandfather but a terrible living reminder of the tragedies and failures of his life, had been bundled off, back to the mother planet. He'd taken her up to the North Polar spaceport himself, put her on an Earthbound ship with the same two hands that had buried his son, to be raised by his unmarried sister.

How old would she be now?

And what was her name?

Even his faithful old foreman, Walter Ngu, was gone, savagely beaten to death by one of the youth gangs that roamed the Project these days, simply because he'd spoken sharply to one of them that morning in the fields. The poor little man had only been doing his duty. What could you do? Watch over people. Encourage them to take care of one another. Offer them every opportunity to live a safe, healthy, orderly, productive life. And they still turned out to be animals.

Rabbit people, indeed. More like degenerate, treacherous, needle-toothed ferrets. Sometimes he looked out over the fields and hated each and every one of them. Sometimes he wanted to—he shook the thought off hastily, before it could consume him.

He'd considered notifying Emerson, who'd been Walter's eldest son, after all, but had finally decided against it. That traitorous, conniving ingrate either wouldn't give a damn that his father had died, or else he'd find some way to twist things, to blame the whole affair on his old enemy, the Senator, just as he'd publicly blamed Junior for what had happened—entirely at the hands of a few drunken, irresponsible Education and Morale counselors—to that little colonial tramp. Altman couldn't always remember his wife's face, but he'd never forget Emerson's when he'd brought Junior's lifeless body back from Vesta. It had been frozen, expressionless. But inside, he'd known, the boy had been gloating.

Ten years.

And now the only one he had left was Alice, Emerson's mother, ironically enough, who brought him a fresh cup of coffee as she always did at about this time, took the cold one away mostly unconsumed, went back into the Residence, and left him alone.

Alone.

He and Emerson Ngu now had more than enough reason to hate each other for the remainder of their normal life spans, and perhaps, if they were "lucky," if this UN science report meant anything at all, they could manage to do it even longer than that.

He felt a sudden chill.

Why had he thought earlier that he was feeling so good?

"Senator, are you ill?"

Irritably, Altman shook his head. He wasn't ill, merely preoccupied with what he was gradually realizing amounted to a severe attack of culture shock. Nevertheless, it took his attorney, shipped out here to the Asteroid Belt from Colombo especially for this occasion, several more attempts to get his full attention.

The hearing was almost over. All that remained to be heard now was the disposition. Each side had exercised its opportunity to state its case over the past few hours, and Judge Aloysius Brody appeared ready to render his decision.

How laboriously—and vainly, as it had turned out—
had the Senator striven to get this matter taken out of that
old buffoon's hands, even to the extent of attempting to import an arbiter from Earth. Brody had no background in
the law. Before setting himself up as a tavern keeper, he'd
been a common laborer. Even now, he had no sense of the
importance of his position as the only available jurist on
Pallas (three others having refused to hear the case at all),
and seemed to enjoy making things more difficult for anyone else who exercised authority.

He didn't even demand that everyone rise as he
stumped back into the room—the same barroom he always
used for these proceedings—on his cane and artificial leg.

Beside him, Altman felt his UN-supplied lawyer tense
as his professional involvement overrode his professionally
assumed detachment. Perhaps he'd done an adequate job;
he'd certainly spent enough time at it, taking ten minutes
to every two the defense had seemed to require. The Senator had never been a trial lawyer himself and didn't feel
qualified to evaluate. The man couldn't help it if he looked
like a weasel, with that long, sharp nose and a case of five
o'clock shadow that seemed to afflict him ten minutes after
he shaved in the morning. But his suit—cheap and ill fitting as the fashion among his peers on Earth currently dic-
tated—and his clumsiness in the low Pallatian gravity
didn't help matters.

For his part, Altman wasn't sure he cared any more
how this farce played itself out. After all these years, after
his long and faithful service, he'd hoped for more support
than this from Colombo. And he could always try again,
later on. In the meantime, like it or not, he had other, more
visceral items to concern himself with. In the first place, he
hadn't been outside the Rimfence since Junior had been
killed—had it really been seventeen years ago?—and the
way things had changed had almost come as a mortal blow.

The two hundred miles of rough gravel from Curringer to the Project (more accurately, between the town and the Ngu Departure plant five miles short of it) were now smoothly engineered and paved in some plastic substance which, excepting lubricants, now represented the only use a fusion-powered civilization seemed to have for petroleum products.

Seventeen years.

Nearly as shocking, the dilapidated rollabout—there had been no more gifts of vehicles or other major equipment from Earth—was pleasant to ride in and managed the trip, which once had taken more than half a day, in just under four hours. It helped that the machine had been retrofitted with a catalytic fusion reactor, but it meant, of course, that his drivers had been deceiving him for years about the need for an overnight layover. He was almost pleased enough over missing the arduous journey he'd expected to overlook it.

Almost.

Along the much-improved road lay one enormous, neatly developed homestead after another of a kind once limited to the town's dusty outskirts, punctuated, at wider intervals than would have been the case on Earth, by clusters of shops, stores, and taverns. He saw nothing resembling a town hall, hospital, firehouse, post office, police station, or school. The Outsiders seemed more determined than ever to do without what every other member of the human race regarded as the minimal amenities of civilized existence. Not for the first time, Altman wondered how they survived, and cheerfully envisioned a series of unmanaged catastrophes for which any physical evidence seemed remarkably (and regrettably) lacking.

Seventeen years.

Almost before it had begun, it seemed, the ride was over. His intention to review the case a final time had been forgotten, along with his fellow passenger, the lawyer from Earth, until it was too late. The center of the Outsiders' pioneering efforts on Pallas and that of his own had never strongly resembled one another. But even here, the basic nature of the contrasts between Curringer and the Greeley Utopian Memorial Project seemed to have changed dramatically.

It was more than just the fact that the town had grown while the Project had not—and, in all frankness, seemed to be withering. He had once thought of it (and who had told him he had no poetry in his soul?) as the difference between corruptible metal and undying stone, specifically between sheet steel, easily derived from native ores, from which Curringer was mostly constructed, and concrete, also manufactured locally, which had gradually replaced the temporary plastic construction of the Project. Now it appeared, however, that hardwood was coming into vogue among the Outsiders as a building material, as trees sown decades ago all over the asteroid were beginning to be harvested.

In some ways, this trend struck him as a curious regression, but whatever it actually represented, the Senator thought with a pang, Curringer, with its brightly painted facades and smoothly paved streets, appeared fresh and new, whereas his official Residence, along with the increasingly shabby buildings in the compound surrounding it, covered as they were with overlapping layers of spray-painted graffiti, were slowly starting to crumble back into the soil from which they'd come.

The screeching of a chair leg across the floor brought him back to the present. "It seems t'me," Brody began, startling no one in the room but Altman, "having given 'em due consideration, that the Senator's long list of complaints an' charges against the defendant here tend t'sort themselves into two general categorics."

Altman glanced over at his adversary, hating the very sight of him. As with everything else on this occasion, he was startled to see, in the place of the nasty little Asiatic brat he always envisioned, a solidly built man in his mid-thirties, battered and prematurely gray from his experiences of life. Altman tended to think of it as the inevitable wear and tear of a profligately selfish existence. Ngu was a trifle scarred about the face, and still affecting the eye patch he'd begun wearing to divert public condemnation for his part in Junior's death. (For that matter, he was always startled to see an old man's face staring back from the mirror.)

After the affair of Vesta, Ngu had returned to what his kind regarded as civilization. Whatever else it had achieved, his flight from justice, wandering in the wilderness, had served a typically evil purpose. From subsurface deposits he'd somehow discovered near the South Pole, he'd started an ice-mining company at a time when there had been a seemingly endless supply of water on Pallas and everyone, including his erstwhile partners, had thought him still a bit crazed by previous events. Within ten years, he'd extended a pipe network all over the rapidly developing and increasingly water-hungry asteroid.

To the Senator's helpless dismay, the slowly dying Project soon became dependent on the network's services. Through a series of infuriating screen conversations and humiliating correspondence, he'd continued to insist that Ngu owed an obligation to his first home on Pallas; yet the younger man had consistently charged all the traffic would bear for whatever water he sold, which was why he, Altman, was here today, trying to set reasonable and humane limits on what Ngu claimed were his rights, in order to achieve the greatest good for the greatest number.

"Lookin' over the Senator's briefs," Brody continued, "no pun intended, it seems his initial basis fer complaint's a bill of articles the defendant's folks signed when they enrolled in the Greeley Utopian Memorial Project. From what we're after bein' told by his counsel, freighted up at enormous expense by the Senator's rich and powerful friends in Sri Lanka and what's left of the United States — an' on that account t'be taken with grave import — certain parties in authority on Earth, if nowhere else, still honor those articles, no matter how ethically questionable or outmoded they appear to us, benighted as we be."

The makeshift magistrate paused in his maddening way to shuffle papers before he went on. With everything else that had changed over the years, Altman had been just as surprised to observe that Brody looked and sounded the same as ever. Perhaps there was something to the longevity reports he'd been receiving for the past decade — and perhaps it was not an unmixed blessing they foretold.

"Later on, the good Senator attempts other forms of chicanery — which we'll not hold against him, bein' a lawyer himself after all an' merely followin' his own second nature — rooted in a UN doctrine declarin' Pallas 'the common property of all humanity' despite the fact that no arbitrator here is likely t'recognize such a claim made by them or any other governmental organization. But we'll be after givin' him points fer gall, as well as consistency."

The attorney was on his feet. "Your Honor, I object — !"

Brody interrupted with a nod. "So would I in yer place, Counselor, bein' associated with silliness like this. I uphold yer objection an' find ye in contempt of client, which is no crime and a view I happen t'share. Should yer contempt extend further, say to this court or meself, all I can reply is that, unlike the planet ye come from, yer welcome to yer own opinion, and that's no crime, either."

The lawyer sat, beyond disbelief or exasperation. Altman wanted to tell him there would be another time, but there wasn't any point, since he'd have another lawyer, as well.

Dismissing the attorney, Brody caught Altman's eye. "Now, this isn't an exercise in malice, Senator darlin', no matter what ye may think of it. It's a question of law I tried t'warn ye about twenty years ago an' overlooked fer all that time until now, when ye force me t'make a rulin'. I've no choice but t'declare the Greeley Utopian Memorial Project's articles invalid, null, an' void, since, among other reasons, most of those theoretically bound by it were born after it was signed."

Brody sighed. "By default, an' lackin' a valid precedent in the matter, I hereby find that this makes you, former Senator Gibson Altman, owner-of-record under the terms of the Stein Hyperdemocratic Covenant, of an enormous, unprofitable, labor-intensive agricultural enterprise, on a planet otherwise populated by high-tech hunters. Worse, you must begin payin' yer former serfs forthwith, whose shares in the Curringer Trust ye may no longer vote—or let them go."

Altman heard ringing in his ears, saw his vision narrow to a hazy tunnel at the far end of which Ngu sat looking straight at him, his face utterly devoid of expression.

"I suspect," Brody droned on, "ye'll have no choice but t'subdivide an' turn most of the Project over t'those who've farmed it so arduously these many years, that they'll turn their new land into game farms or huntin' preserves and, as individual entrepreneurs, promptly begin t'prosper. Yer socialist utopian dream, Senator Altman, yer second most important reason fer comin' t'Pallas, is dead."

He slammed the gavel down. "I assess ye court costs. Yer lucky I don't award damages fer the annoyance ye've put the defendant to. Court's adjourned an' the bar's open!"

XXXV
ALOYSIUS'S RESTAURANT

THERE IS NO "BALANCE OF NATURE." ASK THE DINOSAUR.
NATURE IS A BRAIDED, CONTINUOUS *TRANSITION* THAT WITLESS
PRESERVATIONISM OR RELIGIOUS ECOLOGISM CAN'T HANDLE
INTELLECTUALLY OR EMOTIONALLY, IN WHICH THE PRINCIPLE
OF THE "INVISIBLE HAND" WORKS AS WELL—BEING A BASIC
NATURAL LAW—FOR WILDLIFE AND WILDERNESS AS FOR
INDUSTRY AND FINANCE. CREATE AN ENVIRONMENT TO SERVE
SELFISH HUMAN ENDS—AS LONG AS THAT SELFISHNESS
REMAINS CONSISTENT—INSTEAD OF THOSE OF MARGINAL OR
UNFIT SPECIES, AND IT WILL SERVE THE ENDS OF HEALTHY
PLANTS AND ANIMALS, AS WELL.
    —Raymond Louis Drake-Tealy, *Hunting and Humanity*

D on't wish me luck," Cherry insisted, sniffing back a
tear. "You're supposed to say, 'Break a leg.'"

Emerson blinked, having a little trouble with tears
himself. "Why am I supposed to say that?"

Behind her, he heard a low, thrumming noise and a
contrasting hiss as the TransPallatian hoverbus began to
inflate its pneumatic skirts and warm the motors that
drove its impeller blades. For the first time, he was sorry
he'd invented something.

"Because, silly, it's traditional, I don't know why.
Don't look like you're losing your best friend—"

"But I am!" And they both knew it was true.

She patted his cheek gently. "Look, best friend, I'll
probably fall on my face and be back on the next ship—it's
bound to happen once they find out how old I am!"

Suddenly, in his one good eye, Cherry looked very
small and frightened, and, as usual, no more than half her
real age, although they'd celebrated her fiftieth birthday
the previous week. She didn't look that different from the

day he'd first seen her, sitting around in her "working clothes"—brief swatches of bright, satiny color—with several other girls from Galena's at a table toward the back of the Nimrod, a little blond hardly older than himself, eyeing him speculatively. Her hair was still a golden froth hovering about her head like a pale cloud. She'd long since given up her overpowering perfume. She still avoided makeup and there was still the faintest scattering of freckles across her nose.

She was almost as beautiful as Gretchen had been. She always looked that way. Her face (and her body, he was fondly aware) was as firm, smooth, and lovely as ever. Pallas had a way with people, according to folklore, and the scientific data he'd been receiving the last decade tended to confirm it. He looked only a fraction of his own forty-seven years, although his people were inclined to bear their age gracefully even back in the monstrous gravity of Earth—where Cherry was headed in another minute, via TransPallatian, the North Pole, and Curringer Lines.

She laughed before he could voice a gallant denial. "Don't worry, I'll be fine. The only thing that worries me is—are the three weeks of exercises I'll be doing twelve hours a day aboard that new centrifugal space station before the Curringer Lines' insurance company will let me set foot on Earth! It isn't as if I'll get stranded without any money. You've seen to that with your inventions over the years. In an odd way, I'm the same as our old enemy the Senator." She winked at him. "Or his opposite, I'm not sure. He can stay here on Pallas, mourning self-inflicted losses and nursing grudges in solitude, because his livelihood is secured by investments on Earth. Gosh, I could probably buy this producer and his company outright! It isn't the money at all, it's the compliment, being told I oughta be in pictures, and the adventure. You understand, don't you, Emerson? You've had a few adventures of your own."

He nodded back, inwardly miserable, sorry now he'd never married her. Cherry was the only woman who'd never made him feel nervous the way others did. She'd stayed with him and helped make the most terrible hours of his life endurable. On the other hand, what if they'd been married and this offer had come along? He knew the answer without giving it further consideration. He could never have denied Cherry her own wonderful hazard. They'd either be playing this scene exactly as they were now, or he'd be going with her back to that cramped, dirty, heart-wrecking, bone-deforming planet he and his parents had escaped from.

Even thinking about it made him sick. But he smiled and hugged her to him one last time, his cheek hard against hers as he whispered hoarsely, "I can always say I knew you when!"

"Yeah," she giggled, "in the biblical sense!"

He grinned, the memory vivid of an angel perched across his legs in long mesh stockings and a red satin corset which left her breasts and everything below her navel exposed. On another occasion it had been pink velvet shorts with a matching top, her arms around his neck, his hands resting on the bare flesh of her waist.

I'm tired of looking at you across a Monopoly board, he could hear her saying. *If I see one more little green plastic house or red hotel, I'm going to scream. I'm taking you back to my place and you won't get out of jail free this time!*

For whatever credit it was worth, his image was just as clear of Cherry in the overstuffed office of the overstuffed president of the First Pallatian Bank of Curringer, an elderly .45 automatic in one hand, the prototype of his own invention in the other, hefting each, then swapping them in her hands and hefting them again.

Today she wore a conservative business suit. Her Ngu Departure pistol was tucked safely away in her unpretentious luggage since she was slated for landing at a spaceport in West America, where the surviving politicians were summarily jailed for even introducing the subject of gun control. Her bags were already onboard the machine which, for some reason known only to those who write bus schedules, awaited only the arrival of its opposite number from the other Pole. Clutched firmly in her consciousness, if not literally in her hand, was the preliminary contract she'd been faxed last week from Denver, which, since California had been utterly destroyed half a century earlier, had become the motion picture capital of West America, and therefore of the solar system.

The opportunity was genuine enough—a windfall from a documentary some television network had done the previous year on Curringer's "peculiar" social institutions—and the contract was appropriately signed, sealed, and certified. Being the shrewd businesswoman she was, Cherry had employed a reputable Earthside law firm to check out the movie company and the producer who'd seen and admired her on TV. Unknown to Cherry—Emerson had hired another law firm, he hoped—to check up on them.

At last the second bus whooshed down the street and sighed to a stop in front of Galena's. Curringer had no terminal of any kind and probably never would. Emerson had never envisioned these big, clumsy vehicles as anything but a stopgap until his flying yoke was improved enough to render them unnecessary. He was getting close to that point now, and in that sense, hoverbuses were already on the verge of obsolescence. It would be a few more years, though, before enough of the current generation of personal flying machines were out in the market to put mass transportation out of business altogether.

Cherry gave him a final kiss, one he'd remember the

rest of his life, and climbed aboard, sitting on the opposite side of the machine so they wouldn't be waving good-bye for the next ten agonizing minutes. Emerson understood and approved. He was just turning away to walk back to the Nimrod, where he'd planned to have lunch with Aloysius, Nails, and Mrs. Singh—who had made their good-byes to Cherry in their own way earlier—when he heard a familiar voice.

"Emerson Ngu, is that really you?"

He turned, then eagerly strode toward the arriving bus with his hand out. "Mrs. Drake-Tealy!"

Resting an elbow on the hoop of her flying yoke, Mirelle Stein peered over the rims of her glasses to give his hand a disapproving look he could tell was counterfeit from the way her eyes sparkled. "Whatever happened to Miri—and a big hug?"

He laughed and put his arms around her. Like Cherry, she didn't seem to have aged. In fact, she looked a decade younger. "My god, I haven't seen or heard from you since—"

"Since you sent me the current generation of this." She patted the hoop with a hand. "And you need not call me God when we're alone, dear boy. It has been at least six or seven years. I have toured the planet, thanks to you. I have written one book and have a fair beginning made on another. Would you believe I have even been back to Earth—briefly and never again—this thing does not work at all down there. I was back in a wheelchair and could never breathe right."

Emerson glanced a little guiltily at the departing bus, vanishing in the distance, taking the woman he came closest to loving off to her new life half a billion miles away. There was something important about that thought, some insight he'd never had before, but he didn't have time to pursue it now. "I know exactly what you mean. I was just going to have lunch with Aloysius Brody and some other friends. Would you join me? Where's Digger and what's he been up to?"

Stein opened her mouth, then reconsidered and closed it. "Let us talk of this later, shall we? In the meantime, I would love to have lunch with you and your friends, Emerson, if there is somewhere to wash up and you promise not to announce to the general public who I am. I am weary of feeling like George Washington, and I am especially weary of idiots informing me that they thought I was dead."

Emerson chuckled and made the requested promise.

"After that," she added in a different tone of voice, momentarily losing the sparkle and her ageless enthusiasm, "I had better begin looking for a place to stay."

Worried over what seemed to have gone wrong between his two old friends, Emerson nodded, picked up the bags the bus driver had placed at her feet while they were talking, and led the famous philosopher down the street toward the Nimrod.

Their entrance into the tavern was greeted with exclamations of surprise and delight from the landlord's corner table. Apparently Mrs. Singh had known Miri in the old days, as Aloysius had and even Nails was excited by the presence of a woman who would probably rather not have been referred to as a living legend.

"What brings you to our fair city?" Aloysius asked as Miri and Emerson found chairs for themselves. The process was complicated by the philosopher's flying yoke.

"This." She reached into the large handbag she carried and tossed a book down on the table, the gesture losing some of its expected dramatic quality in the feeble gravity of the asteroid. "It is an advance copy, sent to me for review. The book is not officially scheduled for release on Earth until next month."

What they saw before them on the table was a dreary-looking soft-covered volume, the sort of thing a government printing office in Bulgaria might have produced, Emerson thought. Badly printed on the drab, pulpy cover was, *NonHuman Beings: The Discovery of Alien Artifacts among the Asteroids* by Raymond Louis Drake-Tealy, and just above that, "Uncorrected Proof for Review Purposes Only."

They were all familiar with the subject, one way or another. Preliminary developmental surveys carried out by Emerson's company, following his original "footsteps" in the Pocks, had already brought back thousands of the peculiar objects. As Emerson leafed through the book, he saw that it was filled with full-page photographs and drawings, many of them things he'd seen and handled at Digger's cabin, and some few of which he now possessed himself. He'd even brought back a handful of the first such items, a gift from Drake-Tealy after they'd remained on the mantlepiece in the anthropologist's home for years as simple curiosities.

"With circles and arrows and a paragraph on the back explaining what each one was," Nails misquoted, peering over Emerson's shoulder. He'd examined the objects brought from the Pocks. As a machinist, he was inclined to agree with Digger about them.

Mrs. Singh, on the other hand, was shaking her head. "You think the old boy's lost it, don't you?"

Miri nodded. "He is about to make an utter fool of himself and destroy a distinguished career. Although it is couched in cautious, scholarly language—for example, he grudgingly allows for the possibility that these things are no more than peculiar volcanic extrusions left over from the natural formation of the asteroid—his contentions are straight from Erik von Daniken."

"Who the hell is Erik von Daniken?" Nails demanded,

and Emerson would like to have known, as well, but the machinist's question was ignored by all the others.

"I dusted those damned things, these 'Drake-Tealy Objects,' as he and his hangers-on are calling them, for three decades." Apparently, Emerson thought, Miri didn't recall—or didn't want to—that she had been the first to call the objects by that name, however sarcastically she'd intended it. "And I do not believe there is the remotest chance that they are artificial, the remains of an ancient, nonhuman intelligence, however weather-worn and time-distorted. What I am afraid of is that Raymond is desperate to make one last spectacular discovery, or perhaps worse, that—"

"He's suffering senile dementia?" Mrs. Singh suggested.

Miri nodded sadly.

"Ah, but isn't that what they'd have said of Heinrich Schliemann, in his day?" Aloysius mused. "An' didn't he wind up provin' 'em all misguided by discoverin' Troy?"

Nails laughed. "He discovered nine or twelve Troys too many, in the end, though, didn't he?"

"Indeed he did, my boy, indeed he did—vastly en-richin' our body of scientific knowledge in the process an' bringin' up more questions than he answered, which is the proper vocation of any conscientious an' authentic scientist."

Across the room, customers at the bar who'd been watching a soccer game from Earth—Aloysius, a champion pistol shot in his own time, endured this much exposure to collective sports only for the sake of business—suddenly fell silent as a few faces turned toward the innkeeper's table, then quickly back to the screen, buzzing a little among themselves. Emerson glimpsed the reason for their behavior just as his host yelled, "Turn that damned thing up an' keep quiet!"

The color-saturated, three-dimensional image was of the latest blandly photogenic anchorwoman to visit Pallas. Emerson couldn't remember her name or what network employed her. She stood, to all appearances, directly on the airless, harshly lit surface of a spaceport crater bottom, without benefit of spacesuit. Emerson realized she must be standing in front of a big picture window set in the inward-facing cliff of the ring mountain, level with the crater floor.

On the other hand, it might just have been a matter of the simple if totally deceptive image manipulation at which Earth's mass media seemed so talented. They often seemed to practice lying for its own sake.

But what caught and held his attention, and that of everybody else in the room, was neither the amply endowed newswoman in her shorts and halter top (which for some reason had become a sort of uniform for female correspondents visiting the asteroid, the way bush jackets and pith helmets had once been de rigueur in Africa) or the background she stood against, but the person she was interviewing.

Sitting beside him, Miri cringed at the picture of herself, looking rather old and shriveled, and somewhat ridiculous hanging there in her idling flying yoke.

". . . reaction to the controversial anthropologist's latest sensational claims," the correspondent was saying, "which she refuses to discuss at present."

Here, the camera viewpoint shifted briefly to a close-up of Miri, then to luggage piled around her feet, and finally to her flying yoke, as the other woman continued in a voice-over.

"However, in the savage public battle that's certain to follow once she does break her silence, it's bound to emerge eventually that she harbors other, more personal resentments against the famous figure with whom she lived for so long."

Now the image changed abruptly to old stock footage of a younger Raymond Louis Drake-Tealy, seated at his word processor, lecturing a university class, handling a fossil skull, cutting wood in some rustic setting, and finally, stalking game on the African plains with the same big .416 Rigby Emerson was so familiar with.

"Apparently, Mirelle Stein's original vision of a hyper-democratic society didn't include basing an entire civilization on what others now quote her as calling 'primitive blood sports.' "

At the precise instant that the word "blood" was spoken, Drake-Tealy's enormous rifle recoiled on his shoulder, spouting smoke, and the view cut to a tiny, delicate antelope which fell over and slid as if it had been hit by an invisible truck.

"This was entirely Drake-Tealy's 'contribution,' " the newswoman declared, "to match the philosophical insights of Stein herself and the financial and engineering input of William Wilde Curringer . . . and it appears she's always been sickened by it."

The camera was on Miri once again, looking tired and unhappy.

"Kylie Kennedy at Port Peary, the North Pole of Pallas, for the East American Radio Service."

XXXVI
A BEASTLY PATTERN

A THOUSAND YEARS HENCE, PERHAPS IN LESS, AMERICA MAY BE
WHAT EUROPE IS NOW . . . THE NOBLEST WORK OF HUMAN
WISDOM, THE GRAND SCENE OF HUMAN GLORY, THE FAIR CAUSE
OF FREEDOM THAT ROSE AND FELL.

— Thomas Paine

E merson trudged the long, weary road back to Mrs.
Singh's.

Alone.

Ordinarily, it was a brief, pleasant stroll beside a
freshly paved road quite unlike the dusty gravel track he'd
first followed to freedom many years ago. He'd turned
down the offer of a ride in Mrs. Singh's three-wheeled contraption. Nobody had ever come up with a satisfactory ge-
neric name for the damned things, although they were in
use all over the Curringer area and Nails was getting quite
rich manufacturing them. Usually they just sat out on a
sales lot or were displayed on a video screen, requiring no
more label than a price tag.

Instead, Emerson had chosen to be by himself for a
while. While he was in town—they'd all come in to see
Cherry off—he was staying in his old room, which happened to be vacant. By tomorrow it wouldn't be, since Miri
was moving in, apparently as a long-term resident.

How odd, he thought, *and how discouraging. Here I am, very
nearly half a century old, two-thirds of my normal Earthside actu-
arial life span over with* (although nobody could say for sure
how long he might expect to live on Pallas), *and I still can't
sort my feelings out a bit better than I could when I was fourteen.
And everything still hurts just as much as it did when I was that
age.*

Maybe even more.

He lit a cigar, inhaled, and blew the smoke out in front of him.

He wouldn't have admitted that he nearly worshipped Raymond Louis Drake-Tealy as a hero, and was almost as uncritically fond of the warm, kindly individual Mirelle Stein had turned out to be underneath that crusty layer of bitterness and anger which seemed to have crumbled away the very minute she'd discovered a reason to hope again. But it was true. It had broken his heart to learn that they were at odds with one another, had separated after all these years, and, if that bubble-head on TV had her way, would soon be arguing the whole thing out in public.

The one thing he had managed to learn in his forty-seven years was that you can't live other people's lives for them, that trying only makes you—and them—even more miserable. Not that this insight, for whatever wisdom it contained, offered much satisfaction. On the contrary, it was simply the sort of thing you resigned yourself to.

As always, when confronted with this kind of mentally immovable object, the subject seemed to change itself before he'd made any conscious decision in the matter. For some reason that defied analysis, he found he was thinking more and more often these days about Gretchen, and he was very confused about Cherry. Part of him wished her nothing but well, sincerely hoped that she'd succeed fabulously in her new career, as she deserved to. Yet another part hoped, not without a pang of guilt, that she would "fall flat on her face" and come right back to him.

But if he really loved her, he'd never have let her go back to Earth, at least not without him.

Right?

And if she really loved him, she'd never have gone.

On the other hand, maybe they loved each other enough to let each seek his or her own destiny.

And on the third hand, maybe that was bullshit.

With a rueful grin, he remembered an old poster he'd once seen: "If you love somebody, let them go—then, if they don't come back, hunt them down and kill them."

And with that grin, his mind refocused itself once again on something safer, although no less confusing: what were the Drake-Tealy Objects, anyway, and where the hell had they come from?

For that matter, the same question could be asked about the asteroids themselves. Emerson knew that the question of their origin had never been satisfactorily settled. Some scientists, mostly Earth-based astronomers and astrophysicists relying on mathematical models, had held for centuries that they were simple accretions of nebular matter—dust and gases—which, owing to the disturbing influence of massive Jupiter's gravity, had never coalesced into the planet this region of the solar system should have given birth to.

Others, mostly chemists and geologists, argued back (perhaps a trifle romantically, although they had physical evidence, meteors in the beginning and now actual samples, to support them) that the asteroids were remnants of a planet which, for some unknown reason—possibly Jupiter's gravity again—had shattered into millions of fragments. They also pointed out that the advocates of another romantic theory, continental drift, had been unjustly ridiculed as crackpots by established scientists for a century before not only being proven correct, but seeing their concept become the fundamental fact of Earthside geology.

Their opponents countered, quite logically, that just because Columbus had been made fun of and later proven right, that didn't mean Velikovski was right, too.

For the most part, until recent years, those individuals actually living and working among the thousands of tumbling mountains hurtling through space between Mars and

Jupiter had been far too busy simply surviving to worry very much about where the asteroids had come from, let alone some useless curiosity like the Drake-Tealy Objects which, in any case, had only recently come to light.

Now times were better and people could afford to be curious.

Pallas was still the only body in the Asteroid Belt with a permanent population. However, ship-based mining, such as that pursued by Aloysius's friend Fritz Marshall, was being carried out on an everyday basis elsewhere in the Belt, just as sixteenth century European fisherman had once harvested the Grand Banks off North America, re-turning home after each trip, never really setting foot in the New World. And, as Emerson had observed on many occasions before, there was always talk of new colonial en-terprises being launched from Earth, or even from Pallas itself.

There was always talk . . .

"I'm Hugh Downey, Junior, and this is *Fifty/Fifty,* part of LiteLink's never-ending struggle to get at the real truth no matter what the facts may be. With us this evening, via in-terplanetary video and a bit of careful editing to reduce the time it takes for signals to get back and forth from world to world, is the distinguished former United States Senator— and onetime Union Democratic Presidential hopeful— Gibson Altman, presently Chief Administrator of the United Nations' Greeley Utopian Memorial Project on the asteroid Pallas.

"Good evening, Senator Altman. We feel we were very lucky to get this interview, and we're grateful, with all the other networks anxious to consult you on the current cri-sis."

That wasn't true, of course, but it would be after this— and worth every cent it had cost.

"Good evening, Hugh—although it's morning where I happen to be at the moment."

Even so, he had the drapes drawn here in his office— the one room he'd been able to maintain by himself, now that he was all alone, living in the moldering remains of what had once been his official Residence—so that the brown, dying fields surrounding the building would not be visible to billions of viewers back on Earth. It would be late afternoon before the interview—consisting of questions and answers separated by half an hour's wait each time—was over. It would be a long, arduous process which would leave him exhausted for the next couple of days, but it might well prove to have been worth the effort.

Downey briefly detailed Altman's personal history— brushing only very lightly over the scandal which had taken him to Pallas in the first place—but bearing down on the "beastly pattern of treatment" the Senator and his Project had received at the hands of the brutish colonists, whom he compared to the Boers of South Africa.

"Senator, public curiosity here on Earth—as well as there on Pallas, I understand—has recently been piqued by the mysterious so-called Drake-Tealy Objects, which may or may not be remnants of a lost alien civilization. Even before the infamous and colorful anthropologist wrote his book about them, they were commanding higher prices among this planet's fashionable elite than finds of precious metals. A number of very emotional controversies centering on those objects has begun raging. First and foremost, of course, there's the question of what to do with them."

"Yes, Hugh, that's the crucial question. According to a long-standing position taken by the United Nations General Assembly and broadly shared by academic and government authorities on Earth, such objects are the common property of all humanity, and should be treated as such, rather than being permitted to fall into the hands of unscrupulous individuals, no different from archaeological pot-hunting criminals anywhere else, really, willing to exploit or even obliterate these fragile and mysterious relics, simply to make money for themselves."

Downey nodded sympathetically for the benefit of his Earthside audience rather than for the Senator, who didn't see the gesture until half an hour after he'd made the statement that inspired it. "However, I gather that this position, as you say, broadly shared among civilized people everywhere, has been discarded on Pallas, although it still finds local support in the person of a certain courageous, respectable, but tragically unappreciated elder statesman."

That was laying it on pretty thick, even for this notoriously effusive telejournalist, Altman thought, but Downey knew his own constituency and perhaps he knew what he was doing. He'd been paid enough that he'd *better* know.

But before he could make a suitably modest disclaimer, the man was going on. "Some advocacy media figures and entertainer-activists here on Earth have gone so far as to portray Pallatian colonists as thick-witted, savage louts. I've heard comparisons being drawn between them and the whale hunters of ages past, as well as baby-seal harvesters, commercial loggers, and even industrial polluters."

Stand-up comics, TV and radio talk-show hosts, each had played a part in an overall scheme the purpose of which was to make Altman appear moderate and reasonable.

"Hugh, I think the media may be making a mistake in that regard. I admit there are times when I'm tempted to compare my fellow Pallatians to the barbarians who burned the Alexandrian Library, but in general, I think it's a waste of time to call names or point fingers. What we must all do, instead, is encourage the General Assembly to

pass the Emergency Antiquities Protection Act I've proposed, no matter how much or how loudly it—or I, for that
matter—may be repudiated by certain short-sighted individuals making a fortune here on Pallas."

Downey grinned. Like Altman, he knew that, for all
practical purposes, and with only one significant exception, the interview was over, that it had already achieved
what it had been arranged for, and that the rest of the conversation would be a matter of consolidating that achieve-
ment or merely filling airtime.

"And what of the argument we've been hearing lately
that what began as a matter of mere paleontological curiosity could now become a fundamental question of cultural
conflict and political sovereignty? Does the Emergency
Antiquities Protection Act you've proposed threaten to
trample human rights wholesale, as its opponents claim,
and even raise the terrible possibility of interplanetary
war?"

Altman gave his best, tolerant, statesmanly chuckle.
He'd specifically requested that this question be asked so
that the issues involved could be dealt with now, when
they were controllable. He'd wondered when Downey was
going to get around to it.

"In the first place, Hugh, no lawfully constituted national authority or accredited international organization
has ever granted anything remotely like political sovereignty to Pallas. This asteroid was, effectively, *stolen* by the
Curringer Trust from humanity as a whole, to whom it still
rightfully belongs. Legally—although no one's pressed the
matter for decades—Pallas is still administered by the
United Nations, and its inhabitants are still citizens of
whatever nation they originally came from and therefore
still subject to their laws."

"Which is why," Downey suggested on cue, "LiteLink

and *Fifty/Fifty* were unable to find any duly elected leaders on Pallas to represent the other point of view?"

"Precisely. Under the juvenile lunacy of the Stein Covenant, Pallatians enjoy styling themselves as genteel anarchists—which, under a long and very well-established body of international law, means that this is an 'abandoned polity' and that they're subject to the first real government that comes along and claims them."

There: the threat had been made.

Now to soften it a bit and give the enemy a way out.

"But, setting all that aside for a moment, the UN Emergency Antiquities Protection Act is only one part of a larger overall plan for dealing with this unfortunate situation peaceably and ultimately, I believe, to everybody's satisfaction."

Downey raised his eyebrows in an expression he was famous for on five continents. "A plan? Something new— remember, folks, you're hearing about this first on *Fifty/ Fifty*. Tell us about your plan, Senator, and why we haven't heard about it before this."

Altman raised a hand in a self-deprecating gesture he had once been famous for himself. "Well, Hugh, the plan is simple, but it was necessary first to seek support for it among my old colleagues and other key figures who could help with it."

Meaning that Altman and his partisans on Earth had to see whether the General Assembly still had the spine to lay claim to the Asteroid Belt and revive the long-discredited "common heritage" doctrine. That had taken time and used up a lot of favors. Then, of course, it had been necessary to enlist technophobes and neo-Luddites of every conceivable stripe, environmentalists, and self-appointed consumerists to intrude themselves into the argument over the Drake-Tealy Objects.

At the same time, the ever-cooperative mass media had

to be persuaded to help him promote the plan to Earth's uninformed populace, decide to pass him off as a public benefactor all but martyred by the barbarians on Pallas and much sought after for interplanetary interviews. Above all, no opportunity must be offered to those on Pallas to defend themselves against the charges being leveled against them. That had been the hardest part—and the most expensive.

"What we wanted," the Senator announced to a waiting world, "and what we got in the end, I think, was a plan that's harmless to the traditional rights and customs of Pallatians or the so-called principle of hyperdemocracy which is almost sacred to them, whatever we may think of it ourselves. Under that plan, a special, newly constituted agency of the United Nations will assume nominal ownership and control of all items of scientific or antiquarian interest discovered in space. Civilian employees of that agency will oversee the handling of such objects, assuring that their eventual disposition is completely ethical. Notice we're not taking over Pallas or any other asteroid—as we could do under international law—nor are we seizing anybody's home or farm or factory. The fact is, once this law is in force, no one will even notice it's operating."

"Well, it certainly sounds reasonable and sensible to me, Senator, as well as being in everybody's best interests. I don't see how any decent individual could oppose it."

"Neither do I, Hugh, which is why I urge your viewers to write or call their United Nations representative, demanding that the Emergency Antiquities Protection Act be put in place immediately, along with its various enabling regulations."

Downey grinned his famous grin. "I'm sure they all heard that, Senator, and will do as you ask. We here at LiteLink and *Fifty/Fifty* wish you the best of luck."

"Thanks, Hugh."

"Thank you, Senator, and good night."

XXXVII
ROSALIE FRAZIER

ADVERTISEMENTS CONTAIN THE ONLY TRUTHS TO BE RELIED ON
IN A NEWSPAPER.

          — Thomas Jefferson

E merson slapped at his cheek. A swarm of impossibly fat black houseflies buzzed and battered themselves against the sunlit windowpanes, and some kind of tiny brown weevil had gotten into the cupboard by the hundreds, spoiling both the freeze-dried coffee and the tins of hard biscuits.

It had been that kind of morning. He'd flown three-quarters of the way to the South Pole the day before, ostensibly to inspect a homestead that was up for sale, but actually as an excuse to get away from Curringer, the media, and the latest interplanetary crisis. He was sick of turning on the screen only to see Gibson Altman denouncing Pallatians and everything he accused them of standing for. Emerson was equally sick of being hounded by news vultures; avoiding them only seemed to make them more zealous to invade his privacy and interrupt his work. Of course if he'd actively sought publicity, they'd have ignored him.

His visit with the homesteader had not gone well. The idiot had tried breeding African elephants from zygotes, but his holdings were too far south and offered the wrong forage. What animals he'd raised had eaten him out of house and home, stripping the land to bare soil. They'd been sold to competent breeders further north, and the man was now attempting to unload his overgrazed acreage in order to emigrate back to Earth, where, no doubt, he'd

write a book about the inhospitable frontier which somehow would fail to mention his own ineptitude.

There was ice under that much-abused ground, but
Emerson's hydrologist, who'd met him at the site, had
warned him that the salt and metal content were too high
to make it economical for the pipeline's electroceramic fil-
ters to process. A geologist, who'd also flown up from Port
Amundsen, had informed him that the depth and distribu-
tion of the deposits were all wrong. Extraction would
cause a massive subsidence which might not only generate
local quakes—and on tiny Pallas, the word "local" took in
a lot of territory—but could also get him sued by neighbors whose surface water would drain into the resulting
depression.

The final straw—and he hadn't needed a hired hand to
tell him this—was that extending his network to reach this
far east over the rugged terrain of the Pocks would yield a
dead loss for the next ten years. Convincing the landowner
that he wasn't trying to drive the price down, and that he
really didn't want the land, had proven impossible. All the
time Emerson had been there, inspecting the ruined claim
stake, the man had kept the video in his ATV tuned to another interview with Gibson Altman. Clearly the homesteader agreed with the Senator on many points. They
hadn't parted company on amicable terms. Another unsat-
isfied "customer," he thought wearily, more grist for Altman's evil mill.

Although there were many demands on Emerson's
time and he could have used the last forty-eight hours to
good advantage either in his new offices in Curringer or at
his still-growing Ngu Departure plant, where he had really
wanted to be this morning was Port Amundsen, at a sym-
posium on state-of-the-art spacecraft design given by Fritz
Marshall and companies that maintained the atmospheric

envelope and orbiting solar mirrors that kept the asteroid warmer than nature had intended.

Or he could have been at a similar affair in Port Peary concerning recent experiments in the field of antigravity, the so-called "fifth force" locked inside the deepest recesses of the atomic nucleus. Mankind's future—and his own, he was convinced—lay in space, and he was determined to involve himself in it somehow, if only the press of business left him enough time and energy.

He couldn't even visit Digger while he was down here at this latitude. The anthropologist's cabin was on the other side of the Pocks, half a world away, and the man was rumored to be visiting Earth. In any case, he wasn't answering calls.

Instead, Emerson sat on the steps of a corrugated-steel line shack he'd stopped at for a rest—since he could hardly call on the hospitality of the landowner—and ate a snack from stored supplies. The shack marked the farthest reach of his pipeline in this area. Outside, the flies were mustard-colored and bit savagely if he wasn't watchful. The rough, sparse ground cover was golden brown, punctuated by blue and yellow wildflowers, mostly mountain columbine. He was smoking a cigarette and drinking a warm Coke— at least the weevils hadn't managed to bore their implacable way into that—making virtue of necessity by enjoying the sunshine and the smell of sage and evergreen the breeze carried to him.

There was considerable satisfaction, gazing down the slope along the die-straight path of the pipeline. Where it crossed the holdings of others, it was often painted camouflage colors to match the local surroundings. Here, it gleamed like liquid silver in the sun, reflecting perfectly the cheerful yellow of a tiny caterpillar tractor sitting alongside. The pipeline was a testimony to human purpose, which could be just as implacable as that of any insect and vastly more constructive. He knew what Altman and his friends would say about that shining length of stainless steel, but to Emerson, it was beautiful.

In a few minutes he'd have to resume his journey to Curringer, where more unpleasantness awaited. An individual whose land had held ice of the proper quality was now convinced, mostly by Altman's continuous barrage of innuendo, that Emerson had cheated him. He not only wanted his contract set aside, he wanted damages which he had publicly promised to donate to an Earthside animal rights foundation. Emerson's lawyers—it still shocked him to realize that he had lawyers—had filed for dismissal and, under the Stein Covenant, were confident of getting it, but his own testimony was required, which meant the waste of at least another day.

This wasn't the first instance of his business practices and personality being called into question, and it wasn't any accident. The real perpetrator to be watched on Pallas, Altman had warned an entire galaxy, it seemed, over and over in the past five years, was that ruthless industrialist Emerson Ngu. If one believed Altman, his fast-growing, world-embracing water network—"to name a single, typically exploitive undertaking"—now threatened to destroy millions of priceless Drake-Tealy Objects.

Emerson snorted derisively. He had as much trouble thinking of himself as an industrialist as he did about employing lawyers. He was just a guy who made guns, flying yokes, a few other items, and happened to run a pipeline because his factory and the little town that seemed to be growing up around it of its own accord needed water. To listen to the Senator, one might think he was another William Wilde Curringer.

That seemed to stir an idea, something about mankind's future in space, but the thought eluded him.

As far as the Drake-Tealy Objects were concerned,

Emerson was as romantic as anyone and honestly hoped Digger was right, that they were the product of an ancient alien civilization. It would be exciting, reassuring, and somehow would make the universe seem less hostile and lonely. But there was no telling where the damned things were going to turn up; they seemed to be buried every-where, and if you tried to avoid the almost indestructible items, nothing would ever get done on Pallas. Which may have been the Senator's point.

Nothing substantially new had been discovered on that topic in the past five years. One world-famous popular "scientist," more of a TV personality, in fact, who hadn't done any original scientific investigation of his own for decades, had "reconstructed" the hypothetical nonhumans of Pallas, along with their airy, futuristic cities. This effort made as much sense to Emerson as trying to recreate the human race and its civilization from a handful of paper clips. The aliens stood about five feet tall, had enormous, lovable, moist brown eyes, and soft, glossy fur.

Naturally, these wise and noble beings were pacifists and vegetarians—although, when it served the purposes of the pop scientist and his fans, the benighted creatures had also blown themselves and their planet to pieces in a nu-clear war which unfortunately had left no physical evi-dence, but which must stand nevertheless as a dire warn-ing to a foolish and untrustworthy humanity concerning the iniquities of individualism, capitalism, runaway tech-nology, or whatever else the pop scientist and his fans hap-pened to dislike this week.

Those brown eyes had done the trick. While Altman appealed to what he termed the "collective conscience of humanity," several countries, including East America and the People's Republic of Britain, had outlawed the import of Drake-Tealy Objects, bypassing any need for con-science, making the choice for their subjects via the same

deadly force so vehemently deplored by Altman and his allies on any other occasion. The UN was still pondering the
Altman Plan. That it abrogated the concepts of national
sovereignty, personal privacy, private property, and profit,
on Pallas or anywhere else, was never conveyed to a public
less hostile toward ideas like that than had been the case a
century ago. By now they were growing bored with the
subject anyway, and the media would find them as dis-
tractible by the next well-planned crisis as they always
seemed to be.

Emerson didn't really blame them. In fact he didn't really believe in anything that might properly be called "the
public." There were just billions of preoccupied individuals, coping with their own lives as he was attempting to
cope with his. He knew the media lied about every issue he
was familiar with, and as a consequence he assumed they
lied about everything else, as well. But unless it bore directly on what he was doing, he lacked the time and energy
to discover the detailed truth for himself. That was the advantage the media enjoyed, and the source of their power,
but he didn't know what to do about it any more than anybody else did.

Meanwhile, the prolonged and inefficient assembly of a
UN spacefleet to enforce an Emergency Antiquities Protection Act they hadn't as yet ratified was proceeding in a
bizarre kind of open secrecy, reminding Emerson of what
he'd read of the decade of corruption and incompetence
spent in the creation of the Spanish Armada.

Nobody seemed to know whether the idea was to
blockade Pallas, preventing export of any further Drake-
Tealy Objects, or to seize control of the entire asteroid.
The latter seemed far likelier to Emerson, since the Objects' main value seemed to lie in the excuse they provided
Altman and his ilk to destroy everything Curringer had
ever accomplished. Once a fleet stood in orbit about Pal-

las, it was only a step from blockade to invasion. The art of wringing a credible provocation from an enemy unwilling to fight hadn't changed since the time of Begin or Bush. Pallatians observed what little the media told them of these events in a sort of helpless disbelief, and made what preparations they could for war.

Which was another reason Emerson had flown to the southern terminus of his pipeline, on which all of Pallas had come to depend for its health and growth. He wanted to estimate for himself how defensible it might be. The answer, he admitted gloomily, was that it wasn't defensible at all. How could it be? It had been built in a time of peace for peaceful purposes. It had been meant to bring life to otherwise lifeless regions of the asteroid. Pallas was a growing concern, but it wasn't growing fast enough to make the pipeline profitable if it had to be—what was the word?—*hardened* for war. Somehow, without giving up what Pallas really stood for, that war had to be prevented.

Idly, because he was still looking for an excuse to postpone his journey back to Curringer, Emerson stubbed out his cigarette. He'd also run short of cigars this morning, which might at least have kept the damned flies away, and the thin, acrid smoke was getting in his own eye. He leaned inside to turn on the shack's all-purpose communicator. He didn't really expect it to be in any better condition than the coffee and biscuits had been, so he was actually surprised when a perfect polychrome three-dimensional picture of the familiar bartender-announcer from His Master's Voice sprang into life across its screen.

"*. . . gonna repeat now, an important news conference recorded live earlier this morning here in Curringer and broadcast over KCUF. We don't get to do this kinda stuff very often, folks, so we'd really appreciate it if you'd pay attention.*"

The announcer was replaced by a scene Emerson recognized, the inside of the Nimrod Saloon & Gambling Emporium. Aloysius's people had set up a table by the wall with the enormous antlers, cluttered with large pieces of poster board displaying photographs and computer printouts. There were also items of physical evidence, some of which he'd handled himself. Behind that, and a fat cluster of microphones duct-taped together, stood two women. The one who hung suspended in a flying yoke, he knew. As the unseen camera focused in, Miri Stein spoke.

"Ladies and gentlemen, I am here today to introduce Dr. Rosalie Frazier, who has come to Pallas through the auspices of the Curringer Foundation, an organization few are likely to have heard of, since it was set up in secret, independent of the Curringer Trust, to safeguard the Covenant which bears my name and which some claim is responsible for the unique way of life we share and enjoy on this asteroid.

"Before you ask, I am responsible for having brought this young scientist to Pallas. I believed her presence to be urgently necessary, with warships being prepared, even as I speak, to impose the political will of Earthside politicians on all of us. She is one of a tiny band of 'xenoarchaeologists,' an expert on nonterrestrial artifacts, and she wields impressive credentials, even if her field has so far been forced to struggle along without a tangible object of study. At my request, she has been commissioned by the Curringer Foundation to settle this dispute over the so-called Drake-Tealy Objects once and for all. Dr. Frazier . . . ?"

He'd never seen the young woman before, but as the screen shifted to a close-up, he knew she was too beautiful and lively for the Earthside media to ignore. Looking flushed and excited, she had dark, glossy, shoulder-length hair, large, appealing blue eyes, nice cheekbones, and a nose turned up a little at the end. A good mouth, but it was her self-confident manner he found most attractive. She was slim, in tight-fitting coveralls a movie director might consider appropriate to digging artifacts in a desert, and at the same time intriguingly rounded in the right places.

Best of all, from the standpoint of the Pallatians she addressed, she carried a heavy autopistol in a broad belt slanting across her hips.

Obviously a bit nervous, she cleared her throat. *"Thank you, Miss Stein. To relieve the suspense, I'll begin by saying that the Drake-Tealy Objects I've examined on Earth by neutrino-scan and other recent techniques are not only indisputably the product of intelligent fabrication, billions of years old, they were apparently assembled atom-by-atom to assume whatever shape they have and perform whatever function they once served, in a manner beyond our present technology."*

She held up a hand, trying to silence the uproar she'd provoked. *"There isn't much more to say about that aspect, except to note that certain of my colleagues have been somewhat premature, inferring such things as the makers' size, body shape, hair and eye color—not to mention party affiliation and softdrink preference from a few badly worn tool specimens . . ."* There was general laughter. *"I do, however, have something to say about the disposition of these objects.*

"The legislative program put forth by ex-Senator Gibson Altman is not in the interests either of the people it affects or of science. It's nothing more than backdoor socialism, blatant and regressive, a last grab at power by collectivist politicians on Earth and elsewhere whose time in history is over. I urge Pallatians to take arms—I see you've done that already—and resist this reactionary stupidity. I urge the people of Earth to remove the self-aggrandizing hacks responsible for taking them to the brink of history's first interplanetary war."

The room rocked with cheering and applause and it was some time before it could be quieted down.

"It should be clear to everyone else by now, after the disasters of the last century, that coercion isn't the answer to this or any other problem. Instead of fabricating another statist excuse to beat people up and kill them, I propose to educate Pallatian Object-finders, so that what they bring back from the wilderness will retain its

archaeological 'context' and be of greater value to science and the market.

"To Senator Altman and his allies, if they're so worried about preserving the prehistory of this asteroid, perhaps they should dig deep in their own pockets—rather than those of the taxpayers—and buy as many Drake-Tealy Objects as possible. They can put them in museums—or wherever else they think advisable.

"Thank you."

XXXVIII
A PRECIPICE AT HIS FEET

A MAN IS ONLY AS OLD AS THE WOMAN HE FEELS.
— Groucho Marx

Emerson grinned.
"Well, I can see my help wasn't needed. Inconsiderate of you to conduct your lives without it!"

He'd traveled halfway around the little globe for the second time in as many days in an attempt to persuade Drake-Tealy to see his wife. He'd tried hard to stay out of the archaeological free-for-all when it had been a public matter, but he'd immediately recognized what Miri had really been up to yesterday, and why.

Happily, he was too late. Miri and Digger were sitting on the front porch of their cabin, holding hands and swinging gently back and forth in a rustic glider the anthropologist had built by hand. Now that he'd alighted in the yard in front of the house, Emerson could see that there was a third individual, Miri's video protégé, a beautiful young girl of about half his age, occupying an equally handmade-looking armchair in a nearby corner formed by the porch railing. It had been difficult to tell from above, in the late afternoon sunlight.

With a houseguest ready to occupy the living room couch he'd slept on during his own first stay here, he realized he'd have to sleep out under the trees tonight or fly all the way back to the plant. Well, why not? His work was already done here, wasn't it?

Digger laughed. "Come on up and make yourself to home, son! We've got a venison stew simmering on the back of the stove and Miri just put on a fresh pot of coffee."

Emerson did as he was bidden, leaning his flying yoke against one side of the steps and reflecting that R.L. Drake-Tealy was one of the few people on this little world who would think to call him "son." During his stopover—not brief enough to suit him—in Curringer, Mrs. Singh had reminded him that the previous day had been his birthday, his fifty-second, if he remembered it correctly.

Miri smiled at him as he hunkered down on the padded top of a very old-fashioned wooden keg they kept around as a stool. "You haven't met our other guest. Rosalie Frazier, this is Emerson Ngu. Emerson, meet Rosalie. She's recently arrived from Earth to—"

"I saw you both on TV, Miri. It was a pretty startling and impressive performance." He nodded cordially at the younger woman. "Nice to meet you in person, Dr. Frazier. How does it feel to have prevented history's first full-scale interplanetary war while saving Pallatian sovereignty and hyperdemocracy itself?"

She shrugged. "The reviews aren't in, Mr. Ngu. Possibly I've provoked rather than prevented it, which would make me feel a great deal like Harriet Beecher Stowe. And I prefer to be called Rosalie by friends of Miri's and Digger's."

"Then make mine Emerson," he responded, "and I could use a cup of coffee, if you don't mind, after the miserable day I spent in Curringer and the long flight out here."

It was Rosalie who got up and went into the kitchen at the back of the house for Emerson's coffee. As she passed by him, he inhaled the faintest possible trace of some subtle and pleasant perfume. He'd already noticed that she was considerably more attractive in person than she'd appeared on TV the previous day, and there was a lingering familiarity about her. He thrust the thought aside, however. Whatever her credentials, she still was only a girl, possibly in her late twenties, far too young for an old bird half a century old like himself.

In response to Miri's raised eyebrows, he explained how he'd happened to see them and the reason he'd had to return to town instead of flying out here immediately.

"By the time I got to Curringer and discovered that my testimony wasn't going to be necessary after all—god, I love lawyers—I'd wasted most of the day cooling my heels at the back of the same room where you and Rosalie held your history-making press conference. Aloysius and Nails and Mrs. Singh send their regards, by the way, along with three cheers apiece. I looked afterward, but neither of you was to be found anywhere in town, so I took a chance that you'd be out here, even though there's a story circulating that Digger's back on Earth."

"I am," the old man chuckled. "This is just a hologram you're talking to. I wish I'd seen the ladies in their moment of triumph. Did anybody think to make a tape?"

Emerson explained that what he'd seen yesterday at the line shack had been a recording and that KCUF could probably supply a copy. "You probably ought to have one," he told Miri and Rosalie as the latter handed him his coffee. "You two may just have saved a pair of worlds and the lives of everyone on them."

He knew that a UN fleet could have wiped Pallas out simply by destroying the atmospheric envelope. On the other hand, he was aware that the Pallatians weren't with-

out resources and that anyone with a small spaceship—
Marshall, for instance—could have nudged a county-sized
asteroid from one orbit into another, causing it to plunge
down onto mankind's mother planet, duplicating the catastrophe which had possibly finished off the dinosaurs.
There had been talk of doing exactly that among his ac-
quaintances at both poles, and maybe even some preparations.

He said as much now, omitting the fact that he'd di-
verted some of that hostility by contracting for an ice-find-
ing survey to be conducted among the nearby lesser asteroids.

"Well, before you wax too eloquent in your congratulations, young man," Miri cautioned him, with the same sort
of reference to their relative ages that had startled him in
Digger's case, "you should be advised that I was acting
from no high-flown sense of duty or historic mission. I simply missed my husband and had to see this question settled
before it split us up forever. I knew that, had Rosalie's
findings gone the other way, he would have accepted them
out of respect for the same plain scientific truth that I am
committed to. And even centenarians like Raymond and
myself," she added, "have their passions."

Digger laughed, remembering that he'd once said almost exactly the same thing to Emerson. "I don't believe
this relationship of ours was ever fated to go smoothly, my
dear."

She nodded agreement. "Being misquoted by ax-grind-
ers in the mass media did not help things much," she told
Emerson. "You may already know I heartily concur with
Raymond's notions about hunting and always have—
among other reasons, because they tend to ensure the survival of individual liberty on Pallas. It is hard to oppress a
population equipped to hunt animals the size of a man.

"However, that was all theory. I was raised as a city

girl on Earth, tainted, perhaps unconsciously, by fashionable attitudes toward life and death which have little bearing on reality anywhere, but especially on Pallas. I never
quite adapted personally to some of the more sanguine aspects of the hunting life, and, after being crippled, never
had a chance to try. The time I have spent in the town
where William Wilde Curringer died, among people who
hunt for a living, has helped me deal with problems that
were strictly mine to begin with, and my trip to Earth,
where hypocrites deplore hunting but wear leather shoes,
finished the job.

"Now I understand, as I never did before, the depth of
that hypocrisy. Many of the animals bred to be hunted
here on Pallas, deer, antelope, elk, moose—"

"Rabbits," Digger interrupted, counting off until he
ran out of fingers, "squirrels, pikas, javelina, mountain
goats, caribou, bison, bear, boar, elephant, buffalo, rhino,
quail, pheasant, pigeon, wild turkey, grouse, even ducks
and geese—"

"Along with many of their natural predators and supporting species," Miri regained the floor, "face extinction
back on Earth where they are 'protected,' whereas here,
there is talk of reviving mastodons by cloning and even a
little speculation that the genes of dinosaurs may someday
be salvaged from bird or reptile tissue."

"Or from blood preserved in the guts of biting insects
trapped in amber—somebody wrote a book about that,
once. Damned clever it was, too." Digger grinned, obviously thinking about his .416 Rigby. "Wouldn't that be a
grand hunt?"

Miri smiled. "All I want right now, however, is to be
with Raymond and enjoy the time we have left."

Rosalie sighed. "You love this place, don't you, Emerson?"
He stood with his hands in his pockets, his toes danger-

ously close to the edge of an intimidating precipice at the
southern end of Digger's homestead claim. Off to one side,
the stream running through the anthropologist's land
plunged off the cliff-edge into the crater valley below,
which at this time of evening was filled with colored mists
and shadows. He wondered what it must have been like to
walk rather than fly out here from what passed for civilization in the early days. The thought was more intimidating
than the cliff-edge at his feet.

"I love all of the wild, untamed places of Pallas," he
told Rosalie, "and the violent topography of small planets
in general." He continued thinking out loud. "On Earth,
because of the gravity, I guess, the pioneers traveled the
valley bottoms, mountain passes, and so forth, to get from
one place to another. Here, they had to follow the ridges,
partly because the low gravity allows it, partly because the
valleys are all circular, having been blasted out by impact
with smaller asteroids, and don't necessarily connect with
one another."

From this unexpected plateau, even with the sun
threatening to set over their right shoulders, they could see
not only into the twilit valley below them, but over the next
one and the one after that, taking in at a single, sweeping
glance perhaps a hundred miles of rugged Pallatian geog-
raphy which, for the most part, only Emerson had so far
explored, and then, mostly from the air.

He felt rather than saw her nod in acknowledgment.
They'd hardly looked at one another since they'd made
their way through the dense woods following dinner to get
to this spectacular sight. The idea had been Digger's, with
Miri's enthusiastic approval. They both had realized what
the elderly couple had been after, aside from the chance to
be together for a little while, but they'd gone along, Emerson because the idea appealed to him despite what he
thought he ought to feel.

They'd left their flying yokes at the cabin, but they both wore their pistols. This place wasn't safe and never would be. It hadn't been meant to be safe. Despite the scenery, Emerson would have liked very much to gaze deeply into the girl's eyes if the idea hadn't also embarrassed him. To his amazement, the middle-aged bachelor had immediately found himself falling in love with Rosalie. He was old enough, he lectured himself, to be her father, and the fact that simply being with her like this evoked a fierce burning within his loins was only a perversion on his part, to be suppressed and ignored at all costs.

"Yes, I love this place," he added, as much to bar the forbidden path his thoughts had been taking as anything else. He touched the fabric patch that covered his right eye socket. "I was hurt the first time I came here, in mind as well as body. I'd not only lost everything I had, and everything I'd ever wanted, I'd lost everything I believed in. I was healed here, and I probably grew up."

A faint breeze stirred and she moved closer until she took his left arm, as if merely against the coming chill of the night air. "I know all about that, Emerson," she told him. "A lot of people do, back home on Earth. You may not realize it, but you've become something of a folk hero in certain quarters, especially in West America, where I did most of my growing up, as well as my own . . ."

Her voice trailed off. He turned to look at her—she was so beautiful to him that it hurt—wondering what she'd been about to say, but didn't say anything himself.

"As well as my own personal hero," she went on, visibly mustering courage. Suddenly she was not the competent, self-confident professional he'd seen and begun falling in love with yesterday, but a small, frightened girl he also found terrifyingly irresistible. "I think the reason I came to Pallas was for the chance of meeting you—"

He ran a nervous hand over his face, feeling the lines

and scars of a lifetime of . . . what? Action and adventure? Accidents and mistakes, more likely. "Not to discover a lost alien civilization, that didn't have anything to do with it?"

She shared his laughter. "Well, that might have been part of it. Whatever the reason, Miri didn't have to be any more persuasive than she and Digger were tonight. But you're interrupting, and I'm pretty certain I can only work up to this the one time: Emerson Ngu, I think I've been in love with you, or at least with stories about you, since I was a little girl."

He felt an almost painful tension in his body that hadn't been there for years, perhaps even decades. Most of all, it hurt him—and at the same time stirred him—in a very private, secret place he thought had been permanently scarred over, thoroughly numbed to any possibility of sensation, a place where no one, not even Cherry, had been able to touch him in a long, long time.

"There's usually a difference," he told Rosalie sadly, "between stories and reality."

"Yes," she whispered, pulling his face down to hers, "and in this case, it's entirely to your advantage."

That was all it took to blast his bitter resolve to bits, along with his embarrassment. In a matter of seconds, he and Rosalie lay together on the dried leaves at the edge of a quarter-mile drop into oblivion—which he felt was ironically symbolic of the circumstances. His mouth was still on hers as he slipped the khaki bush shirt off over her shoulders, his fingers having seen to its half-dozen buttons without his conscious attention. He would reflect later that it was nice to be middle-aged after all, to know what the hell you were doing.

She wore nothing underneath, and while he felt her nipples rise and stiffen beneath his palms, and reveled in the scent of her, she struggled, first with the awkward buckle of his heavy gun belt, then with the fastenings of his

Levi's. Women, he had long since come to believe, always knew what they were doing, regardless of age.

They melted together for the first time in the heat and blazing light of freshly discovered passion, and to them it was more than a matter of mere coupling, it was as if the subatomic particles which constituted their bodies, their minds, their very beings, mingled and fused. She cried out with welcome, long-anticipated pain as he exploded, letting go of a lifetime of grieving, anger, loneliness, despair, and frustration he'd never fully realized he'd been carrying around inside him. Everything was right, the feel of her body beneath his, the sound of her voice, the texture of her firm young flesh, everything.

He held her afterward without a word, and, in a surprisingly short time, their second moment of passion was slower, gentler, more relaxed and deeply satisfying. They smoked a cigarette and watched the violently multicolored sunset for which Pallas was famous, then the moon rise over a hundred miles of alien landscape.

There would have been a third moment, but, as he was about to take her again, and she was about to give herself, he heard a low cough behind them at the edge of the trees and tumbled off her awkwardly to snatch up his pistol, expecting to see a chagrined Drake-Tealy with some reason for having interrupted them.

It had better be a *very* good reason.

The pistol had been only a precaution, but it was well advised. Over the moonlit front sight of the massive automatic, he was looking straight into the luminous eyes of an African leopard.

Behind him, he heard the hammer of Rosalie's pistol clicking back to full-cock.

They must have been a hell of a sight, he thought, the two of them, completely naked, guns in hand, startled by the big cat who gave them another polite, if somewhat sarcastic-sounding coughing noise, turned on itself like a rope of silk, and vanished without another sound into the utter blackness beneath the trees.

Neither of them could stop laughing as they put their clothes on in the dark and gathered up their belongings to go back to the cabin, leopard or no leopard. Perhaps, he thought, there wouldn't be a problem now about that living room couch.

There wasn't, and they were married within a week.

XXXIX
HOME TO ROOST

TV—CHEWING GUM FOR THE EYES.
— Frank Lloyd Wright

I *'m Ned Polleck and this is DarkTalk, a feature of the East American Television Service, coming to you on this particular occasion from the studios of KC—of a TV station in Curringer, the principal town on the asteroid Pallas."*

The famous newsman was sitting at a table, shuffling papers, in what was recognizable to any Pallatian as His Master's Voice, the saloon that was also home to KCUF. Around him, the patrons and staff of the place were carrying on with business as usual, although somehow, with lighting or camera angles, the whole scene had been made to look like something from a Robert Service poem about the Yukon. Watching from his apartment at the Ngu Departure plant, Emerson expected the camera to pan down at any moment for a view of the Face on the Barroom Floor.

Rosalie's hand, where it clutched his, was cold and a little damp. He glanced at the automated camera perched atop the TV set like the intrusive parasite it was, and tried to suppress the sour look it engendered and which could only add to the overall disreputable impression given by his scars and eye patch.

"With us tonight from their respective homes on Pallas are former U.S. Senator Gibson Altman, longtime Chief Administrator of the Greeley Utopian Memorial Project, and Mr. and Mrs. Emerson Ngu. Mrs. Ngu is better known as Dr. Rosalie Frazier, a xenoarchaeologist associated with North California's Stanford University. Her husband is also famous, the inventor and industrialist Emerson Ngu, a man who, in his own way, has become as controversial as the industrialist who founded the asteroid colony, William Wilde Curringer.

"Senator Altman —"

The camera's-eye view, which had switched briefly from the bar to a picture of themselves, to a picture of Altman, and then back for a moment to Polleck at His Master's Voice, showed Altman's office at what was left of the Project again.

"Good evening, Ned." Despite his years, Altman looked as photogenic, calm, and composed as ever.

"Senator, for years, you've been advocating a plan under which the United Nations would take charge of alien artifacts found on Pallas, the so-called 'Drake-Tealy Objects,' to ensure that their scientific value is preserved. More than a dozen nations have forbidden their importation, yet a multibillion-dollar business continues to thrive, mostly through Japan, South Africa, and West America. There are rumors that a UN military force stands ready to enforce a global ban, and yet that international body has yet to ratify your plan. Why is that, Senator?"

Altman leaned back casually in his chair and steepled his fingers. *"In the first place, Ned, let me say I'd never have agreed to appear on this broadcast if I'd known that Emerson Ngu and his wife were going to be on it, too. They're simply the most visible portion of a vicious and obscenely well-financed lobby which has been able to block appropriate action in the UN. They repre-*

sent interests which have only profit in mind, rather than the bene-fit of mankind as a whole. As such, they have no legitimate right to speak on this issue."

Polleck gave the viewers the boyish grin he was famous for, then assumed a serious expression. Emerson could never decide whether he more closely resembled Alfred E. Neuman or Howdy Doody, two American institutions which enjoyed periodic revivals.

"I see. That's a rather unique interpretation of the First Amendment, wouldn't you agree? Or doesn't the First Amendment apply on Pallas? And yet those on the other side of the argument freely acknowledge the scientific and historical value of the Drake-Tealy Objects and claim that their free-market methods do more to preserve those scientific and historical values, while at the same time protecting the rights of the individuals concerned. What would you say to that, Senator?"

"Why, I'd say that's Rosalie Frazier talking." Altman leaned forward, frowning. *"She was employed in the first place by Mirelle Stein and the Curringer Foundation to act as their scientific mouthpiece, to lend an air of respectability to the blatant profiteering going on up here on Pallas. If you want more proof, look at the way she married Emerson Ngu almost the instant she arrived. Since then, she's generated one publication after another, apologizing—"*

Polleck interrupted. *"Dr. Frazier, the Senator has leveled serious charges concerning your scientific and academic integrity. What do you have to say in reply?"*

Emerson had felt Rosalie stiffen for a moment, then force herself to relax. "I'd say he's lucky I *do* believe in free speech, which is protected on Pallas by the Stein Covenant, and that I'm not the kind who initiates lawsuits at the drop of an unkind word."

Emerson knew that she was privately furious about the lies Altman had been spreading about her, but had stoically refrained from public comment until now. He wasn't

at all sure why she'd talked him into this particular cha-
rade.

She took a breath. "The fact is that I was invited here
by Miss Stein and the Curringer Foundation to confirm or
deny the scientific authenticity of the Drake-Tealy Objects, and that they didn't care which way it happened to
turn out. I'll also add that SUNC issues my salary checks,
and that I don't work for anyone but them. The fact that I
met and fell in love with Emerson shortly after I arrived on
Pallas is a happy coincidence I don't intend to apologize
for."

She turned and smiled at him as the view shifted back
to Polleck at His Master's Voice.

*"Well, while we're at it, I'd like to ask Mr. Ngu what's so bad,
really, about a UN scientific body supervising the handling and
disposition of Drake-Tealy Objects? Isn't that the best way to
make sure that they're preserved and studied? Why do Pallatians
object to it, to the point that they seem willing to go to war over
what amounts to a mere handful of archaeological artifacts?"*

Now it was Emerson's turn to be nervous, and for a
moment he wasn't sure whether he could force his voice to
work. He felt Rosalie's hand give his a squeeze.

"Mr. Polleck, I understand that if you weren't visiting
Pallas, you'd leave this broadcast as you do any other night
to go home to a farm you own near Fairfax."

Polleck grinned, and this time it seemed genuine. *"Remind me to borrow your research staff sometime."*

Emerson grinned back. "If scientific or historical objects were found on that farm—say, remains of a long-lost
Indian tribe—under the legislation Altman's pushing, it'd
mean a squad of UN goons would move in on you, take up
residence at your expense, watch your every move, search
your safe and dresser drawers at regular intervals, and interfere every time you planted or picked a flower in your
garden. If they wanted to dig that garden up to find more

objects, you'd have no recourse in the matter, and as each object was found, it'd be removed from your property without compensation. If you attempted to interfere, you'd be jailed, possibly killed in the process. I don't know if you'd be willing to go to war to prevent that. I've lived under the thumb of the UN, and I would."

Somehow, he'd maintained an even tone throughout, and he even managed a cheerful smile at the end. Right now he wanted one of his cigars more than life itself.

Polleck shrugged. *"But under United States law, not to mention the archaeological statutes of the state of Virginia, isn't that essentially what happens right now?"*

"It probably is," Emerson replied. "Which is why we're living here on Pallas, where a person's life, liberty, and property—not to mention privacy—belong exclusively to him- or herself, not some gaggle of self-impressed, self-appointed keepers of the public weal."

"But what about the scientific and historical—"

"Excepting Rosalie, I've yet to meet an archaeologist or paleontologist who didn't want a free ride on someone else's back or gave a damn who he had to have shot to get it. To be fair, I suppose that's true of scientists and academics in general. The difference here is that they're not going to get it. If they try, we'll shoot back."

Polleck raised his eyebrows, another famous expression. *"Strong words, Mr. Ngu. Your response, Senator?"*

"Thank you, Ned." Altman shook his head, more in sorrow than in anger, and gazed thoughtfully at the camera. *"I'm glad you've had a chance to witness for yourself the typical violent and aggressive behavior one has to deal with every day on this backward—"*

Emerson interrupted. "Wait a goddamned minute, Senator. Since when does self-defense constitute aggression?" He hadn't been able to help himself, and Rosalie had refrained from interfering. It was one of about a million reasons he loved her.

Polleck took a deep, almost weary-sounding breath, but Emerson was sure the man was getting what he'd wanted all along, a noisy argument. *"I suppose Mr. Ngu has asked a fair question, Senator Altman. Do you have an answer for him?"*

"When it selfishly denies the common heritage which is the property right of all humanity as a whole."

His adversary had assumed such a self-righteous expression that Emerson wanted to smash in the screen of the TV. "With someone like you acting as the executor of the estate," he demanded, "keeping the books, holding the whip? Better hope you do a better job than you did with the Greeley Utopian Memorial Project!"

"Now see here, Emerson Ngu!" Abruptly, Altman seemed to lose control of himself, as well. This made Emerson feel better, and he managed to calm down a little. *"I didn't agree to this interview to be insulted and badgered by conspirators bent on discrediting the Altman Plan and the Antiquities Protection Act!"*

Emerson grinned. "Just because you're paranoid, it doesn't mean you don't have enemies, right, Senator?"

The newsman raised both hands, palms outward to the camera. *"Gentlemen, gentlemen, this isn't* Fire/Counterfire *on LiteLink, and I don't think our viewers are interested in a shouting match. Let's break for a commercial, then we'll change the subject. I'm Ned Polleck, and this is* DarkTalk, *a feature of the East American Television Service, coming to you tonight from Pallas."*

As far as Emerson could tell, nothing changed except that Polleck relaxed slightly and some flunky came to his table to rearrange his hair a trifle. He didn't speak to the flunky or his guests. After a minute or two had gone by, he straightened in his chair, reintroduced the show, spoke of the unusual circumstances under which it was being produced, and mentioned his three interviewees by name, profession, and the part they were playing in the Drake-Tealy controversy.

"I interviewed an astrophysicist last week," he began, *"who claims that, due to a change in solar activity, there's going to be an unusually harsh winter in the northern hemisphere of Earth this year, a brief, cool summer, and then a really terrible winter. You're considerably further away from the sun on Pallas. How do you think this solar activity will affect you, and what plans have you made?"*

The Senator preempted Emerson and Rosalie. *"Clearly, Ned, what's needed is a comprehensive, worldwide plan which only an organization with broad powers can—"*

Emerson shocked himself by interrupting. "This is the first that anyone around here—and that includes Senator Altman, by the way—has heard of this, and it'll have to be confirmed before anyone can act intelligently. We're pretty resourceful on Pallas. If you'll give me the name of this astrophysicist—"

"I will, right after the broadcast, Mr. Ngu." He appeared to turn to Rosalie—some kind of actor's trick, Emerson realized—although he was still looking at the same camera. *"Mrs. Ngu, or should I say, Dr. Frazier, what do you think Pallatians should do to prepare for possibly the worst winter in the asteroid colony's history?"*

She shrugged, hesitated, and then a grin stole across her face. "Well, it's the first I've heard of it, too. I'll probably take up knitting, since I'd planned to, anyway."

Polleck looked genuinely puzzled. *"Knitting?"*

"Sure," Rosalie responded cheerfully. Emerson wondered what the hell she was up to. "Isn't that the traditional response of a pioneer woman to the news that she's going to have a baby?"

"What?" This from Emerson, who peered closely at his wife, then remembered that five billion people could see

him making a complete idiot of himself. His heart was thudding in his chest like that of a schoolboy on his first date.

Rosalie turned to him. "That's right. I agreed to this interview as a surprise, to let my dear husband know in a unique way that he and I will be parents in about seven months. This is the first he's heard of that, too. And I have something else to say, Mr. Polleck, which should finally clear up any charges the Senator has been making about a conflict of interests on my part. The shouting match you referred to was much more than that—it was a family squabble."

Polleck had given up. He lifted his hands and rolled his eyes. *"I don't believe I follow you, Dr. Frazier."*

"Mrs. Ngu," Rosalie corrected him. "You see, when Emerson becomes a father, the Senator will become a great-grandfather. Neither of them knows—or has until now—that Frazier is the name of my adoptive parents, that of the Senator's former wife and a new husband her family didn't approve of and never met, and that I was born right here on Pallas.

"I'm Gwendolyn Rosalie Altman—Gwen-Rose to those who remember—the orphaned daughter of the Senator's son Gibson Altman Junior and of Gretchen Singh Altman!"

XL
SOLAR WINTER

"WINTER IS ICUMEN IN, LHUDE SING GOD DAMN!"

—Ezra Pound

H ey!"
A bone-numbing wind shrieked, tearing at the flap
of canvas where someone had nailed a board to the tent-
post and burned words into it with a laser: *The Brass Mon-
key.*

"Shut the door!" three or four voices hollered in uni-
son, barely audible over the wind, and the one who'd just
entered obeyed, not before a scattering of snowflakes had
entered the tent, a few hissing on the platinum screen of
the catalytic stove.

"Sorry," Emerson muttered as he pulled his gloves off
to hold his hands over the heat. He'd dragged his folded
flying yoke in with him, which was why he'd had trouble
with the flap, not wanting the batteries to freeze. Someone
handed him a coffee mug. Blinded by condensation, he
pulled his eyeglasses off and peered into the grinning face
of Ned Polleck, almost unrecognizable bundled in makeshift winter clothing and with a week's growth of sparse,
untidy beard.

"If it gets any worse out there," Emerson told him, "I'm
going to see if Port Amundsen has any spare spacesuits!"
Even in the heated, insulated tent, his breath formed a visible cloud before his face. He wanted to light one of his cigars, but in this confined, already-smelly space, it probably
wouldn't have been appreciated.

"Too late!" Nails Osborn was smug. "I just got off the
horn with Fritz Marshall. He's sending a dozen in the

morning. It's too cold to fly in what most of us are wearing!" The change had caught them unprepared. Pallas had chilly moments in the quiet, moist hours before dawn, but it had never been a place where much warm clothing was necessary. "I don't think it's going to get any better for a while!"

"The last mini-ice age in history," Polleck observed in his made-for-TV voice, "lasted four generations and killed off an industrial revolution prematurely."

Appreciatively sipping hot, black coffee as he shrugged out of a homemade parka, Emerson grinned back at the former newsman—former *full-time* newsman, anyway— who was now so far away from everything he'd ever known on Earth. For reasons he'd never made clear, Polleck had remained on Pallas following his interview with Altman and the infamous Mr. and Mrs. Ngu. He'd shown up at the Nimrod to publicly sign the Covenant the morning afterward, officially becoming a Pallatian, and had simultaneously resigned as East American Television Service's star anchorman.

As the arctic gale outside shook the entire tent, threatening to pick it up and carry it away, Emerson thought backward in time, fondly remembering quite another variety of storm that Polleck's "defection" had stirred up on two worlds.

Pallatians in general had accepted him as one of their own, especially after he'd strapped on a pistol, a sort of flourish to the signing, provided by his once and future competition, the bartender-announcer at KCUF. Altman had been livid, declaring it to be the same sort of prearranged stunt he claimed had been perpetrated by Stein and Frazier. Although Polleck's former employers on Earth had played the story down as much as possible, it had been too good for other networks to pass up.

The tent flap opened and closed, dropping the inside

temperature another twenty degrees, as Tyr May entered and shook snow from his clothing. Emerson had known him to be a quiet, thoughtful man, but he was even more subdued at the moment. Bitter cold, Emerson had observed over the past weeks, affected some people that way.

Emerson had consulted Polleck's astrophysicist, and events had proven him correct. Before the year was out, Pallas had found itself in the grip of unprecedentedly miserable weather. For the first time in what seemed a long while, he thought about Cherry. With her usual good luck, she'd picked exactly the right time to leave Pallas. He'd gotten a postcard from her a month ago, from sunny Mexico, where she was directing a movie for the production company she now owned.

Within the same few months, partly as a result of Polleck's having sold the Alexandria farm Emerson had asked him about, the Voice of Pallas had competition for the first time in the asteroid's history. WRCS (Polleck had picked the call letters) was temporarily headquartered at Baldy's Tonsorial Parlor, on the shore side of Seyfried Road across from the Nimrod. Polleck had begun constructing his own production facilities, with a beautiful view of Lake Selous, on the unused lot between the barbershop and the White Rose Tattoo as fast as weather would permit. By then, people were skating on the lake. Aloysius had wryly suggested they should build the new TV station in a dome shape, out of ice blocks.

Polleck had done his first broadcast from an old-fashioned leather-and-chrome chair while having his hair trimmed by the grateful proprietor. He was recruiting the rest of his staff by letting anyone try out, on the air, who wanted to. Mrs. Singh had given it a whirl, although she'd complained that the studio lighting hurt her eyes.

For the most part, perhaps not surprisingly, it was girls from Galena's and similar establishments—initially during off-duty hours, although a few were said to be thinking about retiring in favor of a media career—who were proving the most competent and popular news readers, talkshow hosts, and weather reporters, a task of increasing importance as the harsh winter set in. Upon learning of this, Aloysius had mumbled something about Frank Sinatra being ahead of his time, but Emerson had never been able to get him to explain the remark.

However, Nails's remark about Fritz Marshall and the spacesuits registered at last. "Good work," Emerson replied to the machinist. "Tell him he can take back an equal number of frozen deer, elk, and antelope carcasses. With all the strikes and boycotts going on Earthside, they're probably running as low on supplies at both poleports as we are here. Damn, I'm tired of having to euthanize animals because they're too weak to eat! I came out here to keep them alive!"

"So we can go back to slaughtering them when it's over?" Polleck shook his head. "I don't get it. Isn't this *supposed* to be a hunting economy we Pallatians have? And don't winter kills contribute to our increasingly short rations?"

"Whenever you can find them before they've rotted in the sun like road pizzas," Nails told him, snorting with disgust. "It still seems to get warm enough for that, thanks to Murphy's Law. We're used to managing our game better than that, thank you, and what we have to do out there right now is *not* hunting."

Polleck looked at Emerson, but the latter was too tired to explain things further than Nails had. The struggle for survival on Pallas was a phenomenon its residents hadn't faced since the bad old days only a handful of elderly people like Brody and Mrs. Singh remembered. It had returned, however, and in earnest, with a series of massive solar fluctuations which, coming at the moment Pallas was furthest from the sun, had dropped the mean temperature of the asteroid several degrees, damaging field and forest, freezing lakes and ponds, and causing heavy snow to fall in Curringer for the first time since Pallas had been terraformed.

At the moment there were four feet of the unwanted stuff piled up in the town, which was nevertheless much better off, being fusion-powered and located on the shore of a large, weather-ameliorating lake, than most of the rest of the little world. Emerson, Nails, Polleck, and many other Pallatians were airlifting forage to game animals out in the Pocks and weyers, and attempting to rescue human victims of the cold, but their resources had been limited at the outset.

And wouldn't last much longer.

"I killed a man today," May announced quietly. He ran a cold-reddened hand through his graying hair and shook his head. "Maybe ten or fifteen miles northwest of here, where I was dropping hay to a small herd of mulies. I'd set down to get some of it up under a clump of trees and out of the weather. The sonofabitch was on me before I knew it, with one of those autorifles the goons used to carry at the Project. The poor jerk was probably hungry, maybe a little bit crazy. Hell, I would have fed him, but he never even gave me a chance!"

Taking a breath, he tapped the holstered Ngu Departure 10 millimeter he carried on his belt. "Thanks, Emerson." He'd meant it without irony, and Emerson knew it.

Polleck could be heard, muttering to himself in his TV voice, "Frontier justice is swift and final."

Emerson shrugged. It was already starting to be an old story: criminals thought to be leftover inmates—and security guards—from the old Project, singly or in small bands, had begun by attempting to loot some of the less-settled, isolated areas of the asteroid almost as soon as the cold

weather had set in. So far, for the most part, they'd been
disastrously unsuccessful, and many a Pallatian had good
reason to be grateful all over again to a young inventor
who had, many years earlier, made reliable personal weapons cheap and easily accessible.

But now, as the weather grew even more unrelenting,
these new barbarians were moving toward the centers of
population. Mrs. Singh had driven off half a dozen of them
herself only the day before yesterday, Emerson had heard,
at her home in Curringer, and he'd reluctantly ordered a
squad of guards posted at the Ngu Departure plant. Under
more ordinary circumstances, he wouldn't have bothered—these things had a way of taking care of themselves
on Pallas—but Rosalie, while not exactly helpless, was
nevertheless eight months into a pregnancy which had already proven disturbingly difficult, and a full three-quarters of his factory personnel were out here in the field, trying to help starving refugees of one species or another,
because everybody's future depended on it.

"If that's meant for your next broadcast, Ned," Emerson advised the newsman, too weary to assume a diplo-
matic tone, "I hope you'll place it in context for your—"

"*Dozens* of faithful viewers?" Polleck finished. "Don't
worry, Emerson, frontier justice, administered at the scene
and moment of the crime by the hands of the intended victim, is a selling point to me—I lived in Washington too
long for it not to be—and it's no news to anybody else on
this asteroid! "However, there's something else we'd better talk about, before it goes too far."

Emerson raised his eyebrows.

"It's the mirror you've been talking up—to reflect sunlight to the surface and raise the temperature?"

"That's right," Emerson replied. "I was at a space-in-
vestment seminar in Port Amundsen when the subject first
came up. I think that we've been lucky until now, but that

our luck isn't likely to hold much longer. We already have a couple of solar mirrors orbiting the asteroid, several hundred square miles of aluminized microplastic, maintained by the same commercial contractors who manage and repair the atmospheric envelope. What we need now is at least one more to warm—"

"Whoa, pardner, you don't need to sell me! I favor anything that keeps my precious ass from freezing solid. I hate to be the bearer of bad tidings, but somebody should tell you that Altman has been using your idea as a political springboard."

"What?"

The newsman nodded. "He's blasting Wild Bill Curringer—and you, by an association I'd be proud to claim, myself—for not having foreseen this tragedy, and claims that only a Man with a Plan can do something about such an obvious failure of the market system. Unfortunately, he seems to be finding a whole new constituency among desperate settlers who don't like chilblains and frostbite!"

Although he hadn't voiced his suspicions to anyone, Emerson believed Altman was ultimately behind the series of well-timed strikes and boycotts on Earth which were currently interfering with interplanetary trade, hampering Pallatian efforts at recovery. What Polleck was telling him about now was exactly the kind of thing he thought the Senator would follow up with here on Pallas.

He thought back to the morning conversation with his wife, who was under doctor's orders to alternate two hours of complete bed rest with half an hour of limited activity. The asteroid's one flaw was that it wasn't a good place for having babies. Perhaps nature—or, rather, natural selection—would eventually correct that. Perhaps it was being corrected now. Despite all their careful precautions, Rosalie had experienced minor, but very frightening, bleeding, and they'd spent their time on the radio reassuring one another, as expectant parents will.

Later in the day, Mrs. Singh had told him about the hoodlums she'd run off in a hail of carefully misplaced gunfire. Neither had mentioned Altman. Perhaps they were preoccupied with their own problems, although that wasn't like either of them.

Perhaps they hadn't wanted to worry him.

But Polleck was still talking. ". . . in your absence. I'm astonished that nobody else has told you about this, Emerson. Altman's been saying that he agrees with you about the need for an additional solar mirror, but that the only way Pallas can avoid 'free riders'—people who will benefit from the mirror but are unwilling to pay for it—is to set aside the Hyperdemocratic Covenant 'for the duration of the emergency,' in order to levy taxes for its construction."

Emerson had to bite his tongue to keep from saying *What?* again.

"In any case, he claims that Curringer's failure to anticipate the crisis invalidates the agreement represented by the Stein Covenant, and he's broadly hinting that the UN spacefleet is standing ready to back up his interpretation of it."

"I see." Emerson handed his mug to Nails and began pushing an arm into his coat while looking around to see where he'd left his flying yoke. "If anybody calls or comes looking for me, tell them I'm headed back to Curringer, will you?"

"Sure," Polleck answered. "What are you going to do?"

With an effort, Emerson pushed the door flap aside and pushed his face into the blizzard. If anything, the weather was worse than when he'd come in half an hour ago.

He shouted over his shoulder.

"I'm going to kill that bastard!"

XLI
CHRISTMAS FOREVER

AT LEAST THE NAZIS BURNED BOOKS IN PUBLIC. LIBERALS
SUPPRESS OPINIONS THAT DIFFER FROM THEIR OWN THROUGH
INFLUENCES THEY WANT KEPT SECRET. THE RIGHT WING
DESTROYED BOOKS. THE LEFT DESTROYS AUTHORS.
—William Wilde Curringer, *Unfinished Memoirs*

O*nly another three hundred miles to go,* Emerson told himself, as the vicious, freezing wind slapped at him as if
he were a mosquito. In an instant he lost a hundred feet of
altitude and was nearly tumbled upside down, both motors
of his flying yoke straining with a noise that was audible
even above the wind. Level once again, and climbing to
avoid trees he knew were there but couldn't see, he tapped
at his power gauge. *Only another three hundred miles to go!*

He woke up with a start, surprised he'd managed to
doze off for—what, more than an hour? He certainly
didn't feel rested enough to corroborate the testimony of
his watch. He was equally surprised to find that he wasn't
flying around in circles or hadn't flown right into the
ground like William Wilde Curringer.

Only two hundred and fifty miles to go—maybe less!

He was grateful he'd thought to bring a radio along,
the little one with a clock he normally kept beside the bed.
Compasses were useless on Pallas, but he could tune in,
now and then, to either of the stations in Curringer and
correct his flightpath. Even so, he might overshoot and
have miles to double back unless he were careful, and he
was rapidly becoming too cold and tired to be careful.

With that thought, he had to shake himself awake
again, chagrined and a little afraid. Another forty minutes
gone in a twinkling. He'd worked a long full day in the

rugged territory around the camp, after a bad night's sleep, and now he'd traveled an estimated four hundred frozen miles against the wind. He might be no more than eighty or a hundred miles from home by now—but it was still a question of which would fail him first, the much-abused batteries in his flying yoke . . .

Or his own strength.

Come, now, he lectured himself, *who else can stop Altman? And besides, Rosalie and your unborn child are depending on you, too. You want to die and never see your—*

Angrily he rejected the thought and turned on the little radio as he'd begun to do so long ago, holding the tiny plug to his ear. He was almost angry to discover that KCUF was playing Christmas songs until he thought it over and began to laugh. The hell of it was, this particular Christmas might last fifty years, on Pallas.

It might last forever.

The whole goddamned planetful of them might wind up just like Gibson Altman, Junior.

At the last moment he remembered what he'd started to do—at least he hadn't fallen asleep again that time—and turned the little receiver until it nulled out and KCUF could only barely be heard. According to the seam along the plastic case, which he was using as a sight, he was still flying in as close to the right direction as was humanly possible. It was both gratifying and amazing, but if he lived through it, he'd do something about this absurd situation, perhaps with radio beacons intalled on the atmospheric canopy itself. It shouldn't take—

Abruptly, the radio signal vanished from the air. He could still hear a static crackle, which he guessed meant that KCUF was at fault, so he started looking for WRCS, but it seemed to be off the air, as well. That was a bad sign. Curringer had no municipal power and lighting system. Most buildings, residential or otherwise, were equipped with their own small deuterium fusion reactors, the way houses a century earlier had all had furnaces in their basements.

He wasn't sure he wanted to know what it would take to kill the power simultaneously at two radio/TV stations, even across the street from one another.

Too bad these household fusion reactors weren't small enough to power a flying yoke, he thought, and gave the power gauge a tap. His heart sank with the needle, which apparently had been frozen in place. If the damned thing could be trusted even now, he had less than half the flying time left he'd earlier believed he had.

And up ahead, through the blizzard all around him, which was bad enough, he thought he saw the ominous black wall of an even more terrible storm, hanging like a funeral drapery almost from the canopy above to the ravaged ground beneath him.

Fighting off a horrifying urge to sleep, even as full of adrenaline as he was, it slowly began to dawn on him that he might still have a chance. The storm front, which he could make out between occasional rifts in what he'd thought of as a terrible storm itself until now, seemed to be receding from him. If the timing was right, and his power held up, he might make it home tonight, after all.

And maybe only another fifty miles to go!

It was at this point that the whine of his ducted fan motors began to drop in pitch and he realized he'd be lucky if he made it to the ground in one piece.

Emerson never panicked.

He calculated that, with Pallas's minimal gravity and a deep bed of snow almost certain to be covering the ground below, he could easily survive a fall from this altitude. He also remembered that he couldn't be much more than fifty miles from Curringer, and that, even asleep, he'd been staying on course with reasonable consistency.

He had warm clothing and the means of making a fire. He was armed; a brief, unpleasant thrill shot through him as he recalled how much of his now-precious ammunition he'd consumed, humanely dispatching wild game animals over the past several days. If he remembered correctly, he was down to what was left in two full magazines and the chamber of his Grizzly.

Mostly he was worried about human predators. But there were other things down there to worry about, as well. Things driven mad by cold and hunger.

The landing, when it came, wasn't as bad as he'd thought it might be. Good luck placed him precisely between two big evergreen trees. Bad luck dumped him into the middle of a saddle-shaped snowdrift between them, at least a dozen feet deep, where he floundered for some while, sweating under his heavy clothes—which he correctly reasoned was a dangerous thing to do—until he was free of it.

At least he could still move everything, and without pain. He'd been afraid that his legs had been frozen in the air—it had been increasingly difficult to feel them—and even more worried about breaking something when he landed.

He was reluctant to leave his flying yoke, but there was nothing to be salvaged from it that could keep him alive, and its weight and bulk might kill him. He thought suddenly, *I make the goddamned things! I can always get another one—that is, if I don't get fitted for wings and an accompanying harp and halo first!* Actually, the mythical alternative location appealed to him a lot more at the moment, brimstone and all, but unfortunately he'd never believed in mythology.

What he did believe in—and fear—was this tendency he'd developed to wool-gather when he should be in motion. He shouldered the knapsack he'd had tethered to the yoke and looked around. It almost seemed calmer down here on the ground, and it was certainly warmer. He trudged off in the direction of a low, dense clump of oddly familiar trees that might possibly provide both shelter and firewood.

Suddenly, and before he'd taken more than a dozen steps, his worst nightmare was fulfilled as he heard the same snarling and barking which had set the hair on end of the remotest ancestors any human being can claim, a sound which, all by itself, may have propelled humanity from the paleolithic to an age which provided weapons like the Grizzly. To his right, plummeting and plunging through the drifts to get between him and the copse he'd headed for, was an indeterminate number of noisy, furry shapes, black as death in the half-light of the storm.

Emerson struggled to draw the Grizzly from under several layers of clothing, tangled the long tang, hammer, and rear sight for an anxious moment, then shook it free and leveled it on the pack leader, thumbing the hammer back. He couldn't tell yet if they were wolves or simply feral dogs abandoned by their owners with the onset of foul weather. Since there could be no doubt as to their intentions, he squeezed the trigger. The weapon bellowed, the sound oddly muffled by the snow on the ground, and the leader leaped and twisted, not making any noise Emerson had expected, not even twitching after it hit the ground.

Immediately, the pack surrounded their fallen leader and began to rend its gunshot body to pieces, growling and snapping at one another, breaking into a savage fight at one point which left another of the beasts crippled and being torn apart before it died.

Emerson wished briefly that he had full metal jackets in his pistol, rather than softpoints, so that he could shoot through two or more of the animals when they were clumped up like this. He knelt and silently counted two dozen of what he now was certain must be wolves before the majority, left out of the cannibal feast, began to notice that the object of their original attentions still existed.

"Sorry, boys," he told them in a firm, level tone, hoping that the sound of a human voice would make them hesitate. "I'm still the uncooperative pain in the ass that I always was, and I refuse to be dinner!" He also responded by rising slowly as he spoke and backing toward the trees he'd been headed for, keeping the Grizzly leveled at whatever animal seemed to be the bravest and brightest at the moment.

As he made his slow, backward progress toward the trees, he saw that they were beginning to spread out, those on the flanks trying to get behind him. He'd never known that wolves were this intelligent, but it didn't surprise him to be learning it the hard way.

He always seemed to learn everything the hard way.

"But you're too young," he'd protested just after the Polleck broadcast, "to be Gretchen's daughter! She was born in 2036, which would make you—"

"Thirty-eight," Rosalie finished for him smugly. "Not too bad for a middle-aged broad, you think?" She stroked the hand she held with her other hand.

"But you can't be more than—"

"Twenty-seven. That's what my biological clock says, anyway. Don't worry about being confused, Emerson—it confuses me, sometimes. Especially since, in some ways, it's always felt to me like *you* were my father. You should have been, you know. Do you mind?"

Emerson was lost, but he knew one thing for certain: "I don't mind anything that ended up here, with us together. And you know they say that incest is a game the whole family can enjoy. But how—?"

She blinked, her face having suddenly lost its humorous expression. "Simple. When you're stuck with an inconvenient granddaughter, send her back to Earth and have her put into cold storage! It was the Senator's sister's idea, really. They excused it by claiming they couldn't predict the result of returning an infant to a one gee field." She stopped and stared down thoughtfully at their hands where they lay interlocked in her lap.

"And?"

"And," she looked up at him suddenly with tears in her eyes. "That's where I stayed, an experimental cryogenics subject, for eleven years."

It was Emerson's turn to sit in silence. Finally: "Eleven years . . ."

"Until my Grandma Gwen hired a detective to find me, and a squad of mercenaries to get me out. She raised me, Emerson, that wonderful, sad old woman. She had no choice but to move the family to West America, where her ex-husband's lawyers couldn't get to me. In the end it was my Uncle Terry—Altman's younger son—who steered me toward xenoarcheology. He was really only four years older, but . . ."

Emerson nodded. "I get it."

"Well, from the beginning I intended to get back to Pallas somehow, at first to repay Grandma Gwen—I figured if I could make up for what she'd always felt was her failure as a pioneer woman . . . and then there was the matter of confronting a grandfather who let something like that happen to me."

Another reason, Emerson thought, to hate Gibson Altman for the rest of his life.

She laid a palm on his cheek, very gently, having seen the pain she was putting him through. "And then there was you."

He turned his head and kissed the gentle hand that caressed his face. He touched her still-flat belly. "I loved your mother," he told her, "but you'll never know how glad I am that I'm *not* your father!"

She smiled and folded herself into his arms.

Suddenly, he was struck in the back—for an instant he thought one of the wolves had jumped him, but he'd hit a tree trunk which had either been much closer or which he'd been approaching faster than he'd estimated—and only barely held onto his gun. The tree shivered and dumped a tremendous load of snow on him, blinding him momentarily, which the wolfpack, its numbers augmented now by those who'd finished with their dead mates, took as a signal to attack him.

Again the leader died as Emerson's pistol thundered, but this time, it was much closer. Too close for Emerson to let the rest of the animals come devour him. A few tried, and a few more died. The thought ran through his mind that he hoped these weren't the last wolves on Pallas—then he laughed out loud, changed magazines with a single round still left in the chamber, and shot another, and another.

And another.

Five rounds left.

Then four.

Then three.

The enemy closed in.

Forget heaven and hell, he thought; it looked like he was going to Valhalla.

With a pack of wolves for pets!

"Desperate times call for desperate measures!"

Gibson Altman paced back and forth at the front of the saloon, trying to give emphasis to what he'd said and stay warm at the same time. He was angrier than he could ever remember being—odd, how good it felt—because he and everybody else on Pallas had been betrayed. This was just like the business with the sunrises and sunsets nobody had predicted, only, of course, it was far worse.

That old bastard Brody hadn't let him in the Nimrod, where people had gathered to sit out a storm they weren't sure was ever going to end, but the crowd here in the White Rose Tattoo would do nicely. He'd had to come into town anyway, since the Residence, where nothing remotely like nuclear fusion had been tolerated for many years, was like a meat locker. It was that or begin living in the rollabout, which did have its own reactor. Someone was going to pay for what was happening here. Since William Wilde Curringer had escaped justice, it would have to be someone else. Altman knew just who that someone else would be, too.

The last time an estimate had been made, there were fifty thousand people on Pallas, and there were fewer than a hundred in this room, but it was a beginning.

Everything had a beginning.

"There's no storm at the poleports," he pointed out. "And I've learned that there are ample supplies of aluminized mylar to build another solar mirror! All that's needed is the will to order that mirror built and placed in orbit!"

Perhaps the White Rose Tattoo was better, since some idiot at the Nimrod would have been sure to point out that putting another mirror in orbit would take time and money as well as will. It would require the skillful operation of a dozen small spacecraft, which were expensive and difficult to run even at the best of times, and it wasn't strictly true that there was no storm at the poles. There wasn't any atmosphere, and the storm through which they were suffering—and which would make the undertaking dangerous— consisted of deadly charged particles.

"We'll put it to a vote, then act! Suspend the Stein Covenant, take over both TV stations, conscript an army which will overrun any resistance at the poles! By that time, I can have a war fleet on its way from Earth! We'll force them to put up that other mirror, and if anything needs to be paid for to get it done, by God we'll enact some tax law and screw it out of rich sons of bitches like Emerson Ngu!"

Nobody cheered among the huddled masses in the tavern, but nobody argued with him, either. A few eyes, a few faces turned toward him, half in guilty fear, half in dawning hope.

Everything had a beginning.

"All in favor, say aye!"

XLII
Spring Eternal

TO KNOW WHAT YOU KNOW, AND TO KNOW WHAT YOU DON'T KNOW, IS TO KNOW.

— Roger L. Smith

The night held warmth, moisture, and a promise, unmistakable to anyone who could remember it, although there were children grown on Pallas, with children of their own, who couldn't.

Emerson squinted one good eye through bifocals that needed cleaning. Long ago he'd learned the hard way, from the first experience he'd had like this—the ambush in which Gretchen had been killed—never to provide an advantage to the enemy. This time the territory was his— they couldn't possibly know the ground the way he did— and he didn't intend to be caught entirely in the dark.

It seemed a lifetime ago—and it had been—that ugly business with Gretchen and Junior's goons. He'd been, what, sixteen? He didn't remember, although it felt like yesterday. For that matter, it had been a full quarter of a century, he realized with a start, since he'd fought his desperate, snowbound battle with a pack of hungry wolves, back in the early years of Pallas's long solar winter. And he'd thought himself an old man—of fifty-three—even then.

Now—he looked down. The icy claws of winter had been pried loose of Pallas at long last, although the wounds and scars they'd left behind would be a long while healing. And was this the hand of somebody seventy-eight years old? But the sight of an old, familiar weapon in his hand brought him abruptly back to the present. He was seeing it mostly by memory in any case. Through a high overcast, the reflected light from Rosalie, his artificial mylar moon, was insufficient to lend any real detail, and the wellhead's electric lamps would stay unlit.

He needed light for only the merest fraction of a second, something to tell him where the other guy was. What he wanted was a tripwire of some kind, a blasting cap from the toolshed behind him, and a pinch of fine, fast-burning flash powder, the latter unconfined by anything more than the thin layer of transparent plastic wrap required to keep it together. They'd do the trick very neatly.

Rosalie—his own Rosalie—did the wrapping; he prepared the tripwires and caps. The only plastic they had with them, the kitchen variety that stuck to itself whether you wanted it to or not, had always hated him. Then, in the moonlight, he placed as many of the makeshift devices as they could fabricate, ten or twelve dozen before he lost count, around the little fortress of piled sandbags where they would make their stand. Between the rocks and boulders of this stony region where his pipeline started, the soil bubbled with a thaw a generation overdue.

They sat together and ate a final meal.

Hell, he thought, *if I'm seventy-eight, it's a different seventy-eight than anyone ever lived before.* He'd spent all but the first two on Pallas, in a tenth the gravity mankind had evolved under. And he was physically capable in a way an Earthman of forty might envy. Even those, like Mrs. Singh, Aloysius—and Altman, unfortunately—who'd spent most of their adult lives on Earth had benefited on the asteroid, and there was no telling how long those born here were likely to live.

Cherry, who'd returned to Earth and its gravity, had passed away a couple of months ago, although she'd lived a long, eventful life, acquiring LiteLink and other media companies. For thirty years she'd sent him postcards and he'd sent her pictures of the kids. She'd even made a stab at reforming the way news got reported.

His wife looked up from her sandwich and smiled. He was a lucky man, he reflected, to have loved three beautiful, intelligent women, the one he'd married the most beautiful and intelligent of all. That they'd apparently loved him for some reason, each according to her fashion, was little short of a miracle. And that the beautiful, intelligent creature sitting beside him had bestowed upon him eight beautiful, intelligent children while managing an alien artifacts laboratory at the Ngu Departure plant with a crew that still grew every year was utterly beyond belief.

In the distance, a bird—he didn't know what kind—gave uncertain song to the friendly darkness. If he had to die tonight, he could do it knowing he hadn't missed anything very important. But he'd do his damnedest not to die, not only to help keep his lovely Rosalie alive, not only so that their wonderful mob of kids would have a father, but because there remained so much he wanted to do!

Twenty-five years: she'd been eight months into a troubled pregnancy filled with blood and hovering terror, the kind no young woman should have to go through. There being no such thing as a free lunch, it was a price they paid for their longevity on Pallas, a not-so-beneficial consequence of lower gravity. It would result in a winnowed, hardier population. But, as had so often been the case in the two million years humanity had already been around, women had to pay the tab.

Tonight, damp, earthy smells of melting ice and warming soil dominated even the blooming of night flowers. Back then, he'd been feeding animals in the Pocks (not as trivial a pursuit as it might seem), when he'd had a warning through Ned Polleck that Altman was up to his old tricks, this time attempting a straightforward coup against the Covenant under cover of harsh weather, rallying a portion of the populace driven from their homes by the cold, as Altman himself had been. They were desperate enough to listen to him, and he was taking full advantage.

He'd begun in the White Rose Tattoo, planning to seize the TV stations next door and across the street, proclaim suspension of the Covenant, and yell for help to a fleet he swore already stood about Earth to come to their aid. Democracy would be "restored," and he promised an extra solar mirror would be constructed to end the unusual weather. What good seizing KCUF and WRCS would have done, Emerson hadn't figured out yet; their antennas had been blown down in the storm, they were off the air, and Altman didn't know enough to get them back on again. He'd never learned you can't order technicians around the way you can stoop labor.

Meanwhile, Emerson was fighting for his life. He'd fired his last shot, and there were plenty of hungry wolves left, many of which hadn't shared in feasting on their dead and dying pack-mates but were maddened by the scent of blood.

The Grizzly would make a lousy club, he thought, as the starving animals shook off timidity and approached slowly, fur bristled, muzzles accordioned into snarls. He groped inside his coat for the survival knife he carried. It had been Gretchen's, a long, subtly curved weapon with a *tanto*-cornered tip. That he was a dead man, he knew all too well, but he was determined not to die cheaply. A customer or two tonight at Emerson's Diner would get a supper of cold steel.

He dropped his pistol, bracing against whatever he'd backed into as the first wolf leaped. Holding his knife, edge up, in both hands, he took the shock of the animal's eighty pounds on his wrists, lifting and gutting it before he thrust it aside.

Another leaped—then exploded in midair, showering him with hot blood! An instant later came the thunder of a mighty weapon, terrible as the impact of the bullet.

He didn't dare turn to his left, where the sound came from. Part of the pack was distracted, but several still paced a half-circle around him, and he must keep watching. Another, closest to him, blew apart, tossed to his right like a doll of rags and sawdust. At the same time he knew he'd had another shower, a literal bloodbath, he heard a second tremendous blast, closer now, and recognized it.

"Digger!"

"Coming, boy! Keep your guard up—and an eye on the doggies!"

"No problem!"

Another wolf died, and another, and another. Then it was over. As the old man approached on what Emerson recognized were snowshoes, the pack evaporated into the storm they'd come from, leaving behind little but the bones of their dead. They'd even licked up most of the bloody snow around the bodies of their fallen mates.

He groped at his feet for his gun, brushed away gory slush, and slipped it in an outer pocket, unwilling to reholster it. He found a spare magazine where he'd dropped it and, by the time Drake-Tealy was at his side, wondered what to do with his knife. It was stainless, but he didn't want to put it back bloody, either.

"Well, son, I see you almost made it!"

"Digger, what the hell are you doing way out here?"

"Way out's in the eye of the beholder. Don't you know where you are?"

He looked suspiciously at the snow-buried clump behind him. "No idea. When I went down, I figured I was fifty miles from Curringer, but I had plenty of reason to be further off than that." He slipped his feet into snowshoes Digger had brought for him. They were oval, smaller than Digger's, something he'd be grateful for before he took more than a few steps, snowshoeing being a strenuous art.

Drake-Tealy laughed. "You're in Mrs. Singh's backyard! Miri and I holed up here for the duration. When Nails told us you were headed back, we kept looking. Imagine our surprise when we heard gunfire. I thought you'd come to practice where you first learned!"

Emerson sighed, realizing that the long day wasn't over yet. "I could use the practice. I've come to kill the Senator, I think. You want to go with me?"

Drake-Tealy nodded toward the bloody knife clutched in Emerson's fist. "I had an impression you were out of shells."

"I have this—or I can beat him to death with my gun."

Digger nodded enthusiastically. "*That* I'd like to see!"

With a pang of regret over sandwiches and hot chocolate he was sure Mrs. Singh had waiting for them inside, Emerson turned toward the corrugated shed where she kept her three-wheeled contraption. Their snowshoes got them that far. They dug away the door and discovered that the rear of the roof had collapsed. The machine itself was almost pinned in the shed. It got them to the edge of town a mile away.

The trip took over an hour.

It was like a diorama of the end of the world. Snow piled deeply against buildings on both sides of the street had blocked it, forming gently-curved saddle drifts such as he'd landed in between the trees. They abandoned their vehicle, strapped snowshoes on again, and made their difficult, exhausting way toward the Nimrod. Emerson was nearly used up. It was harder and harder to breathe in the intense cold, his chest had hurt since the landing, and the full ferocious weight of a leaping wolf on his knife had strained his arms, which ached.

Before they came to Brody's, they saw a scattering of shadows straggling from the blizzard into the White Rose Tattoo and decided between them to see what was going on. They arrived at the door just as Altman was finishing his harangue.

"... no storm at the poleports, and I've learned that there are ample supplies of aluminized mylar to build another solar mirror! All that's needed is the will to order that mirror built and placed in orbit! We'll put it to a vote, then act!"

Standing inside the doorway, Emerson was disappointed to hear murmurs of assent from the crowd. Drake-Tealy, looking like the Abominable Snowman in his ice-encrusted winter gear, gave him a knowing, cynical nod. Emerson shook his head.

"Suspend the Stein Covenant," Altman went on, apparently not noticing their presence at the back. He looked like he was enjoying this. "Take over both TV stations, conscript an army which will overrun any resistance at the poles! By that time, I can have a war fleet on its way from Earth! We'll force them to put up that other mirror, and if anything needs to be paid for to get it done, by God we'll enact some tax law and screw it out of rich sons of bitches like Emerson Ngu!

"All in favor, say aye!"

Suddenly the barroom exploded with the all-enveloping thunder of Digger's rifle going off into the ceiling, which responded by raining dust onto their heads and shoulders.

"I vote nay!" the anthropologist shouted, "and so does that rich son of a bitch, Emerson Ngu!"

Trying to ignore the ringing in his left ear, Emerson stepped forward, his pistol encrusted with frozen wolf blood. He realized that he, too, was covered with it, and that he must have been a horrifying sight to the people huddled in the room.

"The Stein Covenant is a unanimous consent agreement," he told them all, "signed by every one of you. It can't be cast off by majority vote, and I won't let it be overthrown by a mob!" One-handed, he thumbed the hammer back on his empty automatic and pointed the muzzle at Altman's face. "I'll kill you first!"

Altman took a step backward. "Why, this is . . . this is unthinkable! You can't . . . you can't . . ."

"I can and I will," Emerson told him. "And I'll enjoy it!"

"So will I," Digger added, leveling his rifle at the Senator. Emerson knew he had just fired the last round his .416 Rigby held in its magazine. Even if he had more in his pockets, the crowd would overrun them if he tried to reload.

"But I'll do something else, if you let me," Emerson added, putting into motion an idea he'd had on the way back from the Pocks. "This is all about an additional solar mirror, right? And, if I know Altman here, it's about how to get the thing built and paid for by force. All right, *I'll* build it. Anyone who wants to help can help pay me for it after it's built. Otherwise, I'll foot the bill myself. I'll start as soon as I get Fritz Marshall on the phone. I think it can be done in a few weeks if you can all hold out that long."

"He's stalling," Altman warned them. "He hasn't solved the free-rider problem yet!"

Emerson laughed. "Yes I have, you idiot!" He lowered his gun and shoved it back in his pocket. He'd have to burn this parka, or it would stink once the blood thawed. "To prevent destruction of the Covenant, I'm willing to gamble everything I have and underwrite the construction myself. To hell with free riders, I want the mirror, not the dubious satisfaction of forcing others to pay for it!"

Afterward, he'd learned that the entire crowd had turned their backs on Altman and cheered.

He hadn't seen them do it.

His eye had rolled back in his head, and he'd collapsed.

XLIII
THE FOUNTAINHEAD

THAT GOVERNMENT IS BEST WHICH GOVERNS SOMEONE ELSE.
— Rex F. May

H e was ready when the first of his flash-flares went off. Silhouetted momentarily in the almost blinding light, the lead attacker was confused because something bright and noisy had just happened *behind* him, and sought cover too late.

Emerson's pistol sights rose and aligned themselves on the frozen target. When something happened *in front* of the thug—the blast of the Grizzly—he never knew it. A 260-grain softpoint took him square in the center—Emerson thought for an instant he could see light from the dying flare through a hole gaping in the man's chest—and the thug pitched over on his face, dead before he hit the ground.

Emerson's own short-lived shadow, thrown across the sandbags piled before him and followed by the slap of Rosalie's Mark IV Ngu Departure, told him that another of Altman's henchmen had tripped a wire on the other side of their perimeter. Her silence, rather than profanity, meant that she'd connected and that one less assassin would be collecting blood money from the Senator after this night's work.

Why Altman had resorted to a strategy of outright sabotage and murder worthy of his long-dead son, now that the solar winter was finally ending, Emerson couldn't say. He'd never understood why the man did anything. He only knew that these hirelings were here to contaminate the most important single water source on Pallas and that he, himself—thanks to one thug who'd wanted more money and didn't care whether it came from the intended victim—was here to stop them.

Two more simpletons fell to a combination of flares and carefully aimed gunfire before it finally occurred to them to fall back and come up with some other plan.

This wasn't the first assassination attempt foiled by Emerson's adeptness at self-defense. Perhaps worse, the barrage of injunctions, restraining orders, lawsuits, and other—what had Aloysius called it, chicanery?—had never let up, even while the rest of the planet had been locked in its arctic nightmare.

At one point, working through Earthside holding companies, Altman had even tried to ruin Emerson by manipulating the outstanding loans which construction of the solar mirror had made necessary. Without warning, however, small ice-asteroids, propelled by an experimental application of Fritz Marshall's new fusion/ion drive, had begun arriving at both polar spaceports. It was the payoff on an old investment which, during the emergency, Emerson had almost forgotten. Meant to utilize his already existing pipeline network, it had bailed him out, saving him from Altman's machinations.

Over the next few years, again drawing on Earth-based resources, Altman had tried to launch a series of businesses to compete with and destroy the inventor-entrepreneur. Altman, however, had never understood the workings of free enterprise, and none of his fledgling companies had even made it past the feasibility-study stage. Ironically, Emerson would have welcomed competition, feeling that it would have been just what he needed to keep his managers on their toes.

In any other legal venue, Altman's unceasing campaign would have rendered Emerson's company operations impossible, exactly the way that nuclear fission had been rendered all but impossible in the old United States back in the twentieth century. The Covenant had stopped him short every time, and saddled him with all the costs. Emerson wondered—but only a little—where the man was getting money for lawyers. Maybe he wasn't any more. Maybe that accounted for this swing to outright violence.

Perhaps it was cheaper.

This time, Emerson and Rosalie had entrusted their four youngest children, Mirella, Brody, Teal, and baby Cherry, to the ancient Mrs. Singh. Two of the kids, Henrietta and Gretchen, were in school on Earth, an extremely unpleasant necessity Emerson hoped to do something about someday. Drake was managing company interests in Curringer. And the eldest was somewhere the other side of the line shed, only yards away. They'd stood guard at the pipeline head six days and nights now, almost without sleep. Considering that Altman's hired guns hadn't expected opposition, the bastards had taken long enough to work up their courage.

He heard the whine of the camp's little caterpillar tractor coming up to speed, as well as painful clanking and grinding sounds of men unfamiliar with machinery trying to get its earth-moving bucket into a position they desired. Once it started forward, the vehicle inevitably tripped one of his wires and betrayed itself in a resulting flash, bobbing over uneven ground, crawling slowly toward him.

Casually, Emerson satisfied his curiosity, firing at the tractor, hearing the softpoint clank and splatter harmlessly off the tough metal bucket the way the same kind of bullet, fired for recreation, had on the metallic silhouettes he'd played with as a kid.

In one way, it all seemed so long ago, and in another way it didn't seem so long ago at all. He could still recall the night when his oldest son was born, the very same night he'd crash-landed in the snow, fought a desperate battle with the hungry wolves, staggered covered with their frozen blood into the White Rose Tattoo, and he and Digger had saved the Covenant—with empty guns.

He'd awakened at Doc Sheahan's, knowing instantly where he was and why. She'd warned him on several occasions about the general condition his heart was in, with pointed reference to his habit of working long nights and especially to the cigars he was so fond of. Told that he had to give up every bad habit he loved, he'd retorted, "One quality of life I've pursued with absolute consistency is the liberty to do whatever the hell I want. I was always willing to die for that liberty and now you're saying that's what I've got to do? Well, I was prepared for it all along—now gimme back my goddamned cigar!"

He hadn't really lied to himself about those chest pains earlier this evening; he'd just put off thinking about them because there were things tonight that had to be done.

His first conscious thought was that, if they'd done nothing else right on Pallas, they'd finally combined medical and veterinary practice under the same roof. His second thought was of Rosalie. He'd left her at the Ngu Departure plant almost alone. He tried to sit up. Strong, slender hands pushed him back into the bed.

"You're not going anywhere, Emerson Ngu. Better relax and try to sleep. You've finally had the attack I warned you about, and you're damned lucky it wasn't a bad one."

His one eye was wide open now, and he remembered everything. "Let me up, Heidi—I've got to talk to my wife!" He'd told her before he left the Pocks that he was going back to Curringer to deal with Altman, and he didn't want her worrying.

Doc Sheahan smiled down at him. For some reason, there seemed to be a lot of noise in the hall outside his room, as if a dozen people were gathered there, all arguing with one another. It was funny how he hadn't noticed until now that her hair had gradually turned as white as the snow piling up outside. She'd been one of those Scandinavian blonds whose hair was very nearly white already.

Maybe that was it.

"Any louder," she stage-whispered, "and you'll be doing it through the wall, but I'd advise against it. She's busy now, and I need you to behave so I can get back to her."

Emerson gasped, unbelieving. "What the hell are you talking about? She—Rosalie came all the way here, two hundred miles, in that . . . that mess outside?"

"She didn't consult me about it." Doc Sheahan shook her head. "You've been a bad influence on her, Emerson.

At least she didn't try to fly it, like you did. She came in one of those three-wheeled contraptions, in labor—telling me the road was clear because it had been blown clean by hurricane-force winds."

"In labor? But it's only—"

The doctor smiled tolerantly. "These things happen in their own time, especially on Pallas. Now, will you please settle down and let me get back to her?"

The racket outside the door had swelled to an angry babble he almost had to shout over. Vaguely, he wondered what was going on. "Can I see her? Can I help?"

"You can help by not having another heart attack, tonight anyway. And you can see her soon. Like you, I'm afraid she's in amazingly good shape considering what she's been through. Personally, I don't understand these hardy pioneer types. But if she gets a breather, she'd probably like to see you, and believe it or not, current wisdom says that once you're stabilized it's better to have you on your feet. For now, I want you to rest until your readings settle down."

The noise outside had died abruptly.

"Okay." Emerson finally lay back against the pillows, noticing for the first time the plastic tubes sticking out of his arms, connected to a pump because transfusions wouldn't flow by gravity alone on Pallas. On a table against the wall, some electronic device was counting his heartbeats. "Tell me when—"

"I will, don't worry." She straightened, walked to the door, and left. By reflex, he patted his chest, looking for a cigar, then wondered what they'd done with his clothes.

The door swung, and Digger stuck his snowy head inside. "You look like secondhand hell, old son. I'm going back to Mrs. Singh's house to pick up the womenfolk, who insist that babies can't get born without them. Anything I can bring you?"

"Yeah—a Senator's head on a pike."

Drake-Tealy laughed. "Funny you should ask. How would the raw materials do, with some dis-assembly required?" He reached out into the hall, dragged a figure into the room, and pushed it roughly toward a chair. "Now be good, dearie, understand? Or old Digger'll come back and stuff both your legs up your arse!"

The figure slumped compliantly into the chair. At the center of several layers of improvised cold-weather clothing, Emerson recognized his old enemy, Gibson Altman.

Emerson remained silent; it was up to the Senator to say something. Finally: "The clinic's crowded from wall to wall—it's the storm, I think—and there wasn't anyplace else to wait." He was sullen, apprehensive, as if he expected Emerson to rise from his bed and throttle him. Emerson thought about it, but decided he wasn't strong enough. Yet. Besides, Rosalie might need a husband tonight.

"To wait for what?"

Altman peeled off the first layer, an oversize sportcoat he was wearing over another almost exactly like it. "Maybe she's your wife, but she's my granddaughter. Like it or not, that's my great-grandchild being born in there."

"I'll try hard not to hold it against him—or her."

"How very generous of you, Emerson. You can afford it. You won tonight—by brute force."

"Let's not quibble, *Gibson.*" Emerson tried not to get angry. "You were more than willing to try a military coup yourself, backed by a nuclear-armed UN spacefleet, to throw out the Covenant, return to majoritarianism, and force any number of unwelcome changes on Pallatians. Anyway, no one's ever been able to show me any difference between democracy and brute force. It's just a majority ganging up on a minority with the minority giving in to avoid getting massacred."

He tried to think of something else to talk about, but what could there be between him and this man, except a difference of principle which had driven their enmity for half a century? Apparently Altman had the same problem, because he didn't argue with Emerson's analysis.

Perhaps he secretly agreed with it.

Perhaps all politicians did.

It was an odd moment of uneasy peace, the only one they'd had in fifty years. It was probably the only one they'd ever have. Emerson couldn't see them burying the hatchet and becoming one big happy family. The idea made him sick to his stomach.

In the end, the two old enemies waited together in silence, broken only by the rhythmic beep of Emerson's heart monitor, for news of Rosalie's struggle to bring new life into a world that didn't seem terribly happy to receive it. Emerson was surprised to find himself dozing off from time to time. He didn't know what Altman was doing. He didn't care. Outside, the wind howled and shrieked, sculpting the snow into dunes and, for all he knew, piling more on top of them.

After what seemed like days, Doc Sheahan came back into the room, examined the monitor, then Emerson, and grinned down at him. She'd ignored the Senator.

"I'm beginning to think you're going to live. If you feel like climbing into this *four*-wheeled contraption, I'll take you to see Rosalie—and somebody else."

Emerson sat up straight. "Let's go! What about all this?" He waggled a tube-laden arm at her.

"We'll get that fastened onto the chair before we move you," she replied. She glanced over at Altman. "You're invited, too, although if it were up to me—"

Altman rose without a word and waited while Emerson was transferred from the bed to the chair. He didn't offer to help, so Emerson didn't have to turn him down rudely.

Doc Sheahan pushed him through the door, with Altman following, down the hall a few feet to the next room. As the door swung aside, he saw Rosalie.

An inexpressible joy filled him. He hadn't known it was possible to be so happy, and he was suddenly afraid—for the first time, really—about damaging his heart. He hardly noticed that Mrs. Singh, Digger, and Miri were crowded into the room, as well.

"Congratulations, Papa!" Rosalie's voice was more than a little shaky. She'd had time to wash her face and comb her hair, and she never wore makeup. "It's a boy!"

"It's our baby!" Emerson exclaimed, taking the tiny bundle from her. "Our baby!" His mind had left him somewhere out in the hall and he couldn't think of anything else to say. "What's his name?" he asked, feeling stupid as soon as the words were out. He discovered that huge tears were rolling slowly down his face.

"Funny," Rosalie told him, pressing a palm to his cheek, "I was going to ask you the same thing!"

XLIV
THE STAINLESS STEEL ORACLE

THE THOUGHT OF SUICIDE IS A GREAT CONSOLATION; WITH ITS HELP YOU CAN GET THROUGH MANY A BAD NIGHT.
— Friedrich Nietzsche

A voice whispered, "Nice try, Dad!"

William Wilde Ngu—known to friends and family as Will—flopped down across the sandbags between his father and mother, every bit as curious as they were about the enemy's latest tactic. The elderly caterpillar tractor, of course, had not fallen over like a metallic silhouette when Emerson had fired.

Now Emerson unleashed his second major surprise of the evening, grateful he'd thought to bring along the great weapon. It was the only one of its kind on all of Pallas. He'd inherited it regretfully from his old friend and mentor, Digger.

He remembered the way Pallatians everywhere had been saddened to hear of the death of Raymond Louis Drake-Tealy. It had been followed, almost at once, by that of Mirelle Stein. Only he and Rosalie had ever known the whole truth, and they weren't talking. Aloysius Brody had died in the asteroid's first three-wheeled contraption accident and been buried in space, as he had wished, at a solar-escape velocity that would take him to the stars in a few million years. They were all gone now, or going, all the founders, all the pioneers.

Having practiced with the mighty .416, Emerson didn't look forward to using it, but was more than confident it would do the job. He also wondered a bit absently whether his insurance would cover the damage he was about to do to his own tractor.

Or his collarbone.

As calmly as he could, by feel alone, Emerson lifted the enormous rifle to his shoulder, worked the glassy-smooth bolt upward and backward, forward and down to chamber one of the banana-sized cartridges, and waited quietly for the little earth-moving machine to trip another flare. When it did, he aligned the post-shaped front sight, its square top centered in the ghostly ring of the rear, on that portion of the upraised bucket which he calculated was shielding the driver.

He squeezed the trigger.

The big converted Enfield slammed into his shoulder with the force of a heavyweight boxer's punch. The blast from the front end of the African game rifle momentarily became the only thing he was aware of, the only thing he was capable of being aware of. When his head cleared and he heard the tractor-motor still running, it took considerable courage and determination to reshoulder the weapon—he wasn't consciously aware of having lowered it—operate the bolt to eject the spent hull and chamber a second round, and fire another shot in the same direction, this time guided only by his memory of the first shot.

It wasn't the best or safest technique, he knew, but it worked. This time he heard reverberation as the bullet, almost an ounce of thick copper and alloy-hardened lead, struck the bucket at twice the speed of sound. It was followed by a hideous shredding noise as the tractor's electric motor, damaged and still running at high speed, began to destroy itself. Above that came the screaming of a man hit by bullet fragments or tractor parts, begging to be rescued by his cohorts.

Rescue never came. In a few moments, the wounded man fell silent. "Out of the corner of his ear," as Mrs. Singh would say, Emerson heard Rosalie swapping pistol magazines.

She'd been shooting more than he'd realized.

"I think," she whispered, "that there's only one more of the sons of bitches out there!"

Could it be? She'd been shooting *a lot* more than he'd realized, and apparently so had Will, which was why the young man had joined them on this side of the sandbag fortress.

"All right," Emerson yelled into the darkness, "that's enough! Throw down your weapons now and give up, or we'll come and get you like we did your friends!"

The only answer was the sound of a flying yoke dwindling in the distance. Cautious, Emerson waited a long time before he stood up. Colors had begun to gather on the horizon, signaling the approach of dawn, and it was by the light of this fantastic multicolored display that they searched the camp and found that they were alone.

"Dad," Will told him at last, "I just got off the phone with Mirella, checking on the kids back home. We weren't the only ones who got hit tonight."

"What do you mean?" Rosalie slid close and laid a hand on her son's arm. Emerson held his breath.

"Another bunch of thugs attacked Mrs. Singh's house. They were driven off—you taught us how—but Grandma . . ."

"What is it, Will?" demanded Emerson. "Grandma" was Mrs. Singh.

"She had a stroke or something. They got her to the clinic, but she didn't make it."

"Then neither," his father declared, "will the Senator!"

Among the consequences of what he always thought of as the Night of the Wolves, Emerson had finally produced a flying yoke independent of batteries. The tiny fusion reactor at his back would have taken him through the canopy if he'd soared upward. As it was, it whisked him at high altitude at three hundred miles per hour from the Pocks to the ramshackle slum that was all that remained of the Greeley Utopian Memorial Project. A lifetime of hatred burning inside him made it a shorter flight than it might otherwise have seemed.

Miles behind him, Will and Rosalie followed. He knew she was using her own cellular phone to call for help, probably to restrain him, but he didn't care. He'd lived a long, full life. All he wanted now was blood on his hands.

There was no one to greet him. His mother had died long ago, and there was only one light burning, in what had been the Senator's study. Stooping on the house like the bird of prey he'd become, Emerson kicked his feet out and burst through in a shower of glass. Altman jumped up, face ashen with shock and outrage. Emerson could see the old-fashioned communicator on his desk, its screen showing the same man he'd bribed himself, reporting failure of their mission.

"You one-eyed, slant-eyed bastard!"

Altman raised his cane and swung it down as hard as he could on Emerson's head. His feet actually left the ground for an instant with the force of the effort.

The comparatively younger man was too fast. He dived under the swing, the automatic pistol he carried completely forgotten, his fingers crooked into claws directed straight at his ancient adversary's throat. He was on the Senator, choking the life out of him, before the cane came down where he'd been.

Instinctively, Altman dropped the cane and forced his wrists between Emerson's forearms, breaking the hold. As his enemy's hands left his throat, however, his own arms sprang wide, leaving him open for the fist, rocketing in, that caught him on the nose and upper lip. Both of them heard the distinct *pop!* of Emerson's little finger breaking. Before Altman could quite finish marveling that he was really seeing tiny purple stars, Emerson hit him again.

It wasn't quite so hard this time, because it was the same damaged hand, but it was in almost the same place. After he heard the cartilage grinding on itself inside his nose, the Senator stopped feeling pain. All the older man experienced now was a fury utterly beyond comprehension or containment, a frenzy of outrage which had been building, under pressure, for three-quarters of a century, a destructive ferocity for which something inside him held Emerson responsible, because any likelier, more accurate alternative was unthinkable. His opponent cocked his bloodied, broken fist back for a third and final blow.

Altman suddenly lashed out at him, seized him by the

shirtfront, and, without thinking about it, smashed his forehead down onto the shorter man's upraised face.

Emerson grunted and reeled backward, momentarily overcome, glassy-eyed, with blood spouting from his nose. He staggered, but managed to keep his feet as the Senator charged him, arms outspread, teeth gritted. Emerson thrust an arm out as if to fend Altman off, the fingers extended upward. By accident, the heel of his hand caught the older man in the eye and swerved him off course. As he passed, Emerson, somewhat under control again, swiveled like a bullfighter and hit Altman, backfisted, and with all his strength, over the right kidney.

Altman kept going and fell on his face. But as Emerson lifted a heel to stomp him, the Senator somehow managed to turn over. His hand found his lost cane, which he swung upward, catching Emerson in the solar plexus.

Emerson collapsed.

Both men were on the floor now, crawling toward each other through a litter of broken window glass, snarling under their breath, which came in ragged gasps.

Each man was now reduced to a ferocious, single-minded animal desire to kill the other after a lifetime of mutual hatred. The older of the two had sunk his teeth into the flesh of Emerson's face, and Emerson's thumbs were on Altman's eyes, pressing hard, when Will, Rosalie, and Nails began pulling them off each other.

By which time neither of them cared.

Altman regained awareness in his office, where he'd been left lying on a soiled and threadbare couch, after he and Emerson had pounded each other into unconscious, bleeding pulp before they'd been separated. Feeling more pain than he'd known was possible, he arose and limped to his desk, toppled into the chair behind it which squeaked in protest, took a moment to catch his breath, then reached out with a hand trembling from exhaustion and slid open the upper right-hand drawer.

Bodily pain wasn't the only thing he was feeling. In fact, it scarcely counted.

Yes, there it was, gleaming dully back at him from the dark recesses of the drawer, the very embodiment of evil in two pounds of stainless steel. It had been confiscated, years ago, from one of the peasants and had somehow wound up in his custody.

Altman picked up the pistol, surprised at its weight and by how naturally and comfortably it fit his hand. There was no hammer to cock, no safety, just a sensuously curved trigger begging to be pulled. Feeling nothing in particular, he swung the muzzle around until it pointed at his face. No need to check if it was loaded. He could see the coppery glitter of a hollow-pointed bullet inside the abbreviated barrel, its hungry serrated lips eager to taste blood.

He wouldn't disappoint them. He pressed the muzzle to his temple, felt the cold ring of steel on his flesh, then remembered this wasn't the way. He might destroy his frontal lobes, leaving a paralyzed vegetable hulk still capable of feeling.

For some reason, he couldn't bring himself to put the barrel in his mouth. But he could do the next best thing, aim it at—what was it called?—the philtrum, so the bullet would follow the nasal passages to the cerebellum. It would be fast, it would be final. The problem was, it hurt. Emerson had hit him there, and the punished flesh was crushed and swollen. Sharp pain brought tears to his eyes. He put his finger on the trigger and began increasing the pressure, bit by bit until he could feel small parts begin to move inside the gun.

Suddenly he jerked the pistol away, laid it carefully on

the desk, and stared at the words engraved in the silvery slide:

NGU DEPARTURE
CALIBER 10 M/M
MADE ON PALLAS

Somehow, this changed everything. If he killed himself with one of these damned ubiquitous things, it would mean that Emerson had won. He couldn't let Emerson win, not again.

For the first time in three-quarters of a century, it occurred to Altman to wonder why he always lost when he confronted Emerson Ngu. He had his own problems. Earth's power-hungry politicians, losing their hold on humanity in a way even he could see, yet still embroiled in age-old internecine struggles, had used him as a pawn for decades. The remaining few who supported him in his struggle here had discovered they were in no position to make threats any longer.

Pallas was a long way off, and governments on Earth hadn't bothered even copying the Marshall drive, the development of which Emerson had financed, which made a mockery of the rocket-powered UN fleet, now mothballed in orbit, on which he'd counted for so long. Nor could Earth rely on nuclear weapons. Pallas had particle beams meant for mining but capable of neutralizing atomic bombs at astonishing distances. And anyone in the asteroids could devastate the Earth, simply by altering the orbit of some uninhabited rock. When the public had learned of this, Altman's allies in brinksmanship had been lucky to escape alive.

It hadn't done him any good, he realized, knowing that all this industrial machinery, so useful in defending Pallas, had been created merely to enhance the wealth of his lifelong foe. Beaten in a last effort to destroy Emerson by competition, he'd lost it all: wealth, power, all the favors he'd been owed. The end had come when he'd seen most of his belongings auctioned to pay debts no one would help him with any more. He'd used the last of the proceeds to have the pipeline destroyed.

Until this moment, Altman had always defended a collection of ideas he thought of as enlightened and humane, but which his enemies dismissed as mercantile socialism, living beyond its time in an inappropriate environment. It was an environment to which he'd been involuntarily consigned, from which he'd always believed he would eventually return, vindicated. One thing was certain, he'd never been a "native," not in the sense Emerson and his family were. Altman saw for the first time that this had always imposed a disadvantage on him.

And now, if he decided to go on living, he must try to become Pallatian himself. He must learn the ways, as best he could, of this new frontier, become a genuine pioneer, and defeat his enemy on that basis.

It didn't occur to him that if he achieved that transformation, there would remain no need to defeat Emerson at all.

XLV

A GOOD PLACE TO BE FROM

I DON'T WANT TO ACHIEVE IMMORTALITY THROUGH MY WORK, I
WANT TO ACHIEVE IT BY NOT DYING.

— Woody Allen

D *amnation!"*

The twittering of the communicator on his desk,
coming abruptly as it did, nearly frightened Altman out of
whatever wits he had left. He let it go on ringing a long
while, determined not to answer, unwilling to talk to anyone about anything tonight.

Whom had he left to talk to?

What was there left to talk about?

But whoever was at the other end outlasted him. Anyone could manage that, these days. After more than a
dozen rings, he glanced down at the base of the device, saw
a light which indicated it was a video call, and pushed the
appropriate button.

Across the room, the wall-sized screen was gone, auctioned off to pay his debts. The small screen came to life,
illuminating his otherwise darkened office. At the bottom
of the display, a transitory readout informed him that it
was two A.M.

"What in God's name do *you* want?"

"Grandfather—" It was Rosalie, with an odd expression on her face he couldn't interpret, even given her normally open nature, even after all these years. The oddly
cluttered room behind her image, nearly as dark as his own
office, was unfamiliar.

"Don't you dare to call me that, young woman!"
Which only went to show how things were relative. She

was decades younger than he was, it was true. But back home—on Earth, he meant, remembering his resolution—back in the old days of the welfare/warfare states, Rosalie would probably have been collecting Social Security by now.

He brushed the errant thought aside.

For a moment, he did see anger in her eyes. "Senator Altman, then—Chief Administrator—whatever the hell you want. I need to see you. I need to talk with you."

"You're talking with me now; what is it that you want?" A peculiar chill slithered down his spine and he experienced a premonitory moment—and a surprise at his reaction to it—when he believed he knew what her original facial expression had meant.

She released an exasperated breath. "I mean I need to see you face to face. Believe me, I don't like this any better than you do. It wasn't my choice, it was a promise I made and have to keep. There's something I need to tell you, something I need to show you, and I can't do it like this. Please come. Please come now."

He nodded cynically. "So you and that bastard husband of yours can ambush me like a—?"

"You know better than that, Gibson Altman." She said it flatly, without anger or any other perceptible emotion, and he knew suddenly that it was true, that it had always been true, and that he had always been the one who couldn't be trusted. He was the villain. He always had been. Was there ever going to be an end to the unpleasant things he had to learn about himself?

It was because of that unanswered and unanswerable question that he replied, "Very well, I'll come—against my better judgment. Where should I meet you?"

For the briefest possible moment she almost appeared grateful. In the unfocused background, he thought he saw the glint of some sort of machinery. "You know the

Horatio Singh Research Center, across the street from the main plant building?"

Again the shocking, premonitory chill and sense of loss. Yes, he told her, he knew the place, one of the many scientific philanthropies she and her husband had endowed. Among other things, he recalled suddenly, it served the sprawling Ngu Departure community as a hospital. It was the same place where, in what now seemed to be another lifetime, all but the first of his great-grandchildren had been born. Aside from the first, he'd never seen or touched one of them.

"Come directly to the double doors at the front entrance," she replied, "which will be unlocked. I'll send my flying yoke on automatic to fetch you from the Project."

Without another hesitation, he nodded again. "I have my own." It wasn't really his; God knew where it had come from. But it was one of a few personal articles, like the gun lying on his desk, that no Pallatian auctioneer, or creditor for that matter, would take from a man. "I'll be there in fifteen minutes."

He was there in ten, although it cost him untold pain. He'd stiffened up considerably, sitting at his desk during all those agonizing hours of self-evaluation. On his flying yoke he passed over the abandoned front gate of the Project which, along with the decaying Residence, was almost the only visible remnant of what had once been a noble and humanitarian undertaking. The two landmarks were now separated from one another, swallowed by squalid private development. As he flew, he discovered minor injuries, scrapes and bruises, from his fight with Emerson that he hadn't noticed until now.

He'd be a long time healing, in more ways than one.

The Ngu Departure streets somehow seemed darker than they should have been, although they were usually well lit and the requisite number of street lamps seemed to be operating. Either it had rained in the past few hours — he wouldn't have noticed a raging thunderstorm in the state he'd been in all night — or they'd just been washed. They threw what light there was into elongated, streaky patterns. Pistol in hand, and every nerve on guard, he glided toward the smoked-glass doors of the Horatio Singh Research Center, which had opened at his approach.

"Why, Senator, I'm astonished. If I'd known you were flying these days, and you hadn't hung up on me so quickly, I'd have arranged to meet you up on the roof. As it is, I'm afraid we're going to have to take a more circuitous route."

It was Rosalie herself, still beautiful after all these years to old eyes illuminated as much by memory as by present vision, who met him, rather than the automated guide she'd mentioned. What she'd said, of course, was true. Until tonight, he'd avoided using flying yokes unless absolutely necessary, partly, he supposed, because they were Emerson's invention and a foundation of the man's obscene fortune. Partly, too, because, every bit as much as the handguns Emerson had manufactured, it was the flying yoke that had destroyed the Project.

Hastily shoving the gun he'd brought into a pocket of his old-fashioned sportscoat, he muttered some uninformative reply. It seemed unnaturally cold inside the place, and very quiet. It reminded him suddenly of a high-priced funeral home.

"I decided there was time to come myself," she added. "There isn't any hurry any more."

Somehow these words failed to surprise him. He thought he knew by now what this was all about. He clambered awkwardly out of his flying yoke, folded it, and left it leaning against a wall near the entrance. Not looking at her, he unfolded his cane and leaned on it wearily. The floors in this place were of native meteoric stone, at least half metallic, highly polished, and recently waxed. It would be just his luck to finish this dreadful day with a broken hip.

As it was, if this had been Earth, rather than Pallas, and he'd still been alive at his current hundred and nine years of age, he'd have needed a wheelchair, even in his present battered but essentially healthy condition. The corridors were long, and he was very tired. It seemed to him as if he'd always been tired.

"All right," he told her, "what is it that you need to show me?"

"Just follow me, and you'll see everything."

Expecting what he had, he was momentarily confused as they passed the glassed-in enclosure of the center's emergency medical theater, with its own outside street-level entrance visible across the room. The place was dark and just as unoccupied as the rest of the building seemed, with only the glowing multicolored pilot lights of various kinds of equipment to hint at what it was. He supposed the doctors must be on call, able to get here by flying yoke within a few short minutes, coming down to this level from a separate entrance on the roof.

After what seemed like forever, following the woman through an endless maze of corridors and passing through a heavy security door, he found himself in a dimly lit, cavernous, high-ceilinged room that looked more like an aircraft hangar than anything to do with scientific or medical matters. The walls were crowded with strange apparatus which, Rosalie told him, was just warming up. It was connected with half a dozen big bathtublike fixtures seemingly festooned with electronic instruments.

Standing in the midst of all this arcane technological clutter, she presented him with what seemed, at first, to be a non sequitur. "Do you recall the fuss, years ago, when Emerson decided to underwrite construction of a spaceship of advanced design, intended to explore further out in the solar system?"

"Why, yes." The Senator shrugged. "That would be the *Fifth Force,* built at the South Pole and supposedly using some kind of innovative antigravity drive, wouldn't it?"

He'd paid the stories some attention because, in those days and, for that matter, until only last night, he'd always carefully collected any information about Emerson's enterprises which might betray a hint of vulnerability on the younger man's part. He'd begun with the solar mirror Rosalie, hoping it would ruin Emerson, and it very nearly had. Voluntary contributions still dribbled in, even today, but it would be another quarter of a century before his losses were recouped. This lunatic spaceship venture had appeared promising at first—antigravity was fantasy, not physics—but as far as he knew, nothing had ever come of it.

"Well," Rosalie informed him, "we had some spectroscopic evidence a few years ago that got us interested, and now an isotopic study confirms that the Drake-Tealy Objects are from somewhere out there. We've still no more of an idea, really, what they are or who made them—any more than we know who built Stonehenge or made the giant drawings on the Nazca plain. But several hundred pioneering youngsters have been selected for the *Fifth Force*'s first voyage, and she's leaving Pallas ninety days from now, outbound for the Cometary Halo in deepest trans-Plutonic space."

He wondered wildly what this had to do with anything, but what he said was, "A dark, frozen hell, I think, to send hundreds of innocent young people to die in."

"That's what they said about Pallas in the beginning,"

Rosalie countered. "And didn't people used to refer to the choicest portions of real estate in the old United States, where you and Emerson came from, as the Great American Desert?"

Leaning heavily on his cane, he shook his head impatiently, feeling every minute of his age and beginning to stiffen again from standing in one place. "Rosalie, no one of my years could stand the suspense any more. What's this all about?"

For a moment, she went on as if she hadn't heard him, gazing past him into some nonexistent distance. Her voice was still young, and in this light it almost seemed as if she hadn't aged over the past twenty-five years. "You know that those young people—and they include my own son and his pregnant fiancée, your great-grandchildren, Senator, and your great-great grandchild—will turn whatever they happen to find out in the Halo into the adventure of a lifetime."

He gave her a sour look, probably lost on her in the darkness. "Who was it who said an adventure is something you spend the entire duration of wishing you were home in bed?" At the moment he wished he were at home in bed, although he didn't think he could stand to be alone no matter how many years he'd spent getting used to it.

"Their children," she added, "will make the place over into a paradise—although they won't think of it that way. People never do—they're not built to. And then someday it'll be another good place to be *from*, just like America and Pallas."

"Perhaps," the Senator replied, stretching his new understanding to the limit. "Perhaps they will at that, Rosalie. But you and I will never live to see it."

No, he knew that he was condemned to live out whatever years were left to him—and if he was lucky there wouldn't be too many of them—surrounded by the ruins of a lifetime of tragic mistakes.

It was probably just what he deserved.

As if she could read his thoughts of resignation to defeat and death, her voice sharpened suddenly. "What makes you so goddamned sure, Grandfather? How do you know that's not the very thing Emerson and I asked you down here to discuss?"

"In that case, *Granddaughter*,"—he was feeling that cold prickling up and down his spine once again and he wasn't getting used to that—"exactly where the hell *is* Emerson?"

She sighed, slumped a little, then made a visible effort to straighten her spine. "He had another heart attack, a bad one, shortly after you two fought tonight."

"He's dead?"

XLVI
THE VOICE FROM BEYOND

DON'T DO PATCH-JOB REPAIRS—DO IT RIGHT, OR SKIP IT . . .
AFTER ALL, THE LIFE YOU SAVE MAY BE YOUR OWN.
  —Jerry Kuhnhausen, *The S&W Revolver, A Shop Manual*

F or the time being."

Altman's head whirled. He was still far too preoccupied with the question he'd just asked to have registered the answer. He'd never realized until this moment just how great a part of his life had centered itself on his old adversary.

He blinked, and the next thing he was fully aware of was Rosalie, one slender arm spread wide to indicate the great, confusing mass of chemical and electronic equipment surrounding them, filling the dimly lit room with an ominous combination of bubblings, hisses, and hums, like something out of an ancient horror film.

At the center of this mare's nest of technology run riot was a row of low stainless steel vats or tubs set into the perforated metal floor they both stood on, just the proper size to contain a human body. Each was covered with a shallow dome of sweating sheet plastic and filled with a milky, opaque fluid of some kind.

On one of them, Emerson's pistol belt and holstered Grizzly draped over a corner.

". . . a multiple enzyme-based, computer-directed processing device," she was saying, "with the potential to take a living organism apart, molecule by molecule, repair faulty and faltering biosystems from a digitalized template, then flush out a lifetime of accumulated organic wastes and bad genetic information."

"What?" Altman shook his head, struggling to get it clear. He wouldn't have understood one word in three of what the woman had said at the best of times.

"In short," Rosalie told him brightly, "it's a rejuvenator."

And odd, surprising sort of hope began swelling in Altman's chest, the complement to his surprising sense of loss. "And at the moment, it's rejuvenating Emerson?"

Looking satisfied and proprietary, she nodded. "So far it's been tried out thoroughly on mice, rats, guinea pigs, hamsters, gerbils, pigeons, dogs, cats, pigs, rhesus monkeys, everything we could get our hands on, with a ninety-percent success rate—"

"Only ninety percent?" His feeling of hope suddenly mixed with foreboding. His imagination filled his mind's eye with horrifying pictures. "What . . . happened to the failures?"

Rosalie shrugged, unsuccessfully concealing her own fears in that regard. "The remaining ten percent . . . eventually died—gruesomely, I'm afraid. I saw a few of them. We hadn't tried it out on living human beings before, not until tonight."

The Senator exhaled, not having realized until now that he'd been holding his breath. It also hadn't dawned on him before this moment that Rosalie was implying that she'd consigned her husband to these infernal mechanisms, this infernal chemistry, *before* his heart attack had killed him altogether. It did now, and, recoiling from the shock of it—a part of his mind wondered whether Emerson had been conscious at the time—he sought security in old patterns.

"I don't need to tell you," he told her nevertheless, "that a process like this, involving such a risk factor, would be completely illegal, back on Earth."

"Which is precisely why," Rosalie replied with a grin, "it had to be invented and developed here. We Pallatians are tougher, smarter—and richer—than those pitiable culls who remain behind in the deadly safety of Earth, because we're willing to take risks. We wouldn't be here in the first place if we weren't."

Altman nodded slowly. "I'm beginning to understand that, after all these years." He looked down at his hand, clutching the pistol in his jacket pocket, as if he'd never seen it before, and shuddered with embarrassed self-loathing. Suddenly, and for the first time, he noticed he was still wearing his bedroom slippers.

Rosalie smiled, warming him even in these surroundings. "I believe you are at that, Senator. Emerson and I considered long ago all the contingencies we could with regard to his failing health, even his long-running feud with you. It was according to that plan that I brought him here tonight, after his attack, to perform the final experiment, a complex, intermittent process requiring sixty days for each of us, so we'll be on time to catch the *Fifth Force* out to the Halo."

" 'Each'?" Altman echoed in paralyzed revulsion. "You're going through the process, too?" She still looked like a young girl to him until he realized that he was seeing her, especially in this light, as much with his memory as with his eyes. But the years had flown by without notice, as the years will do, and she must be at least . . . sixty-three.

She nodded, and this time there wasn't a hint of trepidation discernible in her voice or attitude. "Two of these units over here already hold the bodies of Mirelle Stein and R.L. Drake-Tealy, quick-frozen many years ago at the very moment he died. Miri decided to die *with* Digger— something else that would have been forbidden back on Earth—but now, with any luck at all, they'll both live again, to join us three months from now aboard the *Fifth Force.*"

Mirelle Stein and R.L. Drake-Tealy, alive again. Suddenly Altman was suspicious. A chill crept up his spine. "Rosalie, why the hell are you telling me all this?"

"Well—" his granddaughter shrugged as if it were of no particular importance " —we thought we'd invite our old enemy along, if he was interested and willing."

Shock: "I don't understand."

All the same, the weight of the pistol in his pocket was suddenly very comforting. He glanced from one of the evil-looking vats to another, imagining what the first breath of vile liquid would be like, how it would feel to be taken apart, molecule by molecule, and reassembled according to a computer program.

"I think you do," she continued as if unaware of Altman's misgivings, which she probably wasn't. "Right to the end, Emerson insisted things just wouldn't be the same without you. He told me more than once, specifically: 'Even if I wind up killing him—*or he kills me.*' I think he enjoyed the idea of your having to live in a future he'd created. If this process works the way it has time after time with animals, we'll all be twenty years old again, biologically—but with the accumulated wisdom of a lifetime, and a whole new life ahead of us."

Altman, having recently learned something important about life himself, thanks to the Ngu Departure pistol, was intrigued by Rosalie's words, but terrified of them at the same time. At one level, he suspected that this might be no more than an elaborate trick, a wife's revenge for her husband's death.

At quite another level, he was desperately afraid that the whole thing might be true.

He hesitated.

Abruptly, there was a ripple across the surface of one of the tubing-festooned vats beside which Rosalie was standing. An obscene gurgling came to his ears. He shrank back in mindless dread as a wet, shiny hand emerged from the cloudy liquid, followed by a dripping arm. He looked away as someone—or something—coughed, vomited some watery substance, coughed again, and began to speak, a familiar-sounding voice distorted by the plastic bubble that contained it.

"Come on, you geriatric son of a bitch," Emerson demanded, his fluid-slicked hair and naked shoulders rising briefly from the vat. For the first time, Altman saw into his naked, empty eye socket. *"You're holding up progress, as usual! What the hell are you waiting for, a goddamned engraved invitation?"* Exhausted by the effort, the eerie figure slid back into the solution and was silent.

Rosalie reached out and took Altman by the hand. "C'mon, Grandfather— *'For the opportunity of a lifetime and a lifetime of opportunity'*—you wanna live forever?"

Nodding uncertainly, the Senator stepped forward, toward her, into an unknown future.